Mr. Wright

MR.**WRIGHT**
HEROES OF HENDERSON:BOOK 6

Liz Kelly

Published by Kelly Girl Productions
©Copyright 2017 Liz Kelly
Cover design by Tammy Kearly

ISBN: 978-0-9860864-8-9

For more information on the author and her works, please see
www.LizKellyBooks.com

For

Abigail Elizabeth Ford

A truly resilient real-life hero.

Who's Who in Henderson

*Should you like a review, here is a reference to
the primary characters you've met in previous books.
See a complete list of characters at www.LizKellyBooks.com*

Harry the Bartender

Mysterious young country club bartender with an uncanny knack for knowing your drink and reading your mind. His tequila shots have a way of bringing couples together.

Crain Carraway *(Top Dog)*

Dallas business tycoon and Texas A&M star athlete who found his runaway bride, **Tansy Langford**, in Henderson. He's teamed up with Evans & Evans Investments (E&E) to create the upcoming sports academy.

Vance Evans *(Bad Cop)*

Part owner of E&E Investments and high school baseball coach, he's also the mayoral campaign manager for his best friend, Brooks Bennett. He recently married **Piper Beaumont**, defense attorney in Raleigh and his fourth-grade savior.

Brooks Bennett *(Good Cop)*

Henderson's Golden Boy. He's determined to bring economic prosperity back to town and stop the mass exodus of younger generations. He's running for mayor and is madly in love with **Lolly DuVal**, who is now back in Henderson after finishing her graduate degree at N.C. State.

Davis Williams a.k.a. Pinks or the Ninja *(UnderDog)*

Originally from Baltimore, Pinks is now heavily involved in Henderson's economic recovery plan. He's also heavily involved with *Red*, a.k.a. Scarlett Langford.

Scarlett Langford a.k.a. Red

A Henderson native and recent graduate of Ole Miss. She's ambitious and has a passion for fine wines… and Pinks.

Cal Johnson

Rookie MLB pitching sensation, who showed up in Henderson last Christmas to help sort things out for his third-base coach, **Cooper Crenshaw**. He came back in March to help promote Henderson High's Baseball Opening Day Spectacular and created a viral video when he sang at The Situation.

Missy McReady

Imported from Baltimore by Davis Williams to be Henderson High's ladies lacrosse coach as well as the town's Marketing and Event-Planning guru. She's since earned the title CEO of Henderson and has fallen for its resident Army Ranger, Thurgood Watson.

Thurgood Lewis Watson III a.k.a. Thor *(Mr. Wrong)*

Army Ranger back home in Henderson, now owner of a large plantation passed to him upon his father's untimely death. Ask anybody and they'll tell you, Missy McReady is *his* girl.

Hale Evans

Vance's father, who has recently married Lolly DuVal's mother, **Genevra** (pronunciation Jen-evrah), and is part owner of E&E. His mother, **Emelina Flores**, a.k.a. the Big Em, originally from Spain, also lives with them.

Duncan James *(Playin' Cop)*

Fraternity brother of both Brooks and Vance, Duncan is now working as the corporate attorney for E&E Investments. He's presently engaged to **Annabelle Devine**, Henderson's own Keeper of the Debutantes.

Mayor Clint Stevens

Longtime mayor of Henderson up for reelection against Brooks Bennett.

Marcie Watts a.k.a. Viper

Vengeful ex-girlfriend of **Coach Crenshaw's** *(Kissing Cooper)* who is out to destroy Brooks Bennett and Vance Evans.

Marnie

Ten-year-old neighbor of **Thor's** who's being raised by her grandparents. She came to him to learn how to play football and shoot a gun. He introduced her to **Missy** and redirected her interests to lacrosse.

Evie Jackson

Leader of the old guard and matriarch of Henderson society. When she says jump, everyone responds, "How high?"

Garland Langford

Wife of Rye Langford and the next generation's **Evie Jackson.** She a Henderson socialite and former Miss North Carolina. Mother of Tansy and Scarlett.

CHAPTER ONE

Xavier Wright checked his watch, noting the time. Of course, it didn't much matter. He'd wait however long it took. Chase Alexander had been the best damn mentor and surrogate father a stupid prick like Xavier could have lucked into, and the man deserved a proper goodbye.

With the patience of Job, the wisdom of Solomon, the skills of a craftsman, and a bullshit meter that was absolutely infallible, there'd been no getting away with anything working for Chase. He'd certainly called Xavier out on his bullshit often enough back when he was in college and still dripping wet behind the ears.

Yep, he'd learned a hell of a lot from the man. In so many ways Xavier was sorry to see it end. But Arizona had finally lost her appeal just as North Carolina was calling him home. They say timing is everything, and he couldn't deny the timing was working out as well as it could.

Under the circumstances.

Looking out the window of the neat and tidy construction trailer, Xavier saw nothing but desolate land waiting for the Alexander magic to turn it into something livable. Saw that Chase was still busy with subcontractors wanting to bid on his new project. Well, that was fine. Truth be told, Xavier wasn't in any hurry to say goodbye.

So he settled himself down into a padded chair, crossed an ankle over a knee, and pulled out his phone. His thumb scrolled to the folder containing the electronic newsletter his brother had signed him up for when he'd heard Xavier was finally moving home. He began to read.

Henderson Happenings
"May the Fourth ...
Be With You"

The rumors have been confirmed ...

Henderson's very own Lewis Kampmueller and Darcy Bennett's Christmas wedding is being featured in this month's *Town and Country* magazine with ample press being given to our couture designer Lolly DuVal for her glorious bridesmaids' gowns. Get your copy and post a selfie.

#HendersonHappenings, y'all.
~ Your Henderson Hostess ~

"Kampmueller?" Xavier muttered his surprise. *Geeky guy a couple years behind me in school,* he remembered while opening the next one.

Henderson Happenings
May 15
Monday Morning Review

There have never been so many muscles—glorious, bulging, ripped, masculine muscles—gathered in one place in the great state of North Carolina than last Saturday night in Henderson.

No, it wasn't a Mr. Universe competition. (Although I'm now thoroughly committed to bringing one to town after what I witnessed at Thurgood Watson's *Party at the Plantation.)* If Missy McReady plans to hand out ex-Army Rangers as party favors at all of her events, I will find a way to be on each and every guest list.

I don't remember what the weather was like, but I can tell you it was one *hot* time. Check out the pictures on the

Henderson Happenings Facebook page while I continue to fan myself over the memories.

Drive on in, y'all.
~Your Henderson Hostess~

"Fan herself?" Xavier snorted. Alone in the trailer, he cocked an arm, inspecting his own guns and wondering how he'd have stacked up against those Rangers. Because there was a time he didn't hesitate to engage in a little hand-to-hand combat. Now that he'd gained a little maturity, and let's face it, confronted with honest-to-God Rangers? He whistled. Even his balls weren't that big. He went back to reading.

Henderson Happenings
May 19
Lost and ...

Found in the gutter (I am not kidding you) on Main Street. A book: *365 Sexual Positions*. Pages have been earmarked. You lost it and want it back? Harry the bartender has it. I've suggested he make the owner identify the earmarked pages to claim it. I won't be asking for a selfie on this one. But y'all are free to speculate on just whose book it is on the Henderson Happening's Facebook page.

I have my suspicions.

But a good hostess never tells, y'all.
~Your Henderson Hostess~

"Go ahead and tell," Xavier grumbled to himself. "Anybody who needs a damn book—" His mouth slammed shut, the number 365 registering in his brain. Three hundred sixty five sexual positions? Well, hell. Yeah. Even he could use a book like that. He mentally put *meet this Harry* and *nab that book* on his *First few days back in Henderson* list.

Henderson Happenings
May 22
And have you noticed …

Bed and breakfasts, the ultimate in hospitality, have been creeping up all over Henderson to accommodate out-of-towners. Or is it for the late-night rendezvous? One B&B seems particularly popular with not-to-be-named new parents who were caught sneaking off for a bit of adult time.

#AfternoonDelight, y'all.
~Your Henderson Hostess~

"Good lord," Xavier sputtered. "What is this? Gossip Girls gone wild?" At the same time, he couldn't help but want a complete listing of these bed & breakfasts. He flicked the next newsletter open.

Henderson Happenings
May 26
Coming up this Weekend

You did not hear this from me …

Scarlett Langford has graduated from Ole Miss, and if you give a Rebel Yell in the right direction, I daresay you'll be able to sneak into the Friday night celebration at Henderson Country Club. (Wear red and royal to blend in.) This Hendersonian is hoping for a glimpse of Scarlett's famous roommate Natalie Houser and Natalie's more-than-famous rock-star, rock-out, strike-out boyfriend, Major League pitcher Cal Johnson. (The O's do not have a game scheduled. Coincidence? I think not!)

And on Saturday, way out on Major Hunkadoodle-do's farm, I understand there may be more than cow tipping going on. Henderson's fashion designer extraordinaire, Lolly DuVal, snared her graduate degree this week and is being celebrated by this town's future mayor and the entire swanky

Evans clan her momma married into. There is bound to be a police presence considering she's Brooks Bennett's girl, but let's face it. If you can't finagle your way into a party thrown on a wide-open plantation, then you aren't worth the dirt you were raised on. Am I right?

Don't forget to post your pictures. #HendersonHappenings

Drive on in, y'all.
~Your Henderson Hostess~

"Seriously. Who the hell is this *Henderson Hostess?*" Xavier scowled. He thought about calling his brother to find out, but after shooting a glance out the window, he went back to reading.

Henderson Happenings
May 29
Mayor Mayhem

Just when all of Henderson believed we have the one shining star left in the world of politics, our own Golden Boy Brooks Bennett has let us down. *Or has he?* If you believe the outsider Marcie Watts, who seems to have a stranglehold on Mayor Stevens and his reelection campaign, Brooks and his bold plans for building a sports academy here in Henderson will be the ruination of Henderson High—Brooks's own alma mater. Never mind the man is helping Coach Evans take our baseball team into a second consecutive post-season run for the state championship. I think I'll just say Congratulations, Bulldogs on an undefeated season, and good luck in Greensboro next Friday afternoon.

Let's drive to Greensboro, y'all.
~ Your Henderson Hostess~

Xavier stopped and reread this piece of hometown news three times.

Once, because no one had told him that Brooks was running for mayor. Not his parents, not his brothers.

Twice, because now he definitely had to put running this *outsider* Marcie Watts out of town higher on his list than meeting Harry and absconding with that sexual positions book, which completely pissed him off.

And the third time because his beloved Bulldogs baseball team was on a roll toward States. Again.

He scrolled to the next newsletter, hoping for more information about the team.

Henderson Happenings
June 2
Yes, Sports Academy

Congratulations to the Bulldogs on their first post-season win. And a big Bravo to the huge crowd that drove to Greensboro to support them. Put next Tuesday on your calendar as the Bulldogs head to Chapel Hill to face the defending state champs.

Interested in details regarding the bomb Mayor Stevens dropped last week? Brooks Bennett has been interviewed by McKenna Blakely at the *Henderson Daily*. He's spelling out the expected increase in economic growth due to the proposed sports academy. Visit the Henderson website for complete details, including an artistic rendition of the vision our future mayor, Evans & Evans Investments, and CC Dallas have in mind.

Totally looks like it will be worth driving in for, y'all.
~Your Henderson Hostess~

I should have stopped while I was ahead, Xavier thought.
Yep.

Because reading McKenna's name in that last newsletter landed a lightning strike to his soul while ripping him a new one. Just like McKenna was going to do when he set foot back in town.

Shit.

He knew he'd have to face it, but reading her name just pushed *handling McKenna* to the top of his *Things to do* list. There was just no getting around it. His face must have shown his anxiety when Chase opened the door to the trailer and climbed in.

"You've seen a ghost?" Chase asked.

"Just about." Xavier shifted, putting his phone back in his pocket. *Damn.*

"Everything okay with your mom?"

"Seems to be. Last I heard."

"So what then?" Chase nodded to the hand where his phone had been.

Xavier's mouth hung open for a moment before he shook his head and offered Chase a sheepish grin. "I was an asshole back in the day."

"I remember." Chase tossed his keys on the desk as Xavier snorted in response. "Seriously. You were a cocky son of a bitch when I hired you, albeit sharp as shit and with a work ethic I'd kill to be able to clone. But over the years, the asshole in you has softened a bit, allowing all the good stuff to shine through."

"The good stuff," Xavier joked. He stretched his arms over his head and groaned while tilting his chair back on two legs. "Aw, man," he addressed the ceiling. "I was hell on wheels in high school. I mean"—his chair legs came down with a thud— "I didn't burn stuff down or do drugs and shit. But I was …"

"A kid," Chase said. "You were a kid. Cut yourself some slack."

"I was really looking forward to going home until …" His voice trailed off.

"Until what?"

Xavier lifted a shoulder. "Until I was reminded I've got water under the bridge that needs cleaning up."

"Water under the bridge is best left under the bridge," Chase advised.

"Not when it's at flood stage," Xavier countered. He gave a little huff of a laugh. "This particular bridge is one I should have lit a match to before I left town."

"You don't want to burn your bridges, son. Never personally or professionally."

"Well, if it's still standing, this bridge is gonna be a tough one to cross back over."

"You wanna give me some details?"

Xavier considered it. Chase would give him solid advice for sure. And it wasn't like there was anyone else he could confide in. But Xavier didn't want to own the whole of it in his head, much less voice it aloud. "Nah," he said, tossing it off. "Like you said. Kid stuff. Hopefully I'm making a mountain out of what is now a molehill."

"Time has a way of resolving things."

"In small towns?"

Chase shrugged. "Doesn't matter. I want you to go back there and give 'em hell, ya hear? I know you've got your momma to worry about, but let that be the only thing. Whatever you're wrestling with is history you cannot change. And as for the future? Well, boy, I don't know a soul who's got a brighter future than you."

Stomach churning and head foggy with sudden emotion, Xavier stood slowly to clasp the hand of his mentor, his business partner, and his friend, ending an era.

"I'm gonna miss you," the older man told him sincerely. "Trust me. You'll do yourself proud." Those words meant more to Xavier than the enormous check the man was now stuffing into his shirt pocket. Chase broke the emotional moment with, "Though I can't see much sense in trading in a good solid truck for that flashy, ear-splitting piece of machinery I spied outside. Especially if you're driving cross country."

"After fourteen years, that truck was being held together with nothin' but duct tape," Xavier said, looking out the window at the Harley his ass was going to become well acquainted with over the next week. "And I'm hoping that sweet ride is going to clear my head; help me transition from a lone Arizona coyote back into a member of a very large North Carolina wolf pack."

"You'll do fine son. Family is family. Home is home."

"And the time has finally come for me to head back to mine."

"Text me once a day during the trip. I want to know you've arrived safe on that death trap. Then keep in touch. My best to your folks. I'll keep your mom in my prayers."

"I'm much obliged."

He was. Xavier truly was. He was as obliged, and thankful, and grateful … well just about as *full* as a man could get. So he didn't move toward his shiny new bike. He didn't wrap himself up in his leather jacket or don his helmet. No. Xavier Wright stood there a moment before throwing his arms around the man who had taught him *everything*. He promised himself that with every chance he got he would do Chase Alexander proud.

CHAPTER TWO

Standing in the hallway of Henderson Country Club between the closed-off ballroom to her right and the lively Mixed Grill to her left, Dallas-born Adelaide Bartholomew was torn.

It was late Friday afternoon and cocktails were already being crafted by Harry, the club's infamous bartender, and his new steward, Luke. Although Adelaide was a relative newcomer, over the last few months she'd noticed an increase in the club's activity. The sleepy, rural North Carolina town Mr. Carraway had described was seeing a renaissance. At least on weekends. And lately, the weekends seemed to start earlier and earlier.

But she wasn't here for Harry's cocktails or to start her weekend. She was here to snoop. Because during a business lunch that afternoon, she'd witnessed a truly *grand* piano being hoisted up a short flight of steps and delivered to the ballroom not twenty feet from where she now stood. She couldn't hear activity inside the ballroom, so she tried the double doors. And found them locked.

Darn.

"Looking for this?"

Her dark curls whipped around to find Harry standing in the center of the hallway, dangling a key from one finger. In her state of stunned confusion, she immediately recalled her first conversation with the handsome bartender just after she'd moved to Henderson.

She'd been standing right inside the doors of the Mixed Grill watching her co-workers work the room, meeting and greeting the locals. When Harry caught her eye, he'd gestured for her to join him at the bar with a chin lift.

She'd heard stories about Harry, so being summoned by him was a little nerve wracking. She looked right and left, hesitating to take that first step in his direction. But she'd gone, and he'd given her an encouraging smile as she did, pointing to the seat in front of him.

"I'm Adelaide Bartholomew," she reminded him. "We were introduced at lunch on Monday."

"I haven't forgotten you or the rest of Mr. Carraway's contingent from Dallas. You go by Addy?"

She shook her head. "Addy's my momma. For me, my family uses the second half of the name. They call me Laidey."

"*Laidey.*" He grinned in approval. "You looked a little out of place plastered up against the wall like that. Try this." He placed a shot glass, a wedge of lime, and a saltshaker in front of her.

"Oh." She stared down at his offering. "No. No shots for me, thanks."

"On the house," Harry insisted. "Might make you feel a little more comfortable."

Her body slumped as her face lifted to Harry's. "Did I look uncomfortable?"

Harry leaned in and said quietly, "*Adelaide* looked uncomfortable. *Laidey* looked downright bored."

An unbidden laugh escaped as she gave Harry a real smile. "You read people well."

"Trust your family's instincts," he insisted. "Go by Laidey here in Henderson. Adelaide was your grandmother, and you're *not* your grandmother."

Laidey's gaze widened in wonder. "How'd you know? About my grandmother?"

Harry shrugged. "Easy guess. So tell me about yourself. About *Laidey.*"

"Well … I'm here to work. I like to work. Unfortunately"—she tossed a quick glance over her shoulder—"the rest of my crew are third-generation Dallas socialites."

Harry poured her a glass of her favorite sparkling water. "You're not a socialite?"

"Far from it. My parents are, I suppose. If they were here, they'd be mixing it up, wanting to meet the who's who of Henderson and charm them into liking the Bartholomews."

"But you're not interested in carrying on that legacy? Being a charming *Laidey* Bartholomew?" Harry drawled out, grinning.

"I don't have it in me," she confided. "I'm not like my parents. I'm not like"—she threw an indulgent look behind her—"the rest of them."

"So why are you here?"

"There's work to be done. Lots of it."

"And you like work."

"And a challenge. From what Mr. Carraway described, this sports academy is going to be a challenge. *And* it's important to him—Mr. Carraway—so, I wanted to participate."

"Ahh. You smitten with old Crain Carraway?" Harry winked.

"Of course not," she totally lied. "Besides, he's married and almost ten years older than I am."

"Heart wants what the heart wants," Harry insisted.

"Maybe," she hedged. "But you do know the old Rolling Stones song, right? 'You Can't Always Get What You Want'." She quietly sang those lyrics and was tickled when Harry rebutted by singing her the next line. They grinned at each other while singing the final line, each of them holding the end note long enough to make Mick Jagger proud.

After giving her a high five, Harry asked, "So, what is it *you* need?"

Laidey shrugged because that was easy. "To be engaged in work."

"What else?"

Hmm. She thought for a moment and then said, "A good friend. I need one good friend here in Henderson and I'll be just fine."

Harry had extended his hand across the bar. "Consider me your first of many good friends."

And here he was now, proving true to his word by handing her the key to her heart's desire.

"Harry," she breathed. "How did you know? I won't touch it. I promise. I simply want to sneak a peek so I can appreciate, admire, and wistfully recall my baby grand back home."

Harry chuckled as he put the key in the lock.

"Seriously, of all the things I miss in Dallas, my family's dog and that baby grand are at the top of the list." Then she gave a self-deprecating snort. "Actually, the dog and piano are pretty much the entire list."

"Then you're due," Harry said, opening the door and ushering her inside.

Her breath caught at the sight of a luxurious, spanking-new Baldwin semi-concert piano.

"I'll leave you two alone." Harry exited and closed the door behind him.

June's evening sun shone brightly through the tall windows that stretched across the back and far side of the room. In spite of all of the light, the room's expanse still seemed cold with only she and the piano in a space designed to accommodate three hundred. She tiptoed toward the magnificent instrument, compelled to skim her fingers across the virgin keys ever so softly, careful not to make a sound.

She let her pinky finger press the highest C ever so softly, emitting the tiniest of pings. Her eyes drifted closed as her body absorbed that high-pitched note, allowing it to course through her bloodstream. The intense craving was immediate, as if she were addicted to the sound. Her fingers splayed and flexed as she sat on the polished bench. After a moment's breath, she set her fingertips lightly on the keys ...

And played.

An hour later, as the last note drifted away, spent and out of reach, Laidey sighed, happy in a way she hadn't felt in a very long while. With one final smile at her reflection in the polished wood, she stood and headed for the door.

When she slipped from the ballroom, it was into a bustling scene where patrons milled about, no one paying her any mind—per usual. She was as invisible here in Henderson on a Friday night as she'd ever been in Dallas, she thought as she spied her housemate, Poppy.

Poppy was not invisible.

Poppy was strawberry blond, popular, and probably missing Dallas in a way Laidey never would. They shared one of the two homes rented by their boss, Crain Carraway, to house his CC Henderson employees. Their three male coworkers, one of which was Poppy's twin brother Daniel, occupied the other house right next door.

In truth, Henderson suited Laidey. Much more than it suited Poppy or, apparently, the newly wedded Mrs. Carraway, even though Henderson was Tansy Langford's hometown.

Fact was, there wasn't much she and Tansy Langford Carraway had in common. Tansy was a tall, striking blonde with obvious appeal. Laidey was tiny in every way a woman could be. Short in stature, trim in size, pale in complexion, with dark hair and curls she couldn't seem to grow past her shoulders before it all just looked straggly.

Tansy's job was public relations.

Laidey was better suited for a backroom think tank. She didn't like crowds, and she definitely wasn't going to speak in front of one, ever. Her voice was soft, Tansy's was … not.

Tansy always wore the most fabulous heels, even though she was already tall, and Laidey—who'd been told never to set foot out of the house in anything but heels—preferred to wear sneakers. With everything. She loved the fact that the people she worked with in Henderson didn't seem to care.

And you know who else didn't care?

Crain Carraway.

Now that was the one thing she and Mrs. Carraway did have in common. They may not share a bond over the ins and outs of Dallas versus Henderson, but they did share a common dedication to the same man.

Laidey had worked for Crain for four good years before he met and married Tansy. Laidey watched their whirlwind romance evolve so fast her head practically spun off her shoulders. So when he was looking for volunteers for a long-term project, up went her hand. She couldn't stomach the thought of leaving CC Dallas altogether, but now that the man was married, staying in the Dallas office had become an uncomfortable fit.

And really, a married Crain Carraway was just the cherry on top of the sickening-sweet, multi-layered parfait she'd been force-fed all her life. Because as much as she loved her parents and her brother and sister, she was pretty much invisible when it came to being around them as well.

The Bartholomews, unlike most contemporary Dallas families, had actual Dallas roots going back for generations. Though their ancient ancestors' histories may have been a little unsavory, one thing had led to another and now Laidey's heritage included the likes of Carrie Neiman, who started the famed Neiman Marcus department stores, Henry Exall, who was famous for breeding racehorses, and real estate tycoon Tammell Crow. So yeah, being comfortable behind the scenes was not something that showed up in a lot of Rowling-Bartholomew DNA.

While she knew her family and relatives loved her, she also knew they didn't actually "get" her.

As she stepped into the Mixed Grill, her gaze drifted toward the bar because Harry did indeed, "get" her. How he knew she wanted to get in to see that piano she'd never understand. What she did understand was that the rumors Mr. Carraway had spouted about Harry were proving to be true. And when Harry had promised that he'd be her first good friend in Henderson, he hadn't been blowing smoke. Because he'd then gone ahead and introduced her to her second Henderson friend, McKenna Blakely. And that was a bit of a shock. Because McKenna Blakely was even more *Tansy Langford* than the actual Tansy Langford.

Laidey had been at the bar eating a hamburger the night she met McKenna. It was a quiet Tuesday evening, about a month ago, when McKenna arrived for a meeting with Harry. He'd promptly introduced her to Laidey and then claimed to have something to do in the back room, leaving the two of them alone.

Laidey with her hamburger.

McKenna with a Vanilla Vodka Gimlet.

"I hear Harry's the Handy Man," McKenna whispered conspiratorially.

"The what?"

"Are you familiar with that old James Taylor song? 'Handy Man'?"

"I don't believe so."

"Well, it's not about a typical handyman. It's about a guy who fixes broken hearts."

"Harry?"

McKenna nodded, her thick hair dark and shiny under the lights. "I've heard talk."

"What kind of talk?"

"That a certain husband spent a lot of time out of town, leaving his lonely wife at home. When she started coming to the club so she'd have company during the dinner hour, Harry began teaching her about wine. Occasionally they'd share a bottle. Maybe he gave her a little advice. No one is sure, but people saw them with their heads together. Next thing you know, said husband is now panting after his wife's heels."

"Jealous of Harry?"

"That's the rumor."

Laidey smiled. "Well, good for her, whoever she is."

McKenna leaned in and lowered her voice. "It's my aunt. So, I think it's all true."

"Really? Your aunt. And uncle?"

"Yes. She was miserable. Now she's not. I was relaying a story about Harry and one of my friends to Aunt Patricia, and she said Harry was the Handy Man."

"She told you that?"

"Yes. She used those exact words. And there was a twinkle in her eye when she said it."

Laidey gulped. "How … hands-on do you think Handyman Harry is?"

McKenna laughed. "I'm sure I don't know. But I'm grateful for whatever he did for my aunt."

"What did he do for your friend?"

McKenna looked around to be sure no one was eavesdropping. "For the longest time, my friend Seeley had the biggest crush on Harry. She dragged us in here on her birthday back on a night when everyone else was over at The Situation. Harry, who I'm sure figured it all out quickly, told Seeley he'd meet her for a dance over there when he got off work. And he did. She was elated. We all were. But later that same night, Harry introduced Seeley to Tucker Davenport, and it was a love match. She and Tucker have been dating ever since. I swear Harry's got a knack."

When Harry came back to the bar Laidey was shocked that McKenna just busted out and asked him point blank if he'd helped her aunt mend her broken heart. She watched as Harry gripped the edge of the bar with both hands, casting his gaze between the two of them before it landed solidly on McKenna. "Miss Blakely," Harry proceeded softly. "Your aunt's business is her business. But if you need advice, I'm here for you too."

"No. Not me," McKenna backpedaled. "At least, not anymore. My true love left town a long time ago and never looked back. Apparently I'm retaliating by refusing to leave. I'm determined to find a way to make my living in Henderson."

"What do you do?" Laidey asked.

"I write for the local newspaper. I know it's a dying media, but I still love the written word and the feel of the paper between my hands. We publish it online too, so there's that. But it's the *Henderson Daily*, so the circulation is limited. Although, it *is* the *Henderson Daily*, and this town is so traditional that most people still subscribe to the paper and actually read it."

"Well, that's good."

"For now," McKenna agreed. "Harry, you were going to suggest a business opportunity for me?"

"I might have a suggestion. Do you get the Henderson Happenings digital newsletter?"

McKenna rolled her eyes. "Doesn't everyone?"

"Do you?" Harry asked Laidey.

"Should I?"

"Absolutely," Harry said. "It's an idea from Team Henderson that comes out Friday to let people know what's happening over the weekend. On Monday it recounts whatever shenanigans occurred."

"Like a community calendar?"

McKenna snorted. "Not at all. It's a full-on gossip rag. But with a hilarious bent to it. I don't have any idea who writes it. Nobody does." She stopped, her head slowly swiveling toward Harry. "Do you write it?" she whispered, as if the Universe's secrets had just been revealed.

"Do *I* write it?"

"You do, don't you?" she insisted.

"Of course, I don't," he said with his adorable Harry grin.

"Stop it. You do. You write it."

"I just told you I don't."

"But you do. That's why stuff is in Henderson Happenings before it actually happens."

"Like what?" Harry asked.

"The bed-and-breakfast thing. There were no bed-and-breakfasts anywhere in Henderson. Not until Henderson Happenings *mentioned* they were popping up all over the place and then—poof—a dozen. *You* did that."

"I have no idea what you're talking about, *Ms.* Blakely. But if Henderson Happenings can use the power of suggestion to get things done around this town, why can't the *Henderson Daily* do the same?" Harry lifted a brow.

Laidey watched as McKenna fell back, practically struck dumb. Harry turned to Laidey and said, "First time a cat has ever gotten ahold of Miss Bossy Pants by the tongue."

"Bossy Pants?" McKenna protested.

"You and your dark-haired-vixen ways."

"What?"

"You heard me," Harry teased setting a shot of tequila on the bar for each of the girls. "Now I've given you an idea. Don't let me down." He turned away and left the two of them to their shots.

Laidey pushed her shot away before lowering her voice and leaning toward McKenna. "What are these dark-haired-vixen ways?"

"I'm guessing he hasn't forgiven me for trying to set him up with Seeley."

"Maybe he'd rather date you."

McKenna shook her head, gingerly tasting the shot. "Isn't he dating you?"

"Me? No. I mean, he was kind enough to give me a ride home last week, but … no."

"You sure?"

"Pretty sure."

"Well, are you *into* Harry?"

Laidey shot her a sly grin. "Aren't we *all* a little into Harry?"

McKenna grinned back. "Yes. I would say we are all a little into Harry."

And so they'd bonded.

Over Harry.

Because of Harry.

In spite of Harry.

McKenna with her Tansy-like, bigger-than-life personality and Laidey, the behind-the-scenes worker bee.

CHAPTER THREE

With all the hustle and bustle moving through the Mixed Grill tonight, Laidey decided she'd be happy to remain invisible to all but Harry and eat dinner at the bar. She tucked herself into the seat closest to the wall at the base of the L-shaped counter because from that vantage point, she'd be able to covertly observe all those settled down its extended length. Since it was Friday evening and she'd now become invisible to even those she worked with all week, she ate her dinner eavesdropping on some of the men in her life.

"Don't you have a cute, little wife and a baby to get home to?" Harry asked as he placed a coaster in front of an approaching Vance Evans.

He was good like that. Harry.

"I do have a wife and baby to get home to," Vance agreed. "But duty calls, Harry. These two"—Vance threw a thumb to his right—"Golden Boy and the Ninja have now found themselves strangely in the same boat. I'm here to help bail it out."

"Is that right?" Harry asked with a grin. "Do tell."

"Well," Vance said, hitching his dark good looks onto a stool, "it's no secret that Brooks has not-so-patiently waited for Lolly to move back to town." Laidey detected an indecipherable curse muttered into Brooks's beer. "Only now that she's back, she's working full time on her business which means—"

"She doesn't have one damn minute for me," Brooks bit out.

Harry checked his watch. "It's only six o'clock."

"She hasn't had a minute for me all week. And it's *Friday*," Brooks growled in Harry's direction.

"The weekend," Harry assured him cheerfully. "She'll put the work down for the weekend and show up here shortly." Laidey watched as Harry shifted his attention toward Pinks. "Scarlett giving you the same run-around setting up her wine shop?"

"You know it," Pinks said. "Which is fine because I'm busy. Too busy. I'm always at work." Laidey saw Pinks duck his head around Brooks and eye Vance pointedly. "I just thought with Scarlett home, she'd give me an excuse to stop working for more than the dinner hour."

"Harry?" Vance asked. "Did I just hear the Ninja *complain* about work? Because I'm fairly certain a year ago he boasted he could do anything—anytime—I asked."

"Like I haven't lived up to my résumé," Pinks scoffed. "You're lucky I haven't started my own business and left you to do all this nitty-gritty shit yourself."

"You *have* started your own business," Vance accused. "You and Missy with your locker-room-rejects nonsense. Neither one of you has time for that."

"Our *Sports Stop* is eventually gonna be a gold mine. Selling new and used sports equipment is the coming thing in Henderson. We *had* to run with it. Besides, we own it. We don't intend to manage it, thus providing more jobs for Henderson. Which is the whole point, right?"

Right, Laidey thought.

"And it's practically attached to E&E, so quit your bitching," Pinks finished.

"You're not complaining about work. Clearly you *love* work," Vance accused. "The two of you are sitting here crying in your beers over women."

"Just because Piper is perfect—" Brooks scowled.

"Oh, and she is," Vance assured him.

"—doesn't mean you get to sit here and gloat. If she didn't love being Vance, Jr.'s mommy so much, God only knows what she'd be up to."

"Which is why I plan to knock her up again just as soon as I get the chance." Vance looked at Harry. "I do not want to be in the same boat with these two. I want my wife barefoot, pregnant, and in the kitchen baking me her delicious pastries. And if any of you tell her I said that, I will kill you. Slowly."

Laidey took a bite of her hamburger to hide her smile. No doubt Vance didn't want that bit of old-school thinking getting back to his lawyer of a wife.

Pinks chuckled into his drink, shaking his head. "You are aware that Piper is planning to open Henderson's Big Pie Plate Shop, right?"

"I am, but I refuse to acknowledge it," Vance said.

"So, you're actually sitting in the same boat with Brooks and me, you just don't want to acknowledge it?"

"Not if I can help it, no. My plan is to seduce my wife every chance I get, sans birth control, and derail this whole pie plate business before it gets off the ground."

"It's already off the ground." Laidey listened as Pinks's voice rose in amazement. "Do you ever listen to your wife?"

"I listen to her telling me what a great lover I am, and that's all I wanna hear. Sue me for sticking my head in the sand and trying to figure a back way out of this pie plate nightmare."

Brooks's expression was one of delight. "You didn't come here to help Pinks and me. You came here to commiserate."

Vance took a sip of his whiskey.

Brooks barked out a laugh and slapped his buddy on the back. "Welcome aboard, Third Base."

Laidey watched as Harry pulled out a large, squat cube of a bottle. She'd heard stories about Harry's tequila shots, though up until now she'd made a point to decline them. Harry filled three shot glasses.

"The pie plate shop isn't going to take your wife's attention away from you or Vance, Jr.," she heard Harry tell Vance. "She's doing it *for* you. To support your efforts in saving this town." He held up a shot glass and looked Vance in the eye. "Embrace it," he said sternly, placing the shot in front of Vance.

He held up the next glass and addressed Brooks. "Miss DuVal has chosen to stay here instead of moving to New York or Paris. She's opened her business in Henderson to support *your* efforts to save this town." He set the shot in front of Brooks. "Embrace it."

Harry picked up the next glass and looked over at Pinks. But after a few silent heartbeats, he set the shot glass back down and said seriously, "You're on your own with Miss Langford."

Laidey had to choke back a snort.

"What?" Pinks's eyes screwed up in disbelief as Vance and Brooks hooted with laughter.

Harry poured another shot of tequila and set them both in front of Pinks. "Here, take two."

"Shit." Pinks grimaced.

"Scarlett is a handful," Vance smirked unhelpfully.

"If Harry isn't willing to give you any advice at all"—Brooks shook his head in gleeful dismay—"dude."

Pinks shot a dangerous look at Brooks but said nothing. He grabbed one shot and drank it down. Licking his lips, he began to put words to the things that had obviously been messing with his mind. "Honest to God, she's got too many irons in the fire. Scarlett was supposed to come home and open a wine shop. A *virtual* wine shop. *Reds*. But okay, rent is more than affordable right now, and we need shops opened on Main Street, so she's opening a brick-and-mortar store. Only now, she and her father are attaching a gourmet restaurant to it. *Flights*."

"Pretty sure you handed Rye Langford that idea on a silver platter the day he tried to run you out of town."

"I did," Pinks agreed. "And those things together make good sense. What I hadn't anticipated was Scarlett going all record producer on me. I mean, okay, the idea of Cal Johnson making a record? Pure gold. Because the guy is uber-famous in the sports world right now and can sing the hell out of any song you give him. Attaching that whole deal to Henderson by making him record it here, make the videos here? Freaking brilliant. For us. Of course, you've got to get Cal to go along with it, which Scarlett has thanks to her roommate, Natalie. Putting Cal and his album on the cover of Missy's ridiculous *Hunks of Henderson* calendar? That damn thing is going to sell like crazy. You know it will."

Brooks and Vance grunted in unison.

Their grim faces tickled Laidey because, frankly, she couldn't wait to see the finished product.

"And if Molly and Piper truly pull off this QVC thing," Pinks went on, "getting on national television and selling Henderson's Big Pie Plate? I'm not sure we're going to need the sports academy to save Henderson. I think the women in our lives have found easier, faster, far less costly ways to do it."

"Is that what you're worried about?" Vance asked. "That all our work will be in vain?"

"We've been killing ourselves for close to a year. Pushing this academy as fast as we possibly can. But we haven't broken ground."

"We've been at it for ten months, and we've made incredible progress. We're gonna break ground this fall. It's as fast-tracked as it can possibly get. And trust me, all that other stuff will shine a light on Henderson, giving us a chance to introduce our sports academy to the world. There is no downside to Scarlett and Missy, Annabelle and Lolly, Molly and—" Vance cut himself off abruptly.

"Piper's plans?" Brooks finished with a grin. "Face it, Third Base, Piper and her pie plate shop are not going to be left out of this. None of them is. We started it, and they've jumped on our bandwagon."

"Yeah, but I'm scared to death the next step is going to be a televised *Henderson Cooks with Babies* show starring Piper and Genevra with V.J. and Brody in tow. Jesus."

"Don't give them that idea. They will run with it," Brooks warned.

"Where do you think he got it?" Pinks asked. "Face it, man, you're toast. We're all toast. So, I'm out of here," he said, sliding off the stool. "I'm finding Scarlett, dragging her into the pool house, handcuffing her to the bed, and putting the Weekend Rule into effect."

"Weekend Rule?"

"The two of us can work ourselves to death all we want Monday through Friday. But come the weekend, we don't even *talk* about work."

"Hold up there, Fifty Shades." Laidey watched as Brooks grabbed Pinks by his shirt collar. "Before you start hauling Scarlett into your

Red Room of Pain and instituting rules—that one is awesome by the way—I want you to hear this."

"Hear what?"

"The rumor I'm about to lay down on your boss."

"What rumor?"

"Xavier Wright." Brooks turned his attention to Vance. "I understand he's coming back to town."

"Xavier Wright?" Pinks asked at the same time Vance said, "Really?"

At the nod of Brooks's head, Vance released a long, slow, thoughtful whistle. "Well," he said, taking up his whiskey. "We can use him. Him and the rest of those no good Wright brothers."

"True," Brooks said, a little smirk on his face.

"Wright Brothers?" Pinks asked, retaking his seat. "As in Wilbur and Orville? Who's this Xavier?"

"Meanest son of a bitch we ever played ball with," Vance said, staring straight across to the mirrored shelves behind the bar.

"He absolutely was," Brooks agreed with a grin. "He was a couple years ahead of us. So he's … what? Thirty-two now?"

Vance hitched a shoulder in response.

"The X-man was a great first baseman," Brooks told Pinks. "And an even better hitter. He was a junior when we made the team and took the business of hazing very seriously. He was the one who made us eat goldfish. Regularly."

"Oh, shit." Pinks grimaced and squirmed on his stool.

Laidey squirmed too.

"Yep. Big, plump, *live* goldfish," Brooks declared. "We hated that more than all the other shit we had to endure. And when I say endure, I mean *endure*. That's how Vance and I bonded. We were the only freshmen that year. And as much as I loved baseball, I *hated* the hazing. I had never been so mistreated in my life. Frankly, I was ready to quit, but Vance wouldn't let me. Said eating goldfish was minor bullshit compared to playing Varsity ball and that we could endure whatever we had to to be on the team."

"Tell 'em the rest," Vance grunted.

"The following year, we had seven freshmen make the team. Vance was all set to join Xavier in the hazing rituals, making an ass out of himself while mass-producing hatred from our new teammates. No way was I participating. In fact, I decided to put a stop to it."

"Pussy," Vance muttered with a little grin as he threw back his shot.

"That is *not* the way to build a team," Brooks defended. "No way would we have been able to compete for State again if we continued the tradition."

"So it was Golden Boy to the rescue," Pinks offered.

"You know I hate that nickname, right?" Brooks scowled, which made Laidey smile. Poor Brooks.

"Hey," Vance intervened. "If the shoe fits, Goody Two Shoes. He literally knocked me on my ass," he told Pinks. "Leaving me with an aquarium full of goldfish."

Pinks chuckled. "So then what happened?"

"Xavier and a few others were not interested in dropping the tradition. Vance and I had to get in their faces, hard. Xavier gave us the most blowback, and eventually it came to actual blows."

Vance started to laugh.

Then Brooks joined him.

"What's so funny?" Pinks asked.

"It was completely ridiculous," Vance said, as animated as Laidey had ever seen him. "While Xavier was barking at Brooks for being a—what did he call you? An overrated equipment manager embracing far too much of his feminine side?—I threw the first punch. Knocked Xavier on the ground, which was freaking awesome because the guy was bigger than me. That one punch ended hazing at Henderson High forever, but it started our feud with Xavier. The next time Xavier ran into Brooks, he punched him square in the jaw."

"In school?"

"Hell, no. Out of school. Might have been at a party out at the lake. I can't remember."

"I remember," Brooks said, pointedly rubbing his jaw. "It was at the lake. I was trying to get Grace Schutz to kiss me. I'd lured her away from the party. It was dark, and I didn't see it coming when Xavier jumped me. To add insult to injury, he took off with Grace and dated her for three weeks just to spite me before he dumped her for McKenna."

McKenna? Laidey's ears perked up.

"Anyway," Vance went on. "That started a cycle. Xavier would punch Brooks, I'd retaliate by hitting Xavier or pulling a prank, and he'd go after Brooks again. It got to be a game—sort of like Assassin. Swear to God, punking each other after hours somehow brought us together on the ball field. We ended up as leaders of the team, which soothed Xavier's vengeance over not being able to haze anymore."

"True," Brooks added. "But, you know how bossy Vance is right? The way he likes to … ah, control everyone and everything?"

Pinks looked over at Vance. "Xavier like to boss people around too?"

"Asshole thought he ran the place," Vance said. "I let him because he was a senior, and I knew he'd be heading west for college."

"Arizona State," Brooks supplied. "Got an engineering degree. As his momma tells it, he's been working his way up in the building business ever since he got out there. Anyway, there's a rumor he's coming back."

Pinks ducked his head around Brooks to look pointedly at Vance. "This a problem for you?"

"Not a problem for me," Vance assured him, rubbing his right fist. "Just glad I got a heads up."

Pinks laughed in disbelief. "You don't think he'd come at you now, do you? Didn't that trading punches game end when he left town?"

"No way. As I remember, I punched him the day he graduated. And in retaliation, he stopped at Brooks's door the day he left and returned the favor."

"So, you are the one who could end it, right? Just let it lie … back there … in the past?"

"I could," Vance agreed, "but where would be the fun in that?"

Harry barked out a laugh.

Laidey didn't know if she'd ever met anyone as convoluted as Vance Evans, but she hadn't met many she liked as well either. She noticed Harry glanced her way as he laughed. She could tell he'd been making a point to keep an eye on her this evening. Ever since he'd heard one of her colleagues shout, "The mouse is in the house," when she'd walked in the room.

Harry's reaction had been to flinch. Apparently he didn't know she was well aware of her pet name. Her officemates had used it freely for a long while now. It had never really bothered her. She was, after all, the smallest and quietest among them.

Just like it absolutely didn't bother her when Harry insisted she was as sharp as Vance, diligent as Brooks, sweet as Genevra, but truly quieter than anybody he'd ever known.

No. Those high compliments were appreciated, and she was contemplating them when Harry caught her eye again. Only this time he winked and tilted his head toward the door as he untied his apron.

What? What's happening now?

"Luke, my man," Harry called to the other bartender. "You got this crowd?"

Laidey watched Luke give Harry a chin flip.

"Great. Cover me."

Another chin flip.

Harry looked back at her, nodding pointedly toward the door.

Laidey wiped her mouth with her napkin, took a sip of water, then scrambled off the bar chair, following Harry out the door. She met him in the hallway, saying, "What's up?"

"Come on." Harry took Laidey's hand. "There's something we need to do."

"There is?" she asked as he pulled her along.

"Yep."

"Okay." She gave him a smile and picked up her pace, following him down the back steps to the club's lower level.

He looked over his shoulder, smiling. "You're in a good mood tonight."

"Oh?" Her pace faltered as she reeled herself in. "Am I?"

"Whoa-wait." Harry stopped, swinging her around in front of him so they were face to face. His curious gaze trying to penetrate the depth of her eyes. "Laidey?" he asked quizzically. "Who told you you shouldn't have a good time?"

"What?"

"Take a breath," he ordered. "Then blow it out slowly."

She did as she was told.

Harry stepped in closer and gentled his voice. "Now close your eyes. Think back. To when you were really young."

Her mind traveled back to a Thanksgiving dinner when she was eight-years-old.

"Who told you not to have a good time?"

Laidey's right shoulder rose, scraping against her ear as a distinct memory emerged. She rubbed it a few times and then settled. Her eyes remained closed.

"Who?" Harry pressed.

Laidey licked her lips. "Grandmother Rowling. She told me not to emulate my mother. She said my mother had too much fun. That I should do my name proud and be reasonable. Reliable. Respectable."

"But not fun," Harry stated as Laidey slowly opened her eyes.

"The three R's. Not fun," she repeated quietly. "Wow." Her lips twisted in a grimace. "I've never connected those dots before."

"So, this grandmother you were named after. I'm guessing she wasn't the warm, fuzzy type?"

"You'd be correct about that." She grinned at the analogy and felt her mood lighten again.

"You've done her proud," Harry said with no degree of sarcasm. "I mean it. You are reasonable and reliable. And as I understand it, you're very well respected. I've been told by more than one of your colleagues that Team Dallas can't live without you. Not to mention, Team Henderson's lone lawyer Duncan James has been overheard singing your praises. Your namesake would be very proud of you."

"I hope so," she said honestly. "I liked her. I liked that she *wasn't* flighty like my mother. Don't get me wrong, I love my mother. Though where I may be a source of pride to my grandmother, I'm afraid I'm probably a disappointment to my mom."

"But what about you? The moment I mentioned you were in a good mood, you shrunk down inside yourself. As if your grandmother was warning you off a good mood because it might *lead* to a good time."

"I was in a good mood. I just hadn't noticed it. Once you pointed it out, I did feel rather odd about it."

"Work on that."

"Work on what?"

"Feeling odd. Just …" He pulled her along with him again. "Just work on feeling whatever you're feeling at any given moment. Give yourself permission to entertain the feeling. Sad. Happy. *Fun.* Own them. Breathe through them. Good or bad, they'll pass. But only if you acknowledge them."

"Where are we going?" she asked as Harry pushed through the side door of the club and herded her toward the back edge of the parking lot.

"To meet someone new."

The parking area was dark and sporadically lit. Laidey could hear the cadence of a conversation long before any bodies came into focus. One voice was a low, masculine rumble. The words muffled, but the inflections humorous and coaxing.

But the other? The other voice was as outraged as Laidey had ever heard it.

McKenna.

"Everything okay here?" Harry asked as they came upon the scene.

"We're fine," came McKenna's irritated voice.

A bruiser of a guy immediately went from leaning nonchalantly against the seat of a sleek-looking motorcycle, to taking up a towering, aggressive stance. His leather jacket draped opened over a graphic tee as he put his hands on the hips of his jeans. He appeared to be wearing construction boots and Laidey noted his hair seemed rather clean-cut considering his attire and choice of transportation. She may have spotted a short-cropped beard, but it was hard to tell in this lighting.

What wasn't hard to tell?

The man was comfortable in his body. He was also comfortable in the dark and certainly comfortable with McKenna, although she had her arms crossed so tight over her chest it was obvious *she* wasn't comfortable at all.

So this was Xavier Wright, she surmised. Vance and Brooks's gold-fish nemesis.

"And you are?" Xavier questioned Harry.

Harry extended his hand and started to move toward Xavier, but Laidey grabbed his arm, pulling him to a stop. He shot her a quick glance over his shoulder before returning his gaze to Xavier. "I'm Harry. I work inside."

The guy's sharp eyes studied Harry a moment before they shifted to Laidey, causing her to scoot behind Harry.

"I'm not going to hurt you," Xavier said, staring after her. His face snapped toward McKenna briefly ordering—"Tell her"—before he looked back at Laidey. "Tell her she shouldn't be afraid of me."

"I'm not telling her that," McKenna argued. "I wouldn't tell *any* female that. In fact," she focused on Laidey and said, "run. He absolutely *will* hurt you. He will take out your heart, stomp on it with the heel of his big ol' boot, and ride out of town like he owns the whole world."

"McKenna," Xavier's voice warned.

"It's the truth," she tossed at the biker. "You raced out of here and *never* looked back. How is it possible that in fourteen years you didn't come back?" McKenna's voice was shrill, and Laidey felt emotion roll off her.

"My family vacationed in Arizona," he explained. "I've been working, studying. Come on," he said blithely, "it's not like you don't know all this."

"What I didn't know is that you were coming back, *tonight*. I didn't know I'd see you, *tonight*. And you can take whatever apologies you brought with you and shove them because they are *years* too late."

"I hurt you. I know that. But not for fourteen years," Xavier all but implored. "No way your heart stayed broken for that long."

"Don't flatter yourself," McKenna scoffed. "But you trying to fix it all *now* is infuriating. So stop it. I mean it. Just … go home and see your mother. Please."

"McKenna," he growled low and deep.

Where that sound didn't seem to affect McKenna in the least, it sure as hell had an effect on Laidey. She squeaked and bounced into Harry's back.

Xavier turned a swift glare in her direction. "I'm not going to hurt you," he barked out at Laidey. Then he threw up his hands and spun to face his motorcycle. "Christ," he muttered, placing his hands on his hips, staring down at the ground. "I tried," he said, jabbing a finger in McKenna's direction. "I came to you first." He swung a leg over the seat of his Harley and cranked the throttle. "Before I did anything else, I found you." His attention swung to Laidey. His grey eyes glistened as he gave her a cold glare while swinging that big machine around.

Laidey stayed behind Harry, watching the gravel spray from the tires as the bike raced off through the parking lot in search of open road.

"You okay?" Laidey asked as she moved to embrace McKenna. Harry followed after her wrapping both of them up in his arms.

"I'm fine," McKenna moaned in exasperation, extracting herself from the group hug. "He just caught me off guard, that's all," she claimed, brushing tears from her face. "That face of his," she sighed. "I haven't seen it in years and then—wham." Her fingers ran through her hair, pulling it up into a ponytail. "It was a shock. That's all."

"What did he want?" Laidey asked.

"To make amends." She let out an incredulous laugh.

"Let me walk you two back inside," Harry suggested. "I'll spring for a nice bottle of wine."

"No," McKenna declined. "I'm fine, really. I should have taken the time to wrap my head around the return of the prodigal son. I ought to head home and brace myself for the fact that everyone is going to make him out to be the shiny, new hero back to save his mother *and* this town." McKenna's breath hitched. "His *mother*," she sighed, then whimpered, "I really love his mother."

"Okay, yeah, taking the two of you home," Harry proclaimed. "What you need is a couple pints of Ben & Jerry's, a good heart-wrenching movie, and a lot of heart-to-heart girly chatter."

"Oh, God, Harry. You're being *such* a guy right now," McKenna complained.

"Yep. So I'm ill-equipped to handle all the sighing and lamenting. My man card will be revoked if I even try."

"I thought you were supposed to be the Handy Man," McKenna teased. .

"Oh, I'm handy. But I'm not your man. Not tonight. You two are on your own. You want a ride or not?"

"I've got my car," McKenna told him.

"Fine, then. Ice cream, chick flick, wine. Lots and lots of wine," he ordered. "But no tequila. Tonight is not a tequila night. Understood?"

Laidey was surprised at how easily McKenna appeared to brighten when she smiled at Harry and replied, "Understood."

CHAPTER FOUR

Xavier roared away from the country club, letting regret fly off him. He'd done what he'd had to way back when. He was sorry he'd caused McKenna pain, but he was happy to see she could still stand up to him. The girl's backbone had always been made of steel. Which irritated him to no end and was why the two of them didn't work.

That and the fact he started dating her under false pretenses.

Yep, he'd known he and McKenna were doomed long before she did. He just didn't have the heart to face her while he ripped hers out. Instead, he left without ending it. Left for college, for work, for a life outside of their small town. Pulled an asshole move and allowed what the two of them had die from long distance.

Because he couldn't spell it out.

Wouldn't tell her the truth.

Ever.

But McKenna Blakely had grown up even more beautiful than he'd pictured. And frankly, he was curious why she was wasting her clever, snarky self here in Henderson.

She'd told him, "One word … roots."

Roots. Yep, he had 'em too. Growing right next to hers. Which is why he was home after such a long sabbatical.

Pulling into his parents' circular drive, he glided to a stop, parking his Road King off to the side. He flipped the backpack open and took out the few items he hadn't thrown away on his cross-country trek. He figured even if his closet wasn't how he'd left it, with four brothers, he'd find something to wear.

Or else he'd go shopping.

He'd need a black suit at the end of all this for sure. And as that horrible thought came up … he breathed through it.

Allowed himself to feel the pain.

Let his gut toss with the anguish.

Let it engulf him as he'd learned to do every time it happened. He stood there in the grief, owning it. Longing for it to be different but knowing some things couldn't be changed.

When the agony subsided, when he felt it ease up, when it finally dispersed like a whisper, he took a cleansing breath to replenish the well. Then he marched those final steps to the front door, reached for the knob, and … came home.

Lulu was there before he could blink, hugging him tight. Telling him she was blessed to be holding her baby in her arms again. Lulu— the big-hearted, slim-bodied, black woman who had come to work for his mother as a doula when he'd been born. She'd helped a young Anna Beth Wright figure out how to be a mother by helping her tend to his newborn needs and her own needs as well. His mother and Lulu got on so well that she'd returned for all subsequent births and was there in the mix when his mother delivered a stillborn.

That was when Lulu became indispensable.

The two women had mourned his baby sister together, had included his father in the process as best they could. They included him and his brothers as well, and helped the family heal as a unit. After that, she'd come back whenever the Wright family needed healing, physically or emotionally. Lulu would come and work her magic.

He'd heard she'd come when he'd headed out of town. And again after each of his brothers had done the same. He loved her for being there for his mom, and maybe even his dad, when he couldn't be.

But they were circling the wagons now, weren't they? He'd kept in touch with Lulu directly through the years. Needed to since he had immediately distanced himself from his brother—which was like distancing yourself from your right arm. But he'd clung to Lulu through cyberspace, and had been able to read between the lines where others had not. So he'd planned this trip a long time ago. Planned a strategy to work himself loose from his commitments in

Arizona, giving himself time to ride across the country, getting his head on straight before arriving home. Hopefully long before the end.

"How are you?" he asked the woman he loved with all his heart.

"Well, seein' this man walk into the house where I once knew the boy is a little disconcerting, but I'm getting over the shock." She took a step back saying, "Let me look at you."

"I'm the same pain in your ass I've always been."

"Oh," she said, moving in with a whisper. "You know you're my favorite. Though I will deny it with my last breath if you go and blab to the others."

"As if you don't tell all my brothers the same thing." He grinned from ear to ear at her foolishness before getting serious. "How's Ma? And how's Daddy for real?"

"Why don't you see for yourself?" Lu said way too cheerfully for the situation at hand.

"She's having a good day?" he surmised, looking at Lu's stretched out arm, her hand flicking toward the living room.

"We moved her to the first floor guest suite. Easier for her to get around and have visitors. They've been waiting on you, so head on back, and we'll talk later. I'm going home."

"When will you be back?"

"Tomorrow."

They exchanged a look. "You come every day?"

"Go see your momma. We'll catch up over breakfast."

"I'll do the cooking," he said, walking her to the door. "I've brought home a few tricks to dazzle you with."

"If there's a man in this family willing to cook me breakfast, I'm already dazzled."

"Come a little later then. Give me some time in the kitchen by myself. What? You're looking at me as if I'm crazy."

"I'm looking at you as if I don't believe my ears."

"Ah, come on. We Wright brothers aren't that bad."

"Hmmph," she said on her way out the door.

"I'm gonna make it up to you," he shouted after her. "Make you forget all the trouble I caused."

"You were no trouble, Xavier," she called back with a laugh. "Just comic relief."

"Yeah? Well breakfast will be no joke."

Lu waved him off as she got in her car.

Xavier watched her go. God, he'd missed her. Just as much as he'd missed everybody else. It wasn't his intention to stay away for so long. It just … happened. His life. His work. It all just happened.

He blew out a breath and shut the door behind Lu, wondering if people in Henderson were locking doors these days. They certainly were in Phoenix. He strolled into the living room only to be startled by the sight of the grand piano. How long had it been since his fingers had tickled those ivories? How long since he'd been home for more than a couple nights at a time?

Five thousand one hundred and ten days, McKenna had declared.

Days. How did she know how many days?

She didn't, he told himself. She was just spouting shit to make him feel bad for leaving like he did and then leaving her hanging … for years.

Man.

McKenna.

She was too good for him then and too good for him now. And by the way she'd let him have it, he was pretty sure she'd figured that out. No amount of teasing or consoling was gonna work with her. He was going to have to straight out apologize—something a guy like him had always avoided. But he'd have to do it in this case—sincerely—and soon.

All that driveway breathing was not keeping his dread at bay as Xavier approached the first floor guest room. The last time he'd laid eyes on his ma, she was being treated at the Mayo Clinic in Phoenix. They'd chosen that location not only because he could provide a home base for his parents, but also because autoimmune disease was one of the clinic's specialties. His notoriously energetic ma had looked so ill. Just a sunken shadow propped up by pillows, with tubes and monitors hooked up everywhere. When he'd called home over the last few weeks, he'd noticed her voice sounded stronger. Still, he wasn't going to kid himself. He had no hope of finding her looking stronger or any better.

Hearing soft mumbling coming from within, Xavier knocked lightly on the door as he entered. His eyes fell on his father, seated in an upholstered chair next to the four-poster bed. The man's hair was graying, but he sat tall and fit—the picture of health—as he set aside his paper and stood.

Too scared of what he'd find if he glanced at the bed, Xavier moved to wrap his father in a brief hug, squeezing his eyes shut before pulling back. The two of them stood there, eye to eye, sharing a moment before his father nodded. Keeping his head down, Xavier kicked off his shoes, climbed onto the bed, and wrapped his sick mother in his arms.

"You're home," she said quietly, lifting a hand to run it down the side of his face.

"Ma," he muttered into her neck, fighting back tears.

"You're here now, baby."

His dad sat.

The three of them shared a comfortable silence. He'd been away too long. They all knew it. He'd been the one to state it during their phone conversations. His parents always dismissed it, never minding that he'd left town. When his mom got sick, they'd begged him to stay in Phoenix and finish his project. They told him to come home when he could. His ma constantly assured him that she felt his love and prayers all the way from Arizona, and that she'd call him if she needed him. He was only two flights away.

But now he was too emotional to do anything but be here physically. Couldn't ask her how she was doing because the truth was, he didn't want to know. He'd seen the writing on the wall. Heard what the doctors weren't saying. Read between the lines. But his beloved momma felt a little more solid than she had when he crawled into her hospital bed back in Phoenix. She actually smelled like her old self too. A floral scent instead of the aroma of hospital apparatus, medicines, and what not. He took the hand stroking his face into his own and opened his eyes, holding it before him. Her nails were pretty again, long and polished. And her skin was flushed pink, not jaundiced from the liver infection.

He twisted his neck to look into the face of his mother and— swear to God—that thing that made his ma his ma, her life spark?

It was back. The thing which had been stolen from her the last time they were together. It was what had scared him so. The reason he knew he had to finish up and come home.

"You … look good," he stumbled, not quite believing what he was seeing.

She nodded slowly, acknowledging the truth of it. "I'm getting better."

"How?"

"Stem cells. An assortment of trials that have been tailored just for me."

"They're working?"

"Seem to be."

"What stem cells?"

"Bone marrow."

"Bone marrow? As in a transplant?"

"Yes."

"Don't you need some sort of match for that? Like shouldn't we all have been tested?"

"There was a match."

"Who?"

"Does it matter?"

"I guess not," he said on a laugh. "What does this mean?"

"It means I'm probably going to be feeling up to eating that breakfast we heard you promising Lulu."

"Ma," he accused. "This is amazing."

"I know." She smiled gently. "I'm feeling much better, and my doctors at Duke are very happy with my progress. I'm still fairly weak, but that's from lying in bed for so long."

"So tomorrow we get you over to the gym at the high school. See if we can use some of their equipment to get you back into shape?"

"Sure. Why not? My son is home. Let's go to the gym. If nothing else, I can watch the town go a little nuts seeing that the great Xavier Wright has finally come home."

"Oh. Yeah. That might be a problem."

"Shush. No problem at all," his mother soothed.

"Maybe a little problem here and there," his father said. "Starting with our darling McKenna. Tell you what? I'm going to go warm a plate up for the boy while you two talk that out."

His father was halfway to the door when Xavier said, "I've already seen McKenna."

"What?" both his parents asked at the same time.

"I couldn't very well set foot in town without dealing with her first, could I? And true to form, she snarled at me as if I'd left yesterday, not fourteen years ago."

His father stuck his finger out at him. "You did her wrong," he accused.

"I did. And I'm owning it. But y'all need to get over it."

"She's the daughter your mother never had," his father insisted. "Comes around here once or twice a week to check on her. Read to her. Fill her in on what's happening in town. McKenna would have made a damn fine Wright if only you'd had your head screwed on back then."

"I was a kid, and so was she," Xavier countered. "And it sure sounds like she's the daughter *you* never had, as surly as you're bein' right now."

"Well, I like her," his father grumbled, waving him off and moseying from the room.

"Clearly," Xavier muttered.

His mother chuckled softly and the sound brought him back to happy. "We do love McKenna. She *is* like a daughter to us. We're also very happy you're home. My guess is that your father's on edge wondering if McKenna's going to continue coming around now that you're moving back in."

"Well, damn." Xavier slapped his thigh. "Sounds like my own family has thrown me over for my ex."

"You know that's not true," his ma soothed. "Tell me. What did McKenna say when you showed up at her house?"

"I wasn't at her house. I found her in the parking lot at the club. Thanks to you forcing her number on me, I was able to track her down by her phone—do not go telling her that. Understand? I want to be able to see her when I want to and avoid her when I don't. So please. I know you love her, probably more than you love me right now, but if I'm gonna be in Henderson for any length of time, I need some peace of mind about who I'm going to run into and when."

"Isn't that a little ...?"

"What?"

"I don't know. Sneaky? Like a stalker but in reverse?"

"Pretty much. But this is McKenna, *the daughter you never had* we're talking about. The one who just handed me my ass in front of a dude who totally wanted to defend her honor and some mousy chick that I scared to death." Xavier sighed as he sat up, propping an arm around his mother's shoulders. "I'm tellin' ya. That was not my finest hour."

"Oh, dear."

"Oh, dear what?"

"Well, that thing your father was reading to me? That's a print out of the e-newsletter. It's part of the movement to revitalize Henderson, and it's working. Really well. Only ..."

"What?"

"Well, let's just say that your homecoming will not go unnoticed."

CHAPTER FIVE

Breakfast was cleaned up. The *huevos rancheros* and *bunuelos* had gone over so well LuLu had asked for the recipes. Whether she'd done it to feed his ego or not, Xavier didn't care. She'd eaten everything on her plate and asked for seconds.

Slightly disheartened that his mother wasn't as strong as he'd hoped, Xavier helped his father get her back into bed. He had to remind himself that the two of them weren't out shopping for coffins, so no way was he going to start complaining to the man upstairs. He took his dad aside and gave him the day off. Told him to go play golf or drink himself silly. Told him he'd stay and watch over the love of the man's life while he let off some long-overdue steam. Told him to hit the lake and fish a little. Whatever. The man had done nothing but dote on his wife for so long, it was time he had a little R&R.

After ushering his father out the door, Xavier headed toward the kitchen to see what he'd be able to rustle up for himself and his ma at lunch. The doorbell rang and when he opened it, the words, "Oh, shit," dropped out of his mouth. The next thing he knew, he was sprawled flat on his back, his jaw hurting like a sonofabitch, and Vance Evans's ugly mug was leaning down in his face.

"We done?" Vance sneered.

"Hell, no, we aren't done," Xavier argued, rubbing his jaw.

"Let me rephrase that. We're done. Period. The hazing vendetta between you, me, and Brooks is now *done*."

"You can't throw a punch and then declare it's done."

"I just did. It's done."

When Xavier tried to get up off the floor, Vance put a running shoe on his chest. "What the fuck?" he protested.

It was then his ma came racing around the corner in her bathrobe, hand clasped to her throat. She stopped when she saw the two of them and let her arms collapse to her sides. "Oh, Vance, it's just you," she sighed with relief.

"Yep. Just me. Welcoming Xavier home," he said, digging his foot into Xavier's chest.

Xavier rubbed his jaw while thrusting a thumb back toward his mother. "Damn, Evans. Look what you've done now. Gotten my mother all upset."

"She don't look all that upset. And she looks way too pretty to be sick. How ya feeling, Mrs. Wright?"

"Better every day. How's that baby of yours?"

"Smart and hitting 'em out of the park."

"And Piper?"

"Giving me fits."

"That a girl. You two enjoy catching up. I'm gonna catch a quick catnap. I want to be able to attend the grand opening when Piper's shop opens on Main Street."

"How do you know about that?" Vance asked.

"It was in the Henderson Happenings newsletter." The words floated behind her as she made her way out of sight.

"Freaking newsletter," Vance grumbled. He looked down at Xavier, foot still square on his chest. "Gotta tell ya, some kind of miracle is going down in this house. She looks amazing."

"And because the good Lord has blessed this family, I will refrain from retaliating and using your face as a punching bag once you let me up."

"Listen," Vance said, leaning down, bracing an elbow on the knee attached to the foot on Xavier's sternum. "I'm glad you're back. This town needs as many of you Wright brothers as we can get." He grinned. "Why only one of you became a pilot, I'll never know. Feels like a missed opportunity. Anyway, the hazing thing. It's got to end." Xavier pushed up and shoved Vance's foot off his chest. Vance fell back, catching his balance while explaining. "Brooks is running for mayor. He can't be seen rolling around in agony at your feet week in and week out. And we've pulled in a lot of newcomers to help us get this town back on its feet. I don't want you pulling any shit and messing with the newcomers."

Xavier dusted himself off as he got to his feet. "Newcomers, huh?"

"That's right. We've got a crew from Dallas workin' their tails off helping us get a big idea off the ground. There are also a couple of employees at Evans & Evans Investments from Baltimore who are making our lives a whole lot easier with what they bring to the table. These are good, hardworking folks who, for some crazy reason, have agreed to help us get done what we as a town have not been able to do on our own. I am here to tell you, you cannot be messing with that."

"Ye-ah." Xavier's shoulders bunched up and his torso twisted back and forth while he placed his hands in the pockets of his jeans. "Newcomers make me antsy."

"Dude. You do get that after fourteen years of being AWOL, *you* are the newcomer, right?"

"Ah, that's a big negatory. Did we or did we not live, breathe, and die Bulldogs baseball together?"

"We did."

"Did we or did we not win that damn trophy? *Together?*"

"You know we did."

"So where does your allegiance lie?"

"To my wife Piper. And then to Brooks. Then to this town and everyone in it trying to make it something bigger than our damn trophy. Now, are you jumping on board this bandwagon, or am I gonna have to hogtie you and toss you on it?"

"Look. I didn't come home for Henderson. I came home for my mother. So long as her health continues to improve, I'm in. However I can help. But I *will* punch Brooks the first chance I get, you can be damn certain of that." He held up a palm. "And that will be the end of it, I promise. Golden Boy took all the fun out of being mean, so he gets his one more time. Not promising anything about the newcomers, though."

"You've been warned," Vance said.

"What do you mean, I've been warned?"

"One of the newcomers has a double black belt in Tae Kwon Do. Mess with the newcomers at your own peril."

"You're bullshittin' me."

Vance lifted a shoulder. "Maybe I am. Maybe I'm not." He pounded Xavier on the back. "Team Henderson meets Monday mornings at ten. E&E Investments in the center of town. I'll expect to see you there."

"Man, things haven't changed a bit. You're still the same bossy son of a bitch you were back in high school."

"And don't you forget it," Vance said as he took his leave, shooting a welcoming smile back at his old teammate. "Now get on the phone and get those brothers of yours back here. The top jobs aren't gonna hold out forever."

"What top jobs?" Xavier shouted. But Vance waved him off as he got in his Land Rover.

Monday morning, Xavier felt like a deer caught in headlights as he stepped from the staircase into the foyer of his parents' home. The front door had opened unexpectedly to the beautiful but unwelcome sight of one McKenna Blakely.

The girl had not lost her appeal over the last many years. She was still a pretty brunette, but now she knew how to play it up. Gone were the high ponytail and short gym shorts, although her legs still looked smoking in those heels she had on. Those strappy, little, barely there, pale-pink heels he was paying way too much attention to right now. Probably because he still wasn't interested in meeting her eyes.

"I thought you'd have ridden off on that ridiculous machine by now."

Since she was acting ornery and not hurt he glanced up. "That machine is a ridiculously *awesome* Hard Candy, Hot-Rod-Red Road King, and I just got here Friday."

"I figured you'd see how much your mother has improved and hit the road."

"You'd like that wouldn't you."

"I would."

"Why? You made it clear I don't mean a damn thing to you. Wouldn't even let me work out an apology and try to make things easier between us now that I'm back."

"You *don't* mean a damn thing to me. I don't even know you. *You* just look like Xavier Wright, a boy I trusted. A boy who didn't bother to contact me *once* after he left for college. I am pissed as all get out at him. Him, I will never forgive. *You* just remind me of him, and that irritates the hell out of me."

"Then why are you here, first thing on a Monday morning, seeking me out?"

"Don't flatter yourself. I'm here to see your mother. Because that's what I do first thing Mondays. I come see your mother. And as irritated as I am with seeing your face, I refuse to let it interrupt my life."

"She's *my* mother."

"Pfft." McKenna waved him off like he was nothing and strode by him on the way to his mother's bedroom.

He stalked after her. "What's that supposed to mean?"

She whirled on him. "You not being around for fourteen years gives me just as much a claim to her. Maybe even more. I've been a part of her life on a daily basis. So back off you … you, out-of-towner."

"Out-of-towner?"

"It's like you've never lived here, you've been gone so long."

"You take that back."

"I'm not taking anything back."

"This is my hometown same as it's yours."

"Really? Who are the debutantes making their debut this season?"

"McKenna, I wouldn't know that shit even if I'd sired two of them."

"Well, who's getting married at the church this Saturday?"

"Again, unless I was invited, I wouldn't be following. But can you tell me who made the last out of the state championship baseball game?"

"Gunner Hendrix," she declared.

"What was the score?"

"Fourteen to eight."

"Hmm." He twisted his lips.

She moved in with a smirk on her face. "Okay, Mr. Henderson Sports News. Baseball isn't the only winning team in town. Which other Henderson team won a title this spring?"

Xavier had no idea.

"See," she scoffed, turning away from him and heading across the living room floor. "Out-of-towner."

"Bullshit."

"You don't belong anymore, Xavier," she said over her shoulder. "Your mother's doing fine. Pack your bags and head back to Arizona. I'm sure you got along great with all that prickly cactus."

McKenna let herself into Miss Anna Beth's room without bothering to knock. She figured Xavier's mother couldn't have missed the sparring match happening in her living room. She took a deep breath and greeted the woman she considered a second mother with a smile much brighter than she felt.

The gracious belle tilted her head, giving McKenna a forlorn smile in response. "Was that hard?" she whispered as McKenna came over and sat on the bed.

"Not as hard as I thought it'd be," she sighed. She felt Anna Beth's hand caress the top of her head, trickle down her cheek, and linger over her arm before dropping to her own lap.

"I appreciate you doing this. I know it's not easy for you."

"It's not," she admitted, letting out a bigger sigh and falling into the older woman's arms.

She was pulled close and comforted. "You don't have to, you know."

"I know," she mumbled against Miss Anna Beth's shoulder. "I'm okay. I can handle it. I'm doing it for you. And for him. Even though he's an ass, and he doesn't deserve it." They both shared a sad, shallow chuckle over that. McKenna lifted back up to a sitting position, studying the woman who came so close to dying. "You need him here. And if I can taunt him into sticking around, I'm happy to do it for you."

"You sure you don't want to taunt him into sticking around for you?"

McKenna eyed her. "We've been over this. He didn't love me. And I moved on quickly after his departure. It's just ... his face, getting used to seeing him again. That's why I had to come today, and I'll be coming like I always do. I need to get used to seeing him, and then it will all even itself out and life will go on as it always has. When are your other boys coming in?"

"Everybody will be home for the Fourth. I'm praying I keep getting stronger because I'd love to spend the entire day at the club with my family, just like we used to. How's your momma?"

"Good. Fine. Says she'll stop over with some rations from Raleigh later this week."

"I don't know what I'd do without you two. McKenna?"

"Yes?"

"Thank you for being the daughter I never had."

McKenna pulled back, startled. They'd never talked about that. A smile came faster than her words. "I like that. To be honest, all these years I've considered myself more like the daughter-in-law your boys refuse to give you. We got so close when Xavier and I dated, and we were both so sad when he left. I guess our bond just kept growing."

"Yes, we shared the bond of heartache, watching the boy we loved leave town. But, by then I'd already thought of you as a gift in my life. Like God had sent me a wonderful, kind spirit to fill the void of the daughter I lost. You would have been the same age as our Kendra, do you know that? Would have been in the same class. May have even been friends had she lived."

"We've never talked about her," McKenna said quietly.

"I know. Sweetie, am I making you uncomfortable?"

"No. No, I swear. If you're okay talking about this, I'm okay. I've always been curious. You know, you being ... you, with all these boys running around all the time and no little girls to dress or cuddle."

"Which is why I took such a liking to you. You didn't mind me paying attention to what you wore. You even let me curl your hair for that one dance, do you remember?"

"I do. My momma's always worked so hard. She never had time for things like curled hair or prom dresses. She thought those were frivolous. And now … well, now that I'm trying to make a living and mean something to this town, I get it. I still enjoy frivolous things, but I'm finding less and less time to pay attention to them."

"You're a strong journalist. Our paper needs that. We are readers in this town. We like to know what's going on here, in Oxford, and elsewhere. You provide a wonderful, top-notch service. But you still need to be McKenna. And frivolous is in the eye of the beholder." She winked.

McKenna laughed. "So what do you think? Is Xavier going to stick around?"

"He says he is, although he has yet to define his plans. He desperately needs a trip to Raleigh to shop. He's had on the same clothes since he's arrived. I think he believed he had a full closet waiting on him. Men. How do they not think styles change? Or their bodies? He was eighteen when he left."

McKenna wanted to bite off her tongue when the words, "And he did not look like that," came tumbling out.

"No, he didn't," his mother agreed.

"What do you think of him in that trendy beard thing everybody is sporting these days?"

"He looks good," his mother said.

He did. Though McKenna preferred his face clean-shaven, so the beard was a helpful addition. Even if it looked good. Like, sexy good. Like, damn good.

Shit.

"I need a date," she blurted.

"What about that guy from the online dating thing?"

"He was okay."

"Just okay?"

"Yeah. Just okay. Not worth driving into Raleigh for on a regular basis. But I'll try again. Lots of my college friends have successfully dated online. I just need to get the energy up to do it. And with Xavier home, it might light the fire underneath me to start putting myself out there again."

"So you really aren't interested in my Xavier?"

"I'm sorry. I'm really not." She gave Anna Beth a sympathetic smile. "But I relish my status of being the daughter you never had."

"All right. I won't play matchmaker. I promise. But I do appreciate you continuing to challenge him about being an out-of-towner. I can't think of a better way to get my obstinate and stubborn mule of a son to plant his roots back in Henderson. Roots he won't want to pull up this time."

CHAPTER SIX

"Out-of-towner, my ass," Xavier muttered as he slammed the front door.

With McKenna squeezing every last air molecule out of the house, Xavier had no choice but to leave. Only he had no clue where to head. He knew he needed clothes, like a ton of them. He'd thrown out his work wardrobe of stained jeans and ripped T-shirts back in Arizona, and all the shit he found in his closet looked like a toddler had owned them. He'd had to ransack his brothers' old rooms to scavenge a few items that could tide him over.

He wondered who had remained in town from his high school days he could rally for a weekend in Raleigh, giving him a chance to shop and party and see what's what. Or maybe even take a trip to the beach.

His parents could do without him overnight. Hell, his mother was in far better shape than he expected, and his dad seemed to be handling things with Lulu coming and going.

And Lord only knew what McKenna was contributing to the sustenance of his parents.

Whatever.

He was grateful for all the help Henderson was giving his family. Especially since he and his brothers had scattered far and wide.

But now—now he was sticking around.

Had to.

He was the first to go, so he needed to be the first to come back. It was the right thing to do after he'd managed a modicum of success and squirreled away some money. Due to his ambition, his life had gotten away from him in Arizona. It took the harsh-sounding wake-up call of his mother's illness to remind him of who he was.

Somebody's son.

A member of a family.

And that he had old friends he'd neglected and a hometown that could use his help. He'd never really pulled up his roots as McKenna had accused. His heart, his soul, had always been planted in Henderson.

Arizona simply helped him grow up in a way he couldn't here.

He got on his Road King and revved the engine, heading out the drive. He'd intentionally left his helmet home so he could feel the wind in his hair and a little freedom on the road. Being back with his parents wasn't exactly claustrophobic, but he hadn't answered to anyone but Chase for a long time. So, being back in the fold of his family and wanting to respect their home and their feelings, a little bit of helmet-less freedom felt necessary.

Of course, his mom would skewer him alive if she saw it. Apparently just like Mrs. Blakely, who was honking her dang horn and wagging a finger at him. There were only three stoplights in the whole town and wouldn't you know it? He was sitting here stuck at one next to McKenna's momma.

"May as well get this one checked off my list," he moaned, putting the kickstand down and walking over to the minivan. "I know what you're gonna say," he started his defense with an offense, bending low and pulling off his shades as he looked into her open window.

"Good to have you back Xavier," she said. "Even if you did break my daughter's heart into a million different pieces."

"I'm sorry about that," he said sincerely. "How about your heart? Did I break yours too?" he teased.

"Oh you. Why aren't you wearing your helmet? You got a death wish?"

"Yes ma'am. I do."

"Xavier. Please. With what your mother's gone through? What in the world are you thinking?" she scolded.

"Miz B, It's all your McKenna's fault. She came stomping into my parents' home this morning, took one look at me, and declared me an outsider. Told me I ought to pack up and leave because after fourteen years, I no longer belong. Now you know how I love my hometown, Miz B. Broke my heart the day I left to make my way in this world. I always planned to come back. And now that I have, your offspring has stomped all over my homecoming and got me so depressed I'm riding around without my helmet. You really ought to have a talk with that girl."

Mrs. Blakely harrumphed. "Whatever McKenna's putting you through you deserve." Then she gave him a grin and whispered, "But I'm glad you're back. For your sweet mother's sake and the sake of this town. So stay," she demanded. "And get your brothers to come home and do the same. There was a time when the Wright name meant something around here. Now we've got that Evans crowd running things. And though they're good people, they're relative newcomers. Haven't been here for generations like the Wrights and the Blakelys, and they shouldn't have to save this town on their own. Henderson's history is being rewritten. Everything your grandparents and their parents did for this town has all but folded. If you want the Wright family to be relevant, you need to be part of this rebuilding. Your father has spent all of his energy on your mother, as he should. But he's got nothing left for this town. I'm telling you, it's fallen to you and your brothers."

"Well, damn." Xavier ran a hand over his beard. "And here I'm thinking about taking a weekend and going to the beach," he teased.

"The beach? There's no time for the beach. We've got Mayor Stevens and his slinky campaign manager wreaking havoc on Brooks Bennett's campaign for mayor. They're making that wonderful man out to be the Antichrist. I have just heard more than an earful over at the Gas and Go, and honestly, I cannot believe that some folks are buying what the two of them are selling. The talk is starting to scare me, Xavier. So please, get your handsome butt over to the police station, find out what the hell is going on, and *do* something about it."

The woman was frantic. And not because he'd left her only daughter's heart in a shambles fourteen years ago. No. She wanted him to ride into the center of town and with some flick of a magic wand from his back pocket, fix Henderson. *Seriously?* The pull of the beach just got that much stronger. In fact, Xavier felt like leaving right now. Just turn his Harley around and head straight to the beach. Without a helmet.

"Miz B, have you had a few too many cups of coffee this morning? Because from what I understand, things around Henderson are looking up."

"They were. Until Coach Crenshaw overthrew the wrong woman. Now this Marcie Watts—who *is* an out-of-towner—has gotten her claws into our lovely Mayor Stevens. The two of them have set out to make that darling Brooks out to be some kind of no good, low down Henderson High hater."

"Henderson High hater?"

"You heard me. They say he's putting up another school in town that's gonna be the ruination of us all."

"I'm sure that's not his intention."

"No. His intention is to make Henderson the sports capital of North Carolina."

Xavier wasn't following exactly. But the conversation was reminding him that he did have a priority list. And, after reading those Henderson Happenings newsletters last week, he'd put tossing Marcie Watts out on her ass at the top of it.

Miz B was right. Xavier needed to find Brooks and get the lowdown on just what the hell was going on around here. See where the next mayor could use some muscle. "I'm on it," he told Miz B, backing away from her car. "Thanks for filling me in on all this when that daughter of yours did nothing but try to usher me back to Phoenix." He waved as he got back on his bike.

"Don't mind McKenna," she called, driving off. "She's strong. She can handle you."

Xavier didn't doubt that. He just hoped it wouldn't hurt when she did.

At Henderson police headquarters, Xavier was told he'd be able to find Brooks at the weekly Team Henderson meeting.

Right. The one that Vance—of the aforementioned *Evans crowd*—had ordered him to attend.

Xavier checked his watch. If he remembered correctly, he'd actually be fifteen minutes early for a meeting he'd completely forgotten about. Turns out McKenna had done him a solid by showing up at the house. He would look as if he was actually interested in what this *Team Henderson* was up to. And frankly, since McKenna's mom was so frantic over the talk at the Gas and Go, he had to admit, his interest was sparked.

But the sports capital of North Carolina?

He'd bet Chapel Hill would have something to say about that.

He cruised onto Main Street, expecting to find it looking the way it had fourteen years ago. It did not. It looked like a freaking movie set.

Piles of lumber were neatly stacked in front of several storefronts. Every bit of wood trim gracing the brick facades up and down the street had been recently painted. Quarterboard signs dangled over several doors, making the area picturesque with a decidedly nostalgic feel. And the huge pots of brightly colored flowers strewn the length of both sidewalks made the thoroughfare downright cheerful. On top of that, there wasn't a speck of trash to be found. Not even where construction was obviously taking place.

A quick scan told him the pizza place he loved was gone.

Dammit.

The coffee shop was now a hollow shell. Although he'd hated the sonofabitch who'd owned that dump, so good riddance. Still, he wondered why no one else had fixed the place up and taken advantage of the location. Until he looked around at the painfully quiet street and realized there wasn't much need for a breakfast spot. Probably not enough action to make a luncheonette go either.

In fact, even though the place looked good, it was freaking dead. Until one sleek-as-shit sports car turned the corner at the end of the road and cruised toward him. *Whoa.* That thing was a purebred beauty the likes of which Xavier had never seen. Pearly white, glistening in the sun, with a red interior from what he could tell. His need-for-speed cried out, aching to race the sucker for all he was worth. So he cranked the handle of his Harley, wishing it wasn't too big to pop a wheelie, and sped down the road toward the hot rod. Damn if it didn't just get better looking the closer he got.

He circled around, pulling up alongside the sports car, revving his engine, saying hello to the other machine. The guy getting out laughed at him as he pulled a messenger bag from behind his seat and shut the door.

"That's some car." Xavier acknowledged with a head bob, wondering who the guy was. He dressed well, was tightly built, and had brown floppy hair and cool-as-shit-shades. But he was way too young to own something like this. A car of this caliber was usually seen in California or south Florida, driven by men old enough to be Xavier's grandfather. Because those were the only bastards who could afford them. What the hell had this kid done to earn that kind of money? Instead of asking that, he just asked, "What is this?"

"It's an Aston Martin One-77. One of seventy-seven in the entire world. Sweet ride. Crazy sweet."

Xavier blew out a whistle, sitting back on the seat of his own sweet machine so he could absorb the sleek lines and curves of one of man's greatest accomplishments.

Floppy hair came into the street and stuck out his hand. "I'm Davis Williams."

Xavier shook Davis's hand, looking him over. He couldn't be thirty. Probably wasn't even close.

"I work for Evans & Evans." He pointed to the sign over his shoulder. "You Xavier?"

Xavier pulled back in surprise. "How'd you know?"

"Vance said you'd be showing up today. Wanted me to bring you up to speed."

"Up to speed on what?"

"What we're trying to do around here. See where you'd want to help out."

With that, the deserted Main Street burst into activity. From both ends of the thoroughfare cars streamed in, parallel parking one behind the other. At the same time, it seemed people poured from the buildings. It was as if the tide had shifted and was now coming to shore.

While Xavier parked his ride, a mint condition, black Land Rover pulled up behind the One-77. Xavier watched Vance, some gorgeous old broad, and a handsome dude get out, slamming doors and laughing together like they couldn't wait to get to work. And from their expressions when those three pair of eyes came to rest on him, well, you would have thought it was Christmas and they'd found him stuffed into their stockings.

Vance came over and introduced Xavier to his grandmother Emelina and his father Hale. And right on their heels came one of Vance's fraternity brothers from NC State, Duncan James, a lawyer who had recently opened an office down the street.

Before he could follow Davis and the rest inside, Vance introduced Xavier to an athletic blonde named Missy, a thick-necked badass named Thor, and a pack of lightweights from Dallas Xavier couldn't wait to give a raft of shit to, all of whom disappeared into the building with the Evans & Evans quarterboard hanging above the door. When the sound of squealing wheels hit the air, his attention was drawn to a shiny black F-150 as good ole Brooks arrived, sliding into a parking spot along the curb. He came at Xavier with one of his patented broad grins, looking so happy to welcome one of his long-lost teammates back into the fold.

Xavier was certain his own face looked just as happy when his clenched fist landed an uppercut, catching the unsuspecting pitcher underneath his chin. If Vance hadn't seen it coming, Brooks would have hit the ground for sure. Instead, Vance caught Brooks and smiled down into his stunned expression saying, "He owed you."

It all might have ended there, Xavier thought. All of the hazing and fooling around they were known for back in the day. Except *she* was there. The tiny, little brunette. The one who he'd made quiver in the club's parking lot Friday night. He didn't like scaring her then, and he sure didn't like the way she was cowering from him now.

He'd been shaking his hand out, half grimacing, half laughing, when he'd done a semi-turn and caught sight of a fluffy calico dress out of the corner of his eye. His head swiveled further to find the little sprite stopped on the sidewalk behind him, straddling a teal-colored bicycle. His eyes noted that the bulk of her dark curls bobbed above slim shoulders, while threads of wispy tendrils broke away to frame the pale skin of her tiny face. Her eyes drew him in deep, the brown irises indecipherable from the pupils staring back at him with trepidation. Compared to the rest of her face, her eyes were huge and expressive and almost overshadowed the cherry red of her lips.

He licked his own as he glanced down to take in her … sneakers. Her *yellow* sneakers. And then he noticed the wicker basket she'd latched to the front of her bike. The thing couldn't have been more ridiculous. Like something straight out of Estrogen Onslaught Magazine. Silky pale-pink roses adorned the edge of the basket loaded down with a silver laptop, a miniature pink purse, a soft creamy sweater, and he didn't know what all else because his astounded gaze beelined back to her eyes and the fear he saw there.

"You weren't supposed to see that," he croaked out. "We're … friends. It's a … thing," he stammered, wondering why the hell he felt the need to explain himself to this startled little kitten of a girl. He didn't owe her an explanation. Did he? *Shit.* He was trying to change his image so maybe he did.

"Listen," he stepped toward her and a squeak emitted. She and her bike immediately backed up. "Okay," he said, holding up both hands and standing his ground. "Not going to hurt you. Just want to explain." He twisted, looking toward Brooks and Vance, then back again at the timid, little lass and her two-wheeler. "We're old friends. And before I left town … many years ago," he said, turning back to his buddies, "we had a small vendetta going on. I sorta had to get my last licks in when I could. Didn't think anyone would see that. Definitely sorry it had to be you."

"Laidey," Brooks said as he ambled up rubbing his chin. "This asshole is Xavier Wright. He played ball with us back in the day. He's been in Arizona for years building stuff. We're hoping to convince him to build stuff here."

Little Laidey nodded at Brooks. Her enormous eyes flashed at Xavier for a split second before she walked her bike in a wide berth around all of them and laid it carefully against the large picture window. The three men stood watching as she pulled all the shit from her basket and glanced at them before attempting to open the door with her arms full. Vance leaped over and held it open while she ventured inside.

Once the door closed behind her, a dumfounded Xavier asked, "She works here?"

"Works for CC Dallas," Vance said.

"What-What Dallas?"

Brooks chuckled and slapped Xavier on the back. "Welcome home, buddy. You've got a lot of catching up to do. Come on in, and keep that big mouth of yours shut for the next couple of hours. Vance and I'll fill you in on everything you need to know over lunch at the club." Brooks looked pointedly at his jeans. "You got a decent pair of pants back at your parents' place?"

Xavier chuckled. "I don't have a pot to piss in."

"We'll set you up," Vance said, ushering the two of them inside. "What size are you? I'll call Harry. He'll figure out something by the time we get there."

CHAPTER SEVEN

The conference room was barely big enough to hold all the people gathered and Xavier certainly could have done without the grand introduction he was being subjected to. He was made to stand at the front of the room—no doubt in retaliation for the sucker punch—while a heap of shit concerning his teenage reputation rained down upon his full-grown ego.

Yes, he was the worst of the offenders of hazing.

Yes, he objected to pansy-ass Brooks wanting to stop the sacred, time-honored tradition.

Yes, the three of them had come to blows over it, and that had evolved into a sucker-punch fest at any given moment.

Duncan James, Attorney at Law, was requested to draw up a legal document on the spot that all three would sign in front of these witnesses claiming that the aforementioned shenanigans had now come to a complete and utter halt.

Before Duncan was able to get the job done, Lady—who he'd been told spelled it L-A-I-D-E-Y which just added insult to injury, because what kind of name was that anyway?—handed Vance a piece of paper.

Vance snickered as he looked it over. He handed it to Brooks who barked out a laugh and handed it to Xavier.

It read simply: Our stupid shit stops here.

Xavier looked over at the tiny piece of fluff with those big, expressive eyes. Seriously, she was like a cartoon character. "Didn't know stupid shit was a technical term."

He might have thought he'd heard the words, "Shoe fits," coming from those cherry lips, but he'd be surprised if she had the guts to actually say it, given the way she recoiled every time he looked at her. It was as if she was Tweety Bird, and he was Sylvester the cat.

"Give me a pen," he said. He signed and dated the paper and handed it off to Brooks, who did the same before handing it to Vance. Then, just to be as obnoxious as possible, because he wasn't entirely happy about not getting to punch Brooks anymore, he asked the strawberry-haired fella sitting next to *Tweety Bird* to move so he could sit his big, scary ass down next to her.

Damn. Right.

He turned his head and gave her a sinister leer when he did it too. And she pretended not to notice. Yep. She just pretended she was taking notes or something. Her curls hung down, covering her face, while her little floral-covered pencil was scratching away on some pink-paged notebook.

Was this chick serious?

Christ. It was like he was sitting in a fucking elementary school classroom. Of course, she did use the term "stupid shit," so she wasn't all peaches and cream, he supposed.

Still.

And why did he care anyway?

Seriously?

He shook his head, not caring. Not giving one goddamn about Tweety Bird sitting to his right as some pretty thing—who was not height impaired—got up to speak to the group at large. Now this is more like it, he thought, sitting back and crossing his arms over his chest.

Missy McReady introduced herself and welcomed him to the "Team" before going forward with the meeting.

Had he officially joined the "Team?" What "Team" anyway? He should probably start listening to see what the hell he was being shanghaied into. Maybe he didn't want to be on the team. Or, maybe he'd be great on this team—with that pretty one up there—and this little elf scared to death of him right here.

He took another glance in her direction.

Shit.

He didn't care. Truly.

He'd join the team, and she'd figure it out. Xavier Wright was not to be feared. Maybe at one time. But not now. Now he was Zen. Perfectly under control. Hadn't he just signed that paper saying he was done with stupid shit? And he'd been done with stupid shit for a long time now. He had Chase Alexander to thank for that.

So, whatever.

Little ... what was her name? Lady? With an *i* and an *e*? *What kind of a name is Laidey? Really? I mean, kinda cute maybe, but seriously ...*

"Sorry?" he asked when Missy posed him a question.

"What sort of construction were you involved with in Arizona?"

"Housing," Xavier answered. "Single family homes. Some multi-unit dwellings. One high-rise apartment building."

"Are you interested in building in Henderson?"

"I'm considering it."

"Would you mind meeting with our colleagues from Dallas? They've got ideas for housing that would appeal to singles. Henderson could really use something like that. Like, yesterday."

"Sure." Xavier couldn't help but turn his head and glance at little Cindy Lou Who again. She was with this What-What Dallas group, wasn't she? She was probably single since she looked about seven years old in those yellow Keds of hers. And she used pencils. "Happy to," he said, grinning at her.

He watched Cindy Lou bite her pencil. Like a mouse. Bite her pretty floral pencil, bat her deer-in-the-headlight eyes, and then duck her head.

For God's sake. She was truly scared to death of him.

He couldn't help himself. He leaned to the right and whispered. "I am *not* the devil." But it came out so gruff and angry, he probably sounded exactly like Lucifer himself.

She scooted her chair as far from him as she could.

The whole thing was so absurd he began to chuckle. "Fine," he whispered under his breath. If she wanted to believe he was the devil, whatever. He certainly was to McKenna. What's one more female thinking the worst of him?

He turned his back on the Muppet baby at his right and started paying attention to what was going on in his hometown.

"I can't believe y'all are pulling this off," Xavier told Brooks and Vance over lunch.

"We haven't pulled it off *yet*. But we will," Vance assured him.

"So what's going on with all this mayor business?" he asked Brooks. "McKenna's mother was in an uproar when I saw her this morning. Something about people swallowing a load of crap about you turning your back on Henderson High."

Brooks sighed heavily. "I've got an enemy trying to derail my campaign for mayor. A woman who blames Vance and me for talking Coach Crenshaw out of marrying her."

"Well, did you?"

"Not exactly," Vance said with a smirk. "Although we would have. So, she's not wrong. But she is pissed. And vindictive."

"And hell on wheels," Brooks added.

"She's taken up with Mayor Stevens and gotten him rallied up about being left out of the sports academy loop."

"And she's in marketing, so she's good with the spin. She's spinning the academy as the Antichrist. Which we should have seen coming, but we just didn't. Truly, it never occurred to us that Henderson High was going to take a hit with a private sports academy right down the road."

"Well, why should it?"

"It shouldn't," Brooks agreed. "In fact, our defense has been just that. What's great for Henderson is great for our schools. We bring people to Henderson to live and to work, they pay local taxes. Taxes provide better facilities, better programs, and better equipment for all our public schools. The quality of life goes up for all. The sports academy is a large part of the means to that end."

"Plus, it's cool," Xavier said brightly.

Brooks knocked him on the shoulder. "Glad you think so."

"But you want me to build something for singles to live in. Not dorms or any part of this academy?"

"No. We've gone big time. Not that you aren't. That's not what I'm saying. But we've hired an entire team of specialists including architects and builders who will work together for the scope of the project. For the stadium, the classrooms, the dorms, the recreational facilities, everything. One team. But there are many more plans being worked on for Henderson and most of them involve some form of construction."

"You have entered a gold mine," Vance promised. "We need you and a dozen more like you. But we need you cheap. Not that we don't want you to make yourself a fortune, but for the time being, we'd like you to consider doing what the rest of us are doing."

"Which is?"

"Putting the economic growth of the town first."

"All right. Explain that to me."

Vance took the time to explain how the Evanses, the Langfords, the Bennetts, and many others were now onboard with reducing rents, fees, and profits, all in the name of economic incentives for new businesses to transplant to Henderson.

"Okay, I'm willing to see what I can do," Xavier said. "So what's going on other than the sports academy and Brooks's archenemy?"

"Plenty," Vance said. "We desperately need multi-unit housing that is appealing and affordable. We want it to draw the college graduates back to town, and we'll need it to lure teachers to our academy. But right now, we really need it to house the workers who will be arriving to build the academy. So we'd like for you to meet with the group from Dallas. They've got ideas and we've got nothing but those very old, ugly apartments over off Third Street. From what they're telling us, there's a whole culture to these sorts of places."

"I'm happy to meet with them. See what they've got in mind."

"They'll be waiting on you to show up after lunch. Just across the street from E&E. CC Henderson."

"CC?"

"Stands for Crain Carraway. Might want to Google him. See whom we've hooked our star to. You remember Tansy don't you?"

"Tansy Langford? Darn right."

"She married the CC of CC Dallas. Did all right for herself. They'll be in town one of these days, and you'll get to meet Crain.

Wouldn't suggest taking a swing at him. The guy is rock solid and will probably flatten you where you stand."

"Y'all act like I go around punching people willy-nilly."

"That's because you do," Vance said.

"I haven't been in town for fourteen years."

"And knocked me silly just this morning," Brooks complained.

"Because your asshole friend came and laid me out flat first thing Saturday, reminding me that's what we did."

"You did?" Brooks asked Vance.

"Hell yeah, I did. Of course." Brooks and Vance fist bumped.

"Not only am I surprised Vance is married, I'm surprised he's not married to *you*," Xavier told Brooks. "You two ever been separated more than twelve hours at a time?"

"Not often," Brooks responded. "Why'd you stay away so long, anyway?"

"Got a job. Wanted to go to grad school before I came back."

Brooks brows shot up. "What'd ya get a degree in?"

"Architecture."

"Seriously? Architecture. So you can design *and* build?"

"Yeah. Both. I enjoy working with my hands, but understanding the design side makes things run smoother over all."

"Can you draw? Maybe mock up whatever the Dallas crew describes?" Brooks asked.

"Sure."

Vance leaned forward, his forearms on the table. "My wife Piper's got some sort of a pie shop she's been dreaming up. She wants to open on Main Street. I hate this idea, but I love my wife. How 'bout you come to dinner sometime this week and meet Piper? Listen to her ideas. Though I'll warn you right now, she'll make you taste her latest pie and ask for your opinion."

"Her pies aren't any good?" Xavier asked.

"Her pies are amazing."

"Then what's the problem?"

"The problem is you'll want to simply enjoy the pie, and she'll bug you to talk about it. Drives me crazy. Anyway. Do me a favor and listen to what she wants done for this shop of hers. See if it's something you're interested in designing. I'll pay you whatever your normal fee is. This isn't for Henderson, this is for me."

"So, you're offering me a job?"

"If you and Piper reach an understanding, yes. That'll be up to her. But it could get you working while you're figuring out everything else. You do intend to stay in Henderson, right?"

The look on Vance's face was more of a threat than an inquiry. Xavier hadn't realized just how much he was being railroaded.

"I'm here, aren't I?"

"Okay. Now, your brothers."

"What about them?"

"Call 'em. Get 'em here for a weekend. Let's raft up out on the lake. Remind them who they are and where they came from. It's time you Wright brothers fly your lame asses back into town."

"I'll see what I can do. But since not a damn one of them bothered to come home last weekend and see me, not sure I have any pull whatsoever over that throng."

"Your mother, then. Get your mom to do it. Hell, I'll get the Big Em on her. She'll get 'r' done."

"Your grandmother is something."

"Something combustible and playin' with fire every chance she gets." Vance looked at his watch. "Harry," he called. "We're ready for the check."

Xavier did a double take when he looked at the waiter. There was a gleam in his eye when his gaze landed on Xavier. Not a wink, or a smirk, or a chin lift, but there was definitely an acknowledgment. Almost an understanding.

"We met Friday evening in the parking lot," Harry reminded him. "You were teasing Miss Blakely."

"Right, and scared the devil out of Miss …"

"Bartholomew," Harry offered.

Bartholomew. Xavier simply nodded.

"Harry is this town's soothsayer," Vance said, signing the check.

"I'm no soothsayer." Harry grinned. "But I do enjoy how Mr. Evans expounds my reputation and gives me undeserved praise."

"Don't let him fool you," Vance went on. "You need information, a phone number, a party set up on a moment's notice, Harry's your guy."

"You'd be wise not to believe everything you hear. Especially in this town," Harry offered as he picked up the leather sleeve and backed away from the table.

"So you were teasing Miss Blakely, huh?" Vance questioned with a cheesy grin.

"I was apologizing," Xavier clarified. "But she was so angry I tried to lighten the mood. That … *Harry* caught me trying to win her over."

"Win her over?" Brooks questioned.

"Get her to hop on my bike and go for a ride. Something. Anything. Just make her stop hating me for leaving."

"Is that why she hates you? For leaving?"

"No. I'm guessing she hates me for never coming back. Or to be more specific, for not informing her I wasn't coming back."

"You're back now."

Xavier looked back and forth between both men and their dumb-ass hopeful faces. "Not for McKenna. Trust me. Even if I was back for McKenna, she made it glaringly obvious Friday night that ship had sailed. Can't blame her and not gonna try."

"Dude. McKenna is good people. You try hard enough she'd take you back," Brooks said.

"She's not for me. Never was."

"Bullshit. You two were tight," Vance insisted.

Xavier gave a low chuckle looking at the two Bozos in front of him. "People believe what they see. It's rarely the truth."

"What's that supposed to mean?"

He waved it off. "Nothing," he said, standing up. "Come on. Get me over to this group of Dallas yuppies and let me hear what they think I should build. Then I'll take a ride around town and see where things stand. I'll go by those old apartments. See what's vacant, what needs tearing down, and what could be salvaged. After that, I'll stop back at E&E and we'll talk. Deal?"

"Deal," Vance said as Brooks nodded.

CHAPTER EIGHT

Laidey was laughing at Duncan James and his antics once again. For a really smart, really cute lawyer, Duncan was pretty much a goofball. Except when Annabelle was around. Then he was simply Prince Charming.

Annabelle was Duncan's fiancée, and she was beautiful and refined and charming and everything, everything … *everything*, that Laidey wasn't ever going to be.

Ever.

Because Annabelle could talk to anyone at any time about anything. And Duncan could joke with anyone at any time about anything. And Laidey could conduct business with anyone at any time about anything, and that was … pretty much it.

It wasn't that she was nervous or unsure of herself or particularly shy, although she was a little shy. With her parents bringing her up in the Rowling-Bartholomew social world, at twenty-six years old, she'd been primed for any situation. She could hold her own in a crowd when she had to. She just preferred it when she didn't have to.

Henderson wasn't necessarily an escape from Dallas as much as it was a refuge of sorts. From her parents. From a silver-platter social life. From seeing Crain Carraway and his lovely bride in the office on a daily basis.

Yeah. That.

She sighed. And then laughed at Duncan who had clearly made it his job to cheer up the quiet, little mouse who preferred to do her job silently and away from the rest of the pack.

It was true. She liked working with Duncan mostly because she wasn't working with the rest of her peers from Dallas. Not that she didn't like each and every one of them individually, but collectively, it was as if they'd never left Texas. Working two blocks down from them gave her a breath of fresh air. Plus, she was learning all kinds of things about North Carolina. Like Tar Heels and Wolfpacks and barbecue that was completely different from what was grilled up in Texas. She was even learning about Duncan's hometown, Richmond, Virginia, which was only a couple hours north.

Duncan swore Washington, DC, was only five hours away. *Five hours.* You get in the car in Texas and drive five hours, you're still in Texas.

She liked Duncan and his one-man law firm, and she liked his socially-gifted fiancée Annabelle, and she liked his officemate Missy, who had way too many jobs from what Laidey could tell. And she really liked Missy's boyfriend, Thor, who was as big as Crain and just about as handsome.

Her phone buzzed with a text message from Charles Douglas Higginbotham, ringleader of the CC Henderson group. Charles Douglas, whom Vance had immediately nicknamed CD, and now everyone followed suit.

"Can you walk down for a short get together?"

"Sure," she texted back.

"I'm needed down the street," she told Duncan.

"No problem. I'll be here working on all this when you get back. Want to join Annabelle and me for dinner tonight?"

"Maybe."

Duncan chuckled. "One of these days you're going to say yes."

She gave him a smile. He was on to her, but he seemed okay with it. She simply enjoyed the workweek routine she'd fallen into. Stay a little later at the office so she'd have the place to herself. The evening quiet was conducive to getting things done quickly. And for thinking. Then she rode her bike home at a leisurely pace, winding in and out of the roads she hadn't yet traveled, getting a real feel for the town she was now inhabiting. Once home, she'd eat whatever Poppy's twin brother (who'd also come from Dallas to work for CC Henderson) wanted to cook because he was a closet chef and loved to try new recipes. Unless he was going out with the other Dallas guys and then Laidey would eat leftovers on her own. Which she actually preferred because there'd be more quiet. For thinking.

Her job—part logistics manager, part legalese decipherer, and the occasional soundbite technician—required time to think. And even in Henderson, the world with all of its technology, entertainment, and news cycles, was loud. Poppy's brother Daniel liked to cook while he listened to music. And Poppy was all about the latest TV series, so the television was constantly on when she was home. Laidey had her own room and a set of noise-canceling earbuds, but that was not quiet. That was hiding.

So she was grateful Duncan was "getting her" at last. She certainly didn't want to offend him or Annabelle. She liked the two of them, but she needed her quiet, her routine, a little calm in her life when she could get it. There was a time she hadn't bothered to protect that. A time she tried to be something other than what she was, and that didn't go well for her. She'd learned a lot through that experience. Didn't want to repeat any part of it. So she had her routine and planned to follow it five out of seven days a week.

"See you in a bit," she said as she grabbed her purse, her spiral notebook, and the pretty pencil she'd just sharpened and headed out the door.

She turned toward the afternoon sun and basked in its warmth as it whisked away the chill of air conditioning. The walk felt good, stretching her legs and her mind. She closed her eyes, indulging in the heat of summer in a quiet town, wondering what this little Main Street would look like ten years from now. For she didn't doubt Crain Carraway and E&E Investments were going to complete the sports academy and do what they set out to do. With her help and the help of many others.

She hoped Main Street remained charming. Hoped it would be busier, but still … charming. She didn't have a lot of say in how things would go, but she had resolved, not too long after her arrival, that she'd be an advocate for that. For the small town, we're-in-this-together, welcome to the neighborhood, *charming* feel.

"Don't throw the baby out with the bath water," she whispered under her breath as she pushed open the door to CC Henderson and came to an abrupt halt.

Oh. Crap.

She'd forgotten what this meeting was about, or she would have claimed to be swamped and let them hold it without her. She sure didn't need this, she thought staring at the red T-shirt stretched across the back of some very broad, very well-muscled shoulders at the top of the steps.

The motorcycle mega jerk.

Perched high, as if rising out of a dais, his well-worn jeans and beat-to-hell construction boots made him look like the Patron Saint for Rebels Without a Cause. His hair was short in the back and long on top, and though she couldn't see the hair on his face from this angle, she knew exactly what it looked like. Same as all the other hipsters these days … although his facial hair was trimmed pretty short, like it was supposed to be a few days' growth. *Yeah, right.* After being in the close proximity he'd thrust upon her during the team meeting this morning, she knew his beard was too filled in and perfect to be an afterthought.

The guy was a complete loser. Yelling at women, hitting men, riding a motorcycle without a helmet. Why Brooks and Vance bothered with this guy, old friend or no, please. She didn't get it. She just didn't get it. At least that's what the Adelaide part of her brain was spouting.

The *Laidey* part of her brain was stammering complete nonsense. Estimating his height at six foot four inches and his weight at 200 pounds, because he was almost as tall as Crain, but built less like a football player and more like a golfer. A very *fit* golfer. One who worked out hard, and regularly, and therefore looked darn good in his clothes.

Adelaide refused to listen. Especially when the hot-bodied rebel saint glanced behind him, fixated his smoky gray eyes on her, narrowed them into piercing sheets of ice, and began broadcasting all of his loser crap in her direction.

"Oh, no," he said, turning his entire body toward her. He stomped down each step, slowly, menacingly, and came straight at her. "I'm not putting up with this," he said.

"With what?" CD asked from behind him.

"This," he practically bellowed while shoving a finger in her direction. He lowered his voice and told her pointedly, "You do not need to be afraid of me, ya hear?"

Adelaide had a great retort. She really did. But as she willed it to dislodge from the center of her throat, CD chuckled, "Don't mind Laidey. She's a little shy, but she's good. You'll see. We can't do without her around here. Come on, Laidey. He's big, but I'm sure he won't bite. Let's all head into the conference room and tell Mr. Wright what Dallas has that Henderson needs."

"Other than a Starbuck's?" Poppy chirped as they all turned and started to follow CD down the hallway.

At least Laidey thought that was what was happening. She couldn't see beyond the brooding giant because he was invading her personal space. And yep, that was the doorknob digging into her back.

"I'm Xavier, not Mr. Wright," he said to everyone, although he directed it at her. Directed his words right where his icy stare continued to bore. "And what have I done to give you the impression that I'm a mean-ass son of a bitch? Huh?"

Laidey licked her lips.

"Speak," he shouted.

Shouted!

It caused her to jump. Her pencil dropped from her hands, which caused her to squeak, which caused him to huff—loudly— and then they both went for the pencil and bopped heads—hard.

"Shit."

"Ouch."

"Sorry."

"Crap."

"My fault."

"Just … ouch. You've really got a hard head," she accused, rubbing the top of hers, trying to relieve the acute pain.

"You are not the first to tell me that," Xavier said, rubbing the point of his chin. His strong chin. "I'm sorry." He reached out to … what? Try to rub her head too?

She flinched.

"Jesus. Fine. Okay," he said, taking a step back and holding up his hands. "I won't touch you. I won't try to help."

"I'm fine. You don't need to help. Let's just …"

"What?"

"Move along," she said exasperated.

He stared at her a moment more before whirling around and stomping his big boots up the stairs, leaving her in his wake. If she had any doubt whether that interaction had pissed him off, the slamming of the conference room door erased it.

Okay. Maybe she *was* overreacting she thought as she picked up her pencil, rubbed her head again, and slowly made her way toward the conference room. Xavier Wright definitely made her jumpy. And she was naturally jumpy to begin with, so this wasn't good. And he was … tall. And what kind of a name was Xavier, for goodness sakes?

She stared at the closed conference room door with all of her thoughts boiling down to this. Who picks a name for their kid that starts with the letter X?

When she opened the door and scanned the conference table, jumpy or no, righteous indignation swamped her. *No* one sat in Mr. Carraway's chair. Of course, Mr. X-factor didn't know that. Which was why she was forced to watch his behind plopping into it like it was no big deal. Her distraught intake of breath must have been notable, because everyone, including Mr. eXtra-annoying looked her way.

"What now?" he growled.

"That's Mr. Carraway's chair," she told him.

Xavier looked around. "Which one of you is Carraway?"

CD shook his head. "He's not here. Not in town today."

Xavier swung his head back to her. "So the problem is?"

"No one sits in his chair," she remarked quietly.

"He made that a rule?"

"No. It's out of respect. He's the owner of the company."

"Well, is he an asshole?"

There were some laughs at that. "No," Laidey defended. "Of course not."

"Do you think he'd mind if I borrowed his chair for a few minutes?" Xavier's eyes didn't look to Laidey for the answer but to CD and the rest. They all shook their heads.

"He's a great guy," CD said. "Wouldn't mind any of us sitting in his chair while he isn't here. But like Laidey says, we just choose to leave it empty, as a sign of respect."

"Got it. Moving on," Xavier said, not budging from the chair. "Vance said y'all have ideas on the—" He stopped abruptly and addressed Laidey. "Are you going to stand sentry at the door? Or are you going to take a seat?"

It bothered her to death that this man, this rebel saint, had come in and sat in the chair reserved, strictly, for Crain. He didn't know Crain Carraway. He didn't know the man's struggles. He didn't know how hard he'd worked to build this business. He didn't know anything about him or his company, and yet he refused, refused to get out of Crain's chair.

Who does that?

She wanted to protest. That's why she hadn't sat down. She was waiting for him to apologize and get the hell out of Crain's seat. Yet, he was going on with the meeting like this wasn't a big deal. And the rest of the group was letting him. Let-ting. Hi-m.

For crying out loud.

But now he'd called her out. So she was moving her feet and simultaneously realizing that she might be a tad oversensitive when it came to Crain Carraway. She might need to take a good look at that. If CD wasn't incensed that someone ... some mega jerk ...was borrowing Crain's chair, maybe she was overreacting.

Ya think?

Man, all these months out of Dallas and she still was crushing on her boss.

Her *married* boss.

Not that she'd ever be happy with a hoodlum coming in and sitting in her boss's seat, but perhaps her outrage was a bit ... much. *Clearly.* She needed to move on. Get Crain Carraway out of her system. She'd simply work a little harder, focus a little more, and the next time Harry handed her a tequila shot, she'd drink it.

Flipping open her notebook, Laidey focused in on the discussion, listening to the description of the type of housing Dallas offered for their young professionals. She tried to picture what was being described fitting in here in Henderson, but it was like trying to fit the proverbial square peg into a round hole. The thing would stand out like a sore thumb.

She wondered if this XL Harley Boy might not have thought so too because, at some point, he stopped taking notes and just listened as the discussion dissolved from details of the buildings and amenities into stories from her officemates' time living in them.

She'd heard it all before. And once she realized she was doodling, she slapped her pencil down and brought her head up, locking eyes with Mr. XL.

He winked. *Winked.*

Sucking in a big breath, she checked her watch and told herself there was too much work to be done to sit here and listen to old stories all day. She folded up her notebook and quietly left the room. Duncan needed her help on a boatload of contracts, and she'd promised Pinks and Vance she'd meet with them about a couple of new marketing lines later today. She had no time for this nonsense, she told herself.

What she didn't allow herself to say was that as much as she'd witnessed Xavier Wright's reign of terror over the past few days, the scariest thing—the scariest thing of all—was the wink he'd just shot her.

CHAPTER NINE

Ad-el-aide Bar-tho-lo-mew, Xavier mouthed in his head as he drove his Road King at a leisurely pace around Henderson.

Lai-dey Bar-tho-lo-mew.

Little.

Mousy.

Scrumptious.

Antagonizing.

Scaredy cat.

Wait. Scrumptious?

Hardly scrumptious.

McKenna was scrumptious. Xavier laughed aloud at that thought as he roamed the neighborhood streets. He'd put his helmet on because he was tired of getting a stern finger shaking from all the moms he passed. He still enjoyed the sunshine and the ride, even if he didn't like seeing all the for sale signs and unkempt lots.

Things hadn't changed since he'd been away as much as they had just kept deteriorating. People kept moving out. Homes kept getting older. Roads needed fixing. Open lots needed mowing. Sidewalks needed tending. Hell, most of this stuff probably went unnoticed by the population. They'd been living in it so long they hadn't realized how bad it looked to fresh eyes.

It wouldn't take all that much manpower to shape it up either, but he doubted there were funds to get it done. Still, he could probably take care of a few things on his own. Pay back the community for the support they'd been giving his folks. All the tools he'd shipped back should arrive any day now. He could take care of a few things. Do his part.

A flash down at the end of the street caught his eye. A teal-blue bicycle coasting across the intersection from right to left and a dress floating in the breeze that looked awfully familiar. "No way," he said in astonishment, marveling at how his thoughts had conjured her out of thin air. He revved the engine and raced toward the end of the road, turning left and chasing down the little minx.

Only he hadn't planned on sending her up over the curb, crash landing into an enormous lilac bush.

"Shit."

Ripping off his helmet as he leapt from the Harley, he dug into the bush yelling, "What the hell, Tweety Bird?" as he commenced gingerly pulling her, bike and all, from the riot of pale purple blooms. "Are you all right? What happened?" His one hand held the bike upright while his other helped to guide her out from underneath it. Leaning the bike against his right hip, he used both hands to steady her, checking her over from top to bottom as he brushed leaves and flower bits from her arms and legs, making sure there wasn't more severe damage than a few ugly scratches.

When he was certain there was nothing bleeding profusely or— God forbid—broken, he held her securely by her upper arms and looked into her big, startled eyes. "Did I do that?" A strange emotion clawed at him, and he truly didn't understand it. Except that she seemed so frightened of him and … *God*, he didn't want to be *that guy*. Not anymore. He'd fought hard not to be *that guy*, yet here he was, apparently being nothing but *that guy* to her.

"I'm sorry," he stammered. "Look. I'm …" He didn't know how to … what to… do? Say? He was so lost here. He wanted to laugh.

Or cry.

It was the hand on his arm that drew his frantic attention. Her hand. There was a teardrop on her cheek and she was shaking like a leaf, but she'd put her hand on his arm, *intentionally*. And that had him regrouping, settling down, and paying attention. He watched her hold up one finger, like she was getting ready to say something. Darned if he wasn't willing to wait forever to hear this.

"Not your fault," she breathed. Heavily. Like it all came out on a big, long breath. Like she'd been holding hers. Or struggling to catch hers. Or … he didn't know what, but it was … odd.

Maybe that's what he was feeling. Maybe this Adelaide—this Lai-dey—was simply odd.

He sure felt odd around her.

"I scared you again," he said, purposely softening his voice, wondering where the hell *this* was coming from. "You heard my bike coming up behind you, and you freaked."

"I heard the roar of a motorcycle." She nodded. "When I twisted my head to see if it was you, I went up the curb and into the bush. As much as I'd like to blame my klutziness on you and that obnoxiously loud death trap, I have a past that precedes you. *This* was not your fault."

"I'll address your standards for noise pollution later. Right now, I want to know if you're hurt."

"Yes. My ego feels rather bruised."

He grinned at that. "That might be a real problem. A tiny ego like yours probably can't take much of a pounding."

She gave him a smirk. "It's had plenty of practice."

"Yeah? Does it bounce back?"

She shook her head. "Not if there are witnesses and someone has to pull me out of a bush."

"I promise I'll have a short memory on the subject. Here," Xavier encouraged, walking her bike toward the street. "Let's see if we can get you back on the proverbial horse. Where're you headed?"

"Home."

"Where's home?"

"155 Elm Street. This is what I get for wandering."

"Wandering?"

"I've been trying to see a new street each evening. Get the lay of the land."

"I was doing the same thing. Thinking about what your colleagues told me this afternoon. Scouting out the territory."

"Hmm."

"What's hmm?"

She sighed heavily. Again. Then came a shrug. A bounce of curls. An inquisitive scowl. She was like a damn cartoon character broadcasting her emotions with physical inflections.

"Henderson's not Dallas," his brain heard her say, tuning him off her body language and onto her actual words. "What they described would look ridiculous stuck in the middle of this town. A high-rise?" her voice rose. "A big, boxy high-rise? Built around a pool? With retail shops surrounding the bottom? Henderson doesn't have enough retail to fill up Main Street. But what it does have is charm. High-rise buildings serve a purpose, but they aren't charming. It would never be filled and—"

"Why didn't you say any of this at the meeting?" he interrupted.

She took her bike from him and started walking. "They didn't want to hear it."

He reached out and stopped her. "What do you mean, *they* didn't want to hear it?"

"They like their stories and wanted to share them with you. I didn't want to rain on their parade. I figured you weren't breaking ground today, why not let them have their fun?"

He watched as she tucked her leg through the center of the bike, getting set to ride off. "So you let them have their fun. And left the meeting early."

"I'd heard it all before. I had work to do."

"So, what? You'd planned to seek me out after work? Later? Tell me your thoughts, when?"

She looked startled.

"You weren't going to tell me?" he pressed.

"I … honestly … hadn't thought about it."

"Why? Your points are valid."

She looked off to the side as if thinking. "Well, yeah," she said distractedly, before bringing her chocolate gaze back to his. "But you already knew it, didn't you? I mean, you stopped taking notes at some point, and I figured you were thinking what I was thinking. That it wouldn't work for Henderson."

"So you noticed I stopped taking notes."

Silence descended when she locked her eyes with his. They stood face to face in the quiet, Xavier wondering if she was trying to figure him out. Because he certainly was trying like hell to figure her out.

"You don't have to be afraid of me." The words came out of his mouth before he knew he was going to say them.

She shook her head. "I'm not."

Clearly she wasn't. At least in this moment.

"All right." He took a step back. "Glad we got that settled."

She nodded. Then she put her yellow-sneakered foot on a pedal and left him in the dust.

Laidey had lied. Right to his handsome face. It *was* Xavier's fault she'd ended up in the bush. Completely his fault. Not because she was afraid of his ridiculous motorcycle. Well, she'd never get on the thing herself, but it wasn't like she believed he'd intentionally run her over.

She didn't.

And yeah, she'd seen him punch Brooks this morning. But the way Vance had laughed his ass off over that, she knew it was deep-seated good ol' boy nonsense, and she wasn't concerned Xavier Wright was going to hit *her*. Even though he had thoroughly enjoyed bullying her at the conference table right afterwards.

Maybe she didn't appreciate him sitting in Crain's chair, but that had made it darn clear she had issues about her boss she needed to get a grip on—like now. She certainly couldn't hold Xavier responsible for that.

Seeing him trying to console, tease, and make up to McKenna in the dark Friday night didn't actually scare her. None of it *scared* her.

Nope. Every little bit of it had turned her on. And *that* scared her.

Yeah. So. Okay. Xavier Wright scared the shit out of her. But not in the way he thought.

Which is why she tried to put him at ease when he'd chased her into the bushes this evening. She needed him to stop apologizing, or trying so hard, or even noticing her. She needed Xavier Wright to do what everyone else did. Let her be invisible.

That way she could admire him from afar, keeping her head down and her work on point.

Even though McKenna had denied the extent of her feelings for Xavier over their Ben & Jerry's therapy session Friday night, Laidey vividly recalled a particular conversation with Harry. The one where McKenna had admitted that the love of her life had left town and never come back.

Obviously, Mr. X-factor was the one who'd left McKenna to deal with her broken heart.

Jerk.

And as drawn to the authoritative XL jerk's towering height and commanding presence as Laidey regretfully was, she didn't want to try to imagine what it must be like for McKenna, who had actually dated and fallen in love with the guy.

Poor, *poor* McKenna.

Probably.

Laidey had always wondered about the whole *better to have loved and lost than never to have loved at all* quote. True or not true?

Was McKenna better off having loved and lost the very hot, albeit cocky, brazen, and ill-mannered Mr. Wright?

Would Laidey be better off if she'd had the pleasure of experiencing a romantic relationship with the unparalleled Mr. Carraway? Only to lose him forever to Tansy Langford? Would her complete and utter infatuation with Crain be over with by now? Or would the heartache of having loved him and lost him be ceaseless?

She wondered about McKenna and her heartache. Wondered how she was feeling now, having had the weekend to digest the idea of her ex-beau being back in town. Wondered if she could coax McKenna into sharing enough unsavory details about the brute to help Laidey stop being so—face it, girl—*attracted* to such a flawed human being.

Checking her watch, Laidey decided to head to McKenna's.

CHAPTER TEN

"Have you seen this bullshit?" Brooks yelled, holding up a paper as he busted through the front door of E&E later that evening. Xavier had been standing there trying to figure out why this Davis Williams—a guy Vance insisted on calling *Pinks*—didn't just haul off and drop Vance. Seriously? He called him *Pinks.*

"What's Viper done now?" Vance scowled.

"Who's Viper?" Xavier wondered.

"Marcie Watts," Davis informed him.

No way was he calling the guy Pinks. Not until he got the chance to race him in that One-77 hot rod anyway.

"She's the one giving the Golden Boy a run for his money in the election."

"Oh. I've heard tales."

"Well, wait until you hear this one," Brooks said. "Because this is not the *Henderson Daily.* This is the *Raleigh Times,* and I swear to God, this woman has now crossed the line."

"She crossed the line when she tried to get Henry on steroids," Vance said.

"Steroids?" Xavier gasped.

"Oh, yeah," Davis informed him. "Henry DuVal is one of the younger players on the baseball team. Viper pulled him aside after one practice and told him he needed to be bigger, faster, and stronger if he wanted the college scouts to look at him. She had cards from all the top coaches in her hand. She *gave* Henry the card of a well-known website for performance enhancing drugs."

"Shit. Did the kid get caught taking the stuff?" Xavier asked.

"No," Vance told him. "We were on top of it. Once Viper hit our radar, we warned the kids. Told them that if she approached any of them, they were to report to us immediately. Henry did just that. Of course, we couldn't prove her intent. We didn't have the time to work out a sting operation. Wanted to, but we were focused on winning State and didn't want the kids distracted. Still, you should have seen ol' Brooks take the woman down. Swear to God, I thought he was going to strangle Viper right where she stood."

"Wanted to. Should have. Look at this."

"Sweatshop Opens in Henderson," Vance read the headline. He looked up at Brooks. "Lolly?"

"Damn right, Lolly," Brooks growled. "This is not the kind of publicity she or Henderson need."

"Lolly?" Xavier asked.

"*My* Lolly, is a fashion designer. She and Annabelle Devine have recently opened the House of DuVal. This *sweatshop* being referred to is their design center. It's where the gowns are made. She has three employees and pays them as much as she possibly can. This crazy Viper has spun the good Lolly's doing for Henderson—providing jobs, making apparel right here in America—and posed it as a *sweatshop*."

"Give me that," Pinks snarled, grabbing the paper out of Vance's hands.

"Y'all sure seemed worked up for this Lolly." All three heads turned from the paper and glared at Xavier. He held up his hands. "Just an observation."

"What the hell are we going to do about this?" Brooks asked, frantic.

"Nothing," Pinks said, still reading the article.

"Nothing? This is Lolly's livelihood. No way am I doing nothing."

Xavier watched Davis calmly fold the paper. "Brooks, buddy, you ever hear the old adage, any publicity is good publicity?"

"The word sweatshop cannot be *good* publicity," Brooks remarked.

"Trust me. I've got an idea."

"You gonna fill us in on this idea?" Vance asked.

"Not at the moment."

"Okay, then." Vance clapped his hands together and patted Brooks on the chest. "Why don't you just take a deep breath and trust that the Ninja has this covered. Now Xavier, when can I get you out to the house for dinner and a discussion with my bride about her pie shop?"

"Wait a minute. I'm confused. Who's the Ninja?"

"Pinks," Vance said as if it was obvious.

"Why do you call Davis Pinks?" Xavier asked, completely clueless.

"Look at him."

Xavier did. The guy looked sharp. A pastel linen shirt tucked into expensive summer-weight slacks. Good-looking loafers and a canvas belt that was ... light pink.

"Got it. Okay, so if my mother continues to do well, I'm free any night this week. You tell me where and when."

"Fine. I'll be in touch. Happy to have you bring McKenna if you'd like."

Xavier took a step back and looked at all three men. "Boys. Have I not made myself clear? I left town *because* of McKenna. I'm back *in spite* of McKenna. Put McKenna in my path one too many times and I will bolt."

Vance looked stunned. "You're serious."

"Dead serious."

"What the hell happened between you and McKenna?" Brooks asked, sincerely wanting to know.

"It wasn't like that. McKenna's a great girl. She just wasn't the girl for me. And I hated to hurt her, but I didn't have a choice. And I sincerely hope me being back isn't opening an old wound. So please, believe me when I tell you, I am *not* interested in McKenna Blakely."

"Well, that's a relief."

All heads spun toward the back hallway as the topic of their conversation now stood before them in the flesh.

"How the hell did you get in here?" Vance asked.

"The back door," she said.

"And you're looking for?"

"Him." She pointed to Xavier. "The one who is *not* interested in me."

Pinks didn't hesitate to say, "I'm out of here." Followed closely by Brooks and Vance both bolting with a "Good luck, dude," or some such cowardly crap.

Of course, if he'd been in their shoes, he'd have done the same. Frankly, he was wondering how he could escape those familiar blue eyes himself. He heard a lot of banging and stomping until there was nothing but silence, making it obvious they now had the building to themselves.

Xavier scratched his chin vigorously through his short beard. He dropped his hand and took a cleansing breath. "We gonna do this here, or you want to go get a drink at The Situation?"

McKenna's shoulders fell as she let out a short, sad laugh. "You need a drink to talk to me?"

"I tried to talk with you Friday night."

"You ambushed me Friday night."

"You were the first person I wanted to see."

"I was the first thing you wanted to cross off your agenda."

That truth hit him in his solar plexus. He swallowed.

"Wasn't I?" she pressed.

"McKenna."

"You can't hurt me, Xavier. Unless you lie to me. So, I'm asking for clarification. I'm asking for the truth."

He swallowed again. Because McKenna was wrong. If the truth ever did come out, it would hurt them both.

"Come here," he said, pulling her into his arms, holding McKenna Blakely close to his heart for the first time in fourteen years. "What do you want to know?"

"Everything." It was muffled against his shoulder.

"Everything?" he whispered over her head. "I'm definitely going to need a drink, or two, or three, to get through *everything*."

She pushed back from him. "Come on," she said, heading to the door. "We can go to The Situation and get a beer, and you can tell me about college and grad school and this Chase Alexander your mother goes on about."

"Why?" he asked doggedly. "If my mother's already told you about college and grad school and Chase Alexander, why do *we* need to rehash it?"

"Because." She stopped and turned her stunning face his way. "I'm the daughter your mother never had. Which makes us pseudo-siblings," she smirked. "So if I listen to you tell me about your life in Arizona … if I listen while you go over everything … if I listen to you go on long enough, I'll get used to hearing your voice and seeing your face, and then I'll get used to you being back in town … and that will be the new normal."

"And then what?"

She shrugged. "And then maybe I won't have the urge to slash the tires of that badass Harley every time I see it."

"Worth a shot," he said, letting her lead him out the door.

McKenna thought she knew all about Xavier and his life in Phoenix. But she'd been given the facts he'd chosen to dole out to his mother. Not the details. Not the interesting, curious, who-is-this-guy-and-what-has-he-done-with-Xavier-Wright specifics concerning the man sitting beside her at the bar.

"Yoga? You practice yoga? And meditation?"

"When in Rome," he commented.

"But *you?*"

"Come on? What do you mean, *me?*"

"I mean, let's face it. You were *not* mellow. At all."

"No. I was not."

"Xavier. You weren't just a little rough around the edges. You were a bully."

"I wasn't a *bully*. Bullies beat kids up on playgrounds. I didn't beat kids up on the playgrounds."

"Yes, you did."

"Never. I never did that."

"You beat the crap out of your friends all the time."

"My *friends*. And I didn't beat them up, I pulled practical jokes. For fun. I never once teased a fat kid or a dumb kid or a smart kid or any other kind of kid. I only messed with my kind of kids."

"Yeah, but you hazed your teammates, you played horrible practical jokes on your buddies, you were mean as all get out to your brothers, and obnoxious as hell to your favorite teachers."

"Exactly. To my *favorite* teachers. My *teammates*. My *brothers*— whom I love. If I messed with you, I cared about you. That's how I showed affection."

"Yeah, so you can see why the entire yoga, meditation thing is a bit shocking."

Xavier shrugged a shoulder, his countenance changing. He'd been turned in her direction, but now she watched him shift back toward the bar and lean over his beer. "Or it's just glaringly obvious I needed to find a better way to channel my energy in Arizona."

She couldn't help herself. She finally went ahead and blurted out the question she really wanted answered. "You got accepted to Carolina, Wake Forest, Davidson, and UVA. Did you pick Arizona strictly to get as far away from me as possible?"

Xavier continued to stare across the bar. "McKenna, you ended up at State. It didn't matter which school I chose."

"Answer the question."

He took his sweet time, but he finally answered truthfully. "Fuck it. Yes." The look he shot her clearly added an unspoken, *Are you happy now?* Like she'd been asking for him to break her in two all night long.

Well, maybe she had. Because she wasn't stupid. She'd known, deep down, he'd deserted her. But now he'd gone and admitted it. And yeah, it hurt.

"You really had to go there?" he asked. "The two of us have been here for hours, having a pretty good time. Figuring out a new *sibling relationship*. Then all of a sudden ... bam."

"Because the way things ended didn't make sense."

"No, McKenna. The way things *started* didn't make sense."

"What?"

"Look, you're right. About all of the above. I was an ass back in high school. A complete ass. And frankly, *that's* the reason I chose Arizona. That's the reason I didn't come home ... ever. I knew I was an ass. To you, to my friends, my brothers, even my parents. And I had no intention of coming home until I figured out how not to be one."

"I. Don't …"

"Right now, my mom needs us. *Both* of us. And it sure looks like this town needs both of us too. Can you handle that?"

"Of course, I can."

"Then please. Let my apology stand. Let my apology for riding out of here and not looking back stand. I'm sorry I hurt you. I'm sorry I didn't end things decisively—"

"It's not really about that." She shook her head interrupting him. "I mean, it would have been nice to have a definitive end to our relationship. But, to be perfectly honest, what really ended up pissing me off was that you were the catalyst."

"The catalyst?"

"The one who started the mass exodus. You left, and you didn't come back. Which gave everyone else permission to leave and never come back."

"Everyone else? Like who?"

"Your *brothers*. Your *friends*. One by one, year after year, everyone just up and left."

"Christ, McKenna," he said exasperated. "You want me to apologize for leading the masses *out* of the promised land?"

"No."

"Then what?" he snapped.

She placed a hand on his shoulder and quieted her voice. "You are no longer responsible for my pain."

He lifted a brow. "Since when?"

"Since a long time ago," she claimed. "It just got hard to remember with you in my face all of a sudden. But I'm fine. I promise."

"You're not fine," he said, turning back to his beer.

"I'm perfectly fine," she claimed.

"If you were perfectly fine, you'd be married with kids."

"Says who?" McKenna squinched up her face in distaste.

"Oh, so you don't want kids," he scoffed.

"Not tomorrow."

"Marriage?"

"Eventually."

"Then what was that look for?"

"You don't think I'm fine because I'm not married and I don't have kids. What about my career? My friends? I have a very full life right now.

"A boyfriend?"

"Nothing steady. But I date."

Xavier looked away, not saying anything. He just became a little thoughtful looking into his beer. Finally, he said, "All right."

"All right, what?"

"Just made a decision, that's all."

"What decision?"

He turned toward her, exasperated. "You know something? You're as pushy as shit and demanding as hell."

"If that's not the pot calling the kettle black."

"Exactly. I *am* pushy and demanding. Which is why you and I were never gonna work. We're both like my father. And what each of us needs is someone like my mother. For balance."

McKenna lifted her drink. "So says the yogi."

CHAPTER ELEVEN

"Laidey," Thor called as he came through the door of Duncan's law firm Tuesday.

Laidey had learned that at any given moment during the workweek, Thor could appear as a tall, broad fixture in the place. He liked to stop in to steal a kiss from Missy whenever he was in town. So Laidey was used to him blowing through regularly. This, however, was the first time he'd come looking for her.

"Hey," she said, tentatively. "Can I help you?"

"Not me, but there's a ten-year-old tomboy hanging around outside. Won't come right out and say it, but I think she wants to meet you."

"Me?"

"I'm pretty sure it has something to do with your bike."

"Oh, okay." Laidey wasn't sure what she was supposed to do. Drop everything and go outside? Thor nodded as if she'd asked the question aloud.

"Her name's Marnie. She's a friend of mine." His intense neon-blue gaze compelled her to move.

"Oh. Okay. Well. I'll go see Marnie." So she did. As Thor continued to watch. Sort of scooting her out of the office with his eyes. *Were all the men around here pushy? Other than Duncan?*

But stepping out into the sunlight, she found that Thor was not only pushy, he was wrong. There was no one standing outside. No one hovering around her bike. She looked up the street to the right and down the street to her left and saw no one at all. But her ears did note a faint roar in the distance. A hint of the very engine that caused her pulse to lose its shit yesterday, sending her flailing into a bush.

"Hey!"

Startled, Laidey whirled around to face a dusty, helmet-headed adolescent on a retro-styled bicycle. The thing was purple with a banana seat and tall handlebars. "Wow." Laidey's eyes went wide. She'd seen pictures of her mother back in the seventies on a bike just like this. "I like your bike."

"It's purple."

"I see that. Are you Marnie?"

The girl nodded eagerly.

"Are you Thor's sister?"

"Nope. He doesn't have a sister. I don't have a sister either. The two of us are orphans. So if my Mimi and Dadaddy ever bite it, I'm moving in with him. He says he's got enough money to take care of me, and his cooking is getting pretty good. I told him I'd rather live with Coach because she's a stellar athlete and my best chance for getting a scholarship to college. Thurgood says he'd rather live with Coach too, and he's working on that. I told him to work harder."

"Oh." Laidey wasn't sure what to say to all that.

"I like your basket," Marnie said, pointing to the floral-laden wicker sitting on the front of Laidey's teal bike.

"Thank you. It's useful for transporting things."

"Where did you get it?"

"I made it."

"You *made* it?" Marnie's eyes bugged out of her head. "Mimi makes a lot of things, but she's never made a basket."

"Well, I didn't weave the basket. I bought the basket. But I added the flowers with a glue gun because I like pretty things, and that brown wicker was just too dull for me to put on my pretty bike."

"Mimi has a glue gun." Marnie bit her lip as she gazed longingly at Laidey's basket.

"Do you have things you need to carry when you ride your bike?"

"Not yet. But I want a puppy. If I had a basket like that, I could take the puppy with me wherever I go."

"I bet you could."

The dull roar in the distance was proving a distraction. Laidey tried to focus on Marnie, but felt herself becoming anxious wondering if a certain XL maniac was heading this way. She'd rather not be standing out here on the sidewalk if he drove up. Rather not see him again until she had the opportunity to talk to McKenna and stockpile ammunition against him and his ... *size*.

Sure enough, the painfully loud sound of his flashy red motorcycle compelled both her and Marnie to look down the street to their right. They watched as a glistening blur bolted toward them.

"Wow," she thought she heard Marnie say. Laidey couldn't be sure due to the god-awful noise obliterating her eardrums. Not to mention the frantic pounding of her heart. Honestly, she wasn't sure if it was more the man or the machine that had her nerves jumbled.

Xavier raced by, his big black-helmeted head turned in their direction. Was he smiling at them? No way to be sure underneath the tinted visor. On he flew, gunning it to the end of the business section before circling and coming back toward them at a much saner pace, the decibel level now relatively subdued. He pulled up beside them, lowered his kickstand, pulled off his helmet, and turned off the ignition.

Marnie wasn't afraid of any of it. The machine or the man. She'd put down her own kickstand and headed right for him while he was still idling.

"I'm Marnie," she told him. "I like your bike."

"I'm Xavier. I like your bike too."

"Mine's purple."

"Mine's red."

"I like red. But I like purple better. I've never been on a motorcycle."

"You want a ride?"

Marnie bounced up and down on her toes, nodding yes as she turned and whispered to Laidey, "This is so awesome," as if Xavier wasn't standing right there. Laidey couldn't help but give in to a nervous laugh.

"Do *you* want a ride?" Xavier asked Laidey.

"Me?" Laidey gasped.

"Sure she does." Marnie tossed her arms around. "Who wouldn't want a ride?" She bounced toward Xavier. "But me first."

"Is that bike helmet enough to protect her?" Laidey asked.

Xavier grinned and flexed his muscles, showing off some very impressive guns. "I'll protect her," he said. When Laidey gave him a frown, he followed up with, "We won't go too fast. She'll be fine with this thing." He knocked a knuckle against her helmet but leaned over to adjust it properly and tighten the strap under her chin.

"I *want* to go fast," Marnie protested. "I like fast."

"You like fast?" he asked, grinning at the little girl. Then he shot a wicked grin at Laidey. "How about you? Are you fast?"

"Nooo. Does she *like to go* fast?" Marnie corrected.

"You ask your questions, I'll ask mine." Xavier shot Laidey a wink as he moved to grip Marnie around her middle and pop her onto the seat in front of him.

"Thor?" Laidey cautiously called out, her concern mounting.

"Let's go," Marnie said to Xavier. "Before she rats me out to my bodyguard."

"Maybe we should just make sure—"

"Hold this." Xavier interrupted Laidey's protest and shoved his own helmet in her hands. He took out a pair of mirrored sunglasses from his shirt pocket and put them on instead. He flashed her a naughty grin before shooting off like a rocket with Marnie. Laidey wasn't sure how she was able to hear Marnie's giggles over the blistering roar of the Harley.

"Okay then," she whispered, gripping his helmet to her chest, watching, since that was all she could now do. That, and pray that some random armored truck wouldn't cruise around a corner and smash into the two of them, thrusting their bodies high into the air and plummeting them toward certain death.

But to her relief, Xavier slowed and swung them around, heading back in her direction. Then he gunned the engine as he gave Marnie a thrill—and Laidey a bout of indigestion—racing past, using Main Street as his own personal speedway.

If Marnie's wide eyes and huge smile were any indication, she was completely unaware of the potential for disaster. The girl said she wanted to go fast, and Xavier was giving it to her. And now that that was happening, Laidey just wanted it to end quickly. She didn't want Thor to wander out, witness the nightmare, and yell at her for letting a ten-year-old get on a deathtrap with a Kamikaze pilot.

After screaming up and down the road twice more, Xavier finally put Laidey out of her misery and pulled to a halt at the curb. "That was amazing," Marnie cried as Xavier lifted her from his seat and set her down.

"You liked that huh?"

"I *loved* that. How old do you have to be to drive a motorcycle?"

Still astride the beast, Xavier lifted a shoulder. "Sixteen, I guess. Gotta get a license. Though dirt bikes would be a good place to start for a half-pint like you." He reached out and tapped her helmet. "Give you some practice so you'll be ready for a bigger machine. I started out on a dirt bike when I was your age. Might be one left in my father's garage. I'll see if I can find it."

"You'd give me a ride on a dirt bike?"

"Nope. I'm thinking you'll be able to handle a dirt bike all by yourself."

"No!" Marnie gasped in excitement.

"Exactly. Nooo," Laidey interceded.

"What's the matter, Tweety Bird?" Xavier said, all snarky and puffed up. "Just because you're a scaredy cat doesn't mean you've got to ruin everybody else's fun."

"Scaredy cat?"

"You're afraid of the bike. Afraid of me—"

Laidey stiffened. "Who says I'm afraid of you?"

Xavier threw her a look of abject tedium. "It continues to be obvious."

"Maybe it's the dress," Marnie suggested, looking Laidey over. "Don't let that fool you. I have to wear a dress on Sundays. But I still like going fast."

"You got a pretty dress like that?" Xavier asked Marnie.

Both Marnie and Xavier's full attention turned to Laidey's dress. They studied her from neckline to hem. "I like the color," Marnie said.

"Pink is pretty on brunettes," Xavier commented.

"What's a brunette?" Marnie asked.

"It's a girl with brown hair, like yours."

"So I'm a brunette?" She grinned at him in delight.

"You are."

"Like her?" Marnie pointed to Laidey.

"Just like her." Xavier lifted his sunglasses and smirked in her direction.

"I need a pink dress," Marnie decided.

"I like girls in pink," Xavier agreed.

"Your turn." Marnie stepped on to the sidewalk, throwing a thumb behind her like this was no big deal.

"Thank you," she told Marnie. "But I'm going to pass."

"But you just said you like to go fast."

"Did I?"

"You heard her, right?" Marnie asked Xavier.

"I heard something," Xavier agreed. "Not sure it was a declaration of a need for speed. Sounded more like a—"

"I've got to get back to work," Laidey told them both, turning to leave.

"Did you know she spells her name with an i and an e?" Xavier asked Marnie.

Laidey bristled.

"What's your name?"

"Laidey. L-a-i-d-e-y," she spelled.

Marnie looked back at Xavier, crossing her arms over her chest. "That's just weird."

"Right?" he egged her on.

"Did you know *his name* begins with an *X*?" Laidey sputtered, re-engaging.

"X's are cool." Marnie stated.

"Real cool." Xavier crossed his arms over his chest too.

"Like, X marks the spot on treasure maps," Marnie suggested. "That's cool."

"And who doesn't love Xmas?" Xavier offered.

Laidey began rubbing her temples to play along. "All this *eX*aggerating is making me need *EX*cederin for my head."

Marnie giggled.

Xavier snorted. Then he did a chin lift toward their bicycles. "Y'all starting a tiny-girl bike club?"

Marnie was all over that idea. She talked on and on about how they should include her BFF Nancy and how all of them needed baskets just like Laidey's. The kid had big ideas, and while she was rattling them off, one by one, Laidey noticed Xavier pull his phone from his pocket, his brows rising as he read a text. Laidey thought it was sweet the way he continued to look up at Marnie even though it seemed something urgent was transpiring.

He shoved his phone back in his pocket. "It seems your friend Laidey and I have a business meeting tonight." When Laidey's eyes shifted from Marnie to Xavier, he was looking right at her. "At the Evans estate. Said they'd serve us dinner and force-feed us pie."

Laidey was immediately confused. "What?"

Xavier shrugged. "A special project for Vance. He said I should bring *you*." He held up his phone. "You in?"

"Am I in?"

"Yeah. Can you make it?"

"Wha–why me?" she stammered.

"Why not you?" He shook his head, tapping the screen, apparently texting Vance back.

"What are you telling him?"

He popped his head up. "That you're in. You are, right? I mean, Vance says jump and we all say how high, correct?"

"I don't work for Vance. I work for Mr. Carraway."

Xavier stopped texting and searched her face. His expression grew irritated. "Right. I remember now. You're the defender of his chair." He smirked, his attention going back to his phone. "You wanna moonlight for Vance or what?"

Laidey let out an exasperated huff, racking her brain over what sort of project Vance might have in mind, and why in the world he'd have to include Xavier in the discussion. Especially over dinner. She was having a hard time holding her own in a conversation with Mr. X in broad daylight. She couldn't imagine the awkwardness that was bound to emerge if she had to face him across a candlelit table. Sit across from all that masculine, cocky, devilishly handsome, nerve-racking X-tra-tall male.

"So you *are* scared of me. I thought we were done with all that after pulling you out of a bush yesterday."

"I'm not," she hiccuped, "scared of you."

"The hell you aren't," he said, stalking closer. "Your eyes are wide and shiny, your face is flushed, I can tell your pulse is racing, and you haven't taken a breath since I informed you about dinner."

She stepped back, clasping one of her wrists as if to check her pulse. But her eyes never deviated from his.

He held his hands up. "I would never hurt you. I promise."

"You hurt McKenna."

"McKenna?" His head snapped back as his features twisted with incomprehension. "I never hit McKenna."

"No. The blow you dealt her was one of the emotional variety."

"That was a lot of years ago, and McKenna is *fine*," Xavier claimed. "We were kids back then. And what you need to know is that we weren't right from the start. So, you double-check with McKenna, because we worked through it last night," he said intently, pointing a finger in her face. "So you can stop being afraid of me."

"I'm *not* afraid of you."

His eyes studied her face intently. When he spoke, it came out as a whisper. "The hell you aren't." He shook his head and refocused. "Working together will cure you of whatever issues you've got with me. I've already texted Vance, said you're in." He turned, picked up his helmet and got back on the beast. "155 Elm Street? I'll pick you up at six-thirty."

Laidey felt her mouth open in a protest, but she was too stunned, too overwhelmed to actually spit a word out.

Xavier started his engine, gave a thumbs up to Marnie—who Laidey had totally forgotten was standing there—and roared off toward the end of the road.

"So, I guess you'll get your turn on his motorcycle then," Marnie said.

"I guess so," Laidey replied, taking in her first full breath in minutes.

CHAPTER TWELVE

After a few cleansing breaths which helped to relieve his irritation, Xavier road toward home, trying to work out a way to give the mini-morsel in the pink dress the benefit of the doubt. It was hard for him to see things from her perspective, little as she was, because he would have towered over her before he ever entered puberty. Being so much larger, he acknowledged it made sense that she'd be afraid of him. He was a wily coyote to her fluffy baby bunny.

Of course, he wasn't planning to make a meal out of her, so there was that.

Still, his mind locked on the scenario Friday night where whatever energy he was putting off had her cowering behind Harry. Not a great first impression. And at each subsequent meeting, he'd proceeded to wind her into a tailspin, to the point just seeing him had her so flustered she was riding into bushes.

Having one of these newcomers scared of him was not doing his reputation any favors. He'd come back to Henderson for his mother, and in doing so, he knew he'd have to mend some fences and keep his nose clean. And he was fine with that. He was perfectly happy to demonstrate to anyone who was watching that he was no longer a mean, practical-joking, S.O.B.

"Ah, hell," he mumbled into the afternoon sun, realizing he was now oh-for-two.

The evil twin in him didn't bother to suppress a chuckle. Whether it was the look on Tweety Bird's face when he said he'd pick her up or the fact he'd totally pulled one over on her, he wasn't sure. Because

Vance's text had said, *"Dinner tonight to go over Piper's harebrained pie shop ideas. 6:30. The woman has a notebook crammed full of stuff, so I'd suggest you bring your secretary."*

He texted back, *"You're on. Secretary in tow."*

No, little Tweety Bird was not gonna be happy when she found out he was pulling her in as his secretary. But the fallout—now that was going to be fun. There was just something *so* satisfying about ruffling her feathers, he thought, remembering the first time he sent her scurrying behind Harry. Damn. Something about making her squirm truly got his motor running. Because she was so … serious—stupidly so—and that, well that just sang to his antagonist nature. The girl was so whacked and out of balance he figured he was doing the world a favor by shaking her up.

Now, she did have a surprisingly balanced way of looking at things. Henderson things. Where the rest of her Dallas cronies were completely out of touch, she'd been spot-on about the apartment complex. It couldn't hurt to get her take on this pie shop too. Though it seemed she liked to keep her nuggets of golden insight locked up tight inside her serious exterior.

Didn't really matter one way or another, Xavier assured himself, because what he really needed was for Laidey Bartholomew to stop looking at him like he was Jack the damn Ripper. Even precocious Marnie—a mere kid—trusted him. *With her life.*

So, yeah, okay. He might want to see about borrowing his father's car for the evening. As much as little Laidey seriously needed to feel the wind through her hair, the night might go a little better if he offered the fluffy bunny a carrot. One with a lot of steel around it. And a seat belt.

Arriving home, Xavier found his mother in the living room propped up with pillows in a big armchair, playing bridge with Vance's grandmother, Emelina, along with Garland Langford and Evie Jackson. Back in the day, that last face would have brought Xavier to a screeching halt and have him making a quick retreat. But he was so relieved to find his mother out of bed, he moved toward the group as if it were his best day ever.

Frankly, seeing his mother's smile did make it a great day. Even though she looked more fragile than the two who were a generation older, Xavier was exceedingly grateful that his mother was on the mend rather than in continuous decline.

"Xavier," Mrs. Jackson drawled. "Come, let me look at you."

When Evie Jackson wanted to look at you, you stood before her, hands clasped, nodding in acquiescence. "Your mother told me you'd grown a beard," she said, squinting at him, judging his appearance boldly and without remorse. She finally sat back and regarded the cards in her hand once again. "I like it."

Well, that was a shock. A compliment from Evie.

"How's that brother of yours?"

"Which one?" he asked with a grin.

"The one who looks like you."

"Mrs. Jackson, I'm far more handsome than any of my brothers," he teased.

"Hmm." She played a card. "You know, I still haven't forgiven you for bludgeoning my grandson."

He didn't bludgeon him. He gave him a well-deserved black eye. Years and years ago. Of course, he'd come home to make amends, and arguing with the almighty Evie Jackson was not the way to go. "Your grandson and I came to an understanding over that incident long ago."

"That may be so. But you and I have yet to reconcile."

He spread his arms. "How may I make it up to you?"

Her head tilted toward the grand piano. "Play for us while we finish our game."

He hesitated, looking over his shoulder at the instrument. "Mrs. Jackson, I haven't played in years."

Evie's eyes filled with glee. "It will please me to no end to hear just how rusty you are."

"Of course, it will." He turned toward the others. "My apologies."

When he still hesitated, his mother cooed, "Darling. Just play."

Evie Jackson might hold all the cards in Henderson, but his mother's sweet request slayed him.

"All right," he quietly agreed. He turned from the ladies and took a seat on the wood bench looking at the keys he'd all but banished from memory.

Long ago, Xavier wanted nothing more than to play the piano. From the time he was a little kid, his mother had encouraged him. She'd sit and listen to him practice, even when his younger brothers were running around the living room sword fighting. They both just tuned them out.

He became so proficient that when he was in middle school, his mom paid him good money to play during her dinner parties. He'd play her favorite Barry Manilow tunes. Some Carpenters. Some of the early Beatles. Cocktail and dinner music. Soothing. Then his parents' friends would put a dollar on the top of the piano and request a song. If he didn't have the sheet music, he'd try to play by ear, because he wanted the dollar. Turned out he had a knack for high-energy show tunes. More than once his parents and their guests would gather around the piano and sing long into the night. If he got song requests he didn't recognize, he'd track them down the following morning so he could add them to his repertoire for next time. He remembered lying in bed, marveling over the fact that he'd made some serious cash while doing something he would have done for free. He felt like he'd hit the jackpot ... until it got around at school.

That had embarrassed the hell out of him.

Now in his thirties, sitting there becoming reacquainted with middle C, he wondered why he'd been so embarrassed for his friends to find out. Because he'd come home from school that day and told his mother he'd never play for her or her friends again.

And he hadn't.

Yet, here he sat. Full circle. As an old ragtime song came to him, unearthing itself from beneath all the architectural information and all the construction knowledge he'd piled up over his joy of playing. So he poised his fingers over the keys and surprised himself as they started to dance, as if of their own volition, bouncing out the melody of an old-fashioned, upbeat tune.

The ladies applauded when he finished. And that was a shock. He turned and grinned at them, catching his mother's dazzling expression of joy.

"I don't know where it came from," he told them.

"From your heart," his mother responded.

"More," Evie demanded, going back to her cards.

Xavier faced the keys again, hoping another tune would crawl out of his memory, but as he tinkered with scales, nothing came. Nothing but silence in his head, which was sort of crazy. He listened to music all the time.

He got up and sought out the sheet music hidden inside the piano bench, choosing something he thought he remembered. Once he'd discovered he could play by ear, he'd stopped reading the notes, which eventually ended his formal instruction. Being a kid with a modicum of talent, he wanted to do it his own way. Of course.

But none of that was serving him now as he stumbled through a few ballads from Jesus Christ Superstar. Still, the women were kind with their praise even though it had become obvious he wasn't just old nail rusty, he was in fact, barnacle crusty. That ragtime tune was a one-off, and now he was just embarrassing himself.

"Ladies. I refuse to torture you any longer," he said, finishing song number three. "However, I promise to practice and serenade you the next time you're here to entertain my mother. Mrs. Jackson, I'll even let you offer a critique." He stood. "Ma, any chance I can borrow a car this evening?"

"Where are you headed?" Evie asked.

Xavier's smile belied the *"nosy old bat"* comment that was going off in his head. "I'm headed to Miss Emelina's place. Something about a pie shop."

"Oooh," his mother said, eyes brightening. "I've tried Piper's pies. Are you gonna build out her shop?"

"I'm being interviewed for the job."

Em winked at him over her cards. "I'll be sure to put in a good word."

"Since my reputation precedes me"—he grinned at Evie—"I can use all the good words I can get. Ladies, enjoy your afternoon."

CHAPTER THIRTEEN

Laidey stared out the screen door, watching a Cadillac SUV park at the curb.

Was this disappointment she felt? Disappointment because Xavier Wright had the good sense not to insist she give his two-wheeled deathtrap a try?

Seriously?

Laidey truly didn't want to get on a hot-rod-red Harley, even if she had been thinking about it all afternoon. She didn't like the noise, she didn't like the idea of being seen on the back of the thing, and she definitely didn't like the odds for survival if, God forbid, they were in an accident.

Twice she considered tracking down his number so she could call him and tell him she'd simply meet him there. The Evans estate wasn't all that far, and Poppy probably wouldn't have minded dropping her off.

The fact that he was getting out of a very safe SUV should have been a big relief. And it would have been if it were truly the thought of his motorcycle that had been distracting her all day. Unfortunately, it was the thought of wrapping her arms around Xavier that had taken center focus.

Fool.

She watched as he approached, devoid of his badass leather jacket and ripped jeans. No longer appearing as the havoc-wielding roughneck she'd encountered continuously over the past several days, Xavier Wright was cleaned up and polished. A shiny new penny glistening in the evening sun. Long and fit, wearing a dress shirt tucked into a pair of fine trousers.

Damn, the man looked good in his clothes.

Gone were the construction boots, replaced by a stylish pair of woven loafers. Laidey's eyes traveled from his shoes to the leather belt at his waist, up the buttons of his dress shirt—pale blue with the cuffs rolled up—and kept going over his collar to his Adam's apple, right there in the center of his neck, and up past the way-too-cool scruff where his perfectly straight teeth were being shown off by a crooked grin. Eventually, her gaze came to a halt on the mirth glistening from the gray of his eyes.

"Do I pass inspection?" he asked.

Oh, man.

When she didn't respond—because, yeah, what could she say?—he said, "Tweets. You just eye-fucked me."

"What!"

"Don't try to deny it."

"I don't even know what that is," she stammered. "And who are you calling Tweets?"

"You, Tweety Bird. I'm calling you Tweets."

"Why?"

"Because you resemble a cartoon character. Big expressive eyes over a tiny, little body. Like Tweety Bird."

"Tweety Bird is blond."

"The dress you wore Monday was yellow. So were your kindergarten Keds."

Her lips slammed shut. She whirled around and grabbed a satchel, pulling it over her shoulder.

"You got a pen and paper in there in case you have to take notes?"

"Of course," she snapped, coming out the screen door and letting it bounce closed behind her.

"I'm guessing that was a stupid question," he said as she stomped past him—in pink Keds—heading toward the car. "You strike me as the kind of girl who always has pen and paper at the ready."

"This is a business meeting. I assume even you brought a notebook."

He opened the passenger door and said, "Nope." When she was seated inside, he gave her a brazen grin. "Why would I bother when I've got you?"

Just as she began to inform him she wasn't his secretary, he slammed the car door.

The Adelaide part of her threw Xavier Wright a dirty look as he sauntered around the hood of the car—grinning. The Laidey part of her brain noted he had opened and closed the car door for her.

Yeah, *Laidey* seemed to be turning into a foolish, thrill-seeking Xavier Wright groupie, and she needed to get Laidey's act together. But the proximity of being in a car with him was not helping things. He was so tall his head stopped just shy of hitting the roof. His seat was pushed back so far to accommodate the length of his legs that she had a full view of him—and *his lap*—if she chose to look in his direction. Which she did, a lot. She could try to stare at his profile, but that perfect scruff issue just made her crazy. And now so did the outline of his—pants.

This was exactly what Grandmother Rowling had warned her about. Being flighty and boy crazy was not reasonable, responsible, or respectable. *But*, Laidey conceded, *her grandmother had never been trapped in a car with a piece of sculpted gorgeousness like this.* Being closed up with Xavier Wright was—beyond. Beyond what any reasonable woman should have to endure. He even liked classical music.

"Whose car is this?" she blurted.

"My dad's. I thought it might be best not to scare you off our project by forcing you on the Road King."

"*Our* project?"

"Vance's project."

"So your dad likes classical music?"

"Ah … no. I put this on. You want me to change it?" His hand darted to the dial.

"No," she shrieked. *Completely lame and so awkward.* She was careful to adjust her voice. "I like classical music. This is fine."

He nodded, using two hands to turn them onto the Evans's drive.

"I guess I was trying to figure out if you like classical," she ventured.

"Yep."

Yep? Just a yep was all he was going to give her? Nothing more to explain the anomaly or to take her mind off the fact that they were so close she could *smell* him?

Really? So he smells good. And he looks kinda awesome. And he's got that thing about him. That smirky, cocky, commanding thing going on that just …

Drove her crazy.

In such a good way.

Which was so very bad.

She was awkward enough when her life was on an even keel. Klutzy and quiet. She was working on the klutzy thing, and being quiet wasn't exactly horrible when you worked in a world full of talkers. Regardless—she thought as Xavier pulled into the gates of the estate and Laidey took in the architecturally spectacular red brick, white-columned mansion—being attracted to Xavier made her more klutzy, i.e., the bush incident. And being called out for staring at him was just about as awkward as it got.

She needed to rein it in and deal.

So she turned her focus to the job at hand and found herself standing on the front steps of the Evanses' beautiful home. She wasn't nervous. At least not about what she'd find inside. She'd met everyone who lived here over the last several months and had an opportunity to work side by side with most of them. She wasn't nervous about freelancing for Vance. She liked projects and had plenty of free weekends to get the job done. Working was what she was good at, so she'd handle whatever he needed from her. After all, helping out wherever she could spread goodwill in the name of CC Dallas. She was sure Crain Carraway wouldn't mind at all.

Crain. Tall and broad. Similar to this Mr. XL over there, she thought, trying to tamp down the effects of being in such close proximity.

When the door opened and Vance's ready grin defaulted to shock as he took in the two of them standing side by side, her hackles rose. Vance eyed them both, tilting his head and looking from her to Xavier and back again. Finally, he put his full attention on Xavier and said, "Man, you must have some deep pockets." He stepped back and motioned them both to step inside. "Come on in."

Confused—and frankly worried that she'd somehow made a grand social faux pas—Laidey looked to Xavier for an explanation. He was waiting for her to enter first. "What does that mean?"

"Couldn't say." He stood there, towering over her with his gorgeous dark head of hair and his hands casually stuffed into the pockets of his trousers.

"Vance?" Laidey stepped inside. "Deep pockets?"

"Well, I happen to know what Carraway pays you." He closed the door and took the lead up the foyer stairs. "I hope you broke it down to an hourly fee for this guy before you agreed to be his secretary."

"His what?" Laidey screeched, coming to a halt so quickly Xavier bumped into her back. She turned, pressed her hand against his chest, and pushed him down a step where she could look at him eye to eye. "I'm here as your *secretary?*"

He simply put his super-sized hands on her hips and spun her around, pushing at the center of her back to indicate she should keep moving.

She climbed another step, hissing over her shoulder, "I'm getting to the bottom of this."

He leaned in close—way too close—and whispered right against her ear, "Role-play."

What?

"Unfortunately," Vance was saying, completely unaware of what was happening behind him, "Piper is involved in an impromptu meeting out by the pool." Laidey caught up to him inside an enormous kitchen as he waved a hand toward the windows. She glanced briefly in the direction he indicated, but couldn't help a double take at the scrumptious kitchen.

"This is … something," she whispered.

"What? Oh, the kitchen." Vance stuck his hands in his back pockets. "It used to be overkill when it was just my grandmother and me living here. Back when Dad spent most of his time out of town. But now, with the way our family is growing, it suits. But

I'm planning to build my bride a bigger one. Because Piper likes to bake—which is why you're here, I assume."

She watched as Vance looked over at Xavier for confirmation and got a solid nod.

"Was I not included in this dinner meeting?" She really hoped that didn't come out as exasperated as she felt. Spreading the CC Dallas goodwill was one thing—when it was asked for. But she was coming to understand that she'd simply been thrust upon Vance and his dinner plans. "Vance, I apologize."

"For what?" he wondered.

"For arriving on your doorstep uninvited."

"Uninvited? I told Orville here to bring his secretary. Clearly, the man doesn't fool around because he brought you. Your levelheadedness will no doubt help make sense of Piper's many and various ideas so the big guy there can build it into a reality. Truly, I'm relieved to have you on this project."

Laidey threw Xavier a dirty look. *His secretary.* He answered back with a not-so-sheepish shrug.

Disgusted with herself for being duped and still finding him attractive, she turned her attention to the large, umbrella-topped table where Pinks was seated with Piper, Lolly, Annabelle, Emelina, and Genevra.

"What's going on out there?"

"Pinks is handling a situation for the House of DuVal."

"The House of DuVal?" Xavier asked.

"Lolly and Annabelle's joint venture. Special-occasion dresses. Lolly designs and creates them here in town. Annabelle, with her sorority-girl reach up and down the mid-Atlantic, is in charge of sales. Right now, Pinks is plotting a strategy for handling their recent bad press."

"The sweatshop thing?"

"Yep. Viper, in an effort to get to Brooks and rip a hole in his campaign, went to the Raleigh press and leaked word of a sweatshop in Henderson. Made it abundantly clear that one of the owners was connected to the man running for mayor, and that perhaps Brooks was looking the other way."

"It's not a sweatshop, is it?" Laidey asked, nervous for Henderson.

"Not at all. Just three women working hard. All from Henderson, all with skills, and all are grateful for the job. They work in an old textile mill. No air-conditioning so yeah, they probably do sweat. But it's not how the media has portrayed it."

"And Pinks is fixing this *too*?"

"What do you mean, too?" Xavier asked. "What's this Pinks do for y'all?"

"Everything," Vance and Laidey said in unison. They grinned at each other and high-fived.

"And look at that." Laidey pointed out the window. "He's taking his own notes. Doesn't appear he needs a secretary."

"Can I get y'all a beer? Some wine?" Vance asked, moving away from the windows and toward the kitchen bar.

"Sure," Xavier said.

"Water for me." Laidey eyed Xavier. "Apparently, I'm on the clock."

"I take it you're here under false pretenses?" Vance asked as he poured a sparkling water into a pretty wine glass and then went over to a beverage refrigerator to retrieve two beers.

She shrugged. "We're in overtime, so my hourly wage just doubled."

Vance took a sip of his own beer and cocked a brow at Xavier. "Do not pad your fee because you have an expensive secretary. That's on you."

"Tweets is here as a volunteer," Xavier claimed.

"Wha—"

"Tweets?" Vance asked.

"Tweety Bird. Good with ideas. Understands Henderson in a way the rest of her Dallas crew doesn't. And, with all you and your family are doing for Henderson, she's happy to volunteer."

"Is that right?" Vance asked, thoroughly amused.

Laidey didn't know what to say. *Of course,* with all Vance and his family were doing for Henderson, she'd be happy to give her opinion whenever they asked for it. No strings attached. All they'd have to do is ask. But it was Xavier who had said that her presence was requested. Only now it was clear that it wasn't requested by Vance. Vance just told him to bring *his secretary*.

"Do you even have a secretary?" she huffed at Xavier.

"At the moment, I don't have a hammer."

"And without a hammer *or* a secretary, you're doing what for Piper?"

"With you graciously volunteering and my tools being delivered by the end of the week, I plan on renovating one of the vacant shops on Main Street for Piper. I brought you with me because of your vision."

"What vision?"

"The *charming* vision."

"Charming?"

"Yes. Just yesterday, you told me that Henderson didn't have much but what it did have was charm. And you suggested that we capitalize on that."

"I did?"

"You did. So I figured you might be interested in the next renovation project happening on Main Street."

Vance jumped in. "Laidey, just be my guest for dinner. Listen to the give-and-take between Piper and Xavier. If you've got suggestions, voice them."

"And maybe take a note or two," Xavier ordered.

Laidey tilted her head toward the scene out the window. "Again. Pinks. Taking his own notes."

"Well, I'm not Pinks."

One brow rose. "Clearly."

The House of DuVal meeting broke up just as the timer went off in the kitchen. Emelina came rushing in from the outside as Vance finished Laidey and Xavier's tour of the house.

Well, that certainly didn't help my anxiety level, Laidey thought as she brought up the rear. Xavier wasn't exactly the thick-skulled laborer Laidey wanted to make him out to be. Apparently, in addition to being a brute, he was an engineering *and* architectural brainiac. He'd been totally into the design of the mansion. Asked Vance all kinds of questions about the building process that Vance simply couldn't answer. Xavier would then carefully inspect the house in order to figure it out for himself and explain the answer to Vance and Laidey. He paid crazy attention to the details, like the intricate ceiling work and all the imported materials that had been used. Laidey could tell

Vance was impressed with Xavier's extensive knowledge and keen eye when he suggested Xavier consider signing on as quality control officer while the sports academy was being built.

"Definitely be good to have a guy like you checking on things as they progress. I'm afraid the rest of us wouldn't have a clue."

The whole thing left Laidey feeling off-kilter as she watched Em grab a large salad bowl out of the refrigerator. Genevra bustled in behind them, insisting her homemade garlic bread would be ready in a jiffy. The two went about their tasks quickly and efficiently, and once the bread was in the oven, Genevra stopped, wiped her hands, and turned toward Xavier. "Now we can be properly introduced," she said, her smile radiant. "And … Laidey." She seemed completely baffled to find Laidey in her kitchen. Emelina came to stand behind Genevra, both of them glancing between Xavier and Laidey.

"I like it," Em confirmed.

A broad smile came over Genevra's beautiful features as she nodded in acknowledgement. "I'm glad you're here," she said in a way that soothed Laidey. "You'll be good for this project."

"Genevra, this is an old friend of mine, Xavier Wright," Vance said, stepping in. "You know his momma."

"I do." Genevra took Xavier's hand in hers. "How's she making out this week?"

"Good," Xavier told her. "Far better than I expected to find her. Seems to be holding her own right now. Not out of bed much, but does a lot of reading and online shopping." He motioned to the shirt he had on.

"Please tell her I'll be by in the next few days. Piper and I have some recipes we've near perfected. I always look to her for an opinion when we're close."

Laidey watched Xavier tilt his head, not understanding. So she saw when an expression of warmth softened his features, as if he'd been overwhelmed with a gift. "You do it to get her to eat."

Genevra continued to smile her beautiful smile and nod. "We do. We want her to eat."

"Thank you." It came out distorted and choked. "I want her to eat too."

Laidey reached up and touched him on his back. He immediately stiffened.

Yikes. She snapped her hand back like she'd been burned and took two steps away from him before he caught her around her wrist. "I'm sorry," he said. "Didn't mean that."

Though she was transfixed by the steely-gray of his eyes, they didn't shed light on either what he didn't mean or what he meant now.

Obviously, he was touchy for an ogre.

And she was a jumpy little Tweety Bird in his presence.

The chemistry between them was itchy at best and scalding at worst. They weren't going to be able to work together when they could hardly tolerate being in the same room. Her plan? Keep her mouth shut and her head down during the entire dinner meeting. Short. Sweet. Then out the door. With an Uber.

Did they have Uber in Henderson?

Whatever. She'd get in, get out, and part ways with Xavier as quickly as she could.

"Laidey," Genevra called, holding out a hand to her like she would a child. "Let me guide you through the buffet line. We're going to let y'all enjoy dinner out by the pool. Em and I'll stay inside with the babies so Piper can give all of her attention to the plans for her shop."

She was handed a plate and did her best not to stiffen as Xavier came up beside her, took the spatula out of her hand, and dished her a large piece of lasagna, all the while complimenting Genevra and Em on the spread. She went along with it. All of it. Just watched as the assertive jerk fixed her plate, offering up no protest whatsoever. She … *allowed* it. And then stood there until his plate was full and the two of them were escorted to the vacated table, now beautifully set for dinner, complete with flickering candlelight.

Vance was pouring wine and Piper was placing three folders dripping with papers on the table. "Vance and I'll fix our plates and be right out. Laidey, why don't you and Xavier sit on the far side of the table. That way you have the view."

Laidey continued to do as she was told, feeling completely unsure of herself, wondering what she could possibly contribute.

"You're fine," Xavier whispered in her ear as they seated themselves.

"I'm not fine. I'm intruding."

"You're not intruding. I told them you were coming."

"You told them you were bringing your secretary."

"Exactly."

"I'm *not* your secretary."

"You're my secretary tonight."

"You are insane."

"Nope. Just know what I want and am determined to get it. Consider this a role-playing game like Dungeons and Dragons. You're putting on a mask. A secretarial mask, just for the duration of our game."

"Our game?"

Xavier tilted his head as he sipped his wine. "You don't like to play games?"

Laidey gave him her profile and let out a breath. She did like to play games. And there'd been a time she liked to participate in role-playing games. "Okay," she said, finding comfort in his convoluted analogy. "This is a game. I'm your secretary."

"Perfect."

"Your uppity secretary."

"Uppity?"

"Yes. *Your* secretary has spunk. Or she would have left you a long time ago," she said, making up their backstory.

"She would have left me a long time ago if it wasn't for the fringe benefits."

"I could definitely use your handyman skills around my rental."

"Not exactly what I meant," he hedged, grinning through another sip of wine as Vance approached. He leaned over and whispered in her ear, "Fringe benefits of the bedroom variety."

"Oh, please." Laidey put on a show of rolling her eyes.

"You're blushing," he accused as Vance pulled a chair out for Piper and the two of them took their seats.

"What's the mouse blushing over?" Vance asked, placing a napkin in his lap.

"No mouse. Tweety Bird. And I just told her that since I'm good with my hands, as my secretary, she has access to all that and then some."

"Mmm." Piper smiled and licked her lips. "Fringe benefits."

"That's exactly what I was explaining."

"Are we going to say grace?" Laidey blurted. It was a totally lame thing to say. But right now, her skin was sweating, her heart was racing, and Xavier Wright, tall and fit with those muscular forearms, was sitting six inches from her, talking about his bedroom skills. She really didn't need any more encouragement in the thinking about Xavier department.

"Say grace? At a business dinner?" Xavier was grinning so hard he was practically laughing in her face.

"Your secretary is a holy roller," Laidey informed him.

"Perhaps you'd like to do the honors?" Vance offered, his startled expression wearing off.

"Sure," she said, folding hands and closing her eyes, embarrassment cascading from her ears, strutting down her neck, and gripping her chest. She was so mortified she couldn't clear her head enough to think of the first line of any grace, not even one from childhood. Just when she was about to burst into embarrassed tears, she heard Xavier clear his throat.

"Bless us O Lord for these thy gifts which we are about to receive. Thank you for the fellowship of friends, the invention of lasagna, and your guidance while we brainstorm Piper's ambitious endeavor. In addition, we ask for your blessings to rain down on our small town and all its citizens and especially for the healing of our loved ones, near and far. Amen."

"Amen," Piper and Laidey whispered together. In appreciation, Laidey reached out and touched Xavier on his thigh.

"Didn't know you had it in you," Vance said, digging into his lasagna.

"Had a lot of practice this past year."

"Ah. I suppose you have. Your momma still doing well?" The rest of them started eating.

"Seems to be. Your grandmother was over playing cards with her this afternoon. Which means I'm in her debt. So if she ever needs anything, you let me know."

Vance waved that off. "The beauty of a small town."

"Still," Xavier insisted.

Vance nodded.

"Now Piper, tell me about your pie shop," Xavier suggested. And while Piper's enthusiasm gathered with each word she spoke on the subject and each picture she took from her files—pictures of old-fashioned *charming* storefronts, various stone countertops, display cases, samples of flooring, paint chips, and photos of rooms with the feel she wanted to create—so did Laidey's interest in the project. And the man sitting next to her.

By the end of the evening, the four of them had gone through three bottles of wine, Laidey had taken copious notes, and an agreement had been reached whereby Xavier would meet Piper on Friday and the two of them would select one of the available Main Street locations together.

It wasn't until Laidey and Xavier were seated in his car that she remembered her plan to call an Uber. Because even after the night had ended up going well—*especially* because the night had gone well—she was now getting that anxious, fluttery feeling again. It didn't take a brain surgeon to figure out she was terribly attracted to the brute. And yes, he was still a brute, albeit an educated one. Even if the brute saved her from dying of embarrassment by offering up an impromptu prayer, a brute with good manners and stellar social skills was still a brute.

"Thank you," she said quietly as he drove them from the Evans estate.

"For what?"

"That … grace." She grimaced at the thought of her blurting out the suggestion.

"No problem, Tweets."

Her stomach tightened. "Please don't call me that."

"No?" he asked, looking at her curiously. "You're into role-playing but not into nicknames?"

She shrugged. "Laidey is my nickname. And you don't even like that."

"Who says I don't like it?"

She threw him a weary look. "You made fun of it. Today. In front of Marnie."

"I was teasing you." His playful expression changed abruptly into exasperation. "You know that, right?"

When she didn't respond, he looked out the windshield. "No. You don't know that. You still think I'm *that* guy."

"I still think you're *what* guy?"

It was his turn to shrug.

"What *guy*?" she pressed.

"That guy. The guy I used to be. The guy who hazed his teammates and"—he shrugged—"forgot to break up with McKenna."

"You didn't forget to break up with McKenna."

"No. I didn't," he admitted.

"So what was that really about?"

She heard him huff, his fist bumping against the steering wheel. "My intention was to right a wrong. Bring about peace and harmony. Only it didn't work out that way."

"Right a wrong?"

He nodded into the night but kept silent until he was parked at the curb outside her house. He glanced over at the lights coming from inside.

"You got roommates?"

"One. Poppy. The redhead."

"With the freckles," he added. "She's a looker."

Laidey popped open the door and began to exit.

"Hold on," he said, reaching for her, but she snatched her hand away and grabbed for her tote, slamming the car door as she exited. She certainly wasn't interested in hearing him wax poetic about Poppy and her pretty features, her mind leaping to the front row seat she'd have watching Xavier woo Poppy. The same seat she had when Crain Carraway wooed his wife.

No, thank you.

"Laidey," Xavier called out.

When she heard his car door slam, she blew out a breath, forcing herself to walk steadily to her front door instead of bursting into an awkward mad dash. "Tweets," he said over her shoulder as he wrapped a hand around her wrist, halting all forward motion. As he maneuvered her around to face him, his words were gentle. "Aren't you forgetting something?"

Lord, she was a goner. That smile he was laying on her was sweet, his gray eyes practically twinkling in delight. When he reached for the side of her head, she imagined what would come next. Her breath halted in her chest in anticipation of Xavier Wright's kiss.

Using fingers that soothed and tickled, he pushed some hair behind her ear, repeating the motion several times while he licked his lips. His eyes darted from his fingers drifting around her ear, to her lips, and then to her eyes.

"Hand me your phone." Unable to drag her gaze from his gorgeous face, his voice coaxed her to action. She reached into the interior pocket of her tote, pulled out the device and handed it to him. His smile broadened, his eyes still locked on hers. "Thank you."

He used both hands and his full attention to hammer away on her phone.

"Your contact information?" she half whispered, feeling defenseless over this spell he cast.

He nodded as he typed.

Laidey crossed her arms over her chest, essentially hugging herself to contain the yearning being this close to him created. She remembered to take a breath as she watched his fingers, his strong hands, and the musculature of his arms shown off by his rolled-up sleeves. When Xavier finished, he dropped her phone in the tote hanging off her arm, leaned over, bringing them eye to eye, and gently took her face in both his hands. "Type up the notes tonight, email them to me when you're done."

When she opened her mouth to protest, he kissed her. Quick, easy, like it was nothing. And then he left her standing there. She touched her fingers to her lips, wondering if that just happened. "Did you just ... *steal a kiss?*" she shouted at his retreating back.

He shrugged as he opened the car door. "Meet Piper and me at noon on Friday," he said. Then he banged his fist on the top of the roof. "And do both of us a favor," he barked, pointing directly at her. "Stop being a chickenshit and speak your mind. You know the whole internet cooking show idea is bullshit. I'm not paying you to be a yes man for the client."

"You aren't paying me at all," she shouted. "I'm not your secretary."

"Fringe benefits, Tweets. Fringe benefits."

CHAPTER FOURTEEN

Xavier chuckled to himself on the way home. Tweety Bird was so darn easy to rile up he couldn't help himself. Though, stealing a kiss—as she put it—was probably pushing it. He'd just followed his instincts there. Hadn't wanted to hear any protests and definitely wanted all of her notes. He'd put the odds at fifty-fifty of her actually following through.

Before heading up the stairs, he stuck his head in the guest suite to find his father reading a book in his chair and his mother on the bed, propped up with pillows, but sound asleep.

"How long has she been out?" Xavier whispered, checking his watch because it wasn't much past nine.

"She conked out early," his dad told him, making an effort to keep the worry out of his voice. His father stood and arched his back. The drawn look of his face gave him away.

"Go. Take a break. It's early yet. Call Rye. Have him meet you at the club for a nightcap. You two can catch some of the baseball highlights. I'll sit with Ma for a while. All night if you want me to."

"You sure?"

"Yeah, I'm sure." He smiled at his dad. "Happy to. The reason I'm here. Go."

"If she wakes up—"

"She'll be relieved you're getting a break. Go on. Get."

His dad grabbed on to his shoulder and gave him a squeeze as he walked past.

Xavier took his seat, pulling out his phone, checking for messages. There was a text from Chase Alexander and just seeing the man's name gave Xavier reason to smile.

"You got any work up there to keep an old man busy?"

He texted back, *"You thinking of relocating?"*

"Permits have been denied."

"What?" Chase wasn't new to the industry by any stretch of the imagination, and he knew the ropes.

"Politics apparently. Something about redrawing county lines. Our property is caught in a tug of war. Worth nothing to the politicians as a wasteland, but after I work my magic over the location, there will be wealthy voters living here."

"How long is this gonna hold things up?"

"They aren't saying. Which means it could take months. Years."

"Holy shit."

"That's what I said. So, you need any help in NC? I've got nothing to do here but scratch my balls. Happy to help get you set up. Be your second in command."

Xavier snorted. As if. *"Sure. I could use some laborers,"* he texted back with a grin.

"Asshole."

"Yep. Fell right back into it when I arrived home. Not sure you're gonna wanna start all over with the ass-kicking."

"Hell. I'm bored. Happy to kick your ass all you need."

"Come on out then. I'll put you up and have a tool belt waiting for you. Already have a job. Planning to start next week. Henderson is work-permit friendly."

"Don't blow smoke up my skirt. I'm for real. You want me to come and help?"

Xavier looked over at his sleeping mother. Then he texted, *"Yeah. I really want you to come. Text me your flight information when you've got it. If you can get here on Monday, we can hit the ground running."*

When another text didn't come in, Xavier added, *"You're gonna like it here. Please come."*

He tucked his phone away and sat back, thinking about how much he could use Chase right now. Physically, yeah, sure, there was plenty of building to do. But, he thought as he looked over at his ma, Chase's presence would provide emotional support as well. It always had.

"Oh, Ma," he whispered. "You've just got to get better."

He laid his head against the back of the chair and offered up a prayer. He kept praying and praying until he drifted off to sleep.

A buzz in his pocket woke him a while later. It was Chase's flight information. Xavier smiled at that, really happy he hadn't dreamed the whole Chase-coming-to-town thing.

"What's happening?" His mother's warm voice surprised him.

"You're awake."

"I fell asleep around five. What time is it?"

"Just after eleven. You up for a midnight snack?"

The way her face lit up healed his heart. "I believe I'd like that. Pancakes?"

"Sounds good to me. And I've got some news I'll share with you while you watch me make them. Come on. Out of bed."

His mother didn't argue with him. In fact, she seemed eager to be out of bed. "Where's your father?" she asked, tying her bathrobe around her. Xavier held her steady as she stepped into her slippers.

"I wanted him to get a little fresh air," he told her. "Suggested he meet Rye for a night cap."

"Good. Thank you." The two of them walked slowly toward the kitchen, his mother's arm tucked under his. "He's been my rock through this," she told him. "I was so worried he wasn't going to be able to handle it, but he's been my constant companion. My support. And I believe him when he tells me he doesn't mind. Because he loves me and doesn't want to lose me. Still, *I* mind."

"How's that?"

"The man should be out dancing."

"Since when has dad ever gone out dancing?"

"You know what I mean. He … *we* should be out with our friends, visiting all of our boys, traveling for vacations, all of that. And yet, here we sit, side by side, night after night, and the only travel we've done has been to hospitals near and far."

"You're getting better."

"I am. But not fast enough."

"Fast or not, better is good. And I'm here to make sure Dad goes dancing."

That got her to smile as he helped her ease into a kitchen chair. She patted his hand. "You're a good kid, Xavier. The best."

He scoffed at that. "Nowhere near the best. But I am home. Finally. And I can make pancakes."

As he did, he told his mother about the ideas Piper had for her shop and made the announcement that the great *Chase Alexander* was coming to town.

His mother clapped her hands together, delighted at the news, and it appeared, delighted by the dish he set before her. "Sit down," she ordered. "Eat with me and tell me more."

"I thought I'd fix up the room over the garage. I was planning to do it for myself, but it would be perfect for Chase. He'd have his own access, could come and go as he pleased, and we could offer him kitchen privileges where all he'd need to do is come through the side door there.

"But he means so much to you. I want him to feel welcome, like he's a member of the family. Why don't we just put him in one of your brothers' rooms?"

"I'd like him to stay all summer, and I don't think he'll do it if he feels like he's imposing on you and Daddy. Besides, he'll have to stay in the house a week or so until we can get the garage finished. After that, he'll be itching for his own space to watch TV in his underwear or whatever."

"Oh." His mother smiled a knowing smile. "You're right. A grown man needs his own space."

"Is that a subtle dig that I should find accommodations elsewhere?" he teased.

"Don't be silly. I love having you home. Wouldn't mind if a few of your brothers found it in them to move back in."

"Not staying forever, Ma."

"What?"

"I mean, I'm not living in this house with you and Daddy forever. I'll find a place of my own eventually."

"Here in Henderson."

"That's the plan. There's plenty of work for a guy like me. Might not pay enough to make it worth my while since they're asking everyone to reduce their profits. But I've got some savings stashed. I can give it some time. See how things go."

When his father came home, Xavier cleaned the kitchen, letting the man lead his wife off to bed. He was buoyed by the thought that his earlier prayers had been answered. His mother had eaten everything on her plate, which was rare. On top of that, she seemed refreshed and invigorated.

The power of sleep and food. And prayer.

It was close to midnight when he finally made it to his old bedroom, the largest one in the house with two double beds. He undressed and grabbed his laptop, planning to check his favorite websites, when an email from one *AddieBGood@gmail.com* caught his eye.

"Interesting."

He licked his lips as he clicked it open. "Addie B Good, huh?" Only he didn't find the notes from their dinner meeting with Piper. As he started reading, what he found was more like a research paper detailing the benefits of Piper's proposed internet cooking show with enough stats to back it up so far he couldn't refute them.

1. There weren't many internet cooking shows out there, and none that would be done as Piper had detailed.

2. Cooking shows were a hit on cable TV, and everyone was watching everything from their devices now.

3. Every show would be an unpaid advertisement for the town of Henderson.

The list went on and on, into minutia that Xavier wouldn't have thought of, nor did he care about. Yet, Tweety Bird's point was made, and made well.

He grinned as he propped up the laptop against his knees and sent her a short but sweet response.

Tweets. Don't you ever sleep?

He was checking out Rant Sports when he heard a bing. He opened Addie B Good's response.

I believe you meant, thank you.

Little minx. *What's your cell number?*

Why?

Because texting will be faster.

He waited a full minute before his phone vibrated against the bedside table. He picked it up, added her to his contacts, and read, "*Here's my number. But I'm going to bed.*"

Bullshit. "*You gonna send me those notes before you do?*"

"*I'm not your secretary.*"

"*Role-playing, Tweets. It's our game. Our thing.*"

"*Then what role are you playing?*"

"*The hunky handyman you like to eye-fuck.*" His cheek-splitting grin died off when he didn't get a response. He put his thumbs back to work quickly.

"*Tweets? Come on now, don't get shy on me. It's a game.*"

He saw the dots, grinned because he knew she was responding, and then …

"*Go eye-fuck yourself.*"

He cackled as he slapped his laptop closed, turned off his light, and rolled to his side, unable to stop himself from sending one more text.

"*Friday. Noon. Bring your uppity secretarial humor with you.*"

Brooks and Vance stood off in the distance, slack-jawed, watching as the scene played out before them.

"Fuc-king Pinks," Brooks drawled out in awe.

Vance couldn't spare a glance at his best friend. He continued to gape at what was happening, managing only to spit out, "The dude is a freaking miracle worker."

Ever since that headline in the *Raleigh Times* had appeared, reporters had been camped outside the House of DuVal. A very unimpressive low-level building made of concrete with a tin roof. There was a screen door in the center of the thing with a cement "patio" that ran the length of the building. One reporter had turned into two, and two had turned into a dozen. And every one of those dozen reporters was now sitting outside the building at café tables, enjoying Piper's Big Pie Plate Apple Pie and sweet tea while being treated to a fashion show of Lolly's designs.

The men watched as Piper and Genevra doled out Southern charm along with pie slices, and Annabelle sashayed in between tables wearing House of DuVal fashion. They'd hooked Missy McReady into the modeling, along with Audria White and her cousin Amy.

The reporters, who were a good mix of men and women, seemed completely smitten with the pie and the show. They touched the fabrics, asked the models questions, and took notes as they did.

Lolly eventually stepped through the screen door, looking like she was the only one sweating anything. She had a bolt of fabric in her arms and waited as Annabelle introduced her as the designer. Brooks really couldn't believe it when there was a round of applause.

Lolly, who was nowhere near as serene as Annabelle, nodded her appreciation and gave a short welcome speech as if this had all been arranged. As if invitations had been sent out to a group of VIPs and this was Fashion Week in New York. She answered questions about the sweatshop allegations and took her time to introduce the three women whom she'd hired so they could answer questions as well.

Then Lolly introduced Piper, which had Vance eliciting a growl of discontent.

"Third Base," Brooks soothed. "Piper's a natural," he said as they watched her hold up Henderson's Big Pie Plate, extol its virtues, and inform the media about their date for the QVC debut.

"I know she's a natural. She'll sell the hell out of that pie plate given half a chance. Which is why QVC is putting her on the air side by side with their regular salesperson."

"That's great for Henderson," Brooks claimed.

"Sure. Because every asshole from here to the West Coast is going to want to come to Henderson to try to steal my Piper. Look at her," he insisted. "She's perfect. Looks about eighteen years old. No one's going to think she's happily married and the mother of one. They're just going to see all her … assets and come sniffing around."

"That's bullshit."

"Maybe. But it's my bullshit, and I'm drowning in it."

"Is she … not giving you what you need?"

Vance looked over like Brooks was insane. "What I need? That woman is insatiable. Now that she's got her figure back, she's flirting with me every time I turn around. I can't get any work done."

"Oh, so you're worried she's not getting what *she* needs?"

Vance scowled. "I'm giving the woman what she needs and then some. But I'm not interested in her figuring out that she could have anybody ... *any-body* and that she's stuck with me."

"Piper's wild about you."

"For now."

"Loosen up, buddy. Your insecurities are showing."

"Like that's something new."

"Seriously. What are you worried about?"

Vance looked at Brooks again. "Didn't I just spell it out?"

"Well, see. That's where that big hulking diamond you bought up in New York is going to pay off for you. Piper gets on national television, that ring will make an impression. She won't have to announce that she's married, that ring will do it for her *and* you. You got nothing to worry about. And seriously, all of this is great for Henderson. If those crazy pie plates do take off, and if Piper does open a shop on Main Street, the tourist business would be a welcome blessing for sure. Spreading the town's name and its infamy."

"Infamy?"

"Sure. Because we don't care what Henderson becomes famous for. The new academy, Lolly's House of DuVal, or Henderson's Big Pie Plate. We just care that it becomes famous for something. So throwing out all these nets is a good thing. What Lolly and Piper are doing is a really good thing. We are damn lucky to have them on our team."

"And in our beds."

Brooks blew out a slow breath. "You can say that again."

Vance sighed. After much silence, he said, "They're talking about hiring a nanny."

"Who is?"

"Piper and Genevra."

Brooks stood there a moment. Quiet. Then he ventured slowly. "You know, a nanny is a thing, right? A real, reasonable, lots of families need them thing."

"We've got six adults living on the property. We shouldn't need a nanny to take care of Brody and Vance, Jr."

"All six of those adults are intricately involved with Henderson's renewal. You, Pinks, and your father all have more than one full-time job. Henderson's Big Pie Plate is a big idea."

"I know it," Vance grumbled. "But don't tell me you're gonna be good with Lolly pawning your offspring off on somebody else."

"Hell," Brooks grouched. "I've been absolutely, not-so-subtly *warned* that she's not ready for me to put a ring on her finger. I've got mountains to climb before I'm dealing with all that."

"But you get what I mean," Vance insisted.

"I get that your abandonment issue is once again rearing its ugly head."

Vance nodded, looking straight ahead.

"A nanny is not abandonment. I've seen Piper with Vance, Jr. She couldn't be happier to be a mother."

"Then why the hell isn't that enough for her? Why aren't I and Vance, Jr. enough for her?"

"Because she's brilliant. And capable. And loves you. And wants to help our cause."

"Our cause is fine."

"It is. But this academy is not happening fast." Brooks held up a hand to stall Vance's protests. "It's fast for the scope of the project. But we are a couple years out from opening our doors and building a reputation. That's the long-term, sustain-Henderson project. You can't help but admit that Lolly opening up this sweatshop, and Molly and Piper pushing Henderson's Big Pie Plate is giving us momentum. And the town needs it. I need it. For my campaign."

"Your campaign is fine. Do not worry about the election."

"Viper is a mastermind."

Vance actually laughed at that. "She's definitely keeping us on our toes."

"Now how can you laugh off Viper and be so screwed up over a pie plate and a nanny?"

"Because sparring with Viper is nothing more than entertainment. You know it, and I know it. Even Clint Stevens knows it. But when it comes to my personal life." Vance shook his head.

"What?" Brooks prodded. "When it comes to your personal life, what?"

"I'm waiting for a shoe to drop."

"Dude!"

"I know. I know. But man, life hasn't ever been so good. I come home to this woman who is sweet to me and feeds me and puts up with my bullshit. And I've got this tiny, little kid who's amazing. Smiles every time he sees me. Fuck."

"You sound pained."

"I am. I feel so good, it hurts. And then I see this, and I know the writing is on the wall."

"How so?"

"Piper and Genevra are over there smiling from ear to ear. They love this."

"Hell, I love this. Who doesn't love turning lemons into lemonade? Damn Pinks is a genius."

"Piper and Genevra are out here turning bad press into good, but they are not home with the babies."

"Well, why aren't you home with the babies? You're Vance, Jr.'s father."

"I've got a job," he countered.

"And so do they," Brooks shouted. "Look, one of the biggest things we need to do for this town is create more jobs. *Hiring a nanny* fits in that plan. On top of that, it'll make your wife's life easier. And if Piper's happy, she's less likely to figure out that she's *way* too good for you."

"True that." Vance thought for a moment, his eyes scanning the unlikely scene in front of him. "Okay. A nanny it is."

Brooks let out a deep breath and patted Vance on the back. "Good talk. Now let's get to work."

By the time Xavier's meeting with Piper arrived on Friday, he knew exactly which property—make that *properties*—he wanted Piper to invest in. In fact, he was working hard to swallow down the sense of urgency he felt, not wanting to appear too pushy. But the truth was, he'd already spent hours and hours designing her shop—a project for which he had yet to be officially hired. Maybe it wasn't smart of him to put all this effort in before the dotted line was signed and a fee had been agreed upon. But hell, he'd needed something to do with himself other than watch his ma sleep, and frankly, the best parts of his day were his over-written, over-researched emails from Tweety Bird, otherwise known as Addie B Good.

That Lilliputian must have a case of insomnia, because she'd stayed up late brainstorming, researching, and writing out email after email on ideas for Henderson's Big Pie Plate Shop. Lord, he hoped the tiny one showed up today, just as he had continually insisted with every email he sent back. Because he needed her to help sell Piper on all that the two of them had come up with.

Broom in hand, he was sweeping out the abandoned building when Piper and Genevra walked in. In truth, Xavier had spent several hours hauling shit out to make the place look as much like a blank canvas as he could. He'd set up a long folding table in the middle of the room for showing off his latest set of plans.

"Wow," both Piper and Genevra said, surprised to find the place spic-and-span. He noticed that the light coming through the front windows he'd just squeegeed definitely added to the appeal.

"I did some cleaning," he acknowledged, feeling very nervous about this. He set the broom aside and wiped his hands before moving toward the women. He shook Piper's hand and then Genevra's, saying, "I really like this spot for what you have in mind. In fact—"

And that's when relief fell into him. That's when a tiny brunette—looking like a doll, but one of the *Barbie's-kid-sister* variety—walked in, wearing a feathery, little dress in a shade of teal blue. Xavier was pretty sure it matched her bike exactly. Tweety's shoes did not disappoint. Keds. Only this time, they were white.

"Good thing I cleaned the place up," he said by way of greeting. Piper and Genevra's heads spun to find Laidey on the threshold of the open door. "Wouldn't want you to get your new shoes dirty," he finished.

"They're not … new," she defended, completely frazzled by being the center of everyone's attention.

"Ladies," he offered, just to get a rise out of her, "I asked my secretary to join us."

"My, that's a pretty dress," Genevra cooed. "Don't you think that's a pretty dress, Xavier?"

"I do." He took a moment to grin at the flustered, little Tweety Bird. He didn't know why he loved giving her so much shit, because he was truly grateful she was here. He probably oughta be nice to the research maniac who had, so far, made his job a piece of cake, but apparently he didn't have it in him.

"Come on. You're late," he accused, beckoning her to join him at the table. "I was just about to explain why you think this building *and* the adjacent space to our right is the perfect fit for Piper's dreams to be made into fruition."

"Me? Why, I thought—"

"Go ahead. Tell them about your research into the internet cooking shows."

"We-ll," she stuttered, "they're a thing. A—"

"Right," Xavier said, "and now tell them about all the emails you sent me describing the importance of flow."

"Flow?"

"Right, and how you suggested I go ahead and get my butt in the drawing chair and come up with some plans so that we could fast-track Piper's dream into a reality. Here," he went on, bringing all three women's attention to the set of blueprints.

He kept talking, feeling ease with each of Piper's smiles. Becoming more and more certain he was on the right track with every one of Genevra's compliments. Funny how the nods of approval from Laidey granted him the most satisfaction.

Xavier began walking them around the space, describing his vision in great detail. He pointed out where the cameras would go for the production sequences and explained a little bit about what was needed in the way of specialty electrical work. He showed them where the arched entrance into the adjacent space would be placed before strolling everyone out the door and continuing the tour over there.

Within two hours, the four of them had perfected his plans, leaving him with enough detail that he'd be able to work up an accurate bid. Nothing about what Piper wanted would be cheap. But he'd done a little cabinetmaking here and there, even had some talent for it. He could save her money, if not time, by doing that part himself. And with Chase on the way, hell, as long as they could get the raw materials they needed somewhere between here and Raleigh, they could knock this out in a month, maybe. Of course, that was working overtime, but what the hell else did the two of them have to do?

He had no idea that putting Henderson's Big Pie Plate Shop on the fast track was not going to sit well with Vance.

"What the hell are you trying to do to me?" Vance yelled when Xavier gave him the specifics later that afternoon.

"Price range too high? You said I could give you my regular rate."

"No. The price is the price. Whatever. I want it perfect for Piper. I just … figured, man I hoped, it was going to take you months. Like six months. Or more."

Xavier sat down next to Vance at the conference table. "Well, it would have, but I've got my mentor Chase coming into town. His project in Phoenix is being held up by bullshit politics, so he's gonna spend his summer here, out of the desert heat, helping me set up my business. Besides fixing up the room over my parents' garage, this is the only project we've got." He shrugged.

"Fine. All right. Dammit."

Xavier rubbed his jaw, trying not to laugh. "You said you hated this Big Pie Plate idea. I didn't realize just how much you meant it."

"It's a long story."

"Your wife is sharp," Xavier told him.

"She's a lawyer."

"Ah. Guess that's why she asked to see a preliminary copy of my contract."

"Yeah. Sorry about that. I have found that you can drag a girl out of her Raleigh law firm, impregnate her, put a ring on her finger, and give her every reason to stay put in Henderson, but there is no way to extricate the law firm from said girl."

CHAPTER FIFTEEN

Xavier and Vance were still seated in the conference room—shooting the shit as the day wound down—when they heard Brooks holler for Pinks. The unmistakable sound of hurried and heavy footsteps stomped down the hallway and then Brooks's surly expression popped through the conference room door.

"Where's Pinks?"

Vance responded with a raise of his brow. "His office?"

Brooks turned his head and shouted, "Pinks," down the hall again before entering the room. When there was still no response, he turned a stormy eye on both men.

"He's probably on the phone," Vance told him. "What the hell is up your ass?"

"We need a meeting on this Weekend Rule thing. I just finished introducing it to Lolly, which had her asking about the specifics."

"Specifics?"

"Yeah. I told her the basics. Monday through Friday, she can work as hard as she wants, but come the weekend, it's all about fun and games. No work, no talking about work, period."

"Right."

"So she seems to think that means she can work up until midnight Friday."

Both mouths dropped open.

"*And*, she went on to reason that she could start work at 12:01 Monday morning."

"What the hell?"

"Right? And then she asked what our plans were for the weekend. And I was like, I don't know, what do you want to do? And she said, 'work.'"

"Jesus."

"I did not sweat an entire year waiting while she finished her degree in Raleigh just so she could move back home and ignore me."

"I'm sure she isn't planning to ignore you."

"Might not be her plan, but it's the same result."

"Ask her to move in."

"What?"

"Ask her to move in with you. Officially. That way you get her every night."

"First of all, I'm running for mayor of a very conservative town. Shacking up with my girlfriend isn't going to go over well. Having said that, she spends every night with me now. *Asleep*. She's so damn tired from running this company of hers she comes home late— real late—stays up only long enough so I can feed her, and then she passes out in bed."

"Oh. Then I can certainly see why you're a little frazzled."

"Frazzled?" Brooks asked wide-eyed, looking like he was hanging on by a thread. "I'm losing my ever-lovin' mind," he assured them. "Pinks!"

Thankfully, the Pink One arrived, because Xavier was severely struggling to keep his mirth to himself.

"What? What?" Pinks wondered, coming in and searching the faces of all of them. "What's happened?"

"Lolly is having trouble complying with the Weekend Rule," Vance told Pinks, nodding his head in the direction of one strung-out Golden Boy. "Seems she needs some clarification."

"Okay… " Pinks hedged, sounding unsure. "What sort of clarification?"

Brooks sighed, stretching his neck, letting his head circle around his shoulders in an apparent effort to rein himself in. "When you laid down the rule with Scarlett last weekend, how did it go?"

"Fine. She liked the idea. Realized she was working too hard and thought it made sense."

"Yeah—that's not what he's getting from the Lollypop," Vance offered.

Pinks addressed Brooks. "What'd she say?"

"She, ah, did not particularly appreciate the spirit of the rule. In fact, she immediately started drilling loopholes in it."

"Like what?"

"Like if the two of us didn't have definite weekend plans, then the rule was null and void, and she could go in to work."

Pinks shook his head in the negative. "No. Definitely not the spirit of the Weekend Rule. The Weekend Rule is about downtime. Free time to relax. Together. Tell her plans or no, the weekend is the weekend."

"Yeah, that's a problem too. Because most sane people consider Friday night the beginning of the weekend. She's assuming the Monday through Friday agreement means she can work until midnight."

"Come *on*." Pinks made a face of disbelief.

"Swear to God. The woman is focused, and not on me."

"Okay," Vance said, "so we make some plans. Good plans. Plans that will get her off the designing-women treadmill and on to a shot of tequila and taking her clothes off."

"In private," Brooks insisted.

"Take her out on the lake," Xavier suggested. "Supposed to be good weather this weekend. Once you've got her on the boat, she's stuck. She'd have to swim to shore."

"Great idea." Brooks pointed at Xavier. "Can you get your father's boat? I'll borrow my dad's and see who else might want to raft up. You guys in?" he asked, looking at Pinks and Vance.

"I'm not sure Vance, Jr. is up for a boat ride."

"But his momma might be," Brooks suggested.

"True. His momma might enjoy the lake. But our boat hasn't seen the water in over a year. Gonna take some time to clean the thing up."

"Well, apparently I've got until midnight tonight to handle that," Brooks said. "You don't have to do a thing, I am that motivated. Pinks, you and Scarlett in?"

"We're in. You know Scarlett. She'll bring the wine and set up a tasting. I'll make sure there are snacks so nobody falls overboard. I'll also grab the big cooler and stock it full of beer. What's your drink, Xavier?"

"Me? Beer's good. Domestic, imported, anything. Not picky."

"You got friends you want to invite?"

He shrugged. "I'll ask around. See who's up for a day on the lake."

"Good," Pinks said with a nod. "Anybody mind if I invite Missy and Thor?"

"Bring 'em," Vance said. "No doubt Thor will thank us for introducing Missy to the Weekend Rule. I'm sure Piper will have plenty of pie, and if I head home now to give her the news, she'll probably whip up something more substantial for us to feast on." He checked in with Brooks. "Sound like a solid plan to get Lolly out of that sweatshop?"

"Should have let Viper shut the damn thing down with all the trouble it's causing me. But, yeah. Solid plan. Thanks."

Xavier liked the idea of getting out on his father's boat. He also liked the idea of inviting his role-playing secretary on a high seas adventure. She'd come to mind the moment Brooks had started complaining about Lolly. With all the research she'd done for him over the past three days, on top of her regular job, she could probably use a break.

He had an ulterior motive as well. Because even though Tweets had settled into herself during their lengthy session with Piper and Genevra, she was definitely still skittish around him. Probably because he enjoyed provoking her and did it every chance he got.

Since he didn't see that changing any time soon—because he sort of got off on teasing her—he thought it would help if she spent more time around him. Socially. Give her a chance to figure out who he was and find a way to relax around him. Seemed like a plan, he told himself as he left E&E and headed down the sidewalk to Duncan James, Attorney at Law.

"Tweets," he shouted as he stepped through the door. It was after five, and he figured whatever lawyer business that might still be taking place was probably winding down.

He saw those brunette curls stick out from a doorway down the hall.

"Good. Glad I caught you," he said, heading in her direction.

She didn't say a word, just watched him come, her hands gripping both sides of the doorframe.

"What's up, Tweets?" he asked, glancing over her head and into the protected area, wondering what kind of top-secret shenanigans she had going on in there. "Want to let me in?"

"I'm working."

He made a great show of pulling out his phone, glancing at the time, and shoving it in her face. "Weekend Rule. In effect."

"What Weekend Rule?"

"We'll get to that. First, I want to thank you for all the research you did. I'm not sure I adequately expressed my appreciation at our meeting with Piper."

She snorted, taking her hands from the doorjamb and crossing them over her chest.

"Come on. You have to know I'm grateful."

One meticulous brow rose. "Grateful enough to pay me?"

"Sure. Name your price."

She shook her head, rolling her eyes. "Consider it a gift. To Piper. Why are you here?"

"I'm here to offer my uppity secretary some of those fringe benefits I mentioned. After all, Tweets," he stepped in a little closer, lowering his voice, "you've more than earned them."

"Fringe benefits," she deadpanned. "Of the bedroom variety."

"No. I mean, yes—of course—those are always available to you," he said as seriously as he could. "But at the moment, I've got something else in mind."

"And what would that be?"

"A boat ride. Have you had a chance to be out on the lake since you've come to town?"

"No."

"Perfect. Pick you up tomorrow at eleven. Wear a bikini." He grinned to make it clear he was kidding. Sort of.

She dropped her arms in a huff and turned to enter her ample-sized office. The place was as tidy and organized as an office could possibly be, although her desk was covered in stacks of paper, leaving only a small square of space in which to work.

He took a step onto the threshold. "Looks like you're busy."

"I am busy. We're all busy. The sports academy is a huge project."

"Yet you still had time to do a little freelancing for me."

She looked at him over her shoulder. "For Piper."

"Right. Right. For Piper." He winked. And that did it, he noted. That's what set off the fidgety limbs and the change in her complexion. He watched with great interest as the color of her cheeks went from peaches and cream to a slight shade of strawberry. Her lips stayed cherry red but parted like she needed to catch her breath. "Tweets, you still nervous around me? Because spending a day on the boat might help resolve whatever issues you continue to have."

"I, um, don't, um, have issues," she said slowly, almost methodically as she began to collect books from the shelf at the far wall. Big books. Like, law books. She glanced over her shoulder before she said, "Xavier, I appreciate your invitation, I do. But I enjoyed the research, so it's just not necessary. And, since I'm not the type of girl you'd *usually* invite out on your boat, I'll let you off the hook and pass."

"Well, you're right. I've never had a secretary, so I've never invited one out on my boat before."

"I'm *not* your secretary."

"Role-playing, Tweets." He leaned against the doorjamb respecting the sanctity of her working-girl hideout. "But I am curious. What's my *usual* type?"

She threw a look over her shoulder and turned back to her books before claiming, with all kinds of finality, "Tansy Langford."

"Pfft."

"Are you telling me you don't find Tansy attractive?"

"She's spectacular. But I tapped that back in high school."

"Tapped that?" Her head spun toward him.

"Well, not actually. No. But I *told* everyone I did, so there's that. Kissed her. Felt her up. That sort of thing. A date or two. Nothing serious."

Laidey slammed her books on the desk. "You're disgusting."

"You think going to second base is disgusting? Tweety Bird, you have been hanging with the wrong men."

"Telling everyone you *tapped* Tansy when you didn't is disgusting."

"Yeah. That was the asshole high schooler I used to be. Now I'm the fun-loving, keep-it-real, friendly neighborhood mastermind of Henderson's new pie shop."

"Pie *plate* shop. And you're the architect. Piper is the mastermind."

"So, you'll go on the boat."

Laidey's eyes rolled away from him when she said, "What about McKenna?"

"McKenna's old news."

"But *she's* your type, right?"

"There's a story there that I ain't spilling, but no. She's not *my* type."

"Not *your* type. What does that even mean?"

"Told ya. I'm not telling."

"Fine. But she's a friend of mine, and you're her ex, so that's reason enough not to get myself stuck on a boat with you."

"Look, Tweets," he argued, moving off the doorjamb. "This is a small town. People break up and move on. McKenna isn't going to care one way or another if you and I are stuck on the same boat for one freaking afternoon."

Laidey eyed him, flat lining her lips. "You're right," she confessed, leaning back against her desk. "She probably wouldn't. I texted her before our dinner meeting with Piper. Mentioned we might be working together. She told me her old high school self is still pissed at you, but her true self had moved on a long time ago."

"Perfect."

"Of course, she did warn me that you were a total loser."

He narrowed his eyes as he took a step toward her. "She did not."

"No." Laidey smiled sweetly. "She didn't. Still. Working on Henderson's Big Pie Plate Shop is one thing. Spending time together over the weekend is another thing entirely. I'm not sure about being hemmed in with you in a confined space and having no escape."

"Well," he said, stomping across the space between them, trying and failing to rein in his irritation. "If you get this cranky, I'll make you walk the plank. Problem solved. Because, seriously? I thought we'd gotten past this."

"Past what?"

"Your fear of me. It's back. I see it. Big as day, right there in your eyes."

Laidey immediately dropped her face toward the floor, and Xavier watched her chest expand with a deep intake of breath. He really hated that she had to work at calming herself around him. Yet, he stood there, watching in fascination as she breathed in and out, the toe of her tiny-girl Ked twisting against the floor. When she finally glanced back up at him, she was decidedly less ruffled.

"I don't fear you," she said quietly.

Xavier searched her features and then licked his lips. "Well," he said, "maybe you should."

"What?"

He shrugged. "Pick you up at eleven." He turned and headed toward the door. "Bikini. Sunscreen. I'll take care of the rest."

Slamming the main door on his way out hadn't been his intention, but Xavier supposed it was the physical manifestation of everything starting to get away from him. Because truly, if little Tweety in there could have read his thoughts just now, she'd be locking the door behind him.

"Man," he said on a breath, standing on the sidewalk, not knowing which way was up. He got to chuckling, because … "What the hell?"

Watching that girl wrestle with books larger than she oughta and doing breath work in order not to curl up into a ball and hide under her desk—*got him hard.*

If she knew the dirty, *dangerous* thoughts going through his head? Starting with those buttons. All those tiny, little pearl-like buttons running down the front of Tweety's latest cotton frock. Damn if she didn't dress like she spent her days playing hopscotch with Marnie instead of formulating state-of-the-art plans for sports academies and pie plate shops.

Still, those silly dresses worked for her, and man, he was starting to realize they worked for him too. He'd even considered stealing one of those ridiculous floral pencils off her desk and taking it home to his draft table as a souvenir.

And whoa—thoughts of undressing her? He was picturing it. In his head. While she was standing there trying to catch her breath. All he could think about was how easy it would be to separate those buttons from the fabric. Tuck both of his hands in the neck of her dress, and yeah, one fast tug would do it. Buttons would scatter everywhere, and the mystery of what she wore under her clothes would be revealed. Not that he'd worried too much about that up to now. But, boy, did it strike him when his mind conjured up a barely there bra in the same shade as her dress.

Of course, he didn't spend too much time imagining her bra, because his dick hustled his pliant brain right toward the raunchy stuff. Where he picked her up, sat her on the desk—no—on top of the books on her desk so she was higher, and at just the right height for him to—

"Hmm," he huffed. "Damn," he said. "Fuck," he whispered as he headed back up the street.

Yeah. Tweets had a problem.

A big one.

CHAPTER SIXTEEN

Saturday morning, Laidey found herself reaching back for Harry's advice. The advice he'd given her right before the two of them had found Xavier and McKenna in the parking lot.

Laidey had been in a carefree mood, and when Harry commented on it, she'd immediately felt—what—guilty? Which led to the revelation that she'd been taking her grandmother's advice to be reasonable, reliable, and respectable too much to heart.

There was nothing wrong with her mother. At least, Laidey hadn't thought so until Grandmother Rowling had suggested there was. But over the last week, as Laidey kept coming back to Harry's revelation, the veil her grandmother had cast lifted, and for the first time since she'd come of age, Laidey gave her mother the benefit of the doubt.

Yes, Addy Bartholomew enjoyed socializing. Her parents' social schedule was jam-packed. But people enjoyed her. She wasn't unkind or grumpy. She was actually rather pleasant and endearing. She didn't work outside of the home, but she didn't have to. She had plenty of hobbies and plenty of friends, and she added to social situations in a positive way.

These thoughts were all coming to a head because Laidey knew that today she was going to have to be *charming*. And, although she could *do* charming—she'd been trained by the proud Rowlings and Bartholomews after all—unlike her mother, charming did not come naturally.

Awkward came naturally.

Last night, when Duncan had informed her that he and Annabelle had been invited on Brooks's boat, she realized Xavier's invitation to a *Day on the Lake* was actually an invitation to a social function. And she knew, as kind as these people had been to her, they would expect her to be *the mouse*. All except for Duncan, who—you know—got her. And ... well, she didn't necessarily want to be *the mouse* around Xavier.

Not that she was clear on exactly what she wanted to be around Xavier, because—let's face it—the man was fi-iine. There were moments when he was even kinda darling, especially when he grinned that cute-boy grin of his—the one he saved for the moments when he was all-out teasing her. In spite of all the loud, towering, overbearing nonsense she'd witnessed throughout the past week, she'd been drawn to his voice, to his assertiveness, and to his insistent personality the moment she was aware of him. And, as he continued to refuse to let her become invisible or play the role of mouse in his presence, she began to like him. And, since realizing her crush on her boss had grown hella-inappropriate, she was now considering transferring that crush to Mr. X-factor-and-then-some Wright.

Maybe.

If McKenna would answer her stupid phone.

Because Laidey hadn't talked to McKenna about working with Xavier or about anything else. Except for a few brief text responses telling Laidey she was fine but too busy to talk, McKenna had vanished. Laidey worried it had something to do with Xavier's return. And if McKenna's disappearance did have something to do with Xavier, that meant McKenna wasn't over him and probably wouldn't appreciate Laidey turning her inappropriate crush in his direction. So until McKenna came back online, Laidey needed to continue to play the role of uppity secretary where Xavier was concerned.

It wasn't like she believed Xavier actually had a thing for her. She well remembered mistaking Crain's teasing as flirtation. No. She knew she'd be crushing on him in vain. He was too tall, too ... *much* to bother with a girl of her petite stature. She'd learned that lesson. Still, she wanted to be careful not to step on McKenna's toes with their developing friendship.

She had to borrow a bikini from Poppy, because who packed a bathing suit for a business trip? Although since this was a very extended business trip, maybe she should have thought a little more about what the summer would bring. Anyway, Poppy's suit, although terribly skimpy on its owner, fit her well and had a nautical theme going on. The navy-and-white anchor motif was perfect for a sail. Or a motorboat. Laidey shook her head figuring it didn't matter. Although, since she didn't have any idea how to tie ropes or shift sails and therefore imagined herself falling overboard when someone lowered the boom … oh, Lord, please don't let it be a sailboat.

Poppy also had a straw tote she encouraged Laidey to borrow which was now filled with a borrowed beach towel and borrowed sunscreen. Seriously. Even she was starting to find this all-about-work persona boring. Which was why, when Xavier knocked on their front door at eleven o'clock sharp, Laidey was determined to stop role-playing the part of *mouse* and instead indulge in the role of *socialite*.

After all, she knew one thing about the man. Xavier Wright was fond of role-playing.

There might have been a small beat of time between her "Hi" and the smile she tossed him. But it must not have bothered Xavier because his cute-boy grin showed up.

"Tweets. No dress today?"

Channeling her mother, she did a slow spin, showing off her white shorts and pale-blue, off-the-shoulder blouse. "You miss my dresses?"

"I've gotten used to you dressing like a baby doll."

That wasn't a yes.

"I thought shorts would be a better choice on a boat." She also thought she'd be able to get away with keeping her shorts on over Poppy's teeny-weeny bikini bottoms.

"Along with your Keds. Definitely solid boat shoes, and those red ones are my favorite so far. Ready?"

She nodded, slung the beach bag over her shoulder, and followed him out the door, noting, "The weather is beautiful."

The other thing she noted was that he looked hot in his swim shorts. His legs were tan, he had on a T-shirt that might be a little tight but that really worked for him, and his own version of boat shoes. The man was trim and fit, towering over her but walking by her side in an easy, relaxed manner she'd never be able to role-play. Because, of course, the essence of Xavier Wright made her feel nervous and flustered.

Take a breath, she heard Harry instruct as her hands started to fidget.

"It's gonna be perfect at the lake," he was saying. "Sunny. Hot. You worried about something? You do know how to swim don't you?"

"I do. I can tread water for at least thirty minutes."

"What happens after thirty minutes?"

Oh, boy. Xavier and that grin.

She didn't even have to channel her mother when she laughed. "Don't know. That's all I needed to do to pass a life-saving course years ago."

"Good to know you'll be able to save me if there's a mishap. Hop in."

Laidey stopped mooning over the hottie by her side long enough to notice he'd just opened the door of a very new, very robust, silver pickup. "Where'd this come from?"

"Ordered it before I left Arizona. It came in yesterday, and I picked it up this morning. You missing my Road King?" he teased.

"Maybe," she answered, looking at the mountain before her. There was no way to climb in without his help because the wheels on the thing were so big the floorboard sat way off the ground. "Is this normal?" she asked while Xavier hoisted her up and into the enormous cab.

"What?"

"The height. The distance. From here to the ground?"

Xavier took a look between where she was seated and how far she'd fall before hitting the ground. "I wanted some clearance. You never know what the terrain might be like on a new plot of land."

"And I suppose getting in and out of this thing is no biggie for you."

"Nope. Only for the height impaired," he smirked, shutting her inside.

They drove to the lake serenaded by a soothing piano concerto thanks to XM Radio. It was the perfect balm to settle her nerves, all the while stimulating her desire to play.

"I enjoy listening to the piano," she told Xavier.

"You play?" he asked, pulling into a parking spot at the small marina.

"No. Not really," she said automatically as if she needed to keep it a secret. "I mean, yes. A little. I play a little."

Xavier looked over at her with a puzzled expression. "I'm not at all sure what you just said." Then he noticed something out the window beyond her and said, "Come on. They're here."

It was a happy group that greeted them. Ponytailed Lolly and her big handsome Brooks. Curly-blond Piper with Killer-grin Vance. Sweet Missy and her dangerously pushy Thor. Annabelle and Duncan, who were like Laidey's sponsors here in Henderson. Vivacious Scarlett and her Get-'r'-done Pinks. The lot of them, all doing their best to hide their shock that Laidey was the one stepping out of the truck as Xavier's—well—date.

Not that this was a date, but all of a sudden, it did seem rather couple-y. Which unearthed Laidey's earlier distress over not having reached McKenna.

What if this boating escapade got back to McKenna before she had a chance to explain?

Laidey shook it off. Nothing she could do at the moment other than remind herself it *wasn't* a date.

Due to the *Weekend Rule* Annabelle and Duncan were relegated to Xavier's boat, separating Annabelle and Lolly so they couldn't talk business. Then it was decided Vance and Pinks needed to be separated to prevent them from talking shop. So Brooks begrudgingly took Pinks and Scarlett on his boat, and Vance took Thor and Missy with him and Piper.

As coolers and insulated totes were stored on each of the three boats, Laidey felt her companion—awkwardness—descend. She was standing on the pier holding a beach bag that offered nothing to share except sunscreen. Her distress must have broadcasted directly to Xavier, because after he'd opened a hatch to expose the motor of his twenty-three foot Sea Ray, he came over and held out his hand to her. "I told you to bring a bikini and sunscreen and that I'd take care of the rest."

"I could have contributed," she said, still staring at the bounty being stored.

"Relax, Tweets. You're my guest. We'll never go through all this anyway, what could you have possibly added?"

She shrugged, noting the bottles of wine and huge cooler of beer. She drew in a long breath and let it out.

"I do that too," he said.

"You do what?" she asked, still mesmerized by all the supplies.

"Take a breath. Then release whatever's gotten ahold of me."

She turned and searched his blue-gray eyes, finally noting his offered hand. She wondered what could possibly find a hold on him. He was so ... sturdy. So ... solid. And seemed absolutely immobile.

"Thank you," she said, taking his hand and stepping from the dock, to the boat's back seat and then to the floor as directed.

All of the vessels were built for recreation. Perfect for tubing, water skiing, and the rafting up she'd heard them plan. Brooks and Xavier had a discussion on where to head, while Laidey stored her bag as directed by Duncan and then stood in the middle of the boat, not knowing where to sit.

Duncan and Annabelle were cuddled up on the seat spanning the back of the boat, and there were two sets of back-to-back seats on either side of the center aisle. The front-facing seat on the right—the driver's seat—was obviously going to be used by Xavier. Did she sit behind him facing Annabelle and Duncan or in the forward-facing seat across the aisle from Xavier? She heard a quick whistle, turned her head, and found Xavier listening to Brooks but pointing to the seat opposite the driver's.

She was grateful for the direction.

When a destination had been agreed upon, Xavier closed up the hatch, went to the helm, and pressed a button while turning a key. He then began moving forward and aft, releasing lines and tossing them to the pier. He backed the boat out of its slip with such proficiency Laidey said, "I thought you've been in Arizona for fourteen years."

"I have," he answered, swinging the wheel, shifting into forward, and turning them toward open water.

"You handle this boat like you do it every weekend."

He grinned—big—shooting her a quick wink. "You caught me, Tweets. I came down here last night. Reacquainted myself with the Old Dog and took her out on my own so it wouldn't show just how long I've been landlocked."

She feigned surprise. "So the mighty Xavier Wright doesn't do everything with ease all of the time?"

"Pfft." He took a moment to adjust their course, checking behind him to see if Vance and Brooks were following. He increased their speed, and the bow lifted as the water raced beneath them. "I don't think the word easy has ever been a part of my vocabulary," he stated over the wind.

"Really?" She was intrigued by that. "You're so confident. So assertive. Like everything comes easy to you."

His grin wasn't the teasing kind. "A lot of things come easy to me. I just don't feel easy about most of them."

She thought about that while settling herself in her seat, appreciating the feel of the wind and experiencing the freedom of racing over the lake. "I don't feel easy about much," she said, turning his way, holding her hair out of her face as it blew around her. "But it shows. It doesn't show on you."

He shrugged. "I don't give it a chance to show."

She continued to look at him, wanting more. Craving more. Finally, he gave it to her.

"Years ago, if I felt ill at ease, I would pull a prank, knock someone over, or make a joke to disrupt class. That's how I got this stellar reputation you're so scared of." He shot her a brief cute-boy grin. "Then I learned to breathe through the uneasy feeling instead of creating chaos."

Her brows lifted. "Interesting. Harry taught me to breathe. Last weekend. Right before I met you."

"That come in handy? Breathing?" He was grinning from ear to ear.

"When I remember to do it."

"What's up with you and Harry?"

"What do you mean?"

"You his girl?"

She blinked. Looked around. Brought her gaze back to Xavier's on a laugh. "If I were Harry's girl, or anybody's girl, do you think they'd let me out on a boat with you?"

"Hell, no," he chuckled.

"Harry is one of two friends I've been cultivating since moving to town."

"Ah. You like sitting at the bar, telling him sad stories of your youth?"

"No," she laughed. "Is that what you do?"

"I've been known to stretch a bartender's ear now and again."

"Not me. And Harry's not your usual bartender."

"How so?"

"He gets me."

"He *gets* you?"

"Yeah, he understands me."

"In what way?"

"Well, he realized I'm not *un*sociable. Just quiet, for the most part."

"You're shy."

"I'm not so much shy as I tend to shy away from situations where my awkwardness is enhanced."

Xavier's brow furrowed. "Awkward?"

"Resoundingly awkward."

"Like you blurt out embarrassing stuff in a crowd?"

"No," she laughed. "Not like Tourette's."

"Awkward like you run your bike up curves and into bushes?" he teased.

"Yeah, a lot of that."

He shrugged that off. "Eh. You're tiny. The world wasn't built for people like you. It wasn't built for people like me either." He threw a thumb behind him. "It was built for people like them."

Laidey cast a glance at Duncan and Annabelle before smiling back at Xavier. "The beautiful people?"

He laughed. "Pretty much. And those situated anywhere between five-foot-five and six-foot-one."

"And you're what? Seven-two?" she teased.

"Right, and you're four-foot-three."

"We definitely represent the outliers."

He looked her over. "Wanna drive?"

"No."

"No?"

"Correct. No. No, thank you."

"No way. You're driving. Come here."

She stared at him as if he were crazy.

"Yes, I'm Mr. Confidence, and I can teach the awkward girl how to drive a boat. Get over here."

She was compelled to hop down from her seat. Very awkwardly. He didn't laugh at her though. She wasn't even getting a grin. Xavier was now role-playing the captain of his ship, and he was taking it seriously.

"Stand right here," he said, pointing to the space between him and the wheel. She scooted herself in front of him, where he immediately placed her hands on the steering wheel, cupping his over hers so she didn't have time to freak about being in control of something she had no business being in control of.

She nodded. Felt her head bobbing up and down. "Okay. All right. Don't let go."

He leaned down and said close to her ear, "See that bluff across the way? That's where we're heading." He pulled one hand from the top of hers, pointing left to right in front of them. "Not another boat in sight. The only thing you want to keep an eye out for is floating debris. Like a log. You can't run us aground within the next five minutes, and the lake is deep, so no fear there. Keep it aimed toward the bluff and you'll do fine."

He looked down at her. She could sense it. Saw it in her peripheral vision because no way was she taking her eyes off the water in front of her. Or the bluff.

"You good?" he asked.

She bit her lip and nodded.

"You sure?"

At her curt nod, he lifted his other hand from hers. "Right at the bluff," he said gently.

It took about thirty seconds of feeling the vibration of the boat in her hands before she let out the breath she'd been holding.

"That's it," Xavier said. She glanced up at him. "Gotta breathe."

She gave him a brief smile and then went back to watching for debris. Keeping them aimed at the bluff.

"You drink beer?" he asked.

"Sure."

"You gonna be okay if I step away for about fifteen seconds and get us both a cold one?"

After taking another deep breath and channeling her mother, she fed him what she hoped was a dazzling smile. "Take twenty."

He smirked, leaving her to play captain.

Her beer was opened but left untouched in its cup holder for the five minutes she was at the helm. As they neared the bluff, she felt the heat of Xavier's body as he stepped in behind her, closing her in between both his arms. His hands weren't positioned on top of hers, but just to the side around the wheel. In short order, he took her right hand and placed it on the throttle, covering it with his own.

She looked down at his hand, noting the contrast of tanned skin over pale, feeling the warmth, the strength, the confidence he possessed transmitting sensations of comfort and security. She wanted to sink into those feelings. Had a strong urge to lean back against him so she could latch on to even more. It was a struggle not to give in to it now that the yearning had been unleashed.

He was the one to throttle down and reduce their speed, but she got to feel what it felt like to make that happen. What it felt like to share in his confidence, his command over the boat. They came to a slow drift as Brooks idled beside them.

"How close do we want to get?" Xavier called.

"We don't need to get too close. Just want to be out of the way of traffic."

Xavier nodded, pushed the throttle forward a little, and covered another hundred yards at a slow pace before putting the boat in neutral, then reverse, then neutral.

"See how I did that?" he asked Laidey. "I squeezed the button underneath and gently moved the throttle." She nodded. "You try."

Her first reaction was to balk and say no. But she didn't want to appear a coward or inept, so she squeezed the button underneath with her fingers and pushed the throttle forward, putting the boat into a slow glide.

"Nice, Tweets. Perfect. Now put it back in neutral." She did. "Good." He looked behind them. "Now, shift the throttle into reverse."

"Reverse?"

"Pull it back."

She did.

"Reverse is your brake. When you put the boat in neutral, you still have forward momentum, so you have to put it in reverse to essentially stop forward progress."

"Makes sense."

"Back in neutral." She followed his command. "I'm going to go grab the anchor. You keep your hand on the throttle. When I tell you to shift into reverse, do it. I'll let you know when to shift back to neutral."

"Xavier."

"You've got this, Tweets," he told her as he left her at the helm. By herself. After she told him how awkward she could be.

"I don't think you should be trusting me with this."

"Yeah?" he said, grinning back at her as he tossed the anchor over the bow of the boat, holding on to the line it was tied to. "You untrustworthy?"

"I've got no record when it comes to captaining a ship. Who knows?"

"Okay, gently in reverse."

She did as she was told, and the boat jerked badly causing Xavier to catch himself. "That's all right," he coaxed. "Now neutral. A little smoother this time."

It wasn't any smoother.

Xavier ignored her ineptitude and tugged hard on the line. "I think we're good," he said, tying the rope around a cleat mounted on the front of the boat. He came back and told her to turn the key to the left, which stopped the engine.

"You did good. You've earned your beer."

Once the boats were secured to one another, floaties of all shapes and sizes were released from Vance's cabin. Duncan did an excellent cannonball from the backseat, leaping over the swim platform, soaking his fiancée who had been dangling her feet off the edge. Lolly followed Duncan into the water with a shallow dive off Brooks's boat. It was then Xavier noticed Missy motioning Laidey over to the far side of his boat to whisper in her ear.

Secrets made him twitchy. He wanted to know what was happening there.

Scarlett was busy setting up a wine tasting on Brooks's table, while from the far boat, Piper kept handing over a variety of hors d'oeuvres to complement the wines. Xavier pulled his shirt over his head and strolled over to where Missy and Laidey had their heads together. He overheard Missy saying, "No way am I getting in that water. Are you?"

"Sure, she is," Xavier answered for Laidey. "The water's great. Especially today. What's your problem with the water?"

"I just don't know what's in there."

"What's in there? You mean, like fish?"

"Fish and slimy stuff." Missy shuddered.

"Seriously?" Xavier took offense. "It's a lake. Where'd you grow up that you're afraid of lakes?"

"Baltimore."

"Baltimore? Well, that explains it."

"That doesn't explain it," Pinks piped up. "I'm from Baltimore, and I'm fine swimming in a lake."

"*Both* of you are from Baltimore? How'd that happen?"

As Missy and Pinks filled him in on just how well they knew each other, Laidey started to shift and move by him. He grabbed her elbow. "Stay," he whispered. "Another minute." She settled beside him then, seemingly content to listen as he questioned Missy and Pinks on details. When Thor came over to break it all up, pulling *his girl* away from Pinks, Xavier sat down on the closest seat and pulled Laidey between his knees. They still weren't eye to eye.

"The water's safe," he said gently. "Nothing in there that can hurt even a little thing like you."

"Okay." She nodded, lips firmly pressed together.

"Okay, but what?"

She shrugged.

"Talk to me, Tweets. I brought you out here to show you a good time. I don't like somebody *from Baltimore* turning you off our fine North Carolina lake."

"You sound awful proud for someone who's spent most of his time in Arizona."

"And while I was there, I missed exactly this. Friends. Boats. Floating on a lake. Look, swimming is up to you. I just don't like anybody scaring you off."

She laughed at that.

He sheepishly grinned along with her because really, the thing that seemed to scare her the most was him. "We're working on it," he said in response to what hadn't actually been acknowledged.

"Go play with your friends," she suggested. "I'm going to see if I can lend Scarlett a hand. I don't know her or Lolly very well. Let me offer to help and then I'll grab a couple of those noodles and give your fine lake a try. Although, being from Dallas, I will admit I'm more familiar with a cement pond."

"Then you're in for a treat," he assured her.

"So what's up with you and the little one?" Brooks asked Xavier. Their bodies floated, draped over large rubber inner tubes, and each of them had a beer in their hand.

"Yeah," Vance chimed in, his head turning toward them as he floated face down on a raft. "If she's here working overtime as your secretary, you're in complete violation of the Weekend Rule."

"She's the best secretary I've never had. Figured I owed her. She took it upon herself to research a bunch of stuff for Piper's shop. I would have blown off the idea of the internet cooking show if it weren't for Laidey."

Vance rose up on his forearms and whispered vehemently, "I don't want Piper involved with an internet anything."

"That's on you. I'm giving my client what she wants, which includes wiring for three separate cameras."

"When the hell did Laidey have time to do research that's going to make my wife an internet sensation and put me in an early grave?

We're gonna have to institute a no-overtime rule for that little, bitty woman of yours."

Xavier took a swig of beer. "She's not my woman. She's not even my secretary."

"Then what is she?" Brooks asked.

Xavier looked back toward the boat where the girls were finishing setting up what looked like a solid spread. He watched as Laidey pulled off her top, which was the catalyst that prompted him to say, "She's snack-sized, and when I'm around her, I feel hungry."

"Dude." Brooks laughed.

Both Brooks and Vance followed his gaze to the snack in question. "Huh," Brooks said. "Got a rockin' little body for one so tiny." Xavier took another sip of his beer, completely agreeing with Brooks's assessment.

"You gonna tap that?" Vance asked.

Xavier threw a threatening glare at Vance. "She's not a fan of that word." *And neither am I, apparently.*

"Isn't she a little young for you?" Brooks asked.

Xavier dropped his chin and raised his sunglasses. "You sure you want to throw that stone?"

Brooks immediately looked chagrined. "Sorry, man. My bad. I've got issues."

"Well, keep them to yourself, will ya? I've got plenty of my own issues. I don't need yours heaped on top."

"She just doesn't seem your type."

"Evidently, she agrees with you. She thinks my type is tall, blonde, vocal, and annoying."

"Annoying?"

"She mentioned Tansy Langford."

"Ah, yeah," Vance said. "Definitely annoying."

"So you've had this conversation?" Brooks asked.

"No. It came up when I invited her to join us today. This isn't a date. It's payback for doing me a solid."

"But you're into her?"

"I'm a little into her. I mean, I scare her to death, but hell, I'm used to that reaction." Xavier grinned, delighted with himself as he looked over at Brooks. "Especially from you."

"Asshole."

"Honestly, the fact that I seem to scare *her* might be one of the things that's pulling me in. I don't know." He sipped his beer. "She's a klutz, but a cute klutz. She's easy to tease but not easy to offend. Y'all know she's a hard worker. Apparently doesn't like to do much else. Got mad writing skills, something I decidedly do not have. So … I figure I'm either gonna hire her away from this Crain Carraway character or I'm gonna marry her."

That last bit shocked the hell out of Xavier. It was like his brain and mouth hadn't consulted with him before they decided to out him to the world. He looked to both Brooks and Vance. "Ah—that was said in jest. Even so, I'd appreciate y'all keeping that comment to yourselves. And by yourselves, I mean do not share it with your significant others."

"Circle of Trust, man." Vance said. "Starting a new one up right here."

"Yeah," Brooks added. "Because the old circle has gotten unwieldy. Way too many irons in that fire."

"'Preciate it. Probably just the beer talkin'," Xavier claimed.

"You've only had one," Brooks pointed out.

Xavier splashed a shower of water at Brooks. "I'm grasping for excuses, asshole. Quit pointing out the obvious, will ya?"

That started a battle that ended in beer cans floating away and started the game Who Can Jump Into the Farthest Inner Tube, which turned into Who Can Land on the Raft and Remain Standing?

After a whole lot of energy had been expended, and Missy had been introduced to the lake by Thor gathering her up in his arms and jumping ship, the whole crowd pulled themselves back on board to dry off and settle in for a mid-day feast. Everyone was scattered about Brooks and Xavier's boats and therefore pretended not to notice when Vance and Piper went missing inside his cabin.

Once the men started chatting baseball, the women pushed them off onto one boat while they began straightening the buffet table on the other, disposing of empties and trash, and making it all look pretty for round two—dessert. Only one pie but several types of cookies and bars were brought forth by Piper, who admitted she'd been excited to get back to creating other desserts while she and Genevra worked on their recipe book.

"Recipe book?" Lolly asked. "Mom didn't mention a recipe book."

"Oh, the *Henderson's Big Pie Plate Recipe Book* is one of a long list of ideas we have for the shop. Which, thanks to Laidey and Xavier, should turn out to be really something."

Lolly took that opportunity to set squinty eyes on Laidey and lower her voice. "So, what's up with you and *Xavier*?" She said his name like it was ridiculous. "My mother mentioned you showed up with him for dinner the other night. And now you're here."

"I was pranked into being his secretary," Laidey said with a grin. *Must be the wine.* "Your mother was extremely gracious about it. She made me feel right at home."

"So, you and Xavier are …" Lolly dragged the sentence out, obviously hoping Laidey would complete it.

She licked her lips, casting a glance at the men chatting around the huge Yeti cooler. "I don't know. Friends? Frenemies? I mean, I know he duped me into going to dinner so I'd take his notes, but then I became enamored with the project. I ended up doing some research that he was able to put to good use. He seems to be quite the clever architect."

"His plans are intriguing," Piper agreed. "I can't wait for Molly to see them. But I'm with Lolly. I'm eager to hear about his plans for *you*."

All of a sudden, very aware that she was the center of attention, Laidey took a breath and channeled her mother. "He invited me today to repay me for the work I've done. I'm sure he'd never admit it, but I think he feels a little guilty." She lowered her voice, "Frankly, I enjoy work. And"—she turned to Piper—"your shop, the cooking show, the tea room—all of it—it's a compelling enterprise. I hope you won't mind if I continue to stick my nose into it."

"Please do," Piper said. "Genevra thinks you're the muse in this project. *Xavier's* muse."

"Mmm," Lolly said, crossing her arms over her chest. "What do *you* think of that?"

"Being his muse?"

"I mean, he's gorgeous and all, but I for one refuse to jump on the Xavier Wright bandwagon. I don't like him, and I don't trust him."

"Don't trust him?"

"He's a bully. He *hit* Brooks."

The urge to defend Xavier was great, yet Laidey bit her tongue. After all, she had witnessed the incident Lolly was talking about firsthand. It was a fact she couldn't deny. On top of that, Lolly was intricately woven into the fabric of this group. Laidey was an outsider. She didn't want to tussle with anyone, most of all Lolly. Lolly could definitely take her down in a mud wrestling battle, and she'd enjoy doing it. Besides, in the week she'd known Xavier, he'd bullied her plenty. So defending him was not an option.

Still, a good offense?

"I can't defend him. Though I know for certain Xavier is extremely aware of his less-than-sterling reputation. He's not happy—at all— when he thinks he's scared me in some way, so maybe the bullying thing is behind him."

"We can only hope," Lolly said, her skepticism obvious.

"Apparently Vance was just as bad about throwing punches back then," Piper interjected. "He and Xavier had some good laughs as they reminisced about it over dinner." She addressed Lolly directly. "You may be interested to know that your mother and Em really approve of this match." Piper's eyes shifted to Laidey. "They believe Laidey is the yin to Xavier's yang."

"The yin to his yang?" Laidey wondered.

"The calm, quiet, steady force to his rough, emphatic, explosive nature."

"Hmm." Lolly studied Laidey intently before lightening up. "I can see that. I can definitely see that. Have you met any of his brothers?"

"He has brothers?" Laidey squeaked. She didn't know why that scared her, but it did.

"I knew the youngest one," Lolly told her. "Following in his older brothers' footsteps, he took out a lot of different girls one time and one time only. Like he thought it was his duty to spread the pleasure of dating a Wright brother around."

"A Wright brother?" Laidey questioned. "How many are there?"

Missy interrupted, "Didn't he move back to town, like, a week ago? How did the two of you meet, anyway? Oh. Yeah. At the Team Henderson meeting," she answered her own question. "I forgot."

"Actually, I met him—well—it was more like I *saw him in action* Friday night. My first impression was, wow. Not because of his looks, though. I mean, to me he looked like an enormous badass. It was dark, and he had on a leather jacket, jeans, and huge boots, and he was leaning against that monster bike of his, making it look like it was an extension of him. He'd sought McKenna out at the club and wanted to smooth things over with her. He was … teasing her, I think. But when Harry and I appeared on the scene, his demeanor changed. He wasn't necessarily aggressive, but he definitely took charge of the situation, even though he'd just arrived from out of town."

"Ah," Lolly said. "McKenna Blakely. I hear she was the last girl he dated before he left for college."

"Were there others?" Laidey was instantly curious.

"Plenty of others, apparently." Annabelle nodded her head when Lolly looked for backup. "But McKenna and he went out for a few months or something."

"Well, McKenna and I are friendly," Laidey said quietly. "I'm concerned about her reaction to me, you know, hanging with Xavier."

"Why?"

"He broke her heart."

"Really? I don't remember it that way," Lolly said, her face indicating she was searching her memory. "But I was younger, considerably younger. My cousin Molly would remember better."

"I like McKenna," Scarlett said. "I can see her with Xavier. But that was so long ago. I'm sure if you want to be the yin to Xavier's yang, she won't stand in your way. I mean, it's not like the two of you are *sisters* or anything." She finished by tossing a disgruntled look toward Pinks.

Laidey looked between Scarlett and Pinks as the women around them bit their lips, trying hard not to grin. "Am I missing something? Did your sister date Pinks?"

Scarlett rolled her eyes over an exasperated expression. "No, apparently my sister just wanted him for a one-night stand. I'm trying to get over it because really—whatever. I'm just saying McKenna isn't facing a hurdle like mine, and if she gets moody about you and Xavier, I'll remind her what a true hurdle looks like."

"First, I'm not sure there is a me and Xavier. Second, who's your sister?"

"Tansy. Langford. Carraway."

Laidey's brows rose to her hairline. "Crain's wife?" she whispered in disbelief.

"That's the one," Scarlett said.

"*She* ... had a one-night stand ... with *Pinks*? When?"

Scarlett gasped. Her eyes going as wide as everyone else's. "Oh, shit."

"Yeah," Lolly said. "Cat out of the bag, much?"

Scarlett started pleading with Laidey immediately. "Please, do not repeat that. I'll get in so much trouble. I just thought everybody knew. I mean, everybody in Henderson knows. I just assumed y'all did too."

"What did you think we knew?" Laidey questioned.

"About Tansy sleeping with Pinks while she was married to Crain."

"What?" Laidey was outraged—like—*genuinely* outraged.

Piper hip-checked Scarlett out of the way. "Laidey, trust me. Scarlett is making this sound way worse than it was. However, I'm certain neither Crain nor Tansy would be happy if this got around his place of business. So, can we count on you to keep his secret?"

"Crain is *aware* of Pinks and Tansy?"

"He is. It was an unfortunate misunderstanding. All has been forgiven. Tansy loves him intensely. I know that for a fact. Now, will you keep his confidence?"

Of course, she would. He was *Crain*. Laidey just felt a little blindsided by the news.

"Annabelle," Xavier called. "I'm trusting you to have a handle on that hen party. What's happening over there?"

"I ... don't know," Annabelle said anxiously, looking between Laidey, Piper, and Scarlett.

"Looks like you're lettin' 'em all browbeat my date."

"No," Annabelle supplied. "Laidey's good. She's fine. We're just filling her in on local ... stuff, you know."

"No, I don't know," he groused, starting in their direction. "Hey. Tweets. You good?"

Was she good?

She was certainly feeling indignant on Crain's behalf. She now liked Tansy Langford less than she had before, which was saying something. She was also stuck thinking about her boss while she was out in the middle of a lake in North Carolina and he was in Dallas with his cheating wife. No. She wasn't good.

But for the purpose of avoiding more *awkwardness* she was willing to channel her mother and table her indignation for a time when she was alone and could sort through what she'd just heard. She turned away from Piper and Scarlett and threw the imposing Mr. Wright one of Addy Bartholomew's dazzling smiles.

"How about you come float with me a bit?" he suggested.

She nodded before turning back to the circle of women who anxiously awaited her response. "Mr. Carraway's secret is safe with me."

There was a collective release of breath, then Laidey found herself pulled into Scarlett's arms, a whispered thank you in her ear.

Scarlett pulled back, scolding herself aloud, insisting she needed to let the Tansy–Pinks thing go. "My bad," she insisted. "Please, just forget I said anything."

Laidey assured her she would and maneuvered through the group toward the swim platform, where she grabbed a couple of noodles.

"Tweets." Xavier stood on the adjacent platform. "We can both fit on this." He held up what looked like a floating lounge chair. "I'll get in and paddle over to you." Which he did with complete command of his body. Because getting into that thing from the boat was something very few could manage to make look graceful or easy.

He demonstrated both. Once he was in place, he told her to climb down the ladder and simply fall backward into his lap.

If she wasn't so interested in getting off the boat and away from the present conversation, she might have balked at his suggestion. Because *in his lap* in front of *all these people*? As it was, she figured sitting on Xavier's lap would provide her with a needed distraction.

However, she didn't so much as settle *herself* into the float with him as she was settled. Cautiously backing down the boat's short ladder, she felt his cold hands clasp around her middle before she was swooped off the ladder and placed on top of him. He paddled backward, moving them away from the crowd on board.

"There we go," he said. "You okay?"

"Sitting on your lap or being grilled by your friends?"

"Ah, I was mostly talking about the grilling part. Here." He pulled her around so that her legs dangled over the arm of the chair and she was sideways to him. "Better?"

Since she was now sitting on his thigh instead of nestled between his legs, yeah, she was better. Not that she was a prude or that lounging against his firm body was a hardship, but it was impossible not to notice the many glances being tossed their way.

Invisible she was not.

Fortunately, it wasn't long before a few others decided to get back in the water, and she and Xavier drifted from their attention just as they drifted out of earshot.

"So what was that all about?" Xavier asked.

"Did you know that Scarlett's sister slept with Pinks? While she was married? To *Crain*."

Xavier ducked his chin and fixed a steely gaze on her. "And this is making you flip out, why?"

She sputtered. "She *cheated* on him."

"*She* didn't know that *they* were still married. At least, that's the way my mother tells it. I swear the woman has made it her mission to fill me in on all the gossip from the past fourteen years. She lives for that Henderson Happenings newsletter."

"I really need to sign up for that," Laidey sighed.

"You sweet on your boss?" Xavier wondered.

"Ahhh—he's *married*," she sang in an effort to make it seem like the suggestion was ridiculous.

"Okay. Still, you seem pretty irritated by a story that's been resolved for months. And I'm not gonna soon forget you chewing my ass about sitting it in his chair."

"I'm sorry about that," she said, honestly, taking a breath. "Mr. Carraway hired me out of grad school. I've been with his company for several years. I like him and the work he does. And," she sassed him, "I didn't like *you* way back on *Monday*. So my loyalty went to my employer."

"No, you didn't like me on Monday. Or Tuesday. Come to think of it, I'm not sure you like me much right now."

She smiled saucily. "You've got a nice boat and friends who know how to throw a party. And the sun is shining. I'm not going to complain." She stretched her arms over her head and kicked her feet in the water. "Truth is, I haven't spent a day like this in a very long time. So yes, Xavier Wright, I believe you're growing on me."

He let his hand fall to her hip and gave it a squeeze. "Tweets, you had me the moment you let me off the hook for riding you into that bush."

"I keep telling you, that wasn't your fault."

"I think it was." He lowered his voice. "I'm sorry about that. About scaring you. About sitting in your boss's chair. About hurting your friend, McKenna."

McKenna.

He frowned. "What'd I say?"

"I don't want to hurt McKenna. I'm not sure she'd appreciate me sitting on her ex-boyfriend's lap."

"McKenna and I were wrong from the get-go. You gotta trust me on that."

"Ohhhh, how could Mr. *Wright* be wrong?" she teased.

"Trust me. *This* Mr. Wright"—he pointed to himself—"all wrong. She and I spent a couple hours hashing things out Monday evening. She tell you about that?"

Laidey shook her head. "I haven't been able to get ahold of her."

"She's okay with me being back in town. She's strong, that one. A lot of backbone. I honestly don't think she's going to care if you and I become ... friends."

Oh.

Friends.

There was a moment of disappointment as some form of hope dissolved in her gut.

"Maybe ... more?" Xavier asked quietly. "I mean, I owe my uppity secretary more than a solitary boat outing. I'm thinking I must owe you a couple dinners at least for all the research you did to make me look like a star."

She grinned back at him. "Dinner would be lovely," she said, giving him a green light as she felt herself going from sad sack to giddy schoolgirl in the blink of an eye.

The index finger of his right hand started drawing circles over her knee. "The guys were talking about meeting up for dinner at the club tonight. You in?"

She nodded.

"Okay," he said, looking at her knee. He pulled her back against him, the way she'd been earlier. She felt him place a kiss on the top of her head, felt his arms come around her, holding her comfortably. "Usually newcomers make me twitchy. But you? Hell, first time I saw you ..." she felt him shrug. "I don't know. I just wanted to stop fighting with McKenna and get on with life."

And there it was. The transfer complete. Laidey's crush had just shifted from her cuckold of an employer to a bossy, self-proclaimed *reformed* bully.

Yep. She sure knew how to pick 'em.

"How much time do you need?" Xavier asked as he pulled his new truck—deemed the Silver Hulk by his buddies—to the curb in front of her house.

"An hour? But take your time. Would you rather I meet you there?"

"And deprive me of watching you struggle in and out of the Hulk? Hell, no. Cracks me up. Wait there."

He stepped out of the truck like a real person steps out of a car, because the Hulk fit him. Of course, it was like scaling a rock wall for her. As she opened her door, he was there, offering his hand, which she imagined would make a good first hold. She wet her lips, heating up at the idea of scaling his body.

"I'll be back for you in an hour," he said as he reached in with one arm, easily plucking her from the truck and setting her down before him. "You need more time, just text me. The night's young. We aren't in any hurry."

"But, didn't Vance say they wanted to make it a quick evening? Get back to Vance, Jr.?"

"That's Vance's agenda. You got kids you need to worry about?"
She shook her head.

"Me, either. The rest of them can rush through their evening. You and I have been rushing all week. Tonight, we get to take it slow."

The breath that caught in her throat was telling. Xavier Wright had moved in on her with such finesse she hadn't realized it was happening. Not only did he have her backed up against the side of his truck, his hands were settled on either side of her head, squeezing the edge of the truck's bed. His voice had gone sultry when he started talking about taking things slow. If she hadn't decided to transfer her inappropriate crush to Xavier, she might feel a bit nervous or … trapped, like the air around her had been extinguished due to his proximity.

He bent his head low, his arms doing a pushup move to bring his upper body close to hers. His nose rubbed against the side of her hair, and then his lips dipped to the base of her neck. His kiss there tickled, shooting chills across her shoulder.

"Tweets," he rasped. Everything stopped for a brief moment before he pushed himself off the truck. "Slow. Yeah." He stepped back, pointing a finger at her. "Just, ya know, got a little ahead of myself there. Just …" His words died off as he moved back in, clasping her face between his hands, bringing their mouths together for a kiss. A good kiss. A fantastic, breath-stealing first kiss. It was soft, but way past the edge of sweet. His lips were a luscious delicacy, and their kiss had the essence of an eager start and a satisfying destination all bundled together. Her hands grabbed on to his T-shirt, her body's response to being swamped with the combustible reaction she'd felt bubbling below the surface since she'd first seen him.

Xavier.

Xavier Wright.

Finally.

CHAPTER SEVENTEEN

"Okay, so—that's moving things forward," Xavier said as he pulled his lips from hers and gently untangled the two of them. Laidey's disappointment was tangible. She was so not ready for the kissing to end. Of course, Poppy yelling at them from the front door was the equivalent to her turning the garden hose on the two of them. "I'll be back for you within the hour. Good?"

She wobbled a nod, feeling blindsided.

He grinned. "Kinda knocked you for a loop there, didn't I?"

She pulled herself together to give him a smug look. "As if," she tossed off, picking up the bag she'd dropped to the ground, loving the deep sound of his low-level mirth.

"Okay, then," he said, running a hand down the side of her cheek before backing up and turning away. "An hour."

She stood on the sidewalk, waved, and watched as he drove off. One glance at Poppy—grinning from ear to ear—let her know that she'd have some explaining to do.

"You saw that?" she asked, coming toward the door.

"You mean the way he tried to swallow you whole? Yeah, I caught that." Poppy held the door open.

"Sorry. Wasn't planning on making myself a spectacle."

"No problem. He's some kind of force, that one. Handsome. Solid. Dictatorial."

"Dictatorial?"

Poppy shrugged. "You know, large and in charge." Laidey couldn't deny that. "So, this is happening?"

"Mmm. I need to get McKenna on the phone, like now. Because yeah, apparently this is happening, and I don't have the sense to stop it."

"Why would you want to? He's killer-licious. He's also the man everyone's been talking about. But I guess that's the problem."

"Hmm?"

"It's not in your nature to want to be the one everyone starts talking about next."

"No." She shook her head. "But I'm beginning to like him. A lot. So." She sighed. "I need McKenna on board or at least not yelling at me before I can let my guard down and really start enjoying this."

"Call her."

"I plan to. Right now."

Laidey headed down the hall to her room, pulling her phone from the straw bag. "Thanks for all your beach supplies," she threw over her shoulder. "As you can probably tell, I had a good time."

"Yes. From the street performance the two of you put on, I'd say that's an understatement."

Laidey waved her off with her phone pressed to her ear, immediately getting McKenna's voicemail. "McKenna, this is Laidey. I need to talk to you immediately. It's like, an emergency, so please, please, call me back."

She hung up and proceeded to the shower, knowing exactly the dress she planned to wear.

"I love that dress on you," Poppy exclaimed when Laidey exited her bedroom forty-five minutes later. "Your dark hair pops when you wear white, and that low V in the back is sensational. Mr. *Wright* will love it." She laughed. "Perfect name, isn't it?"

Laidey returned her smile as she heard a text bing on her phone. She dug into her purse expecting to find a text from McKenna. Except it was from Xavier.

"Something's come up."

She read it twice, because the first time the meaning didn't register. After her eyes tried to decipher the words a second time she stood there, staring at the phone, waiting for something more.

An explanation.

An apology.

Something.

She got nada.

And then a text from McKenna came in.

"I'm available to talk for the next fifteen minutes. Call me."

It took Laidey only a moment before she texted back.

"Never mind."

Xavier was behind the wheel of the family SUV, his father in the backseat with his ma's head on his lap. She was wrapped in a blanket and barely conscious. The fear that gripped his chest was real, and it was horrifying. But it couldn't begin to touch the guilt.

He'd moved back home to take care of his mother. Support his father. Yet, he'd been out of cell range, drinking beer and floating in a damn lake like he didn't have a care in the world.

Of course, his father hadn't thought to call him. He'd had his hands full while his mother's condition crashed—violently. Xavier walked into the house to find his very tough father shaking like a leaf with the phone to his ear, explaining his mother's symptoms to her doctor. The doctor wanted her at Duke as soon as they could get her there.

Thank God, Xavier had stopped drinking a couple hours ago. He didn't trust his dad behind the wheel in his present state. The fear in the man's eyes—Xavier couldn't think on it. So he'd focused on hustling both his parents into the car and getting them where they needed to be.

The radio was silent, as was the entire ninety-minute ride to Durham. Plenty of thinking space in which to berate himself. He'd been out partying while his mother—the one he was struggling to improve his reputation for—slipped into what appeared to be a coma. He'd never felt more like an asshole than he did in this moment. And he was never—never—going to let himself forget it.

Because if she died? On his watch?

Hell, he'd taken her improvement for granted. Went about town like tragedy wasn't lurking over his shoulder. Was out *sucking face with a girl* while his father was frantically trying to revive his mother.

That's it, he decided.

He wasn't building any damn pie plate shop.

He certainly wasn't doing shit for Team Henderson.

And Laidey Bartholomew could take a flying leap, for all he cared. Until his mother was back on her feet, her health was all he planned to focus on.

Twenty-four hours later, his mother changed that plan, clearly and concisely. "Baby, you need to leave so I can stop worrying about how worried you are. You heard the doctor. My blood count is responding extremely well to this treatment. I'm feeling much better, and your father is good company. *You* are not."

"Excuse me?" Xavier shouted.

"Darlin', you scare the doctors. You scare the nurses. And frankly, you're starting to scare me. Now, Mr. Alexander arrives tomorrow. I would greatly appreciate you going home and preparing a guest room just as I would if I were able. Please."

Xavier stared at his mother, not believing she was sending him away. "Chase is a grown-ass man who can fend for his damn self. I don't care about Chase. I don't care about anybody but you. I'm *not* leaving."

"You are, sweetheart. You're going to leave so I can breathe. I can't heal if I can't breathe, and you, my darling son, are sucking up all the oxygen in this room. So git."

"Ma. You can't be serious."

"I'm totally serious. When your father gets back from the cafeteria, I want you to make your excuses. I want you to go."

"I don't want to go," he insisted, swallowing his outrage and lowering his voice. "If I go, I'll just worry about you. I'd rather be here where I can keep an eye on things."

"Sorry. You can't handle this. And I need you looking out for the house and getting things set for Mr. Alexander. I am eager to meet him, so you can be sure I'll be working on getting out of here fast. They say tomorrow. I feel well enough to believe them. This is a blip in my healing process. You heard the doctor. This is not a setback."

Xavier nodded. He'd heard the doctor. He'd been clinging to those words. "Ma. I love you."

His mother's mouth dropped open in surprise. Then her face lit up erasing all the markings of illness. "Xavier," she sighed. "Thank you for that. I love you, too."

He gave her a short nod. "I don't tell you enough."

"You've never told me."

"That's my point," he said, shooting her a look. "But you've known it, yeah?"

"Of course," she said, soothing him. "But it's a thrill to hear it coming from my oldest son. Come here."

He went to her bedside and looked for a way to crawl in with her. It was too narrow and there were too many machines close by. So he leaned down and hugged her as best he could. "I love you, Ma. You mean everything to me. Please get better."

"I will," she promised, squeezing him tighter than he would have anticipated.

"Good. I'll go, so you can get to that. I'll take care of the house and see that *Mr. Alexander* is set. Make sure you have someone do your hair before you come home. I've been telling Chase you're a looker. Don't want him disappointed," he teased.

"There's my baby. Thank you. We'll be home tomorrow. Your brother said he'd drive us."

Laidey heard nothing more from Xavier Saturday evening or all day Sunday. About midway through Monday, she stopped expecting to hear from him ever again.

As if he'd been a mirage, everything had gone back to the way things were before he'd come to town. She worked all day, stayed late at the office utilizing the quiet, and then rode her bike in a new direction for about thirty minutes before heading home. There she'd converse with Poppy and her brother, eat dinner, retire to her room, and realize … she was *desperately* lonely.

She hadn't known that she was lonely until Xavier stormed through her life for one week, exiting as if he were a hurricane that had simply moved up the coast.

No one had mentioned his name.

Not to her.

Not at the team meeting.

It was as if she'd woken up from a dream and everything she thought was real simply faded from memory.

On Tuesday, she took a lunch break. She rode her bike to the club and got Harry to open the ballroom. Then she locked herself inside with the piano, intent on playing her heart out. Because her heart had become so heavy it needed a way to scream.

On Wednesday, she did the same thing.

On Thursday, she strolled by the site of Piper's shop finding it exactly as it had been left.

Xavier had not been busy with work.

On Friday, she flew home to Dallas to see her parents. A visit home was overdue, and since Henderson wasn't feeling as charming as it once had, she figured she could use the change of scenery. Which, unlike last weekend, she wasn't going to get at the lake. She wasn't sure she could take being cooped up in her house while imagining everyone else at the lake. With Xavier.

She was back at work early the following Monday, where she tried not to notice that Xavier the Phantom was missing from the Team Henderson meeting for the second week in a row.

Maybe he's left town and moved back to Phoenix. At least she'd gotten one helluva make-out session from "The Week of Xavier Wright." She surmised that was far more than she'd gotten out of the three-year mad crush on her boss.

Still.

So she returned to her first love, the piano, and played the blues again at lunch.

CHAPTER EIGHTEEN

Xavier's reunion with Chase on Monday morning was a balm to his belabored soul. A widower in his sixties, the man was an expert in his field. Xavier considered him an expert at life as well. After giving his mentor the grand tour of his hometown, the two of them discussed ideas to resolve Henderson's housing needs as they worked together to improve the room over the garage.

Chase had been impressed with the plans Xavier had drawn for the space, and with one suggestion—removing the original ceiling to allow the vaulted roof and rafters to show—the two of them were now working side by side on a very cool man cave/guest suite. One that Chase was eager to put some muscle into since he was going to be the beneficiary.

On Tuesday, Xavier was finally able to introduce his mentor to his parents. He was especially pleased to note the color in his ma's cheeks and the energy she maintained for conversation during the cocktail hour and on through dinner. Both Anna Beth and Connor Wright who were a decade younger than Chase, got on well with him, exactly how Xavier had hoped.

However, after that dinner, his ma's energy faded, which Xavier didn't like one bit.

From then on, she stuck to her bed unless Xavier agreed to play the piano. Then and only then would she make the effort to move out of bed and on to the living room sofa. So he agreed daily, yet continued to play poorly. It became apparent to both of them that playing an instrument was not like riding a bike or treading water.

Practice was a necessity he'd gone years without. And with Chase in the house and their focus on getting the man cave finished, Xavier couldn't squeeze out the time to do it.

Still, he played at his mother's request, wishing he could give her a better performance. Which was why his ears perked up as he darted up the club's foyer stairs heading toward a quick lunch meeting with Vance and Pinks.

Someone was playing the piano.

Beautifully.

He stuck his head in the bar area. No piano. The sound was resonating from across the hall. He turned and headed for the ballroom's double doors, curious as all get out because it wasn't so much the piece being played as it was the *way* it was being played. Smooth. Easy. Melodic. Exactly the way he'd never been able to master.

Unfortunately, the doors were locked. *Locked? What the hell?* Xavier pressed his ear to the door, his heartbeat pounding.

"Can I help you?"

Startled, Xavier turned to find Harry. "Yes. Thank you. Do you know who's playing?"

"That would be Laidey Bartholomew."

Xavier's head reared back. "Really?" He tuned in more intently, having trouble imagining her tiny fingers producing such mastery.

Harry produced a key that had Xavier backing out of the way so he could unlock the door. The bartender signaled him to be quiet.

The two of them peered inside, and yep, there she was—Tweety Bird—with her perfectly postured back to them, wearing her yellow dress and Keds, playing the beautiful instrument like she was born on stage at Carnegie Hall.

All kinds of guilt kicked in, squeezing the area around his heart. As he stared at the bounce of dark curls and the gesticulation of her body, he watched and heard passion being translated into heartbreaking melody.

He'd forced all thoughts of Laidey from his mind the moment he'd seen his mother lying lifeless in her bed, his father's face anguished with fear. He'd blamed himself for not being there, for letting the two of them slip so far. And he'd blamed Laidey for his distraction—

for diverting his attention from the job he'd come home to do. With Chase arriving two days later, it was easy to continue tuning out thoughts of Laidey. But now?

Shit.

Standing here? Listening? Watching? This was the worst form of torture. Because the way she played and the emotion he heard, danced him down the path of greed. The sounds pulsated through him down to his toes and woke him the hell up to an intense and selfish desire.

His mind swirled with her melody and the memory of their kiss. Those arms, her hands, now busy creating lyrical ambrosia had gripped him fiercely the last time they were together. His eyes treasured the meager glimpses of her fingers springing over the keys with such rhythmic dexterity, exactly the stuff he could never hope to achieve. This diminutive girl was an artist as large as the sky, and he yearned for more of her songs, for more of *her* as Harry backed him up and out of the room, stealing her from his sight.

"Hey. Wait a minute," Xavier objected.

Harry shook his head. "She needs this."

"Needs what?"

"Space. To play."

"I wasn't planning to disturb her space or her playing. I just want to listen."

"She's good, isn't she?"

"Yeah. Yeah," he agreed, all kinds of surprise leaking into his voice. "She's quite good."

Harry nodded. And then grinned.

Xavier scowled, not liking Harry or his grin at the moment. "What exactly is going on with you and Tweety Bird?"

"Miss Bartholomew?"

Xavier gave a sharp nod.

"I see that she gets the time and space she needs to play. What's up with *you* and Miss Bartholomew?"

"I like to tease the hell out of her." Xavier wondered why he continually admitted that aloud. Then his stupid mouth asked, "Does that make me a bully?"

"Nope. I'm pretty sure she doesn't mind being teased. She says she doesn't mind going unnoticed most of the time, but I think that's a wall she's built. You're an architect. What do you think?"

Xavier squinted. "What the hell are you talking about?"

"You here for lunch?"

Realizing he was now running late, Xavier felt all kinds of frustrated. "I've missed a couple Team Henderson meetings. Vance has summoned me here to either chew my ass or update me. Probably both."

"He and Mr. Williams are in the card room. There won't be witnesses."

"Do me a favor," Xavier asked as they made their way into the Mixed Grill. "Don't let Tweety Bird fly the coop. I need to talk with her. I'm … well, among other things, I'm hoping she might agree to play for my ma."

"I'm sure Miss Bartholomew will be happy to play for your ma. Among other things."

"Laidey," Xavier called, clearing his throat in an effort to tamp down his anxiety. Yep, he'd been right to worry. The look she threw at him was one that not so subtly said, *"Asshole."*

So he pushed himself off the bar and crossed the room, going to where the irritated, little pixie stood her ground.

And since he couldn't take his eyes off the girl or her pretty dress as he approached, her growing discomfort was not lost on him. He watched that sweet shade of strawberry color her neckline and cheeks. Couldn't help but notice how her fingers curled and rubbed at her palms before she shook them out. Apparently, no amount of finger twitching was able to stop her rockin' little body from trembling. And damn if she wasn't looking everywhere but at him. He didn't like any of it, but he especially didn't like that.

"Eyes on me," he said softly, the grin she always brought out in him plastering itself on his face. "I apologize for not getting in touch after my family emergency." He stopped, and cocking his head, he shifted gears. "Are you still afraid of me?"

"Family emergency? And no," she insisted, her eyes darting around the room.

"No? Hey." He tried for her complete attention. "Eyes on me. That night, after we got off the boat, I had to drive my mom to the hospital. To Duke. All the way to Durham."

"I'm not afraid of you," she said, returning his gaze. "And I do hope your mother's okay."

"You sure about that?"

"About hoping your mother's okay? Yes. I'm sure."

"About not being afraid of me."

"I'm not afraid. I'm not *anything*."

"Oh. Well, that's a shame." Refusing to let her see the effects of the knife she just settled in his gut, he stepped forward and bent low to whisper in her ear. "I was getting used to you being just a little afraid. I kinda liked it."

"Liked it?"

He shrugged. "You stammer, you blush, you shake a bit. It's cute."

"So you, being the town bully, get off on making people shake?"

"No. Being the *reformed* town bully, I only get off on making you shake, Tweety Bird."

"Stop with the nickname. That's a ridiculous nickname."

"It's perfect," he argued. "Especially now that I've heard you make music."

She lowered her eyes, whispering, "How did you know it was me?"

"Harry."

"Harry?" she grumbled. "That man needs to learn how to keep a secret."

"Why keep it a secret? You know what? Never mind. Listen." Xavier decided not to use the word *need*, as in *I need you to do something for me*. Instead, he went with the word *want*, because the word *want* was throbbing in his head. "I want you to play the piano for my mother. I won't tell anyone it was you in there if you do me a solid and play the piano for my mother."

Tweety handed over that big-eyed expression he was so fond of.

"I'd like you to come to our home," he explained. "Our piano isn't new like that Baldwin in there, but it was recently tuned, so you'll find it adequate. Will you do it?" Before she could answer, he added, "She's sick, you know? Well, she's in recovery. From a really bad autoimmune disease. And she keeps begging me to play for her but—"

"You?" Tweets spouted. "*You* play the piano?"

Xavier held up his large hands and wiggled ten long fingers. "Like a champ," he claimed. "Although I'm rusty. Haven't played since I moved to Phoenix, so all I do is irritate myself and probably my mother with my rust. After hearing you play, I figure she might enjoy listening to someone with actual talent."

"So you don't play like a champ," she clarified.

"Champ? I meant chump."

That got him a smile. *Finally.*

"In all seriousness, I'll pay you to do it. She's been sticking to her bed lately, and the only way I can get her to leave it is to promise to play."

"Xavier, you're not paying me to play the piano for your sick mother."

"I will. I'd be happy to."

She huffed at him. That cute, little chest of hers rising and falling as she no doubt fought for an excuse that wouldn't make her seem callous. "Fine," she gave in. "I enjoy playing and don't get to do it enough."

"Great. I'll pick you up. What time are you stopping work today?"

"To-day?"

There it was again. The blushing, the stammering, the shaking … God, was she cute when she did all that. And though he really did get off on teasing her, since she was agreeing to help him with his mother, he didn't belabor her discomfort. Instead, he offered, "I won't bring the Harley. I'll pick you up in the truck. Nothing to get your feathers ruffled over, Tweets."

"Fine," she sighed, her eyes cast to the ceiling in thought. "What time do y'all eat dinner?"

"What's that got to do with it?"

"I've got a lot of work I want to have ready for Mr. Carraway when he arrives tomorrow. I was planning to work late. But I can cut out and come back to it if need be."

"Tweets. You work too hard."

"Well, since Mr. Carraway pays me with actual money, not fanciful fringe benefits, he deserves my best."

Xavier rolled his lips between his teeth and crossed his arms over his chest, knowing she had every right to be pissed off. He'd practically felt her up on her front walk ten minutes before he dumped her with no explanation. Still, this Carraway thing was a thorn in his side.

"Right. Right. I remember. He pays you to stand sentry over his chair."

"You don't know the man. He's kind, and he's brilliant—"

"And he doesn't want a disrespectful ass sitting in his chair."

"*I* didn't want a disrespectful ass sitting in his chair."

Xavier took a breath, hoping to soften the situation. "You've refused to show me this kind of loyalty, you know."

"What?"

"As my uppity secretary. I get the feeling you'd let anybody sit in my chair."

"Do you even have a chair? An office?"

"Good point. Okay, what time am I picking you up so you can bring harmony into my parents' home and joy into my mother's heart?"

Her body stiffened, causing her curls to bounce atop her shoulders. "That's a tall order."

"I've heard you play," he soothed. "You can deliver."

"I'll … I'll work my schedule around yours," she stammered.

"How about you just text me when you're finished. I'll make sure there are leftovers to feed you after you perform."

"Perform?" She literally went pale in front of him.

"Tweets. You play like a professional. Buck up. You've got this."

It was seven o'clock that evening, and although Laidey desperately wanted to get one more thing accomplished before she called it a night, a text from the XXL pain in her ass brought her ambition to a screeching halt.

"You gonna work yourself to death? Or you gonna honor your commitment to my momma and show up and play the damn piano before she falls asleep?"

Shit. She texted back. *"Sorry. Clock got away from me. I can leave now. Give me the address, and I'll ride my bike over."*

As she packed up her tote, another text came in.

"I'm outside."

Her gaze swung to the door. His earlier words, *I apologize for not getting in touch after my family emergency,* came back to haunt her for the umpteenth time that afternoon.

Even though the mystery of "something came up" had been resolved, belated apology or no, the truth was he hadn't bothered to get in touch with her.

Not after their day on the boat together.

Not after their kiss.

Not after standing her up for dinner.

In retrospect, transferring the inappropriate crush she had for her boss to Xavier Wright had been a classic "Addy" move. It wasn't any of the three R's. It certainly wasn't reasonable. It had proven to be completely unreliable. And Xavier himself was far from respectable, proving her grandmother right. Channeling her mother was not the way to go.

She reminded herself that even though Xavier was big and commanding, *she* was armed with superior intellect. One she planned to keep lodged between herself and his stupidly cute grin. Resolved—another strong R word—she stepped out of the office, locked up, and turned to find the Holy Grail of Hotness astride his Hard Candy Hot Rod Red, Road King. The thought that she knew the color and make of that thing sent a tremor up her spine.

"Quit being a chickenshit and get your tiny, feathered ass over here," he demanded. "I should have dragged you out of there an hour ago. We'll be lucky if my mother isn't sound asleep."

"It's only seven."

"She's sick," he stressed. "Has shit for energy."

"Well, then," Laidey stalled, looking over his Harley. "Let's do this tomorrow night. Give her my apologies."

"We're not doing this tomorrow night. I go home empty-handed, she'll think I've scared you off."

"You brought your motorcycle. Wasn't that exactly your intent?"

"Not exactly, no."

"Then you chose it because …?"

"You're a dull woman who needs a thrill. Get on."

Laidey's breath caught.

She felt her eyes well with tears.

For all of her *resolve* to be reasonable, reliable, and respectable, she *was* a dull woman who needed a thrill. Xavier may have been trying to yank her chain, but he'd hit upon the truth good and hard. So hard she felt it in her solar plexus.

With more determination than she'd ever embraced, she marched forward to the Machine of Impending Doom and asked, "Okay, how do I do this?"

Xavier stood and scooted forward. "Climb over. Watch that. It's hot. Put your feet here," he indicated.

With her tote thrown over her shoulder, she placed a Ked on the footrest and lifted a leg over the seat, scrunching up the skirt of her dress as she sat on the upper part of the seat.

He sank into the cradle and told her to hang on.

She gingerly grabbed the back of his T-shirt and bunched it up in her fingers.

"Tweets. I *know* you can grip me harder than that, and you falling off this thing will not benefit my reputation." He reached back and took both her hands, pulling them forward and wrapping her arms around his waist. "Clasp your hands together and don't let go," he ordered.

She was straining to keep her head away from his broad back, but as soon as he said, "Ready?" he took off. With a squeal she really hoped he didn't hear, she gripped him harder, laid her cheek against his back, shut her eyes, and hung on for dear life. She may have felt his stomach ripple with a laugh, but the motorcycle was so loud she couldn't hear anything over the din. Her hair flew behind her as she breathed into the fear, telling herself that if he had ridden this thing from Arizona to North Carolina, he could probably get the two of them to his parents' place without incident. Then, solely in order to distract herself, she focused on all that she was leaning against. Length. Plenty of it. Lean and solid. And she found a sense of security in having her arms around him. Like he was one of her childhood teddy bears.

Only ... Xavier Wright was no teddy bear.

Like he was her lover.

Only ... yep, sadly not that either.

Like he was a knight on a white steed, saving her from the advancing enemy.

Only ... *Come on,* she scolded herself, rolling her eyes at all of the Addy-like thoughts.

Unfortunately, that had no bearing on her next big idea, which was to take advantage of their proximity and *sniff* him. As she turned her head, the motorcycle leaned in the opposite direction, causing her to bang her nose against his back, hard. Instinctively, she released one hand in order to rub it, but that caused Xavier to reach for her arm and tuck it back around him. His face turned to the side, and he said something—shouted something—but she couldn't hear it. And that's the moment she realized that neither of them were wearing helmets.

Holy Shit. Grandmother, forgive me. I know not what I do.

Thankfully, it was only moments until they pulled into a circular drive. Once Xavier shut the motor off, she started in. "I can't believe you got me on this thing without a helmet," she cried, trying to hop off without getting tangled up in her dress or hitting that hot thing with her bare leg.

"I can't believe it either," he chuckled.

"What?"

"Tweets. I had a world-class persuasive argument ready to go. But you leapt on my bike so fast I didn't get a chance to put it to good use."

"I'm not getting back on that thing without a helmet."

He grinned. A big, leery, proud grin.

"What?" she snapped.

"Just happy I'll be getting you back on it."

"I didn't say that."

"Yeah, ya sorta did. Come on," he said, taking her by the arm and pulling her to the front door. "My ma is ready for her concert."

She skidded to a dead stop, pulling out of his grasp. "A concert? I don't. I haven't … *prepared* a concert."

"Just an expression, Tweets. Don't take everything so literally."

"Oh, you mean like the time you said you'd pick me up in an hour?" She regretted the words the moment they flew from her mouth. But she regretted them more when she saw the look of pity on his face.

"Look," he said, his voice rough. "I owe you a conversation about that." He drew close, grasping both of her upper arms gently. "I also know I've railroaded you into this. But not being a doctor, I struggle for ways to help my mom. I do some cooking, but she's not real big on eating right now. I babysit to give both her and my dad a break, but I'm realizing the two of them enjoy sitting quietly together. They've gotten used to that. Her only request is to hear me play the piano. But, like I told you, I'm way out of practice. Yet she claims to enjoy it. So, I'm thinking if she has the chance to hear you play, she would be in heaven. And sitting in heaven has gotta help with the healing."

"That's … kind of you to say."

"Just stating the facts."

"All right. I'm … sorry I'm so late."

"You ready to role-play the part of concert pianist?"

"As ready as I'll ever be."

She followed him into the foyer of his parents' impressive home, noticing the grand instrument immediately off to her left. She waited for Xavier to lead the way, and her attention was pulled from the piano when he said, "Ma. This is Adelaide Bartholomew. She goes by Laidey, but I call her Tweets."

His mother, looking frail even though her hair and makeup were in place, sat on the couch wrapped in a blanket, blinking at the two of them in confusion. "Please call me Laidey," she suggested, moving forward to take her outstretched hand. "My friends call me Laidey."

"And this Tweets?" she asked her son.

"A pet name."

His mother looked between the two of them. "A pet name?"

"Long story," he claimed.

"I'm certain I'd like to hear it."

Xavier leaned in to kiss his mother's cheek while loosening Laidey's hand from her grip. "I'm sure you would. But I promise you'll be much better entertained if we just let Tweets—I mean, *Laidey*—get to the piano." He shoved Laidey toward the thing like she was a child. "I heard her play this afternoon, but I'm starting to wonder if I heard correctly."

"Oh," Laidey said airily, "you mean you're not sure if I play like a champ or a chump?"

"Something like that," he smirked.

Laidey sat at the piano. Smiling. *Aware* that she was smiling and feeling very relaxed. And even though coming to that awareness started to shift things, making her less relaxed, she poised her fingers over the keys and played her favorite classical piece. It wasn't impressive, but it was soothing, and from the looks of Xavier's mother, she could use some soothing. So she played Pachelbel's Canon in D and eased into other soft, flowing pieces as they came to her, finishing the fourth piece on a tinkling riff before she snuck her first glance in the direction of Xavier and his mother.

Xavier had his arm around the woman, snuggling her into him. His mother's head rested against his broad shoulder, and her eyes were closed. But she had a sweet smile on her face, so Laidey was pretty sure she hadn't fallen asleep. She wouldn't have minded if she had. Sleep healed, and this woman needed healing.

The way Xavier was looking down at her broke Laidey's heart. It exposed the worry pouring off him and was the first time she'd witnessed any sort of vulnerability. He was so … brash. Most of the time out-right annoying with his pompous, overinflated ego. She began to play a more contemporary piece, which she noticed had Xavier's head snapping up. She couldn't help but lift her gaze to meet those gray eyes.

His grin was slow in coming, but it was directed right at her.

Her regard went back to the keys, while her mind went a little crazy in a totally different direction. A direction in which it liked to run wild and free, no matter how she tried to corral the thing.

Xavier was too smooth, and for all his declaration of changing his brutish ways, he was still a bully. He'd bullied her into being his secretary. He'd bullied her into a fantastic date that ended poorly with no word from him in over a week. And even so, she was now sitting at his parents' piano, playing an impromptu concert after he'd gotten her on his Machine of Decibel Madness.

Obviously, there was nothing he couldn't get her to do.

He'd stolen a kiss just to rile her up. Two days later, he kissed her like it meant something, only to break her heart minutes later. Apparently kissing meant nothing to him.

But to her …

It emphasized just how much time had passed since she'd been kissed. Which, was probably why fighting her attraction to Long and Lean over there was futile. And really? What was the harm in another latent infatuation she wondered as she moved into another John Tesh piece. It wasn't like she'd act on it. Seducing McKenna's old flame would still be the height of bad form, not to mention the man in question clearly wasn't all that interested.

Maybe she'd take a look around. Go have a drink with Harry later. Harry seemed to like her okay. Not that she could see herself seducing Harry or anyone else. She wasn't like McKenna. Bold and fearless. But putting herself out there socially might inspire a more appropriate attraction. That Josh guy from Team Henderson, the one who ran the football team and the computer classes. He probably knew some nice, solid, interesting men who he'd be willing to introduce her to. Take her mind off Xavier—

She let out a gasp as solid hands landed on her shoulders.

"Keep playing," Xavier urged quietly. She felt his fingertips drift from her shoulders as he seated himself beside her on the piano bench.

She scooted to make room as hip brushed against hip. He scooted too, re-establishing the contact, looking down at her with a wolf-like grin—totally teasing her.

"You like to do that," she whispered as she continued to play.

"Do what?"

"Tease me."

"I do," he agreed on a soft laugh. "Forgive me, Tweets, but I really do. And I'm tired of you having all the fun, so do you know any duets?"

She stifled a grin, ending the piece she was playing, letting her fingers drift lightly upon the keys. "Duets are the best kind of fun."

He snickered. "I suppose a kindergartener like you'd think so."

"You don't think so?"

"I think they're good fun," he said. "But not anywhere *near* the best kind of fun," he leered.

"You're such a … man."

"You say that like it's a dirty word," he whispered over her ear. "Yet you sat right here, not twenty seconds ago, giving me another eye-fuck."

She shot a look toward his mother who appeared to be sleeping before she gave him a scathing set down. "Will you stop with this eye … stuff?"

"Just call 'em like I see 'em. Come on, Tweets. Let's see if we can make beautiful music together."

She choked back a retort, not wanting to encourage him. "Okay. Show me what you can do."

"Name a song."

"Classical or what?"

"Anything? Show tune. Rock and roll. Country. Beethoven. Try and stump me."

"What? Are you a piano savant?"

"Not hardly. But I've got a good ear. So put it to the test."

"'I Write the Songs'. Barry Manilow."

"Too easy," he said, his fingers skimming along in an introductory phrase. "That's one of Ma's favorites."

He played it … well. At least his version of it. Which was nothing like the sheet-music version, though if you were listening, over on the couch, you wouldn't be aware. Xavier wasn't lying. He did have a good ear. Even if his technique was crap.

"My technique is crap," he said, mimicking her thoughts. He eyed her while he finished the ballad, looking as honest and candid as she'd seen him.

"Your technique *is* crap," she agreed. "But if no one is sharing the bench with you ..." she shrugged.

"You want to teach me? Technique."

"No."

"Why not?" His hands stopped moving, and for the first time since she'd started to play, the room fell silent.

They heard his mother shift, drawing their attention. Xavier left the piano bench to help her stand.

"I'm okay," she protested, but Xavier helped her anyway. He didn't let go of her, and he didn't give a look in Laidey's direction either, even when his mother addressed her directly.

"Laidey, it was a true pleasure to hear you play. The meds I'm taking make me sleepy. I beg you not to take offense."

Laidey stood and clasped her hands in front of her. "None taken," she assured Mrs. Wright with a bright smile.

"Will you come back? Play some more? Your touch is lovely, very soothing to listen to."

"I'd be honored."

Mrs. Wright nodded, as if she didn't have the strength to say more.

"Perhaps you wouldn't mind playing us out of the room," Xavier said, winking when he caught her eye.

"Absolutely." She reseated herself on the piano stool, one that now felt too large after having Xavier's body tucked up against her.

She started a Beatles song. One of the first she'd learned when taking lessons.

"That's another one of her favorites," Xavier's voice floated back to her.

She smiled down at the keys. It seemed she and Mrs. Wright had several things in common.

"Where did you go?" His text came in twenty minutes later.
"I'm fine. I didn't want to overstay my welcome."
"So you LEFT."
"You were taking care of your mother. I can take care of myself."
"Where the hell are you?"
"I'm halfway to the club. Harry will give me a ride home."

Laidey watched her phone as she strolled on, waiting for a reply. When none came, she rolled her eyes in disappointment—and then rolled her eyes again at being disappointed. She stored her phone in her tote, wondering how she was going to shake loose this unfathomable attraction to a total ass.

Although, she considered, he was certainly sweet to his mother. So he wasn't a complete ass. And he played the piano and liked piano music, so—yeah—not a complete and total ass. *And* he was worried about his brutish reputation. Well, around town. Not so much around her. Not that *she* counted. Except for one day on a boat, she was invisible. An out-of-towner here to do a job. Whatever.

Harry wasn't originally from Henderson, she thought as ... "Oh, hell."

She turned and faced the music as it came roaring up the road to greet her.

"Get on."

It was an order. One issued as soon as Xavier stopped beside her.

Resigned, she climbed on without hesitation.

"Hold on. Tight this time." Another order.

"Fine," she mouthed, following his demands. She didn't resist the urge to press her cheek to his back this time. The night was falling into darkness, which gave her the illusion of anonymity. If no one saw her do it, she could pretend it never happened.

The ride was quick and ended back in the Wrights' driveway.

"But I thought ..." she said, moving to hop off.

"That I forgot I promised to feed you?"

She blinked at him and smirked. "No. *That* I hadn't even remembered."

"I was taking care of my mom," he explained completely exasperated. "Dad's at the club making up for lost time with his friends. He needs that. And I need to feel useful around here," he said, pushing open the front door. "What I don't need is for you to run out on me."

"Xavier," she whispered, chagrinned. "I didn't run out on you."

"No? Well, you sure as hell weren't playing the piano when I came back."

"I just figured you had enough to worry about without adding me into the fray."

"The fray?"

"You know what I mean."

"I have plenty to worry about," he said taking her hand and tugging her down the hall after him. "I don't need you disappearing into thin air in the dead of night, adding to the *fray*," he mimicked. She was pulled through a narrow family room and into a large, square kitchen.

"The dead of night," she scoffed.

He spun and threw his hands in the air. "And why would you run to Harry?"

"Harry's ... Harry. Why do you even care?"

"Why do I care?" He stood tall and took a momentary step back. Then he came at her, shaking a finger. "Because you were here. Playing the piano. And then you vanished." He pulled back abruptly. "And now I'm scaring you."

"Just a little," she said, eyes darting around the kitchen.

"Hey. Tweets. Eyes on me."

She folded her arms across her chest and moved her head in his direction, but her eyes took their own good time. When they finally did land on his, she saw how his gray irises glimmered with satisfaction. She immediately looked away.

"Take a seat," he ordered.

Her feet moved of their own volition. In her head, she tried to reason that following his orders simply made things easy. She didn't have to think about how to act around him because he told her. She wasn't required to say much, like now. So fine. She sat down at the kitchen table and put her thoughts to noticing her surroundings.

The kitchen was a large, interesting space. It was also terribly outdated with old cabinetry and aging appliances. It didn't necessarily look tired, and it was clean as could be. Still ...

"What are your plans for this kitchen?" The inquiry surprised her almost as much as it surprised him.

Xavier immediately turned his head away from the stovetop, his gray eyes gleaming with excitement. He wiped his hands on a dishtowel before asking, "Can I show you?"

She nodded, pleased she'd instinctively known he'd already given plenty of thought to renovating his parents' kitchen.

Large sheets of paper were unrolled on the table before her. In order to see them from a better angle, she stood and pushed the chair out of the way as Xavier placed marble samples at the edges to hold the schematic drawings down. He moved behind her, bracing both his hands on the table around her. She felt his chin rest lightly against the top of her head, as he no doubt peered down at his architectural vision. He first gave her an overview and then began pointing to the specifics, explaining his ideas in detail. Laidey's mind eventually fell away from the details. At least those of the drawings. The details of his rugged hands and brawny arms as they moved to help him explain—those she was exceptionally interested in. And how his voice got low and smoky, tickling her senses as he spoke with such passion.

Eventually, he fell silent, and she felt his warm breath at her ear. "I'm sorry our dinner date blew up." This came out throaty and low pitched, like it was coming from somewhere deep within him. She found herself being turned around as he switched their places. His backside now resting against the table, his hands holding her elbows, while his grey eyes studied her face. "When I arrived home, things were"—he shook his head—"not good. And, ah, I felt guilty that I'd been distracted while things around here went to shit."

Her eyes dropped to his chest as she nodded, understanding what he wasn't saying. That she'd been the distraction. The reason he felt guilty. She felt her ears get hot and her chest tighten at the thought. She had hoped she'd been more than distraction.

"I hadn't planned to call you."

She winced hearing those words.

"But after seeing you today—"

What had Harry said? Feel the feelings? Yeah-no. Because beyond the heartache and deep, deep sadness, what Laidey also felt was a whole lot of D words.

Discarded.

Dispensed with.

Dumped.

Ditched.

Yeah, she couldn't let herself feel all those feelings. Not here. "Take me home."

"Tweets. Please. I'm trying to explain how my fear got the best of me. Come on, now. Eyes on me," he coaxed.

Laidey shook her head vigorously, physically holding herself around her middle, willing herself to keep it together.

"You can't bolt. Just talk to me."

What she absolutely couldn't do was talk to him. Not right now. It would be like opening her chest, exposing her heart, and letting him see the cuts, the bruises, the emptiness, and the longing.

"Tweets?" he barked.

Her head snapped up, and she glared at him for forcing her to look at his handsome face.

There was a blistering moment of silence between them. Then he scowled, "Chicken."

She nodded. The words *I am. I am a chicken*, ran through her mind, but she couldn't bring herself to voice them. She was too afraid to admit how much he'd just hurt her. How vulnerable she'd become after knowing him barely a week.

"Tweets," he said on a groan of frustration. He rotated, reaching to lift a set of keys from a nail on the wall. Resigned, he said, "You're gonna have to grow a pair eventually. Come on."

She followed behind, feeling awkward and cowardly. He didn't lead her to his truck. Probably didn't want to have to help her get into it. This time they rode in his mother's car. A sedan of quality. No music, just silence. It didn't take long to get to her place, but the tension was thick when they arrived. So thick it held the both of them down, stuck where they sat. Xavier's wrists lay across the top of the steering wheel, his head bent toward it. Finally, he stirred, looked out the windshield, and asked, "How old are you?"

She wet her lips in order to answer. "I'm twenty-six."

He nodded into the night.

"And you're?"

"Thirty-two."

She nodded.

"I'm guessing you'd enjoy teaching me to play the piano about as much as you loved role-playing my secretary." He threw a brief glance in her direction. "You want me to leave you alone, I'll leave you alone."

She didn't want him leaving her alone. But she did want to be more than a mere distraction.

His head turned, as if he heard her thoughts. And the gaze he laid on her through the dim light of the street lamps sizzled with energy. It sparked a jump in her heart rate and a flurry of short staccato breaths. He noticed those too, because for the first time ever, she watched his gaze travel to her breasts.

"Tweets," he said after a moment, reaching an arm in her direction. "Get out of the damn car," he said, pulling the handle and then pushing her door open.

CHAPTER NINETEEN

"You wanna tell me what's going on?"

Anna Beth Wright was sitting at her kitchen table, watching her son clean up their breakfast dishes.

"Nothing's going on," he grunted, furiously scrubbing out a pan.

"You haven't said three words. Something is definitely going on."

Xavier stopped what he was doing and sucked in a breath. "I'm not particularly pleased with your gender right now, Ma. So don't push it."

"What happened with Tweets?"

He threw a glower over his shoulder. "Seriously?" He started loading the dishwasher.

"She has quite the way with a piano."

"That she does," he grumbled. "What she doesn't have is a spine."

"A what?"

He turned around and shouted. "A spine. A backbone."

"Like McKenna."

"Yes. Like McKenna." He closed up the dishwasher and began drying the pots and pans.

"But you never really liked McKenna. She wasn't ever the girl for you."

That had his movements slowing down. "Why do you say that?"

On a long, thoughtful breath, his mother sang the words, "Oh, where to begin?" He turned to find her body rocking in the chair, her gaze cast toward the ceiling as if deep in thought. He finished drying the last pan but kept looking in her direction as she began to talk.

"For one thing, you called her McKenna. Always McKenna."

"So?"

"No pet name. No, babe. No, honey. No … Tweets."

He scowled at her.

"You and McKenna argued about everything," his mother went on, undaunted.

"Adelaide Bartholomew argues with me about everything," he insisted.

"Does she? What I witnessed last night was flirting. Never saw that side of you with McKenna."

"I was eighteen when I dated McKenna. I'm a grown-ass man now. Too old to be dealing with kindergartners who wear colorful Keds and write with floral-printed pencils on pink-paged notebooks."

"She writes on pink-paged notebooks?" His mother smiled into the air. "I love that."

"Then you'd love the ridiculous posies she's got sprouting all over the basket on her bike."

"So she likes pretty, colorful things."

"She's silly, and ridiculous, and childish, and young. And, oh, by the way, I scare her to death. For reasons completely unknown to me. I mean, yeah, she saw me hit Brooks and has no doubt heard of my former reputation, but it's not like I've thrown a punch since then. I mean, I may have shouted at her once, so there's that. I also didn't bother to call her after I did my best to compromise her reputation in broad daylight last week, but I was just trying to feed her last night when she shot up and declared she was going home."

His mother sat back, looking at him. "You ever try to feed McKenna?"

"I was eighteen with McKenna. I didn't know how to feed myself."

"True. But you make a point to feed me, as often as possible."

"Because you're underweight, and I want to do what I can to get you well."

"And you wanted to feed Laidey."

"Because she missed dinner in order to play the piano for you. It was the least I could do. By the way, she's also underweight."

"Is she?"

"Did you not see her with your own eyes?"

"I did. I think she's darling. Petite yes, but not frail. You don't have to worry about being gentle with a girl just because she's so much smaller than you. Look at me and your father."

"Ma. Enough."

"Sweetheart, she likes you."

"Not anymore."

"And you like her."

"I think she's quirky. And it's gotten under my skin. Like a form of bacteria you need a pill to get rid of."

"Don't give up on her."

"Already have."

His mother sat back and gave him one of her disparaging looks.

"Already have," he repeated.

"She plays the piano. She's clearly not put off by your overbearing ways. And, she's very attractive."

"If you like tiny, silly brunettes. And what do you mean, my overbearing ways?"

"You're intimidating."

"Not necessarily a bad thing."

"Yes, but as you mentioned, she's tiny. And you're decidedly not. So for her, you're two-times intimidating. And, on top of that, you're demanding."

"So's dad," he snapped.

"Exactly. And once I got to know your father, it never bothered me. Not one little bit."

"Well, it bothers the hell out of me," he said.

"In your dad? Or in you?"

"I don't like the way he bosses you. I never have."

"How does he boss me?"

"Like he's trying to tame you."

She sat back and smiled.

"Oh, come on, Ma. You're not a docile, little doormat."

"Of course, I'm not. Nor would your father want me to be. But he likes being bossy, and sometimes I like to let him."

"Please."

"I'm just saying …"

"I know what you're saying," he shouted.

"Do you? Because you can't be less than you are, Xavier. You can't come back to your hometown and not be Xavier Wright, no matter how hard you try."

"I am trying. For you," he stressed. "I'm going out of my way to right my wrongs, to play nice with all the new faces in town, to wind back my reputation so my name doesn't end up in your precious Henderson Happenings newsletter and bring you any undue stress."

"But I didn't ask you to do that," she insisted. "I asked you to come home. Because I love you. As you are. You're perfect. You're exactly like your father, and I *love* your father."

He didn't know what to say to that.

"What I can't figure out is why you believe you don't deserve to be happy."

Whoa—what? And ouch! Because *that* just struck a nerve.

And apparently, it showed all over his face because his mother's voice immediately softened. "Tell me. What did you do that was so bad you think this town can't forgive you?"

His chest got tight, and still the words leaked out of him. "Got nothin' to do with this town."

"Then who? McKenna? I assure you, she doesn't hold a grudge."

"Well, you'd be wrong about that."

"I'm right about that. She and I talk."

"Which completely irritates me. Look, Ma, we're done here."

She latched on to his hand, and as frustrated as he now was, he still didn't have it in him to shake off his ailing mother.

"Be yourself, Xavier. Be the son I love from every hair on your head down to the bottom of your soles. There is not one thing I would change about you. Except to have you stop walking on eggshells around the likes of Evie Jackson or anyone else. You don't want to play the piano for me, don't. I'm not going to regress because you aren't fulfilling my every wish. What will make me sick however, is seeing the way you looked at Laidey last night and then hearing you've let her slip through your fingers."

She tossed up her other hand to halt him before he could tell her she'd lost her ever-loving mind.

"You're bossy. Use it. You're intimidating. Own it. You've got a good head on your shoulders. Trust it. And above all"—she released him and sat back—"have fun."

Five minutes later, Xavier was sprawled face down on his old bed. The one his seventeen-year-old self had slept in when he'd thought up his bright idea.

Maybe it was time to get a new bed so he'd stop reliving the stupid shit he did back then. Because tearing himself up over what he pulled back in high school was not getting him anywhere. And the truth of it was very little of that shit actually haunted him. None of the practical jokes, the trash-talking, not even the goldfish hazing ritual bothered him enough to offer any more than a simple shoulder shrug and an admission that—yeah, I was a pain in the ass.

There was really only one thing he'd ever done that was completely calculated and mean. And he'd done it to the person he loved most—regretting it with his whole heart. And staying away hadn't solved a damn thing. The situation had not resolved itself as he'd hoped. Instead, his brothers had followed his lead, leaving his parents to rattle around in a big house and suffer through this adversity alone.

He rolled over and stared at the ceiling.

His mother was right. He was who he was, and he did what he'd done. Walking around the streets of Henderson a pussified version of himself wasn't fixing a damn thing. As much as he'd come home determined to make amends to McKenna and others, his ma didn't seem too enamored with the Zen-like version of himself.

He checked his watch. Chase was probably back from Raleigh with the lighting fixtures. He needed to shake off the pansy-ass wuss that had swallowed him and whip out his man card. After all, in a couple hours, they'd have the man cave ready for furniture. Then he'd take Chase for a celebratory lunch at the club. After that, he'd march him down to Piper's shop, and they'd figure out what they needed to get started there.

The polarity of the projects made him grin. Tricked-out man cave versus Suzy Homemaker pie plate shop.

At least Chase was proving to be a much more productive distraction than scrumptiously tantalizing Ad-el-laide Bar-tho-lo-mew.

Yep, building out the room over the garage was far more productive than floating in a lake with a cute girl in your lap while your mother's health went to shit. Of course, that debacle had now turned into a nagging, irritating, *I-should-have-called-her-last-week* distraction. Because now she really knew, firsthand, what an asshole he was. Which, you know, was just in slight contrast to her selflessly disrupting her own work schedule to come play the piano for his mother.

Fuck.

His gut churned.

He could feel a confession coming.

Probably knew it was inevitable the moment Chase had texted from Arizona.

He was going to fall on his sword. He was going to spill his guts to Chase. Had to. There was no way he could keep this shit bottled up anymore.

Two hours later, after they'd hardwired the fixtures and mounted the flat screen, Xavier did what he'd feared most in the world. He sat Chase down and confessed the worst thing he'd ever done.

It wasn't eloquent. Certainly wasn't pretty. But it was the truth, spoken aloud for the first time. And somehow, dumping it onto his trusted mentor's shoulders brought such relief that Xavier went right on talking about how he'd stupidly blamed his attraction to Tweets for his mother's decline, and that, in many ways, he was finding it impossible to be "Arizona Zen" now that he was back in Henderson.

"All right. Well," Chase hedged, obviously taking time to temper his response. "I know for damn certain you're not the first man to do what you've done. Hell, I believe there's a similar story recounted in the bible, so you know, cut yourself some slack. It's far from an *original* sin. The fact that you were a hot-headed teenager is enough of an excuse to let you off the hook in my mind."

Xavier had a feeling Chase would let him off the hook no matter what he'd done.

"Coming home can stir up a lot of stuff. Probably the reason I'm sitting in your hometown and not mine," Chase joked. "And when you are home, it's notoriously easy to fall back into old patterns of behavior. But you've got a sixth sense of some kind that makes you the wiliest son of a bitch I know. I mean, the two of us are in a meeting and what *you hear* is everything *not* being said. I've relied heavily on that. You're the first to sense when the buyers are liars, and you can sniff out the padding on any given bid. Now, yes, that intuition of yours is what got you into this McKenna trouble in the first place. So this time, I suggest you use your powers for good, not evil. Use it to get the girl you really want—this little Tweety whatever—not to just one-up somebody."

Xavier twisted his lips. "Novel idea."

"Listen, son, I know you about as well as I know anybody, and I'm telling you the truth when I say being Xavier Wright is nothing to hang your head over. You've got plenty to be proud of. Don't waste another minute doubting it. Believe in your capabilities. Trust your instincts. Own your limitations and your gifts fully and show up for your ma and this town by being the freaking architect of your own life."

Xavier chuckled at Chase's emphatic plea. "Fine. I will be the architect of my own life. The perceptive, *somewhat* intimidating"— he grinned at that thought because really, he was who he was, and added—"older, definitely wiser, and intentionally kinder Xavier Wright."

"And stop beating yourself up over the past," Chase insisted. "Nothing to be gained by it."

"That's the truth," Xavier agreed. Then he took a breath— resolved.

Until he came flying down the steps after grabbing his wallet from his bedroom and skidded to a halt because—once again— McKenna Blakely was waltzing in the front door like she was part of the family. He figured one way or another he'd better start being okay with that.

"Whoa," he said, catching himself on the handrail so he wouldn't collide into her. "Hey."

She smiled that all-American, girl-next-door smile at him and said, "Hey, yourself."

"How are you?"

She blinked twice. "How am I?" she asked cautiously.

"Not a trick question, McKenna."

"Oh. Is this small talk? Because we don't have to do that. I'm here to see your momma."

"I know," he said, trying to tamp down his irritation. "And I don't think I've taken the time to express how much I appreciate you being part of my ma's—well, both my parents' lives."

"I like them," she said simply.

"And they like you. And they definitely don't want me scaring you away. So, please, feel free to come and go without fear of me making you uncomfortable."

"I don't understand."

"I'd like you to visit Ma whenever you're able. I don't want you not showing up here because you're worried about running into me."

"So you're really going to play nice?"

Xavier snapped up to his full height. "After we did that thing at The Situation, why wouldn't I play nice?"

She shrugged. "It's not your nature."

Instead of getting down in the mud with her, he took a breath and let it out, adding on a smile at the end. "Yoga, McKenna. I told you. Works wonders. Now, I'll get out of your way, so you and Ma can visit. Thank you for coming by. Sincerely," he said as he stepped around her, going through the open door.

"What's going on?" Suspicion clouded her voice.

He turned his head, realizing in that moment *exactly* what was going on. "Not one of my brothers has come home since I've arrived. Not to see me, not to see my mother or my father. I mean they all showed up at Duke last weekend because shit was hitting the fan, but so did you. You're pissed at me, and yet you come. You come for both of them." He changed his stance, turning his body toward his ex, honoring her with his full attention. "I'm sorry I mucked up your life back in high school."

"How did you muck up my—"

He didn't let her finish. "McKenna. I want you to be happy. You deserve it."

"Well, so do you," she said lightly, breezily, as if she was uncomfortable with the conversation and just wanted it to end.

Fine. He'd use his super intuitive power of perception and end it. "Have a great day." He turned and pulled the door shut behind him.

CHAPTER TWENTY

"*What* is going on with you and Xavier?"

That voice.

Those words.

The combination of the two struck dread in the center of Laidey's heart.

She turned from her desk to find McKenna standing there with her mouth hanging open as she tossed a thumb at the door behind her. "I've just come from visiting his mother, because I've been out of town, and I missed Monday with her. She tells me that Xavier brought you over to meet her last night." She sat down in the vacant chair beside Laidey's desk, looking curious and expectant. Maybe even ... hopeful?

Laidey fell back in her chair with an exasperated sigh. "Where have you been? I've been desperate to talk to you."

"I was out of town. On an assignment for the paper. Which was totally cool, because I don't pull those jobs usually. And I ... well, I had the chance to catch up with some old friends." The last bit was blurted out and followed by an abrupt silence. The kind of silence where something wanted to be said. Longed to be said. But whatever it was, it was obvious McKenna couldn't bring herself to say it.

When they both started to speak at the same time, McKenna overpowered Laidey. "It would benefit me if something were going on between you and Xavier."

"Benefit you?"

"Yes. It would. I mean, even though I warned you off him, and he's certainly nothing like our Harry, it would be a huge help—no an actual relief—if you'd go out with him. Just once or twice. Just to get him off my back."

Laidey blinked. "Off your back? Is he pressuring you to get back together or something?" Laidey hadn't taken a breath since McKenna walked in and it was starting to pinch.

"Oh, God no." McKenna shook her head like that was the most ridiculous idea in the world. "But he's *trying* to be nice to me. He's overcompensating, and it's making me feel guilty."

"Making you feel guilty?"

"Yes." She sighed. She looked around, making sure they were alone before she lowered her voice. "Look, I'm going to tell you something I haven't told anyone. It's actually a confession."

"A confession?"

"Yes. I need to confess something. You know, 'fess up. Get something off my chest."

Laidey held up her hand. She pulled in a long, deep breath and expelled it slowly before saying, "Okay. What is it?"

McKenna didn't bother with a breath. She was all full steam ahead when she confessed, "Right after Xavier left town for college, I cheated on him."

"What!"

"I know," McKenna groaned, sinking her face into her hands. "I'm an awful person. Truly awful. And yet, it was amazing."

Laidey sat back in her chair, crossed her arms over her chest, and wondered *what the hell?*

"Look," she eventually said, struggling to come to terms with McKenna and Xavier's convoluted past. "No judgement. I mean, it was over a dozen years ago, and you two were kids, right? And you never heard from him after he left so … where was the harm, really? But I did see you rake him over the coals two weeks ago with a lot of holier-than-thou shenanigans. You made it sound like you were the one *he* cheated on."

"Yeah. I did that. Because when I saw him, I was completely discombobulated."

"You were what?"

"You know, confused. Messed up. Reeling at the sight of his face suddenly back in town. And yes, I played the scorned-woman card loud and long, but to be honest, all that huffing and puffing was really the guilt bubbling up inside me over what I'd done."

"What did you do?"

"Gave someone else my virginity."

"No."

"Yeah."

"Who?"

"His"—she balked—"his … best friend."

"His *best* friend?"

"Pretty much. Yeah."

"And Xavier doesn't know."

"No, and I don't want him to know. *Ever.* So him being nice to me has got to stop. He wasn't *nice* to me when we dated. Him doing it now will just get on my last nerve."

"And by that, you mean, make you feel even more guilt-ridden."

"I need you to go out with him," McKenna pleaded

"How will that have any bearing on him being nice to you?"

"I'll be able to act as if I'm taking the high road. I'll be all, 'Sure, go out with my friend, Laidey.' And then if his *best friend* ever makes an appearance in town, Xavier will have to reciprocate by pretending not to care I'm hanging around him."

"Him who?"

"Him who, what?"

"Who is Xavier's best friend?"

McKenna's head shook vehemently. "I'm not saying. Not right now."

Laidey sat back, suddenly realizing what this was all about. "You saw him didn't you? This Him Who," she accused. "While you were out of town."

"I did," McKenna squealed.

Her friend looked so happy, Laidey couldn't help but feel her joy. "You're being silly," she laughed. "Xavier isn't going to care. You'll be letting him off his own guilt track."

"He'll care. Believe me, he's gonna care. That's why I need leverage. I need his focus way off me and on to someone else."

"And you think I'm that someone else?"

"He introduced you to his mother."

"Yes, but with the way things ended last night, I doubt he's interested in speaking to me. You may be on your own with this."

"His mother is certain he's interested in you. She really likes you, by the way."

Laidey pretended she wasn't remotely curious. "The poor woman was worn out when I got there, and we didn't have a chance to exchange more than two words before Xavier pushed me toward the piano and demanded I play."

McKenna fell back, forlorn. "He's so overbearing. He's always had to be in charge of everything. That's what's going to keep you from going out with him, isn't it?" She sighed.

Laidey laughed. Oh, McKenna really didn't know her at all.

"McKenna," she whispered, leaning in close to confide in her. "That Friday night when Harry and I found the two of you in the parking lot, and you were furious, and Xavier was feeding off your fury and making it out like it was nothing? And then he barked at Harry, demanding to know who he was?"

"You saw him at his worst. Just give him a chance. He's doing yoga now."

"I'm not interested in yoga. But I was drawn to Xavier. That night. When he was bossing Harry, and you, and even me around. I mean, I was a little startled, I'll admit. But there's something about tall, boisterous men that turns me on."

"Turns you on?" McKenna eyes were wide with disbelief. "That kind of behavior just makes me roll my eyes."

"Because your nature is to butt up against all that gale-force wind. But mine is to let myself go with it and enjoy the ride."

McKenna sat back, contemplating her words. "So? Harry's not your guy?"

"No. Harry's not my guy."

"But Xavier could be?"

"Xavier could be," she nodded. "In my dreams. Because I'm here to work," she said, standing and showing McKenna to the door. "Not to role-play with Xavier. Not to date a man to ease your conscience. I'm here to work. And my boss, Mr. Carraway, who is also big—like a mountain big—and boisterous, but in the most charming of ways, is coming to town today. And I need to be ready. So … get out."

"Oh," McKenna grinned. "Look who's bossy now. So, Xavier and his domineering personality sort of does it for you?"

It was obvious McKenna was having a hard time believing it. "That and a sixty-hour workweek will get me a very large paycheck."

"I need to meet this Mr. Carraway," McKenna said.

Laidey nodded, "You do. You really do."

"Shouldn't you be eating lunch at home?"

Too much McKenna wasn't good for Xavier's mood, and twice in one day was definitely too much. He didn't bother to look in her direction as he responded. "Why should I be eating at home?"

"Because your momma's there," McKenna said.

"The woman has lunch visitors every day of the week. I figured that out when I did go home for lunch—regularly—and I was just in their way. So now, I come to the club for lunch, with my buddy Chase. Chase Alexander, meet the thorn in my side."

Chase, who sat beyond Xavier at the bar, took the time to wipe his hands on his napkin before extending an arm in front of Xavier. "McKenna?"

McKenna pressed an ear to her shoulder and smiled sweetly at Xavier. "Aww. You still talk about me to your friends. Hi." She took up Chase's hand. "You must be the handsome man from Phoenix Anna Beth couldn't stop talking about it."

"Anna Beth. Since when do you call my mother Anna Beth?" Xavier scolded.

"Since forever," McKenna said, climbing up on the bar stool next to Xavier. "Harry, I'll have what they're having."

"A burger and a beer, coming right up."

"Exactly, except make it a Cobb salad and an iced tea. Unsweetened."

Xavier gave her a side glance as he sipped his beer. "Pain in the ass."

"Takes one to know one. Harry," McKenna called as he typed in her order, "What's the next theme party Missy McReady is whipping up?"

"Champagne and Shackles." Harry poured an iced tea and set it in front of her. "The weekend after the Fourth. You got a date?"

"I won't be in town. I'll, ah, be doing a little more research for this feature article I'm working on."

"Shame you're gonna miss it."

"Are you working the party?"

"I am not. Missy wants to try a catering service from Oxford. It's been requested I attend the party as a guest."

"That's great. Will you be taking Laidey? As your date?"

Fuck.

Harry's gaze shot to Xavier as if he'd said that aloud. "That depends."

"Oh?" McKenna asked. "On what?"

"Mr. Wright? You got any plans for that weekend?"

Xavier looked between Harry and McKenna then shook his head, bringing on the Zen. "First I've heard of this nunchakus in shambles party."

"Champagne and Shackles," McKenna corrected with an eye roll.

Xavier squinted. "What does that even mean?"

"When you arrive, you and your date are given two bottles of champagne and a pair of handcuffs. You have to stay handcuffed—to each other—until you each finish a bottle."

Xavier chuckled. "Who thought this disaster up?"

"Matt Collins," McKenna said. "He's awesome. Went to Tulane. Brought it to Raleigh. Missy caught wind of it and has put it in the summer lineup."

"Summer lineup?"

"Summer party lineup," Harry explained. "A way of getting people to Henderson for the weekend. It also ensures there is something to recap in the Monday edition of HH."

"HH?"

"Henderson Happenings."

Xavier took out his phone and scrolled to the folder. "Is this what you're talking about?" He held his phone up to Harry.

Harry leaned in and took a look. "Yeah. That's it."

"My brother forwarded it to me when he found out I was moving home. Say, whatever happened to that book? That"—he slid a look toward McKenna, cupping his cheek so she couldn't see him mouth—"365 Sexual Positions book?"

"Ah," Harry pulled back, understanding. "Picked up by the owner."

"They give you proof?"

"Rattled off the earmarked pages so fast it made me blush."

"You happen to take a good look at that book before you gave it back?"

"Wouldn't you?"

Xavier nodded. "We'll talk later."

"Well, by all I live and breathe," the lilting Spanish accent of Vance's grandmother had all three heads turning. "Right here in Henderson." Her smile was directed at Chase. "A cover model for Men's Health magazine."

Xavier and Chase came to their feet. "At your service," Chase said smoothly. "And I recognize you from your Glamour and Vogue covers."

Xavier's eyes went wide.

"Oh, I like you," Em tittered, offering her hand to Chase. She didn't bother to take her eyes off the man when she asked Xavier, "Is this your brother?"

After clearing his throat, because *What the hell?* Xavier said, "Em, allow me to introduce my good friend and mentor, Chase Alexander. I've had him shipped in from Phoenix, Arizona to help with Piper's shop." He turned to his friend. "Chase, this is Emelina Flores. Originally from Spain, she's been a long-time resident of Henderson and is obviously"—he let out a breath—"an incorregible flirt."

Em batted her eyes at Chase. "He says that like it's a bad thing."

Chase's eyes twinkled in delight. "I beg you to join us."

"No begging necessary."

While Chase helped Em onto the barstool on his other side, Xavier and McKenna exchanged amused looks. They both looked to

Harry, who winked as he opened a bottle of wine. "Mr. Alexander," Harry said. "Can I offer you a glass of Ms. Flores's favorite varietal from her home country?"

Chase nodded. "Please."

In the dozen years Xavier had known Chase, he'd never seen him with a glass of wine or a woman. So he was frankly dumfounded by this sudden turn of events.

"Do you enjoy champagne as well?" he heard Chase ask Em.

"I simply adore it," she said, taking a glass of wine from Harry.

"I understand there's a party in a couple weeks. Perhaps you'd like to be my date?"

Xavier turned his head with a snort. "You know that party is for kids, right? Foolhardy, lust-crazed twenty-somethings."

Chase turned his head and spoke directly to Harry. "Seeing as this one"—he threw a thumb in Xavier's direction—"doesn't think being shackled to a beautiful woman sounds like fun, it appears you've got a clear shot at Miss Bartholomew."

Xavier shot his mentor a chilly stare before firing off a *just-try-it* glare at Harry.

Harry smirked, reaching underneath the bar and pulling out a large square bottle. He poured a shot and pushed it toward Xavier. "Kind of a ritual around here when someone finally figures out it's time to go after the right woman."

Is that what he'd just done? Decide to go after Tweets? Because wasn't she the one who got away—like—last night?

He turned his head, catching McKenna looking at him. "This going to be a problem for you?"

"Me?" She seemed startled. "Not at all."

Xavier downed the shot and felt the heat of it relax him. Yeah. He was going after Tweets.

God help her.

"Okay then," he said, slapping his hands on the counter and turning toward Chase. "While you and Mrs. Flores get acquainted, I'm going to run an errand." He looked at his watch. "Shall we meet at—"

"Taking the rest of the day off," Chase said. "Don't wait up."

Xavier chuckled and slapped the keys to his truck on the bar. "Make sure the lady gets home safely," he said, getting off his stool. "Harry, thanks for the kick in the ass. McKenna, you enjoy that burger and beer."

CHAPTER TWENTY-ONE

Xavier walked home, not really sure what just happened. Chase and Em? Vance was probably going to try to kick his ass for that.

The only thing he knew for sure was that the twist in his gut meant he wasn't going to be able to tolerate little Laidey Bartholomew handcuffed to Harry or anyone else. So he picked up his bike and two helmets and headed to Main Street, where he knew the miniature-sized workaholic was bound to have chained herself to her desk.

The good thing about Tweets? He'd always know where to find her.

At three o'clock in the afternoon, he wasn't sure what he'd be walking into at Duncan James, Attorney at Law so he came in quietly, ducking his head as he did, finding quite the picture standing atop of three short steps. Laidey had her back to him, appearing to sort and pile papers across the barren desk in front of her.

"Tweets," he whispered in appreciation of how sweet she looked in pink. For a big, bossy, construction worker, he sure had a thing for soft petals and tiny blooms. She wore his favorite dress, her dark curls piled on top of her head stuck through with floral pencils. The exposed skin of her neck looked so creamy and tempting his brain rerouted, conjuring up vivid images of what his rough, tanned hands would look like stroking over the pale flesh of her torso. Those thoughts sent a tingling directly to his nuts.

She turned, her cherry lips open in surprise before his name slipped through them on a breath. "Xavier."

Acting like his own cartoon character, he gulped.

He took another moment to gather himself, saying the first thing that came to mind. "Chase and I finished the man cave."

Her lashes fluttered. "You and who finished the what?"

Shit. "Didn't I mention Chase or what I've been doing?" The tips of his fingers vigorously scratched through the stubble on his cheek while his brain strived to sort itself out. Yet he didn't miss how Tweets's anxiety was surfacing *again.* The pretty flush of her skin, her fidgety fingers, the blinking of her eyes—it was all there.

Well, hell. Shackling her to him for a good four hours ought to help that along. Help her get past whatever fear she had when it came to him. He was bolstered by remembering their day on the boat and how she'd managed to settle herself. And then his mind drifted to their kiss and his nuts stirred again. He started up the steps toward her. Slowly.

"Tweets, as cute as I find all these little tells of yours, it's time we work out a way to get you over them."

"Get me over what, exactly?"

"Your nervous idiosyncrasies. Probably be helpful for the two of us to attend the Ramshackle and Nunchucks party together.

"Ramshackle and Nunchucks?" She bit that juicy bottom lip of hers, trying not to grin. "I think you mean Champagne and Shackles. I read about it in Henderson Happenings—which I finally signed up for. Sounds entertaining," she said, turning around and going back to stacking papers as he approached. "But I won't be needing a date."

"Right. Because you've already got one. Me."

"You? You who threw me out of the car last night?" she said over her shoulder.

"I threw you out of the car last night because you're a chickenshit, and you wouldn't let me feed you."

"Well …" she stumbled, turning away from him. "You're not the boss of me."

"I am the boss of you," he whispered as he leaned into her ear, bracing both hands against the desk, caging her in. "Don't you remember? You're my uppity secretary."

"Xavier," she sighed, pushing back against his chest and moving herself out of his proximity. She flounced around the desk and sat like a prissy schoolgirl. "I'm not interested in being shackled to someone who considers me nothing more than a *distraction*," she insisted. But then she cast a flirty eye his way. "Even if I kinda liked playing your uppity secretary."

Figuring he needed to man up and give her at least a little of what his heart kept shouting at him, Xavier came around and sat on the corner of the desk. "Look, Laidey," he started, only to have his words trail off as her attention was seized by something behind him. Something over his shoulder.

He tuned in to her face, assessing her expression as her gaze latched on to whoever just came in the door. Watched as she swallowed and rose slowly from her chair. Watched as she licked her lips. Noticed the pretty blush—*his blush*—creeping up her cheeks and how her fingers began to flutter. He noticed that her eyelashes fluttered as well. Watched as she greeted whoever was behind him with a trembling smile.

"Laidey," a booming voice called from behind him.

"Mr. Carraway." Her greeting came out breathy and—*holy fuck*—captivated. Xavier whipped around to find a broad chunk of Texas dwarfing Duncan James's foyer. Then he looked back at Laidey who stood stock-still, hadn't shifted her stance at all, her big, expressive eyes coveting the man behind him.

No fucking way.

He snapped his head back to the intruder in time to see him take the steps two at a time and offer up his hand. "Crain Carraway. I don't believe I've had the privilege."

"Xavier Wright," he responded quietly, standing slowly to shake the man's hand as new knowledge downloaded into his brain. "So *you're* CC Henderson."

"Guilty as charged."

"I've sat in your chair," he said, pointing at Carraway.

Laidey sucked in a breath.

"Glad it's being put to good use." Crain patted Xavier on the shoulder. "I hear you're pretty good with a set of blueprints. Might even consider being our quality control officer for the sports academy."

"I'm considering it," Xavier said, finding his full voice as he assessed the guy's height, weight, and other assets before looking back at Laidey.

"And you've hitched your wagon to my top associate, I see." Crain tossed his chin in Laidey's direction.

"On her off hours."

"Mr. Carraway, it's good to see you," Laidey interrupted. "Mr. Wright was just leaving."

"No, I wasn't."

Both Laidey and Crain regarded Xavier with stunned silence.

He shrugged. "I wasn't."

"Not a problem," Crain told them both. "I just wandered down the path to say hello to my favorite Laidey." Then he addressed the schoolgirl in pink specifically. "Elizabeth and I will be in town for two weeks nailing down details for the sports academy. We'll have plenty of time to catch up and have dinner." He turned and offered Xavier his hand again. "Nice to meetcha."

Xavier took it. "Thanks. You too. I've heard a lot about the legend of CC Dallas."

"Aww, shucks," Crain feigned humility. "No legend at all. Everything you've heard is true. Laidey," he said before taking his leave. "I'll see you at the meeting."

Xavier watched as Laidey nodded and blinked and stammered, apparently much too enthralled by this CC whatever to be able to form words.

What the hell?

He became even more incredulous as he continued to study her as she watched Carraway leave. Because he'd seen her in this exact state. Many times.

He turned his head to watch the last of Carraway before he swung his gaze back to Laidey, curious. "You scared of your boss?"

"What?" she stammered, finally taking her gaze from the wake Carraway had left. "Of course, I'm not scared of my boss."

Xavier slowly started to make his way around the desk. He squinted, taking in every detail of her face. "You sure about that?"

Laidey took a step back, the chair rolling out from behind her. "I've worked with the man for years. He's kind and happy and pays me more than I deserve. Why in the world would you think I'm scared of him?"

"Because when he came in, you got all flustered."

"I did not," she claimed, standing up straighter but continuing to step back as Xavier stalked her.

"You did. You got fidgety and nervous, and your eyes did that thing they do."

"What thing?" she stammered, bumping her back against the wall.

Xavier's hand came up and gently cupped the side of her face. "That thing," he whispered. "The same thing you do with me."

Her gaze dropped to the floor as he stepped further into her personal space, his mind being blown as the truth emerged. "I've been reading you all wrong, haven't I? You're not afraid of Carraway. You're smitten. In fact, he turns you on."

"Don't be ridiculous."

"Which means"—his gaze trailed from the pencils in her hair to the laces in her Keds—"*I* turn you on."

"What?" she scoffed. *Feigned* a scoff. He wasn't being fooled any longer.

"Yep." Xavier took a step back, letting his hand fall from her face. He pivoted, looking back at the front door. "All this time, I thought the blushing, the fidgeting, the running yourself into bushes meant you were *afraid* of me." He turned back in wonder. "And it's not that at all, is it?"

"Xavier, I've told you. I'm not afraid of you. And I'm certainly not afraid of Mr. Carraway."

"Because you are *into* Carraway," he accused. "I mean"—he straightened—"that's just a fact. One that should have been obvious to me when you busted my chops about sitting in his chair. I've never boasted about being the quickest guy in the room, but man for all my"—he air-quoted—"intuitive skills, I did *not* see this coming. You're hot for me." He pointed to his own chest, not meaning to smirk, but come on, she totally deserved it. "Here I am, working my ass off to get you to go out with me and drink a little champagne, and you *want* to go."

Laidey sighed. A big, over-the-top, dramatic, *fake* sigh. So when she tried to open those tantalizing lips of hers, he said, "Uh-uh. Don't bother denying it. I *know* you, Tweets. I mean, I've gotten to know you pretty well over the last couple of weeks, but those last remaining pieces of your puzzle? Well, they just fell into place."

"Xavier."

"Shh. Baby. It's okay. You're into Carraway, I get it."

She shook her head vehemently. "You don't get it."

"Oh, yeah. I do. Now, I really do." Xavier felt a little giddy. Was fairly sure his smile was a bit manic. "You're in love with your boss."

"He's married," she protested.

"Yep. So you can't have him."

"I don't want him."

"After the way you were looking at him, I'm pretty sure you do."

"Well, you're an idiot."

"I was. All this time frettin' over you being afraid of me. I was reading it all wrong. Wasn't I?"

"I need to get to work."

"Sure. Sure you do." He started backing toward the door. His hands pointing back and forth between them. "So, you, me, handcuffs, and champagne. It's a date."

"It's not a date."

He stopped. His arms dropping in exasperation. "Really? We're still doing this?"

"Doing what?"

"Pretending you aren't hot for me."

"What?" she sputtered with a half-laugh, half-cry.

Xavier came forward, placing his hands on the desk between them. He leaned over it, leveraging his chest close to hers, his voice low and serious. "I don't care that you're mad for Carraway. He's married. What I do care plenty about is that since we've met, you've been looking at me the same way I saw you look at him." His eyes narrowed. "You were never *scared* of me, were you? All this time, you were *attracted* to me. Probably from the get-go."

"You're crazy."

"I'm right," he exclaimed. "As sure as I know my last name, I am *Mr. Wright* about this."

She chuckled and then caught herself.

"It's okay. You don't have to admit it. Hell, you're probably embarrassed as all get out from being caught red-handed."

"Red-handed?"

"You all mean-faced, telling me you don't want to date me, and then having your secret sprung like that."

"Sprung?"

"Darlin'. You're hot for me. You don't have to admit it. Doesn't matter if you do. Just know that I'm okay with it. You are welcome to roll all that unrequited lust you've got stored up for Carraway right onto me."

"Now you're just embarrassing yourself."

He stood tall and leveled her with an appraising look. "I don't think so." He started shifting around the desk, slowly. Stalking Laidey and her sassy pink frock. When she tried to make a run for it, he grabbed her wrist and pulled her in close. Then he slowly brought her hand to his mouth and kissed the pounding pulse point at its base. "Thinking back on our kiss," he said in a husky whisper. "Things got decidedly steamy pretty darn quick. You gonna tell me I don't have that right?"

She gulped, her eyes telling him she remembered it just like he did.

"I'm sorry I didn't show up for dinner that night. Wasting a week trying to put you out of my mind was stupid and futile. And it was completely based on fear over my ma's health. Had nothing at all to do with what I feel for you." He tucked his other arm around her waist and drew her up against him. "You hear what I'm saying?"

She blinked. Then nodded.

He looked over his shoulder at the front door. "That thing have an interior lock?"

She licked her lips.

"Lock it," he whispered. "Now."

Xavier held his breath as he tossed all of his proverbial cards on the table. Would she or wouldn't she? That was the question. And oh, boy, he wanted to know the answer.

He didn't let his gaze falter. Just stood his ground, expecting—no—*willing* her to do as he requested. And man, he had to give it to her, because she stood there with her chin raised in defiance.

Tiny, little spitfire was going to make him beg.

"Tweets," he coaxed. "Lock the damn door."

He remained still, even as she moved past him, because a very large part of him believed she was going to walk down the steps and right out the door. And fuck, he didn't want to see it if she did. But he heard the latch shift and turned to find her leaning against the door, biting her lip.

He was pretty certain that now—right at this moment—she actually was scared of him.

"Laidey," he whispered, taking a slow step in her direction. "I promise you one thing," he said as he sauntered down the steps. "I am going to do my damnedest to steal your heart from that boss of yours."

As he moved in, all of those priceless symptoms returned. The fluttering of her lashes, the breathtaking hue of her cheeks, and the trembling of those perfect lips, though he noticed that for the first time she managed to keep her eyes locked with his.

She had no clue of the power she possessed, just as he was astounded by the discovery of the influence he had over her. His little Tweety Bird was fragile. In stature. In confidence. In whatever was going on between them. But so was he. And she had to trust him on some level to have followed his … *suggestion* to lock the door.

"He ever kiss you?" he asked, curious to know.

"Crain?" She shook her head.

His gaze drifted to her hair and those damn floral pencils that kneed him in the balls the day he joined Team Henderson. He gently reached up and tugged one loose and then the other, pocketing them both as her dark curls fell. He pushed his fingers through it, dragging her curls back from her face, cupping her head as he leaned down. Down. Way down.

Damn, she's short.

His free arm snaked around her waist, lifting her up against him while he spun the two of them around. He placed her feet on the second step, giving her a much-needed boost and Xavier's neck a far better angle to do what he'd intended.

"Tweets," he promised. "This is going to be good."

His lips touched down then, his big wide mouth to her plush and supple one. He tamped down the need to plunder, because her lips were softer than he remembered—what with all the sharp wit they liked to spout. And they were gentle, so he was gentle—at first. At first, he just wanted to put his lips against hers and remind himself what all the fuss was about.

After all, everybody had lips. But, he thought as he touched the tip of his tongue to the seam between hers, his didn't *need* anybody else's. Hadn't been particularly interested in anybody else's. So what *was* it between their lips?

Well, his tongue at the moment.

She opened on a sweet breath, and he took full advantage. Loving that he was getting a second taste of this woman. Because this one? Man, this one he just wanted to devour.

There was a rattle at the door behind him. He heard a muffled, "What the—?" come from the other side as Duncan must be rooting for his keys. He opened his eyes as he stopped kissing Laidey, looking down into her pretty features. When her eyes met his, he grinned like he'd just won a prize. Her smile was sweet and bashful.

And then Duncan busted through the door.

An "eek" went up as Laidey fell backwards over the last step, her Laidey-like dress landing way above her knees. Xavier scrambled to pull the dress down at the same time he tried to help her up, causing him to stumble and bang his knee into the edge of the second step. His momentum propelled his body forward, but he managed to break the fall with his palms at either side of Laidey's head, stopping him from squishing her to death.

"What the—? Get the hell off her," he heard Duncan shout.

Xavier felt his shoulder being pulled back as he maneuvered himself backward, off Laidey, off the steps. "It's okay. She fell. I fell. We're okay."

"Why was the door locked?" Duncan growled.

"I was making a confession. Didn't want anyone to overhear," Xavier lied as he offered his hand to help Tweets up.

"Do I look like I was born yesterday?" Duncan pestered.

Xavier turned a scowl toward the intruder, making a show of looking him up and down. "Frankly, yes," he snapped.

"What the hell does that mean?"

"It means"—Xavier bumped his chest up against Duncan's—"I can kick your ass from here to Oxford."

Duncan thrust his own chest back against Xavier. "And you're gonna have to do it too if you've laid a hand on Laidey."

"Okay." Xavier stood down, contritely putting his hands in the air. "I'm glad you've got her back. I really am. That right there"—he shuffled his hands in front of Duncan's chest—"is the old me. Ya know. The kick-someone's-ass me. Sorry."

Duncan threw him a look before shoving at him to get to Laidey. "You okay?" He helped her up. "Tell me what happened here."

"Duncan," Laidey said, wiping at her dress, "you know very well I'm a bit of a klutz. I fell, and then he fell, and then you walked in and assumed the worst."

"Did I? Or was *this guy*"—Duncan stuck his thumb out at Xavier—"taking advantage of you."

Laidey's eyes lifted, capturing Xavier's. The edges of her lips tipped into a pretty, pretty smile. "Yes and no," she said without diverting her eyes.

Xavier lowered his gaze to the floor, grinning.

"Yes and no?" Duncan questioned.

"He was taking advantage of information he's recently unearthed."

"As in?"

Laidey pulled her gaze off Xavier and directed it toward Duncan. "He figured out I'm, ah, smitten with my boss."

"Oh. Well, that's not news."

Laidey's mouth dropped open in horror. "What do you mean, that's *not* news?"

"Everyone who's ever seen you around Carraway knows you're gaga about your boss."

Tweety Bird went red. Hard candy red. Like his Road King. And she must have felt it too, because her hands went straight to her cheeks.

"Now look what you've done." Xavier pulled Duncan out of the way. "You made the poor girl blush." Blush, hell. She was about to die of embarrassment. "Tweets," he whispered as he went to her, taking her hand and intentionally blocking Duncan from her sight. "He's just teasing you. Aren't you, asshole?" he growled over his shoulder.

"Yeah. Sorry," Duncan claimed. "It's not how I made it sound. In fact, it's only Annabelle. I," he stammered, "you know, never would have guessed. But Annabelle is intuitive like that."

"See, Tweets. Just Annabelle. And me. Because I'm intuitive like that too." He grinned. Couldn't help it. Because she wasn't afraid of him. She liked big, bossy men, and now he knew it. Good thing he was big and pretty damn bossy. "And," he went on, "your boss, the one who pays you in actual dollars, has no clue. Whatsoever."

She looked at him, hoping against hope he was right. "You don't think so?"

"No. The man is clueless, which ya know, makes me wonder a little bit about his capabilities."

Laidey frowned. "So you're saying my crush was so obvious he should have known?"

"I'm saying," Xavier said, quieting his voice, "I don't understand how Tansy turned his head when you were standing right in front of him."

She tilted her head as if to say, "Aww," her brown eyes softening. "That's really sweet," she gave him before her eyes hardened. "And total baloney. Get out. I need to lick my wounds. I don't believe a word either you or Duncan said. And"—she held up a hand to stop his protest—"I have work to do."

He stepped back, his grin replaced by a scowl. He started shoving his finger in her direction as he laid down the law. "Tweets. I'm picking your ass up at six. Not a minute later. You will play the piano for my mother, you will let me feed you, and then we're getting down to the serious business of shaking you loose from whatever hold Carraway has on you."

He turned and left her there, forcing himself not to kick Duncan's ass on his way out the door.

CHAPTER TWENTY-TWO

"Ma," Xavier called as he ushered Laidey inside. "Tweets is back."

"Please don't call me that in front of your mother."

Xavier blew it off. "It's fine. She knows."

"She knows what?"

"That you're hot for me."

Laidey sputtered in exasperation, watching him make his way into his parents' living room. *This has got to stop,* Laidey thought as she followed him.

A tall man with a full head of gray hair was escorting Xavier's mother from the hallway. The difference between the robust man and Xavier's mother was astounding.

"Dad, I didn't know you'd still be here."

Xavier's father winked at the two of them as he settled Anna Beth into the corner of the sofa. "I wanted to meet this Tweets your mother keeps talking about," he commented quietly. Laidey felt her cheeks heat. Then came a tug on her limbs as Xavier pulled her around in front of him, his large hands landing on her shoulders anchoring her there.

"Dad, this is Ad-el-aide Bar-tho-lo-mew." She noticed he always said her full name like that. Definitive and sing-songy. "She's from Dallas and works for CC Henderson. Been in Henderson a few months now. She's a bit of a workaholic, but she plays the piano like it's her superpower. I'm hoping listening to her play will help heal Ma."

"Happy to know you, Ad-el-aide." He threw a quick grin toward Xavier as he repeated his take on her name perfectly. "It appears you've made quite the impression around here." There was a kind twinkle in his eye. "Mind if I listen in?"

Laidey absolutely did mind, although she never would have said so. In fact, right now she was wishing her superpower was more along the lines of invisibility. Because playing for Xavier's ill mother was one thing. This situation screamed *recital.* For Xavier's *parents.* Holy stage fright, Batman.

Her discomfort must have translated itself up into Xavier's palms, because he immediately said to his father, "Sure thing. While you two get comfortable, I'm going to show Laidey to the powder room and be right back."

It was sweet the way he took one of her hands in both of his, backing his way out of the living room, his eyes on her the whole time.

"Thank you," she breathed as he led her into the ornate bath. "I wasn't prepared …"

He leaned back against the cabinetry, pulling her to stand between his long legs. "I know you weren't, and I'm sorry about that. If I had any idea he'd be sticking around, I would have tried to head it off. It sounds like my mother is as smitten with you as you are with Carraway."

Her mouth hung open, her brain searching for a retort.

His index finger gently lifted her slack jaw while he said, "Yeah. And after we shake the nosy duo in there, we're gonna fix that." He kissed her then. Soft, sweet, deliberate. "Got it?" he whispered over her lips.

He was so firm, in both physique and demeanor, she wanted to give into temptation and allow herself to melt into him. Body and soul. Just let him handle all the parts of life she didn't want to be bothered with. She wouldn't have believed she could fall so easily for a bossy, old bully, but Lord, he really did it for her on so many levels. She dug deep for the strength to stay on her own two feet and nod.

"Now, I'm going let you collect yourself. Take all the time you need, Tweets, but when you come out, come out swinging," he warned. "My father's skipping happy hour at the club for this," he said through a teasing grin that was nothing but sexy.

"Go," she ordered, coming back into her senses. "That is not helping."

"No?" he teased. "Maybe this, then." He reached an arm out toward the door, quietly closing the two of them inside. He pulled her around as he sat on the lid of the toilet. She watched his rugged hands fuss with the skirt of her dress. "You in this pink thing, all lacy and sweet, sort of slays me," he whispered. Her heart ignited when his gaze moved slowly up her body until he'd captured her eyes. "Since that day on the sidewalk with Marnie, it's been my favorite. Come here." His hands cupped her ass before sliding down to the backs of her thighs.

"What are you doing?" she whispered frantically as he pulled her up and settled her on his lap.

"Giving you something to really worry about." He pulled her hips firmly against his and rocked his pelvis.

"Oh," she whispered. The slow brush of his cock sliding intimately between her legs shot heatwaves throughout her body, short-circuiting her brain and making her delirious. He felt exactly how she expected. Strong. Firm. Big. She felt herself go pliant in his arms, not caring a bit about the self-satisfied smile on his lips.

"Playing the piano for my parents doesn't seem like such a big deal now, does it?" he whispered, moving against her, watching her face.

"Stop looking at me," she insisted on a sigh, closing her eyes to relish the sensations he was igniting.

"Not a chance, Tweety Bird. It's the only way I can be sure about what's going on in that head of yours."

"Nothing," she panted. "Nothing is going on in my head." She braced a hand on his chest, ceasing their movement. "Not even a piano score. We need to stop. Now."

"In a minute." He wrapped his arms around her and placed his open mouth on the ticklish spot between her shoulder and neck.

"Xavier." Her arms wrapped around his shoulders as she teetered on the brink of forgetting where they were. She relished the feel of his body pressed hard against hers. The sensation of his wicked smile on her neck. The whole of it felt surreal because she'd given up her dream of Xavier Wright. *Twice.* On the verge of drifting off into oblivion, she heard him whisper in her ear. "We'll get rid of my parents, I'll fatten you up with lasagna, and then the two of us will work on a duet."

"Hmm," she sighed, struggling to come out of her daze. "Okay," she said, remembering where she was. "A duet. Whatever you want. Let's just get …"

"The recital over with. I know."

"I hate that word," she confessed as she stood, smoothing her hands down her dress.

"Me too."

After introducing her to the most erotic part of his anatomy in the bathroom, Laidey was a bit surprised that the *duet* Xavier had in mind was one of the musical variety. True to his word, they were back at the piano after dinner, him playing a raucous ragtime tune, daring her to jump in anywhere and complement it. Since his fingers were bouncing all over the keyboard in a cheerfully brisk tempo, she wasn't exactly sure how to jump in, until—without missing a beat— his left arm circled behind her and his fingers began playing at an octave lower. Encompassed inside the circle of his arms, Laidey now had easy access to the keys surrounding middle C.

She also fell into an out-of-body experience.

Since her *Crain-ful* crush, Laidey had become a master at the art of daydreaming. Eighty percent of the thoughts she'd been having about Xavier Wright over the last two weeks fell into the category of delicious and decadent. So with Xavier's arm around her now, she wasn't entirely able to comprehend what was happening. It wasn't until she started playing, harmonizing with his lead, that she came into herself and then … let herself go.

She played with an abandon she'd only experienced when no one else could hear. Because she felt happy sitting hip to hip on the piano stool with Xavier, secure in the circle of his arms. And mostly because at this moment, life seemed amazing, far more intoxicating than any daydream she'd been able to conjure. With their intention focused and in sync, with their hands working in opposition but on the same wavelength, the music just happened. And it was vibrant, and strong, and certain of itself, far more so than Laidey could have ever created on her own.

Deep in her soul, satisfaction rooted. Fresh joy blossomed. Love expanded and enveloped the man at her side.

He understood her. Really *got* her. And even better than that? He *saw* her.

Never once had he allowed her to be invisible. From that first night when he called her out—told her not to be afraid of him—he'd been aware of her presence.

Of course, he'd read her all wrong, mistaking awe for fear. But he'd figured that out today, hadn't he? And if this was the result of her secret crush being revealed, well, she'd own it. Sink into it. Relish it.

For the better part of an hour, the two of them spoke through the notes of the music. Ragtime turned into pop. Pop turned into classical. Classical turned into ballads that stirred her emotions until a single tear fell, landing with a splat on the F key as they brought their musical interlude to a soft and poignant end.

They sat inside the silence. Breathing. Experiencing. Vibrating. Then, as if all the passion they'd released through the music descended back upon them twofold, Xavier took her face in his hands and laid his mouth to hers in a kiss so sincere and enraptured the rest of the world fell away.

It was the intentional clearing of a masculine throat that had them breaking apart. Xavier's parents, arms around each other at the other end of the room, smiled brightly at the two.

"We heartily approve," Mr. Wright said with a nod before pulling his wife with him down the hall.

"Always good to have your approval," Xavier called after them, playing a riff to accompany his sarcasm before throwing down some ominous cords.

"Tweets," he said, pulling her from the bench, "let's go upstairs."

"What's upstairs?"

"Privacy."

"Like a recreation room?"

"Like my bedroom."

She balked a quarter of the way up the stairs. "We're not going to your bedroom."

That cute-boy grin became ridiculously sexy as he came back down a step. "Do not try to tell me you aren't interested in seeing my bedroom. I'm on to you, remember? Hot for Carraway, hot for me. Carraway is married, and oh—lucky for you," he held up his left hand, pointing to his ring finger, "I'm not."

"Exactly. We aren't married," she whispered adamantly. "And your parents just caught us tongue wrestling. I'm not compounding the embarrassment by following you upstairs."

"Did you not just hear them give us their stamp of approval?"

"Which didn't sound at all like *Please feel free to have sex under our roof.*"

"Sex?" he shouted. "Who said anything about sex?" he bellowed so loudly anyone within the far reaches of the house could hear. "I just want to show you my vintage Matchbox collection."

"Wha—?" she stammered.

"Oh, no, you don't." Xavier caught her around her middle as she spun with the intention of flying down the steps and sprinting out the door. "You are not running away from me or what's about to happen again."

"What's about to hap-*pen*?" she shrieked as he tossed her over his shoulder.

"I'm carrying your tiny ass to my room, tossing it on my bed, and introducing you to each and every car in my collection. You're gonna hear all about each piece, and you're gonna pretend to be fascinated." He was halfway up the stairs.

"I won't have to pretend," she croaked out. "I like miniatures of any sort."

"Makes perfect sense, since you're a miniature person and all." He leaned forward and dumped her onto his bed. She landed on her back and shimmied up to her elbows to watch Xavier pull the skirt of her dress down, protecting her modesty. "Second time I've had to do that today," he commented. "You look great in pink, by the way. Have I told you that?" He didn't wait for a response. "Okay." He rubbed his hands together with prideful excitement. "Stellar collection coming right up."

It wasn't until the third diecast vehicle sat in the palm of her hand that she realized Xavier had indeed brought her up here to see his Matchbox collection. Or, if that hadn't been his original intention, he was faking it damn well. The door to his room stayed open, and he had a full story on each car. "And this one is exactly like Vance's father's orange 'Vette," he said as he replaced the 1970 Dodge Charger with the Corvette. "Vance has offered me a fortune for it over the years, but my grandfather gave me this one, so I can't part with it."

"Did your grandfather start your interest in collecting them?"

"Sort of. Whenever we'd visit, he'd have a new Matchbox for each of us. My bros and I. We'd trade them right then, and if there was more than one I liked, I'd offer money or to do one of their chores. If they weren't interested, I'd find a way to, ah, add it to my collection eventually." He motioned to the large strong box he'd opened with a key. "Thus the security, and um, the deniability."

"Deniability?" She asked taking the 1977 Armored Jeep from his hand and placing the 'Vette back in the box.

"The cars my granddad gave me were lined up on my book shelf, along with the ones I bought myself. The ones I didn't want anybody to know I had went in here. I kept the box locked and under my bed."

"Are you telling me you stole your brothers' Matchbox cars?"

"Only if they wouldn't make me a deal." He didn't look the least bit remorseful.

"Xavier."

He sat down next to her, thumbing through the goods in his metal box. "I haven't been lying about my vintage asshole status. This is probably one of many reasons my brothers have not rushed to Henderson to welcome me home."

"Were you really that bad?" she asked, moving to her knees behind him. She felt compelled to wrap her arms around his shoulders and lean in to kiss his cheek. "I just can't see you being that much of a jerk."

He shrugged, his hands coming up to stroke her arms. "I wanted what I wanted."

"So did you want to create an impressive Matchbox collection, or did you simply want to one-up your brothers by having something they didn't or couldn't?"

Xavier's head twisted sharply, looking at her over his shoulder. He unwrapped her arms from his neck and pulled her around onto his lap. "You cannot know me this well after only two weeks."

"One week. Last week you were in denial that I existed."

"Yep. My bad. I didn't figure on Tweety Bird having talons long enough to sink into my heart. But ..."

This was said so casually it took Laidey a moment to register what he might be saying. "But? But what?"

"You *know* what," he said, smoothing a hand over his stubble and mouth while looking her right in the eye. "How many women do you think I've shown my Matchbox collection to? You're in trouble, Tweets. Big trouble."

She laughed. "Trouble?"

"Vintage-asshole trouble."

She drifted a hand over his cheek, giving into the urge to feel the soft stubble along his chin. "You've assured me on several occasions you have *reformed*."

"I have, and I am. Even so, if you plan to hang around, whatever my prior misdeeds reap might rub off on you."

"I'm a little sturdier than I look," she said, granting him a soft smile.

That brought out his wicked-cute grin. "Good to know." He kissed her. Quick-like. And then started scooting both of them off the bed. "Ready to go?"

She stood, a little taken aback. "So you really did bring me up here to show me your Matchbox collection?"

"Pfft. Tweets. My parents are right downstairs."

She chuckled. "I just assumed from all your bravado you didn't care."

"Seriously, it's going to be way more fun sneaking you up here when they have no idea."

"What?"

"Yeah. Like after our date Friday night. We'll climb in the window the same way I used to climb out."

"We have a date Friday night?"

"Yeah. It's the one that comes after our date Thursday night."

"Thursday night?"

"Which follows tonight's and Wednesday's dates."

"That's a lot of dates."

"Making up for last week. Come on." He took her by the hand.

"Why are there two double beds in here?" she asked, following him from the room.

"One's mine, one's my brother's."

"How many brothers do you have?"

"Four."

"Four?" Laidey asked in dismay.

"Too many?" he joked as they started down the stairs.

"Your mother's given birth to *five* boys like you?"

"Yeah. But I'm the worst," he boasted. "The rest of them aren't nearly as good looking or as scary."

CHAPTER TWENTY-THREE

Xavier had lost count of the lies falling out of his mouth.

He hadn't wanted to hustle Laidey up to his room so he could show her his Matchbox collection and confess his childhood sins. He didn't give a goddamn whether his parents gave a thought to what they might be doing up there. And he definitely wasn't making up for lost time by harnessing all of her nights this week and into next.

No, he'd been role-playing. Fell into it the moment those big, Tweety-Bird eyes went into high alert as soon as she'd figured out his plan.

Hell, yeah, he wanted her in his room. Was aching to grind up against that scrumptious, little delicacy. After their piano interlude, his dick was hard and throbbing for Tweets. But one look into those panicked brown eyes, all sweet and innocent in her pink baby-doll dress, he knew he and his inner bully needed to simmer down.

Not for good. Hell, no. But, yeah, at least for the moment.

Of course, the heat stroking his balls roared to a boil when her dress all but flew over her head as he'd dumped her onto her back. Her lying *in his bed* with those creamy thighs whispering come-ons to his raging stiffy? Tweets and those dark curls of hers had been nothing but a come-fuck-me mess all jumbled up in his comforter. He was never going to get that image out of his head.

Thank God, the toy collection provided something to talk about, giving him a chance to drag his brain out of the gutter and off the peek he'd snagged of her basic pink undies.

Basic pink. Like that wasn't going to turn him on.

Then she'd knelt behind him, pressing her breasts against his back, engulfing him with the sweet smell of her perfume and the soft skin of her arms around his neck. The girl had truly taken him at his word, believing he was now a *reformed* asshole because otherwise she never would have gotten close to him. Not with the dirty thoughts blowing up his mind.

And then she slayed him with her *one-upmanship* question.

Talk about intuitive. Little Laidey Bartholomew from Dallas saw right through him, down to the truth of his scary, dark soul. And yet, she didn't run away screaming.

So he wasn't kidding about sneaking her through his bedroom window Friday night. That future scenario was written in stone. All he needed was the couple of nights in between to give his PYT in pink a little romance.

That, and keep her away from her goddamn boss.

Fucking idiot. Tansy over Tweets? As if. He snorted aloud as he squeezed Laidey's hand, walking her down the steps and back toward his parents' room.

He knocked and then stuck his head in, finding his parents in their respective reading positions. "We're heading out. Tweets is in love with her boss, and since he's in town this week, she wants to get her beauty rest."

His parents laughed like he was making a joke as he closed the door. Tweets blushed and stammered as he pulled her away. "Wha— why did you tell them that?"

"Is it true? Are you in love with Carraway?" he asked as nonchalantly as he could muster, returning them to the living room.

"No, it's not true. Of course, it's not true."

"But you think he's hot?"

"Xavier. I had a little crush on my boss. It's not a big deal."

"Seems like a big deal to me. How long has this *little crush* been going on?" He swung her around to face him as they reached the piano, suddenly very interested in her answer. Although *fuck*, those eyes of hers told him everything. "Come on," he said, pulling her toward the door. "I'm gonna need the full story."

Xavier drove them toward the lake, listening to the lively recount of Laidey being hired by the illustrious Dallas sports star and the type of work she'd done for the man over the years. Instead of just parking by the docks, he coaxed Tweets out of his truck and onto his father's boat, motoring them well off shore before he cut the engine. No need to bother with an anchor, it was dark and the lake was quiet, a perfect place to catch a breeze on a hot June night. A perfect place to get to the bottom of this irritating conflict of interests. Mainly his interest in her and her interest in *him*.

Finding the candle his mother kept stored in the hatch, he set it on the table, lighting it to add to the glow of the running lights. He led Laidey by the hand to the bank of seats spread across the stern of the boat. He actually heard her cheeky grin as she asked, "What exactly is going on here?"

Hell. Was this peanut teasing him? Her grin was blatant under twinkling Tweety eyes.

"Oh, Tweets," he warned, pulling her to him as he sat, grasping both her hips, and tussling her onto his lap. She let out a squeal of delight as she settled in front of him, her legs straddling his thighs.

"I do love that you're rough-and-tumble strong," she told him, her hands gripping his shoulders.

"I didn't realize how much I like pink," he said, wrapping his arms around her hips, tugging her lower body in close. "Or crayons."

"Crayons?"

"Keds. Bikes. Baby-doll dresses. You know, all of your juvenile penchants."

"I really do like crayons," she admitted. "Probably because my job is nothing but black-and-white print. I'm either reading it or creating it. The thing *I* didn't realize is just how attracted I am to overgrown bad boys."

"I wasn't *bad*. More like obnoxious."

"I've heard you made people eat goldfish."

"Goldfish are as edible as any other freshwater fish. They're a delicacy. Like sushi."

"Sushi?" she laughed. "Is there anything you can't spin in your direction?"

He hoped not.

"I like you, Tweets. And as happy as I am to have figured out you aren't afraid of me, but rather out-of-your-mind *hot* for me, this information is a double-edged sword."

"Out-of-my-mind *hot* for you?"

"No need to deny it. Just want to get to the bottom of why you're looking at your boss the same way."

Laidey's curls swung as she shook her head vehemently. "Strictly a work relationship."

"He never tried to offer you fringe benefits?"

She leaned in, pressing her breasts against his chest. "Only my pseudo-boss has offered me fringe benefits."

"Which you really should consider taking him up on," he said, loving the feel of her body against his. "Seeing as you're so hot for him and all."

"Mmm. I'll admit to being lukewarm."

"I'm going to stick with lust-crazed and completely hot for me. It's going to work out better in this scenario."

"What scenario?"

"You. Me. A boat float in the dark."

"Hmm. It is dark."

"Seriously. How bad do you have it for this CC Whatever?"

He felt her body deflate just a little and didn't like how that boded for him. "I'm not ... I don't have it *bad* for him." Laidey placed her fingers on his lips preventing him from arguing. "The truth is, at one time I sheltered a hope that since we worked well together in the office, something might develop socially."

"Like he didn't know that was a sexual harassment suit waiting to happen. Come on, Tweets, the guy is freaking old."

"He's three years older than you," she argued.

"Well, you're a baby. Those additional three years form a gigantic divide that should never be breached. Especially by someone in a position of authority."

"Says the boss to his uppity secretary." She laughed. "It didn't matter anyway. As soon as he laid eyes on Elizabeth Tansy Langford, my hopes were dashed. He might not have asked her out right away, but I saw how he looked at her. I swear there was drool falling from his lips whenever she was in the office. I knew I wasn't going to measure up to tall, blond, and you know ..."

"What?" Xavier prompted.

"Tall, blond, and ... voluptuous."

"You mean big tits?"

"Yeah, those," she snorted as if she couldn't believe he'd say the word aloud.

"No, Tweets. If the man was looking for long legs and breasts big enough to fill his all-star basketball hands, you were not going to fill the bill. Of course, now he's stuck with a snarky former beauty queen when he could have had a sweet, young workaholic with pretty brown eyes capable of running his ever-expanding empire. The man's a fucking idiot."

"Thank you," Laidey said, leaning in to peck his lips. "That's very, very sweet of you to say."

"It's the damn truth." His hands massaged her hips, starting to feel their way up her back, liking how soft she was, soft and cuddlesome. "I can't imagine him overlooking this bit of feistiness I have sitting in my lap. You're like a featherweight boxer. Small, but packing a powerful punch. I think I started to fall for you the minute you wrote up that, "Our stupid shit stops here" contract. Such a contrast to that fluffy dress thing you've got going on."

"You were so annoying that day."

"Not even close."

"What?"

"You were totally into me. Probably loved it when I came and sat next to you."

"I promise you, I did not love it."

"I think you did."

"Because you're smug," she laughed.

"Look who I've got sitting on my lap."

She shrugged that off like it meant nothing. "It's a good, sturdy lap."

"Is that why you're so hot for me, uh?" he teased, rocking his pelvis into her backside. "Because of my big, sturdy *lap?*"

"Wha–?" she stammered. But then she gathered her wits and said in a haughty tone, "Clearly, I like large men."

"Carraway and I might be the same height give or take, but he's got that middle-aged belly thing going on, and Tweets," he said, smacking his own abs, "I do not."

Laidey chuckled. "He's super huge where you're sufficiently huge. I don't know what it is about big"—she cut herself off and corrected—"*tall* men. In fact, I'm not sure height is actually the attraction for me. I mean, it's kinda silly, you and I."

"I don't know. This seems to be working pretty well." His hands continued to roam, finally having the time and space to get a feel of her.

"Truthfully what *drew* me to Crain is not what—ya know— made me *hot* for you," she mimicked him. "He's kind and decent, and really, really likable. And you're …" she trailed off.

"I'm what?"

"Not."

"Not?"

"Well, come on, Xavier, you're not kind or decent or all that likable."

"Bullshit," he laughed, not believing what he was hearing.

"You're bossy and demanding, and you get things done by sheer force of will, not letting anyone or anything stand in your way. Case in point, you making me your secretary on Vance's project."

"That was fly-by-the-seat-of-my-pants, pure genius. I liked what you shared about Henderson. About what you thought would and wouldn't work. I wanted you at that meeting with me. Didn't think you'd go if I just asked."

"Because I wouldn't have."

"See how perceptive I am? So come on, Tweets, 'fess up. If it's not my size, what is it about me that gets you going?"

She sat there in his lap, staring at his face so long he said, "Don't make me kiss it out of you."

Her brows rose. "I like the way you kiss."

"Yeah? Good to know. But once I start, I'm not likely to want to stop, so give it to me straight. Why me? If not because I'm as tall as your boss and therefore an easy substitute?"

"Like anything about you is easy," she teased.

"I know, right?" he admitted with a grin. "I'm not easy. I'm trying to be. I was, in Arizona after a time, but coming home to Henderson, I'm just the same ol' me."

Tweets tilted her head, her big eyes sparkling with mirth. "But see, I like the you you're trying so hard not to be," she admitted. "I like how you are with your mother, how you're sweet to her, want to do everything you can for her. You're like that with me, only you give me a lot of lip," she teased. "I liked how you tried to tease McKenna into not being mad that you came home. I definitely liked how you stood up to Harry. And I even liked how you called me out on being nervous around you all the time. Whether you're talking business or boating with your buddies, what I see in you is a man who just can't help but shine."

Well.

Hell.

He did not see that coming.

Instead of being able to respond with a traditionally flippant, ego-centered comeback, Xavier's heart broke open. Everything he'd been worrying about spilled into his chest overwhelming him with emotion.

God's honest truth, he wanted to cry over the lousy chance his ma had of surviving. He wanted to wail over the damage he'd done to his relationships with his brothers by staying away so long. He felt like he could weep because this silly, brilliant, way-too-good-for-him girl thought he had the ability and courage to shine.

Instead of relinquishing his manhood, he pulled the one good thing he had going for him in close and kissed her lips. Thank God the taste of her short-circuited his emotional breakdown. He was pretty sure if Tweets was attracted to a badass, blubbering over his family drama wasn't going to be a big turn on. So he allowed this island he'd found in the storm to fill his senses and push his fucking worries out to sea.

Her scent reminded him of the floral bush he'd pulled her from a few weeks ago, but her skin prompted the memories of luxurious Italian sheets in a Lake Como five-star resort. Her lips were sensual, full, a treasure he indulged in by sucking and biting. The feel of her tongue against his performed the miracle of stuffing his heart full of joy and ease. He *loved* her tongue, the taste of her mouth, the smell of her neck, and the sounds of her appreciation.

Oh, the *sounds* of her appreciation.

Tweets wasn't one to hide her emotions or her thoughts, and bully for him that she didn't try to do so while his hands and mouth were on her. He hungered for more of those signs—ones that came in the form of whimpers and sighs. He wanted to get lost in those.

So the fact that he pulled back and made the strangest of suggestions—"Let's have a double date with Carraway and Tansy. Tomorrow night"—shocked even him.

"Wha—What?" she stammered, totally love drunk from their make-out session.

Good. Damn good. Still, he needed to be sure of her affection before he was the one struck love drunk and left to wallow in it alone.

"Dinner. Tomorrow night at the club. I'll set it up. I just want ..."

"You just want what?"

"To know ..."

"Yes?"

"That you're moving on from him."

She leaned forward to reengage, kissing him on his cheek, on his chin, on his upper lip, and at the edge of his mouth. She quietly assured him, "He's married."

"Doesn't mean you don't have feelings for him," he whispered.

"I have feelings for you," she whispered back, applying more of her mind-bending kisses.

Finally, he grasped both of her shoulders and pushed her back far enough she couldn't get her mouth on him. *What the fuck am I doing?* he wondered, but that didn't stop him from making this a thing. "For me. Just do this for me. I need to see you and him, and you and me, together."

Exasperated, she said, "Xavier Wright, you can't possibly be worried about me and my boss. That's ridiculous."

"No. *He's* ridiculous. Choosing Tansy over you makes no sense. I can't wrap my head around it. So humor me. I want to make sure you're over him."

"And on to you?" She smiled, sneaking back in, wrapping her arms around his neck, definitely doing some shining of her own.

"Exactly," he said, giving her lips a nip. "Over him and on to me," he whispered, reengaging because it felt too damn good not to.

Her kisses weren't tentative, they were no-shit serious. Xavier relished the contrast between the cool night air and the hot, little number in his arms. Things were heating up good when he whispered, "Really wanna get you out of your dress."

"Hmm," she whispered back. "I've kinda been wondering what's underneath this shirt." Her hands hadn't been shy about feeling him up. Now her fingers skimmed underneath the hem of his T.

He reached both arms behind his head, pulling the cloth barrier off and tossing it to the floor of the boat. But when his fingers went to the line of buttons down the front of her dress, she shook her head in the negative.

The disappointment he felt was acute.

"Just pull it over my head."

"Yeah?" He grinned as his libido hit reboot.

"Yeah," she whispered. "That's how I always put it on and take it off."

His eyes skimmed down the front of her, not believing they'd actually gotten to this point. "Tweets," he said in awe, his hands skimming her sides all the way down to the hem of her dress bunched up around her thighs. He decided *this* was worth taking some time to accomplish. No need to rush the moment he first got Adelaide Bartholomew out of one of her fluffy dresses. He heard her giggle and looked from the hem back to her eyes. "What?"

"Just you," she told him, happiness all over her face. "I didn't count on you being ... sweet."

"Hell. You're like a tiny, little bird, Tweets. I don't want to crush you or rush you. I wanna take my time with you. Pet you." His eyes danced at the thought of that, causing her to laugh again.

"Okay. So, tonight we ... pet."

He heard exactly what she was saying and wasn't going to push. At least, not right then. "Still want to sneak you into my bedroom Friday night," he told her.

"Kinda counting on it." She smiled.

He smiled back. "So you're game for whatever this is between us? Willing to out us to your boss over dinner tomorrow night?"

She nodded. "Badass and all."

He burst out laughing. "Tweets. I am not your walk on the wild side."

"You sorta are."

He probably was, knowing her and all her fluffy dresses. "I think I want to be more than that," he whispered.

Her expression went soft.

Then she clasped a hand over her heart.

"Xavier Wright," she whispered. "You aren't a bad boy at all, are you?"

"Been trying to tell you that, Tweets. Although I'm definitely willing to role-play if that's what you need." His eyes stayed latched on to hers as he began to pull the hem of her dress up.

She met him stare for stare, raising her arms over her head, a visual he was never going to forget.

Fuck. Me.

Her bra and underwear weren't frilly, but they were skimpy as all get out and the sweetest fucking shade of pink he'd ever seen. Of course, they were. Ad-el-aide Bar-tho-lo-mew, his mind sang. Gonna be the fucking death of me.

The two of them sat there, studying each other with open admiration.

"So you really are a construction worker," she said.

"What?" His mind was elsewhere. Way elsewhere.

"Architects who sit behind desks don't have bodies like yours."

"Tweets, you saw me without a shirt on the boat a couple weekends ago."

"And you saw me in a bikini. Not really the same thing, is it?"

"No," he agreed. "It's definitely not."

"So I guess you're right."

"About what?"

"I *am* hot for you."

He grinned. "Really want to lay you down right now," he whispered, moving her from his lap to the bench seat. He followed her down, leaning over her as she relaxed onto her back.

As much as he wanted to take his time and revel in this moment with Tweets, his drive to touch her could not be beaten back. He slipped her bra straps down from her shoulders, loosening the cups hiding her breasts from his view. His eyes longed for better lighting, but his mouth didn't require any light at all when it nudged her bra cup aside and swallowed her whole.

Almost a mouthful.

Certainly enough for him to enjoy.

He manipulated his tongue around her flesh, mapping out the peaks and valleys. His hand plied her other breast a little more aggressively than he'd intended. He hadn't thought much about it, but it'd been quite a while since he'd gotten his rocks off without playing solitaire. Hadn't even noticed until his body reminded him how good the skin-on-skin thing felt. He tuned in to her hand clasping the back of his head, the other one running fingers through his hair. He heard her whisper something. It sounded sexy, so he stopped what he was doing and lifted his head.

"Tweets?"

"That stubble of yours. It tickles."

"Oh." He pulled up. "Sorry."

"No. No," she insisted. "I like it. I thought it would be scratchy, but it's soft. I like it. I definitely like it."

He smiled, going back in to give her more of what she liked.

Fuck. His head popped up. "Shaving it off for the Fourth of July. But I'll grow it back afterwards."

"Why?" she complained.

"Ma wants it off for the family picture."

"Oooh," she said, sliding the palms of her hands along his jaw, feeling his beard. "But it's so badass."

Shit. He totally dug this chick.

"I'll grow it back. Promise. You want a badass, you get a badass, Tweets. Pretty much anything you want at this point." Her eyes lit up so big and bright Xavier thought it was probably his greatest achievement. "Now, can I get back to making you whimper?"

"I don't whimper," she protested.

"Oh, Tweets. You fucking whimper. And you sigh. And when you do, it grabs me by the balls."

"Is that a good thing or a bad thing?"

"Good thing. Very good thing." He ducked his head to go back to doing what he'd been doing. "Whimper away."

"I'm not sure I like the idea of whimpering."

"Then moan," he said around a mouthful of boob.

"Like a porn star?"

His head bounced up. "No. Like you. Like, you know, *you.*"

"Like me?"

"Shh," he insisted. "Enough talk. Let's do."

"Now I'm feeling self-conscious," he heard her say as he went back to her breasts. Deciding he'd fix that, one arm snaked down her body as he rolled his hips to her side, giving him direct access to the area he figured would either shut her up or give him what he wanted. Her lust-laden Tweety Bird sounds.

With *this,* he took his time, petting her just like she'd suggested. At first, his fingers enjoyed the feel of whatever soft, girly material she had on down there. Then he started paying attention to what lay underneath by using his fingertips to gently tickle her hot zone. She might not be moaning, but she was starting to shift and move. Her breathing was becoming labored.

He felt evidence of her desire, wanting so bad to slip his fingers inside but determined to make her crazy first. See how turned on he could get her by teasing her like this. The scent of her sex compelled him to slip down her body, his lips teasing her belly button before he replaced his fingers with his nose. He slid over the cotton, relishing her heady aroma, wallowing in the proof that her body responded to his.

His mouth ate at her though the fabric, giving her time to prepare for where this was heading. He looked up at her face as he slipped a hand into her panties, his fingers drifting over her sex, slowly stroking up and down, tickling the spot that caused her hips to lift every time he touched it.

Coaxing Laidey along this sensual path was like unearthing a powder keg buried beneath a formal garden. The blooms, although colorful, were grouped together and minding their manners. No one would suspect—hell, he hadn't suspected—that underneath her colorful accoutrements, lay a short fuse aching to be lit. Her penchant for color had camouflaged this sensuous side, leading him to translate her reaction to him as fear.

Because from what was going on beneath him right now, the only thing she might be afraid of was him not taking care of business. Tweets wanted badass, Tweets was going to get badass.

Xavier kissed the sexy-sweet skin revealed as his hand slipped down into her pink lingerie. His middle finger slid into the heat of her body as he moved his mouth lower and tasted his girl for the first time.

Like hell, she didn't whimper.

He had to remind himself that this was strictly a petting session, so he proceeded to pet her with his tongue, his lips, and the scruff on his jaw. A lick here, a kiss there eventually turned into an unadulterated, full-on feast.

She came hard.

Then came again.

Then begged him to stop, where he promptly told her, "Badasses don't stop until they feel like it," and kept on making Tweety Bird sing.

Fuck, he loved that sound.

His dick was painfully hard. He'd been jacking himself against the seat through his jeans while he took care of Tweets. Pain never felt so good. However, he didn't have a condom and didn't feel badass enough to rub one out in front of her. Of course, she might not notice since he'd reduced her to the state of a rag doll, and her hands now covered her eyes.

Lifting his gaze to make sure she wasn't watching, he unzipped his pants and shoved his hand inside, grasping his cock and giving it a rough tug. He wanted nothing more than to unleash himself and rub his raw length up and down the hot, slick crevice of Laidey's body. Fuck, he really did. Was desperate for it.

"Laidey," he gasped.

"Yessss."

"No. Just gonna …" He pushed those sweet pinks of hers back into place and laid himself down on top of her, kissing her lips as he moved against her one time.

That's when she sort of did moan like a porn star, which he would have totally given her shit about if he wasn't so caught up in the mind-bending sensations below his waist. He braced his forearms at the side of her head, lifting his chest off hers, giving himself leverage to move as he pleased.

"You've got one sexy, little body, Tweets," he told her. "Got me losing my mind," he panted. "Crazy hot. Can't imagine what it's going to feel like when there's nothing between us," he whispered, his face all squinched up with his eyes closed. He fought off the orgasm as long as he could—"Don't think it can get much better"—until he fell into it. Groaning into the pain. *Baby.* Into the pleasure. *"Laidey."* Falling into the brink.

Yep.

He did it.

He made a fucking mess all over pretty, little Tweets and her slender, little belly. As soon as he could move, he reached for his T-shirt, cleaned her up, and then cleaned himself up, laughing with her as he did.

Pants still undone but now all tucked in, he tossed the shirt overboard and pulled Laidey into his lap as he sat. Fuck, she was a mess. No longer pink and innocent, she was hot as fuck and sexier than sin. A goddamn wet dream of a mess. He might not be able to go at her at the moment, but give him five minutes and he'd have her flat on her back. Again. "More than you bargained for, I'm sure," he said, pushing hair from her face and kissing her lips.

"I didn't expect anything less from a bad-boy bully."

"You getting off on my former reputation?"

"No. I got off on your fingers, and your mouth, and—" He cut her off with a bruising kiss.

"Kinda lovin' this naughty side of you, Tweets. But right now, I don't need more motivation to want to drag you underneath me and take this to the next level."

"Mmm," she said against his lips. "Such restraint."

"You pushing my buttons?" he growled.

"Hmm, I've become very fond of the way you push mine."

"That a fact?"

She matched his buoyant grin with one of her own. "It is."

CHAPTER TWENTY-FOUR

"What the fuck?"

"What? What's wrong?" Laidey stood bewildered in the middle of the family room, wondering what in the world could have put such a scowl on Xavier's face. His incredulous expression was directed at her, not Poppy, who'd let him in the door. It also overshadowed the delicious dress shirt, the had-to-be-new sports jacket, and the crazy-hot sunglasses he sported.

"What the fuck do you have on?" he growled.

Laidey looked down at the black, clingy, one-shouldered dress Poppy had lent her for tonight's dinner date with the Carraways. "What do you mean?"

"Tweets. That is not your usual fluff. In fact, there's no fluff there at all. It's just, you know, your body—like—right there. Screaming at me. Curves and all." His menacing gaze traveled down to the strappy three-inch heels she'd also borrowed. "And where the fuck are your Keds?"

"Why does the word fuck keep falling out of your mouth? We're going on a date," she insisted. "I didn't bring any date clothes from Dallas, so I borrowed some from Poppy."

"We've been on plenty of dates, and you've never dressed like this."

"Never dressed like what?"

"Flat-out sexy."

Laidey shook her head in disbelief. "That doesn't sound like a compliment."

"Should it? You *trying* to look sexy?"

"Kinda," she admitted. "Definitely wasn't going for this reaction though. I wanted to dress up because—you big bully—we haven't been on *plenty* of dates. This is actually our very *first* date."

Xavier's body jolted, his gaze shifting from her torso to her face. "This is our first date?"

She nodded.

"Fuck. I mean, excuse me," he said to Poppy, who stood at his side, witnessing the entire scene. "My language. I know. Forgive me." He looked back at Laidey. "It's just that I feel like we've been on a dozen dates. And that dress is great," he addressed Poppy again. "Really great. I mean, man." He turned his attention back to Laidey. "Darlin', you look smokin' hot in that tiny thing, and those legs of yours look awesome in heels. I like the added height on you, I really do. But I was expecting, you know, Keds and those dresses you summoned from the 1950s."

Laidey's mouth dropped open, and Poppy covered a snort. The two women looked at each other, Laidey in shock, Poppy close to hysterics. "I told you," Poppy said. She looked at Xavier. "Totally a throwback to the fifties. Though she's able to pull it off."

"Yeah, she does," he insisted. "I mean, at first I thought she was in grade school, dressing like that. But now I'm used to it. Hell, I like it. Not that I don't like this," he said, eyeing his date. "I just don't like the motivation behind the change."

Laidey blinked. "Motivation?"

Xavier put his hands on his hips and threw a chin lift in her direction. "You put that on for Carraway or me?"

"What?"

"It's a legitimate question. Did you get yourself all sexed up for Carraway, or for me?"

"I'm not *sexed up*."

"Does she look sexed up to you?" Xavier asked Poppy, both of them studying Laidey from head to toe.

"She does look hot," Poppy admitted.

"She borrow all that makeup from you too?" he asked.

"The makeup is her own."

"I like the shoes," he told Poppy.

"Thanks. What about the dress?"

"On any other night, I'd think the dress was fucking awesome. In fact, if it were any other night, that damn dress would bring me to my knees. But since we're having dinner with the man she's been lusting over for years, I'm not convinced I'm the one she's trying to impress."

"You've been lusting after Mr. Carraway for years?" Poppy wondered.

If Laidey could have shot fire through her eyes, Xavier would be in cinders.

"Shit," he said. "I didn't realize it was a secret from your housemate."

Laidey took a deep breath and calmly turned her attention to Poppy. "Xavier is under the impression that because I am *fond* of my boss, that because I think he is one of the kindest, most generous, and innovative men I know, that I am *smitten* with him."

Poppy shrugged. "Yeah, then we're all smitten with him," she assured Xavier. "But Laidey's totally into you," she went on assuring him. "She said—"

"Poppy," Laidey shouted. "Thanks for your help. I'll take it from here."

Poppy broke into a self-deprecating grin, realizing she'd been about to divulge state secrets. "Yes. I'm sorry. You two have a good time."

"You sure?" Xavier teased Poppy. "I wouldn't mind knowing what she said."

"Later," Poppy winked, moving toward the kitchen.

After a moment of quiet, Laidey bobbed her head toward Xavier. "What's with the sunglasses?"

"What's with the dress?" he countered.

"I wore the dress for you. Wanted to look sophisticated since you've finally gotten around to taking me to dinner."

He nodded. "Sunglasses are badass. I wanted to be the biggest badass sitting at our table."

"You're not wearing those at dinner."

"Might," he said. "Not sure what I'm walking into."

"This was your crazy idea. We don't have to do this. I can call him and say we're—"

"What do you mean, you can call him?"

Laidey blinked. "I work for the man, remember?"

"But you have his number? His personal number?"

"Of course."

"Why?"

She shrugged, teasing him with a haughty grin. "I'm a *key* employee."

"Yeah. About that. What's it going to take for you to come work with me once I get my business up and running?"

"You aren't serious."

"Of course, I'm serious. I'm just worried I won't be able to afford you with the profit restrictions Vance is placing on me."

"You can't afford me," she assured him. "But you don't have to. I like Piper's project. I'm happy to text you at all hours of the night with suggestions."

"It's the multi-unit project I'm thinking about. Your insight into Henderson and your spooky-good research skills would save me time and money if I could nail it right out of the gate."

She finally crossed the distance he'd kept between them, sneaking into his personal space, feeling very sly. "Why don't you just relax about me working for Crain? He can pay me to do my job, and in my off hours, I'll see what I can do for you."

"There's plenty you can do for me in your off hours. None of it has shit to do with building out Henderson."

She gave him a grin. "Still. I think we'll be able to work something out. No need to coax me into jumping ship."

"Hmm," he grunted. "Come on. Let's go meet the captain of that ship." Xavier held the door open as she grabbed a sweater and her little clutch from the couch.

"I think you're going to like Crain. Although I'm still open to calling and canceling. It's not like I'm all that excited to be having dinner with *your* ex."

"That's right." He grinned, following her out into the evening. "I forgot I swapped spit with Tansy."

"And felt her up," she reminded him.

"Carraway ever feel you up?"

That deserved nothing but an eye roll, which she gave him thoroughly.

"Just checking," he said, lifting her into the passenger seat of his truck, stealing a kiss just like he did after she became his uppity secretary. "Always good to know exactly what I'm up against."

Harry intercepted Xavier and Laidey as soon as they entered the Mixed Grill. He was dressed as a waiter, not in his usual bartender gear. "Harry?" Laidey wondered.

"The Carraways are already at the table. Right this way."

Her eyes darted over to Luke, who had been left by his lonesome. "Why aren't you behind the bar?" Her voice was full of suspicion as she and Xavier followed Harry into the dining room.

"Because the *Carraways* are waiting at your table," he said, eyeing her.

"Yes, but ..." Her question trailed off as Crain, seated at a small, round table on the far side of the room, stood and greeted them boisterously.

"Adelaide," he called as they approached. "And Xavier Wright," he said with a broad grin and open countenance. "We meet again." He shook Xavier's hand vigorously.

"Mr. Carraway," Laidey acknowledged, suddenly feeling very awkward and acutely aware that every move she made, and every word coming out of her mouth, was being scrutinized by Xavier. She also felt odd—as in, falling-back-into-her-old-self *odd*—seeing Tansy, or as Crain called her, Elizabeth. It occurred to her that she hadn't felt *odd* like this since Xavier crashed into her life.

"Call me Crain," he told her. "Now, in the office, forevermore. I've never really liked the formality."

"I'm not sure I'm comfortable—"

"Sure you are," Xavier prodded. "The two of you have been working together for how long?" he asked as he went around the table to kiss Tansy on the cheek. "Hello, Tans."

"Ah, she goes by *Elizabeth* now," Crain made a point to tell him.

"So I've heard," Xavier grumbled, shooting an eye at Laidey as Crain helped her into her chair.

"Adelaide and I have worked together for over four years," Crain said, answering Xavier's question.

"She goes by *Laidey* now," Xavier corrected.

The two men squared off with the table between them. Each one eyeing the other. Crain eventually nodded. "I understand."

Xavier nodded back.

Both *Elizabeth* and *Laidey's* brows were raised as they watched the interaction. Elizabeth was the one to speak up as the men took their seats. "We went ahead and ordered cocktails. Harry said he knew what the two of you needed."

Laidey looked around the table from Crain's Old Fashioned to Elizabeth-Tansy's wine. Her gaze landed on the decorative shot glasses in front of her and Xavier. It was all there on tiny silver platters—limes, salt—all the telltale makings of Harry's infamous tequila shots.

Elizabeth nodded toward the platters, wearing a grin. "Looks like things are getting serious between you two."

"Why do you say that?" Xavier asked, putting a hand on Laidey's thigh underneath the tablecloth and giving it a squeeze.

"The tequila. Harry doesn't serve it to just anybody."

"That right?" Xavier asked, picking up his and holding it out toward Laidey.

Laidey grabbed her own, remembering her vow to accept Harry's shot the next time it was offered. Considering the company she was keeping at the moment, her boss, his *wife*, and a reformed bully who brought his bullying out of retirement whenever she was around, she couldn't think of a situation that better required a quick dose of alcohol.

Like a pro, because she'd seen it done plenty of times, she licked the skin of her hand and salted the wet spot. Xavier stopped her at that point by clasping her wrist.

"May I?" he asked, his voice quiet and low. It took her a second to get it. In fact she didn't understand at all until he offered her the salt on his own hand.

Without waiting for her response, he leaned in and chewed on the skin between her thumb and forefinger, closing his eyes as if it were the most sensual thing he'd ever done. She followed suit, sucking on his skin, drawing the salty flavor onto her tongue, into her mouth. The two of them clinked glasses before downing the tequila. Then, as if rehearsed, they entwined their arms before sucking on their own lime wedges.

Laidey grinned like the smitten female she was. She didn't care that Xavier was making a show of pissing on his territory in front of Crain. The fact that he wanted to had her falling further under his spell.

He was so bad.

And yet, darned if it didn't make her feel good.

Crain cleared his throat. "So, obviously, you two are a pair."

Xavier nodded, taking the wedge of lime out of his mouth and setting it on the plate in front of him. "Unfortunately for her. I keep warning Tweets that my reputation is stuck at the level of reproach. As hard as I try to redeem myself, I can't seem to get out from under my stupid-high-schooler's shadow."

"Tell me about it," Tansy agreed.

"Darlin'," Crain addressed his wife. "As I understand it, your high school persona was squeaky clean. It wasn't until you made the poor decision to run out on our elopement that *your* reputation landed in the crapper. Still," Crain went on, clinking his own glass with his wife's, "I'd go through every bit of what this little filly put me through twice over, as long as I was guaranteed the same result."

It was the first time Laidey had felt happy for her employer when it came to his marital status. Seeing the affection he had for his bride, and seeing it returned, well, that was good enough for her. She reached over and gave Xavier's thigh a squeeze, shooting him a quick smile.

"Everything going well here?" Harry asked as he passed out menus.

"Exceptionally," Xavier told him.

And on it continued. The two couples had plenty to talk about, sharing their stories from growing up in Henderson versus Dallas. Even with Elizabeth's balls and beauty, Laidey was surprised they had much in common in the vulnerability department. It shocked her to discover how far Elizabeth used to bend to please the influential people in her life before she found a way to be true to herself. In Dallas. After leaving her hometown.

Laidey understood all that perfectly. Only for her, she had to leave Dallas and move to Henderson to be the person she was meant to be.

"So you like it here?" Crain asked.

"I do," she said honestly.

Crain glanced in Xavier's direction before he captured her eyes again. "You okay staying indefinitely?"

Laidey wasn't sure why she looked to Xavier. She loved her job here. Liked the autonomy of it. She enjoyed the small-town atmosphere, and she believed in what Team Henderson was doing. She liked being a part of the big picture. Besides, getting home to Dallas for visits wasn't difficult. So yes, whether she'd met Xavier or not, her answer would have been the same.

Still, she found herself looking over at him, curious if he had an opinion. The man didn't flinch. Just nodded like he was the one making the decision. Like if he wanted her here, then by God, she was staying. Case closed.

Although shocked to find her feminist instincts falling by the wayside, Laidey was less surprised with the speed Xavier and Crain bonded. After all, they were both captains of their own destiny. And they shared a common interest—seeing this town flourish. They both had history with each other's dates, which was touched on briefly as Elizabeth admitted to her husband that she'd been on one date with stupid-high-schooler Xavier and his overblown ego.

Harry had waited on them all evening, serving, clearing, fetching drinks, and refilling water. He'd winked at her when he brought out the entrees, seeming more relaxed and satisfied that everything was as it should be.

The night proceeded brilliantly, and Laidey realized to what extent when Xavier whispered into her ear while reseating her. "You are stealing the show," he said. She didn't know about that. What she did notice however, was that her Rowling-Bartholomew society upbringing was coming out naturally for perhaps the first time.

"Because I'm with you," she told him.

Simple.

Succinct.

And apparently, exactly what Xavier wanted to hear. His sexy grin shined while his gray eyes sparkled with mischief, like he wanted to eat her up. She was so turned on by all that he beamed in her direction, she actually pictured herself crawling up the side of his parents' home and into his bedroom window, tight, clingy dress and all. Xavier actually made Crain seem old and predictable. Maybe even staid. If her crush hadn't already transferred itself onto Tall, Scruffy, and Dastardly over here, it would have jumped at the chance tonight.

After the four of them shared an oversized dessert, they adjourned to the bar. She wondered at the sight they made. Laidey, towered over by three of nature's finest specimens. She wasn't sure how she'd managed her way into this group, until Xavier spelled it out by sharing her "Go eye-fuck yourself" story.

Apparently, that's when Xavier fell for her. Who knew?

"Who's that?" Xavier shook his drink toward the tawny-haired woman standing at the end of the bar.

By the look on Crain, Tansy, and Laidey's faces, Xavier knew exactly who it was. "That's Viper, huh? The one who outted the sports academy, tried to get the baseball team on steroids, and told the *Raleigh Times* Henderson had a sweatshop?"

"That's the one," Crain said. "Quite a piece of work."

Xavier shrugged. "Surprisingly attractive." He downed the rest of his whiskey, gave a brief nod to his companions, and headed straight for trouble.

"Clint," he said, shaking the mayor's hand. "Xavier Wright."

"Hello," Clint said merrily. "I heard a rumor you were back in town. How's your mother?"

"Thanks for asking. She seems to be holding her own this week. How's Henderson?" His eyes drifted from Clint to Viper.

"Good. Lots going on, as I'm sure you've been made aware."

"Indeed."

"Let me introduce you to my campaign manager, Marcy Watts," Clint offered when he noticed where Xavier's gaze stayed.

"No need," he commented. "I literally picked *Viper* out of the crowd."

Her saucy brow quirked. "Now that's interesting, Mr. Wright. Because I did the same for you."

"Doesn't surprise me in the least," he said. "I'm the old bully in this town, and you're the new one."

"Oh," she dipped her eyelids. "I wouldn't say that."

"It's the damn truth, isn't it? You like to get your licks in on our Golden Boy the same way I used to. Hell, we've probably got lots in common. Did you know he was the one who put the brakes on hazing newcomers?"

"Sounds like good ol' Brooks," she said.

"Doesn't it just?" Xavier's face scrunched with distaste. "Nearly ruined all my damn fun back in the day. Kinda like he's trying to do to ol' Clint here. Isn't that right?"

Clint held up his hands. "Hey, I'm happy for the competition. Brooks and I go way back. Nobody's done more for Henderson."

"So you're a fan?" Xavier asked, surprised. He turned back to Marcy. "Get a load of this one," he scoffed, tossing a thumb at Clint. "Too nice. Doesn't have that killer instinct."

Marcy grinned, sipping her drink. She looked over at Clint and shrugged. "When the man's right, he's right."

"Which is why it's a good thing he's got you, correct?" Xavier asked Viper. "Because you've got what it takes. You've got what Clint doesn't have. The drive. The desire. That fire deep down in your belly to not just defeat Brooks in this election, but to systematically rip the fabric of Henderson apart, bit by tiny bit."

"Not at all," she cooed. "I'm simply representing my client to the very best of my ability."

"By wedging a divide between the two men who've done nothing but live and breathe for this town? You just heard Clint tell you he's not angry about Brooks running for mayor. He's embracing the competition. But you, being an instigator and a bully like me, you've set out to destroy what Clint considers a friendly competition. By the time you're done, the two of them won't be speaking."

"The spoils of war, I'm afraid."

"You're not afraid. You're ecstatic at the thought. But you have no plans to stop there do you?"

"I've been hired to win a campaign. That's what I'm here for."

"Bullshit. You're here to ruin Brooks and do as much damage to his plans for Henderson as you possibly can. Not to mention the rest of the people in this town. Well, I'm here to tell you that now that I'm back, *that* shit's going to stop. Pit a bully against a do-gooder, bully wins every time. But let's see how you do going up against one of your own."

"That your sweetheart over there?" Viper gestured. "The *newcomer?*"

Xavier turned his head to see that she indeed indicated Laidey. *Are you fucking kidding me?* He eyed Viper. "Never seen the girl before," he claimed.

Viper nodded, allowing her devious grin to say everything she wasn't. "Always fun to meet a kindred spirit." She winked, and then turned her attention to the mayor. "Clint, I believe our table is ready."

Xavier backed out of their way as they headed to the dining room.

Fuck.

Fuckity, fuck-fuck.

That did not go as planned.

CHAPTER TWENTY-FIVE

Very early Friday morning at the Evans estate, Pinks walked into the kitchen to find a fully decked out Emelina humming her way around the coffee maker. "Em?"

"Oh," she exclaimed, grabbing at her throat as she spun toward him. "Dear boy, what on earth are you doing up at this hour?"

"Em," he chuckled. "I'm up at this hour every morning. Scarlett sneaks back into her parents' place before dawn so I'm the one who starts your coffee. The real question is, what are you doing up at this hour?"

"Today, I'm making the coffee. Can I pour you a cup?"

"Sure." He sat himself on a stool. "So what gives?"

"Gives?"

"Ah, you're dressed to kill at"—he checked his watch—"5:45 A.M. We've got clients coming in I don't know about?"

Em batted her lashes as she set a mug of coffee in front of him. "I've met a man."

Pinks felt his brows rise. "A *new* man?"

"Yes. A new man. A wonderful man. A *younger* man."

Pinks chuckled at the deep pitch in her voice and the eyebrow wiggle over the word *younger*. "How old is he? Thirty? Forty?"

"Sixty-five. I'm not a cougar. It's a respectable difference in age since we're both considered old by the world's standards."

"No one would ever describe you as old, Em. You're too out-there to be old."

"I'm out-there because I'm bored. Now I'm excited." Her eyes glistened with the truth of what she said.

"Should I be worried?"

"About me, no." She waved that off, walking back to fill another mug.

"Well, who is this *new man*?"

Em looked around and lowered her voice as she came in closer. "His name is Chase Alexander, and he's from Phoenix. Quite dashing and very quick-witted. He's staying at the Wright's place, in a darling bachelor pad over their garage."

Pinks glanced at Em's attire once again and then leaned his body over the counter between them, whispering. "Emelina Flores, have I just caught you doing the walk of shame?"

"No shame," she assured him, a sly grin forming around the lip of her mug as she sipped.

"You little hussy," Pinks teased. "Who knows about this?"

"No one. And I know you'll keep your mouth shut."

He held up his hands. "I've got your back. You can count on that."

"I'm planning to invite Chase over for dinner tonight. So when I lay down the 'all hands on deck' order, you'll know what that's about."

"Does Mr. Alexander have any idea what he's walking into?"

"None at all. It'll be baptism by fire."

"Are you going to let Genevra or Piper in on this secret? Oh, and can I bring Scarlett?"

"No on the Genevra and Piper thing, yes to Scarlett. But let's keep her in the dark, shall we? I'm going to set out notes right here," she tapped the counter, "suggesting a dinner menu that will have Genevra and Piper salivating to help me in the kitchen. Something wonderfully Italian. Four full courses."

"They'll be all over that. What can I do to help?"

"Why, dear boy. You'll tend bar like you always do. And of course, you'll set the tone for the evening by being the first to welcome my Mr. Alexander with open arms."

"I will indeed, Em. If you like him, I like him."

"And I do like him." She licked her lips, causing Pinks to blush.

Across the way at Laidey's place, the morning went a little differently.

"Adelaide, can I borrow your bicycle pump?" Poppy asked as she busted through Laidey's bedroom door, studying her phone. "I want to buy this," she said, holding it out, showing off a picture of a huge blow-up raft in the shape of a pink flamingo.

The rustling and scrambling that ensued was the kind that only happened when you got caught with your pants down.

"Oh, my God," Poppy said, "I'm so sorry, I didn't know ..." But instead of turning away and skedaddling out of the room, she just stared.

"Poppy," Laidey said, while pulling the sheets up to her neck. "Get out."

Poppy burst out laughing. "Sorry. Yeah. Going." She turned on a blush and a giggle and left the two of them alone.

Laidey looked at Xavier, the hair on the top of his head all mussed, his gorgeous chest bared for the world to see. She fell back into her pillow with a huff. "Now she's going to tell everyone we're doing it."

"Let's humor her then and go ahead and really do it," he said, rolling himself on top of her.

"I hate being the center of attention, and unless you snuck out in the middle of the night, we still don't have condoms."

"Fuck the condoms. I'll pull out," he promised, kissing her neck, working his way down to her breasts.

She was tempted.

Oh, so very tempted.

"You're smooth, Mr. Wright, but the answer to that is still hell, no."

His head popped up. "You don't trust me."

"Ah, no. Not in the pull-out department."

He fed her a wicked grin. "Then suck me off again."

She batted her eyes, feeling heat flare up over her face.

He kept grinning, dipping his head to kiss her nipple. "Last night was hot, Tweets. Your naughty, little mouth." He sucked air between his teeth with a hiss. "Damn. So good."

"I needed to distract you out of your virile, badass, growly mood."

"Growly?"

"Yes, growly. Baring teeth and everything. I would have been concerned it was directed at me except for the way you kept me attached to your hip. And I know it wasn't directed at Crain. The two of you are like besties now." She rolled her eyes. You ready to share what it was all about?"

"It's nothing. Nothing I can't handle. Just you know, do your job, keep your head down, and come to me right away if anything seems squirrelly."

"Squirrelly?"

He sighed, rolling to his back, tucking an arm around her to pull her in close. He tucked the other behind his head as he spoke. "I just don't like this Viper chick, and until I can figure out a way to run her out of town, I don't want you caught in the crosshairs."

"She's not gunning for me."

"She might be now."

"What?"

"I wasn't going to say anything, but hell, the truth is I screwed up royally by trying to bully a bully. I thought I was safe going up against Viper because my business is still in the planning stage. She can't come at me like she did Lolly, yelling to the papers that my employees are all illegal aliens or shit. But I didn't realize I have something much more valuable to protect."

"What's that?"

"You."

"Me?"

"Yeah. She threatened you, Tweets."

"In what way did she threaten me?"

"In the midst of our heated discussion, she pointed to you and asked if you're my girl."

"And you take that as a threat."

"Hell, yeah, I do. And I want you to take it that way too. I doubt she's out to harm you physically, that's not her style. But professionally? Personally? Absolutely. She'd be only too happy to air your dirty laundry."

"I don't have any dirty laundry."

"Still. Probably good you're aware," he grumbled. "You can keep your eyes open now. I'm sorry I didn't tell you last night. I hate that I'm the one who brought you to her attention. I'm sorry about that, I really am."

"Xavier, stop. She can't possibly hurt me."

"I hope not. But she's definitely making me think about standing down."

"Which is obviously her plan. If you're distracted by what she could do to me, you're too busy to work proactively against her. She's very good at her job."

"Too damn good. My intention was to let her know that I had Brooks's back. Instead, I handed her you."

"So that's why you were half beast last night?"

"Yep. Although," he said, snuggling down into the sheets with her, his hands going everywhere, "it worked out pretty well, considering it got you to put your hands, *and your mouth*," he growled, "right where I wanted them. Ought to write Viper a thank-you note for that."

Laidey rolled with him, her hands enjoying his body as much as he was enjoying hers. "I'll be fine," she said into his chest. "But I'm not buying condoms. That's your job."

"Number one thing on my To-Do list. Listen, about the Fourth of July. Please don't think I didn't want to take Crain up on his offer ..."

"Xavier, I understand. Your mother wants your whole family seated together. I don't blame her."

"Yes, but I'd rather be sitting with you."

"Separate tables, same event. No biggie."

"Oh, there's a biggie. You're going to be meeting my brothers. All my brothers. You won't be able to miss a-one of them because Ma's forcing us to wear matching shirts."

"What?" she laughed.

"Yeah. For the family portrait she's commissioned to have taken at the club. Polos. Navy with a red stripe. White shorts. We'll look like the freaking USA sailing team."

"It'll make a great picture. You can't blame her for wanting one. Ooh. Lolly's making me a dress. Maybe we should ask her to make something for your mother to wear in the portrait. A red dress so she'll stand out. Like a rose among you thorns."

"Thorns is right. Look, Laidey." Her eyes immediately lifted to his, tuning in because he used her name instead of calling her Tweets. "My brothers are a lot like me. They're all fairly imposing. And things are a bit strained between us right now. That's on me. I know it. I plan to fix it. Still, when I introduce you, you being so tiny and all, I'm worried …"

"That they'll tease me? Or tease you in front of me?"

"Yeah. I don't want you to be offended or take any of it personally. I want you to know that it's all about me."

"Not everything's about you."

"This will be."

"You seem pretty stressed about this family reunion."

"Because it should have happened already. Not four weeks after I returned home."

"Look, Xavier. I'm not interested in adding any stress to you or your mother's situation. So I'm fine with us sitting at separate tables. If you want to focus on your family over the holiday weekend, that's fine with me too. I've got my Dallas peeps to hang with. I've got Harry."

He growled at that.

"I'm just saying don't worry about me. Hang with your brothers, make your mom happy, and take a great picture. I'll be waiting for you when it's all over."

He kissed her nose. "Tweets, I wanna show you off. Just thought I should give you a little warning that my brothers grew up in the same Wright Family House of Charm that I did."

"Ha," she spat out a laugh. "Were you *all* bullies?"

"Nah. But smart asses? Yeah, every last one of them. Especially to each other."

"Siblings. That's how it rolls."

"I just don't want the Wright brothers to roll all over you, leaving my little Tweety Bird flattened on the pavement."

"I'll handle it. I promise."

"And you'll stay away from Viper," Xavier insisted.

"We were warned to stay away from Viper soon after we moved here. We aren't to talk with her or engage. Orders from Team Henderson."

"Good. Fine. Let's just keep it that way. I'm starting Piper's shop this afternoon. Do you think you can unchain yourself from your desk long enough to stop by and meet Chase?"

"How about I bring you both lunch?"

Xavier drew back, his eyes blinking. "You'd do that?"

"Why so shocked?"

"You're a businesswoman."

"Businesswomen eat."

"But do they fix hungry construction workers lunch and bring it to a job site?"

Her brows rose. "If the job site is two doors down, yes."

He kissed her again. "That'd be great. How much time do we have?"

"For lunch?"

"No. Now."

"Oh. We're done for now. This businesswoman needs to get in the shower."

Xavier grinned. "Construction workers do some of their best work in showers."

Laidey uttered a startled gasp as she entered her office. Frozen in place, she stared at the scene before her.

The building was supposed to be empty.

Duncan and Missy were down at E&E having a pow-wow with Crain and the heavy hitters on Team Henderson. Knowing that, and having the conversation with Xavier floating around in her brain, an acute sense of fear permeated her entire body.

Marcie Watts wasn't just *sitting* in Laidey's chair. No, the infamous Viper had her expensive heels propped up on Laidey's desk. Her ankles were crossed, and she appeared to be reading a hard copy of the research Laidey had compiled for Xavier regarding Piper's shop.

The woman may have looked harmless in her pricey business attire, but finding her like this, physically taking over her office? Sheer terror.

"How did you get in here?" Laidey whispered, unable to unearth her full voice.

"I have a key." Viper dangled the object between her painted nails. She licked her lips and smiled. "How are your parents, Miss Bartholomew? Addy and Philip, correct? Are they still happy in their place on Preston Road?"

Obviously, Laidey wasn't the only one good at research. But mentioning her parents' names and their street pushed out her fear and brought on her anger.

"*Why* do you have a key?"

Viper simply tilted her head and grinned.

"Did Mr. James *give* you that key?"

Marcie slowly pulled her killer heels off Laidey's desk. "You don't need to worry about this key," she advised. "What you need to worry about is the law."

"The law?"

"Yes." Viper gave her a short smile. "I understand you're well acquainted with the law."

"As it applies to business proposals."

"Oh, don't be coy. You and I both know just how familiar you are with criminal law when it comes to teenage indiscretions. But if you prefer a business proposal, here's one for you." She stood, pocketed the key, and smoothed her hands down her awesome green skirt. "At eleven o'clock this morning, I will be at the courthouse filing for a restraining order against Xavier Wright. If things go my way, which they will since the mayor will be there to recount the unfortunate incident at the club last night, Mr. Wright will be forbidden to stray anywhere close to me."

"I doubt that will hurt his feelings," Laidey quipped.

"No, but it might hurt his ability to earn a living." Viper took a deep breath and sighed, "I'm feeling compelled to open Mayor Stevenson's campaign headquarters here on Main Street." She checked her watch. "I'm meeting an agent to look at an available space just a couple doors down."

"Please don't let me keep you."

Viper held up the research papers. "If you think Mr. Wright would like to keep working on that ridiculous pie plate shop, you'll suggest he get down on his knees and apologize to me before my court appearance. I'd like an assurance, in front of witnesses, that he and I will be able to put aside our differences and work together to make Henderson great again."

"Ah. I think that slogan's been used."

"The law, Miss Bartholomew," Viper threatened as Laidey stepped aside, letting her move through her office door. "The law is on my side."

Laidey followed in the wicked woman's footsteps, making sure she found her way out of the building. For a brief moment, she stood there and considered keeping her own ass covered.

Nah, she thought. Better to suck it up and become her own brand of badass.

Her first call was to Duncan, confirming he didn't willingly give Marcie Watts a key to the building.

Her second call was to Michael Sterling, the town's locksmith.

Her third call was to 911.

CHAPTER TWENTY-SIX

Brooks Bennett stood in the hallway, observing. The last thing he wanted to do was chance that a conflict of interest would be called into question and jeopardize what was going down.

But he sure didn't try to hide his glee.

Vance came up and smacked him on the back. "What's doin'? Your text said Courthouse STAT."

Brooks motioned his head toward the open double doors.

Marcie Watts, who in the very astute, official, and succinct way she had of speaking had, only moments earlier, been describing for the judge how one Xavier Wright had bullied her mercilessly at the Henderson Country Club, was now being handcuffed and read her Miranda rights.

"Ms. Watts, you're under arrest for trespassing, harassment, and a number of other criminal violations. You have the right to remain silent. Anything you say can and will be held against you in a court of law …"

Marcie's head flipped around, her glare landing directly on a notoriously quiet, hardworking CC Henderson employee.

"Laidey?" Vance breathed. "Laidey made this happen? How?"

"She called 911," Brooks chuckled. "Said Viper had broken into her office and threatened her parents, Xavier Wright, and herself. I made the captain take the call. Wanted everything done by the book. Who knows if we can make this stick, but at least we can sit her butt in a holding cell for as long as the law will allow."

"Or until some fancy attorney shows up."

"Or until then," Brooks agreed. "At least she'll be cooling her jets for a bit." Brooks grinned as he looked out the front door. "Glorious day in Henderson, wouldn't you say?"

"The sun does look brighter, all of a sudden."

Vance high-fived Brooks before the two of them walked out front where Xavier came running up the steps. "I just heard Laidey had an altercation with Viper," he said. "What's going on?"

"It's cool," Brooks told him. "Like so many before her, she was accosted by Viper's vicious words and threats. But Laidey knows the law. Well enough to figure out which ones Viper broke. Not sure how much is going to stick."

"Especially when some high-priced attorney gets ahold of this," Vance added.

"But it's totally made my day," Brooks said. "Anybody who gets Viper off the streets for any amount of time is a hero in my book. Who knew our little mouse had it in her? Sorta a Dorothy Gale moment. Dropping a house on the Wicked Witch of the East."

"Here she comes," Xavier said, watching his precious Tweety Bird being escorted out of the courthouse by uniformed police. "You okay?" he asked, moving to her.

"She's a smart one," Chief Lumblad complimented. "Was able to recount the story in great detail, knew what laws had been broken, knew how to preserve the crime scene for fingerprinting, and also knew exactly where we could catch the culprit."

"What's Mayor Stevens have to say about all this?" Xavier asked. "The man can't have a suspected criminal running his campaign."

"Mayor Stevens has yet to comment on the situation," McKenna's journalist-mode voice came from the back of the entourage before she stepped forward. "Laidey texted me about the impending arrest so I could be here to report the full story for the paper. Photos and all." She beamed her joy at having a real scoop to print.

Xavier wrapped Laidey up in his arms. "Are you hurt?" he whispered.

"No," she said, hugging him tight. "Just freaked out."

"No doubt. Are you done? Are you free to go?"

"She's free," the chief said. "She's given us a full report. You think of anything else, Miss Bartholomew, you just give us a call."

"Thanks. I will."

Vance and Brooks were clapping as Xavier escorted Laidey down the courthouse steps. "I couldn't find a way to take her down," Brooks said, pointing to himself. "Vance couldn't find a way to take her down," he said, pointing to his buddy. "And believe me, we've been looking. She breaks into your office to intimidate you and you've got the wherewithal to call 911?"

Laidey shrugged, breathing deep. "If this ever goes to trial, which, let's face it, it probably won't, it will come out that I was once *briefly* incarcerated."

"What?" Xavier shouted as the men's faces fell into disbelief.

"You?" McKenna laughed.

"Yes. I never thought that unfortunate event would lead me to know enough about criminal law to help put a nuisance behind bars, but it did."

"Wait? What's the story?" Xavier pressed.

"I was a kid, trying to be cool, following along with the cool kids doing dumb stuff, knowing full well I should just say no and head home. Because even though Joe Peterson had a key to the main door of his uncle's building, the comic book store within that building was deemed a separate entity. Thus, my office—paid for by CC Henderson—is separate from Duncan James, Attorney at Law. Even if Duncan had given Viper a key, which he says he did not, she was trespassing once she set foot in my office. That's the technicality I knew about. What scared me was her intimidation techniques. She knew my parents' names and address. That didn't sit well with me. Not to mention that she threatened Xavier's livelihood. I'm sure a good lawyer could file more claims against her. I told the police everything that happened. They'll look into adding additional charges."

"How was she threatening my livelihood?" Xavier asked.

"After your little conversation last night, she was going to get a restraining order against you and then rent a place on Main Street right next to Piper's shop, which would prevent you from working there."

"Bullshit she was."

"That's what she said. Unless I convinced you to apologize in front of witnesses. That was her plan. That's why I knew where she would be at eleven o'clock."

"You fightin' my battles for me, Tweets?"

"No. But if I can head them off, you can be sure I'm going to do it."

He hugged her close, squeezing her until she squeaked.

"Nice work, half-pint," Vance said, offering up a high-five, which Laidey took. "Didn't realize we had a miniature badass in our midst. To think it was little Laidey who brought down big, bad Viper. We need to celebrate," Vance insisted. "My place. Tonight. Pool party, barbeque, the works. Spread the word, ding dong the witch is jailed. We're celebrating. I'll text Harry and Pinks and get them to handle the details. Oughta be epic."

"Uh-oh," Piper said, looking down at her phone.

"Uh-oh?" Emelina inquired. "There's no uh-ohs happening today."

"Vance has planned a party. For tonight."

The three women stood around the mammoth kitchen island surveying all their work. Fresh pasta rolled out ready to be cut, a mixture of the finest cheeses in a bowl, fresh herbs and spices everywhere, Genevra's signature sauce boiling on the stove.

"Well? What kind of party? For how many?" Genevra asked.

"A blow-out," Piper read. "According to Vance, Viper has been handcuffed and tossed in jail." She lifted her head. "That does sound like a reason to celebrate."

"Yes, but my beautiful dinner," Em moaned.

"Tomorrow night," Genevra said cheerfully. "We'll wet and cover the pasta to keep it fresh. The sauce will keep, and it will give us time to go get that prosciutto we love so much from that Italian deli over in Oxford. Along with fresh melon to wrap it around."

"But …" Em hesitated, full of woe.

"What's wrong?" Genevra wondered. "You love a good party."

Em took a breath. "It's just that … well, I've met a man. And I wanted to introduce him at dinner tonight."

"A man?" Piper's eyes widened. "Like someone other than Mr. Monaghan?"

"Or Mr. Purvis?" Genevra added.

"Or Mr. Harvath?" Piper went on.

"Yes. Yes. Someone other than the usual suspects. There is a *new* man in town, and I've got dibs. He's ..." she paused dramatically, "*younger*. In his sixties."

"Em," Piper exclaimed. "Who is he?"

"A Mr. Chase Alexander. I met him at the club. He's a friend of the Wrights. Staying over their garage for the time being."

"For the time being?"

"He's in town to help young Xavier establish his business. I believe he'll be doing some physical labor on your shop, Piper."

"And you like him?"

"Trust me, there is nothing not to like about Chase. You two will adore him."

"I'm sure we will," Genevra said, practically biting her lips trying to hide a smile.

"Invite him to the party tonight," Piper suggested. "And then to the family dinner tomorrow. Let your son and grandson get used to seeing the man around here before they realize you've ..."

"I've what?" Em asked haughtily.

"Started dating?" Piper asked cautiously.

"Yes," Em sniffed. "Dating. Right."

When Em turned her back, Piper mouthed, "I think she was with him last night," to Genevra.

"Stop talking behind my back," Em ordered.

"Right. Okay," Genevra said anxiously. "Let's get all this put away, and see what we can whip up for the party tonight."

"Vance says he's put Harry on the burgers, brats, and beer. He's put Pinks on everything else. All we need to worry with is dessert."

"And maybe an appetizer or two," Genevra insisted. "Em, you okay with this?"

"I am. But if you don't mind, after we clean all this up, I'd like to head over and hand Mr. Alexander a personal invitation."

"You do that, Em." Genevra smiled. "We can handle things here."

∽⋙⋘∽

Xavier scraped a hand through that gorgeous hair, his T-shirt, worn jeans and work boots all causing flutters in Laidey's stomach as the two of them were left alone on the courthouse steps.

"I'm heading into Raleigh to check on Piper's fancy-ass wood order that keeps getting delayed. I might have to make a couple stops to find what I need if I get the sense this supplier is jerking me around."

"All right. Will you, ah …"

"Will I what? You wanna come? Need me to pick up anything for you in Raleigh?"

"No. No, not that. I'm just …" She tilted her head. "Are we going to the party tonight?"

"Hell, yeah. You're the reason everyone's celebrating. Why wouldn't we go?"

"No. I mean, yes, of course. But, I guess what I'm asking is, are we going together? Are we, together?"

He pulled her in close, smiling a giddy smile over her head. "Tweets, what part of the last few days have been unclear? Yes, we're going to the party together. And yes, we're … together. Whatever you want to call it. You're not going anywhere are you? Back to Dallas or anything?" He pulled back slightly to watch her shake her head. "Then yes, baby. As long as I'm here and you're here, we go to parties together. You don't need Harry," he insisted. "Harry is now off limits."

She pushed at him, pfft-ing. "Harry is a good friend."

"Yeah, one who wanted to shackle himself to you and drink champagne all night. Not gonna happen."

"Go to Raleigh. Call me when you get back."

"Hey," he said, causing her to turn around and look at him. "While I'm there, I'm gonna do what my ma's asked. I'm going to cut my hair and get a shave." He stood there scratching at his jaw like he was regretting it already. "You gonna be okay with that?"

Laidey stared at the stubble she used to find so irritating and felt a little twitter flutter around her lady parts. She was going to miss the stubble.

"It'll grow back," he said, reading her mind.

"I know. I'm just committing *this* Xavier Wright, reformed bully, to memory." She gave him a smile.

He smiled back. "Text you when I get back to town. Sorry about lunch, but I guess local heroes have other stuff to keep them busy."

"Local hero?"

"You're the itty, bitty thing who took down big, bad Viper. Once the story spreads, everybody is going to know your name."

Laidey saw her invisibility status fly out the window. "That doesn't make me particularly happy."

"It'll be fine, Tweets. I'll protect you from all the paparazzi."

As it ended up, Xavier got caught up in Raleigh, texting her a dozen times about how infuriating his day was and then apologizing over and over for making her late to the party. Laidey texted back that she'd catch a ride with Poppy and meet him there. No problem.

Only it was kind of a problem.

Laidey hadn't anticipated the attention that was thrust upon her the moment she walked up the bank to the Evans's pool. They started applauding. All of them. Team Henderson and their fans, yelling for a speech, which she somehow managed to pull off in a few vivid sentences. She even got a laugh. Then McKenna pulled her inside the mansion, announcing to one and all that she was getting an "exclusive interview" for the *Henderson Daily*.

It all seemed like such a fuss. With Xavier by her side, it would have been a lot easier. She could have stepped behind his tall frame when she needed a moment to regroup. But with him showing up late, she was pleasantly surprised at how she'd managed to handle the limelight on her own. Though it wasn't how she preferred to conduct business—i.e., invisibly—she didn't feel particularly awkward or odd either. Perhaps the last few weeks of forging a relationship with the town's former bully had awakened her social side. Strengthened her confidence. Beat back her awkward nature. Whatever the source, she felt changed and emboldened.

The news came that Viper had posted bail and then turned on Mayor Stevens with a scathing verbal assault as she ducked into a black town car. Brooks had reportedly reached out to Mayor Stevens, offering an invitation to the night's festivities but Clint had declined.

Everyone hoped this was the end of Viper's reign of terror, but no one counted out a repeat performance.

Laidey was in the kitchen speaking to Lolly about a dress for Mrs. Wright and the family portrait she planned to have taken. "She's terribly thin," Laidey said. "I was hoping you'd design something that would camouflage the fact that she's been sick. She's very short compared to her husband and Xavier. If the rest of the Wrights are as tall, she'll be swallowed up in the picture."

Lolly stood in thought, as if she was visualizing the portrait. "The photographer should have her sit on her husband's lap. That would give her a boost and make the picture less formal. Give it a carefree and happy feel. You say they're wearing navy blue?"

"With a red stripe and white shorts."

"Red would be the way to go. She'd disappear in navy."

"I don't actually know if she's planned something to wear, but it's been on my mind. Maybe when Xavier arrives, we can talk to him. I'd be happy to pay for the dress. Anonymously."

Lolly patted her shoulder. "I'd love to have the opportunity to dress her, just for the publicity."

"Still. Whatever costs you incur, count on me to cover them."

Lolly smiled. "I appreciate that. Let's go talk to Xavier about it. My brain is already starting to flow with ideas."

"He hasn't arrived."

"No. I saw him come in."

The two women looked out the kitchen windows, searching the crowd gathered around the pool. "There he is. Standing near Vance."

Laidey's gaze scanned the crowd for Xavier. She didn't see him. She scanned again, snagging on to his height first as he accepted a beer from Vance. Her greedy eyes slid down his long body dressed in fancy slacks and a gorgeous button down. Laidey licked her lips, her mouth going dry.

The man certainly looked good in his clothes.

Her gaze drifted to his hair, noting the sides had been groomed and the longer length on top had been cut. From the back, he was her ruthlessly irritating Xavier. But when he turned in her direction, she hardly recognized him. The lack of beard—well, the lack of groomed scruff—was … wow. It *totally* changed his look. He didn't look nearly like the badass he was.

No doubt about it, clean-shaven Xavier Wright was drop-dead gorgeous. He just didn't look like the guy Laidey had fallen for. Though apparently, he looked exactly like the guy *McKenna* had fallen for.

Laidey saw it go down. She'd been content to watch through the window, her eyes narrowing in on Xavier as he spoke to Vance and sipped his beer, contemplating her response to this … new man.

She watched intently as he looked around the party. Saw when he turned back to Vance with a question. Watched as Vance gestured toward the house, which led to a nod and fist bump from Xavier.

Standing at the far end of the island as he came through the French doors, Laidey's peripheral vision caught McKenna stepping into the room from the opposite side, stopping abruptly as she caught sight of Xavier. The two of them faced one another at the top of the kitchen while Laidey was poised way down at the end of the island, paralyzed. Afraid to look away.

McKenna seemed startled. Startled and then delighted. Happy. Giddy, even. Laidey's stomach lurched as McKenna licked her lips like she wanted to devour him.

Xavier reached up to rub at the smooth skin of his jaw. "McKenna?" he whispered. She moved forward, placing her hand on his cheek, going in for what couldn't be mistaken for anything but a kiss.

Xavier turned his face so her lips landed on his cheek. He was grinning until he spotted Laidey.

"Hey," he called, shaking McKenna off.

Laidey gulped. "Hey, yourself," she replied, seeing the guilt crawl into McKenna's eyes once she realized Laidey was standing there.

"I thought …" McKenna said, trailing off as if confused. She shook her head and laughed. "You shaved," she accused.

"At Ma's request," he told McKenna, all the while looking over at Laidey. "You look pretty," he told her, his cute-boy grin working its magic on all her thrill zones. Her breath seized up, taking in his clean-cut gorgeousness up close. It was so odd seeing him like this.

He looked downright civilized. Easy. Not at all the bad-boy bully impatient to redeem himself.

Dressed in new clothes, clothes that actually fit him and weren't worn or torn, he looked like he belonged to the Wright family and to the upper echelon of Henderson. He even looked like he belonged in Dallas society and would be exactly what her parents expected.

Hmm.

"Xavier," McKenna called. "Your mother asked me to have a word with you."

"I just got here. Haven't even said hello to Tweets. Give us a minute, will you?"

He'd said all that staring directly into Laidey's eyes. As if he felt her uncertainty.

Yeah, she was uncertain.

Not sure what to make of this stranger in front of her, turning her on at the same time he was flipping her out.

She was also uncertain that McKenna's feelings for Xavier hadn't magically resurfaced. It made perfect sense, really. When he'd come back to town, he hadn't looked like *this* at all.

But now? Now Laidey was betting that he looked a whole lot like the Wright brother McKenna had fallen for. In fact, the words she'd heard McKenna admit to Harry a while back sprung to mind.

"The love of my life left town and never came back."

Well, after a shave and a change of clothes, it sure looked like *McKenna's* Xavier had just arrived back in town.

As much as Laidey really wanted to concentrate on the gray eyes shooting the come-on vibes her way, her eyes continued to dart between the old sweethearts. McKenna was still struck dumb over his face.

"Laidey?" Xavier asked around a grin as he licked his lips. "It'll grow back, I promise."

She shook herself out of her internal rumination and remembered where she was.

"Tweets," he said, starting toward her. "You going shy on me?"

As Xavier stalked over to her, McKenna whirled and dashed out of the kitchen, fleeing into the party.

McKenna, her second friend here in Henderson.

Crap.

"I think McKenna—"

"Let's not talk about McKenna," he said, taking Laidey into his arms. "Why are you standing there when my hairless face needs a kiss?"

She smiled then. His long arms, that confident swagger, his devious grin, and his sexy-as-hell voice all reminding her that yes, scruffy beard or no, this was still Xavier.

Her Xavier.

She just couldn't help feeling a little bad for McKenna. And suddenly she found herself standing in McKenna's shoes. Feeling what it would be like to lose him.

Her arms wrapped him up tight, squeezing him briefly. "I didn't recognize you," she told him.

"I could tell."

"I didn't think your short beard would make you look so … different."

"Which is why Ma insisted I take it off for the portrait."

"Right. Because she thinks of you without it. Like McKenna does."

"But you think of me with it."

She nodded.

"Then I'll grow it back."

"You don't have to grow it back for me," she said, reaching up and touching his face. His jaw felt so smooth. "Did you have a professional shave?"

"It was awesome," he said, picking her up and plopping her butt on the end of the island. "First …" He took her face between his big hands and brought their lips together in such a soft, poignant kiss, Laidey's essential parts fluttered in anticipation of what might lie ahead. "I bought condoms," he whispered as he kissed the side of her mouth, his tongue stroking over the edge of her lips.

Her essential parts stopped fluttering and started pole dancing.

"How's the hero of Henderson holding up at her own party," he asked, sneaking in more kisses, preventing her from responding. "Sorry I'm late," he eventually added. "Vance said you held your own pretty good for a wallflower. I told him wallflowers don't give head the way you do."

"You didn't."

"I didn't," he chuckled. "But I thought about it." He continued to kiss her. "In my head." He kissed her some more. "You ready to get out of here?"

Yes. Yes, yes, and another yes. "Don't you want to mingle?" she asked instead.

"Mingle with you, Tweets. It's been a long day." He pulled back from the kissing. "I had to go clothes shopping," he said, showing off his new look. "My mother insisted. Said she was tired of me looking like I lived under a bridge."

"She wants you looking like you come from the *right* family."

"Cute, but I'm afraid you're correct. She's tired of seeing me dragging my ass around in ripped jeans and soiled T-shirts. Thought it was offending her visitors." He moved in between Laidey's legs and stroked his hands up her arms. "This from the woman who insisted I be Xavier Wright and the likes of Evie Jackson be damned."

"Well, she's your mother. Not Evie Jackson. She's also not at this party," Laidey smirked.

"See this is what I was afraid of, Tweets. The beard, the jeans, the motorcycle. I *am* your walk on the wild side."

"You're definitely walking all over my wild side. I don't really care how you dress. You look good in your clothes. These clothes. Ripped jeans. Out of your clothes too," she whispered, reaching her chin up to kiss him.

"You are just begging to get fucked, aren't you?"

"What?" Laidey pushed him away as he laughed.

"Tweets, you should see your face."

"Because I'm not … begging to be … you know …" But she sort of was.

"Fucked," he mouthed the world. "You can say it. It's not like it's a dirty—oh, yeah, it is a dirty word. One that little kindergarteners like you probably aren't aware of."

She looked down at her attire. "I dressed as you requested."

"I know. This little, white number is getting me hard."

"Aww, too bad you're all dressed up. Probably too worried about getting a grass stain on those expensive slacks to take a tumble down the hill."

"I'll tumble you down the hill, pricy slacks be damned."

She lifted her arms to wrap around his neck when they kissed this time.

"Oh!" came a female voice.

The two of them broke apart, Laidey hopping down from the island and feeling very embarrassed by being caught by Vance's grandmother, Emelina. The handsome man who stood next to her looked ready to bust out laughing.

"Sorry about that," Xavier said as contrite as Laidey had ever heard him. "I was just, um, kissing Henderson's latest hero hello."

"Looks like you were getting ready to do more than that. Boy, don't you have your own place you can whisk your little gal off too? Oh, I forgot. Thanks to me, you don't." The man grinned like he couldn't be happier. "Is this the one you and Harry are fighting over?"

Xavier no longer looked chagrined. Now he looked pissed. "Laidey," he said begrudgingly. "This is my boss and mentor, Chase Alexander."

"Oh. *This* is the elusive Mr. Alexander," Laidey said, pulling out all her momma's charm as she and Xavier moved toward the other couple to say their hellos. "Mrs. Flores, I apologize for sitting on your—"

"No apologies, darling," Emelina cooed in her Spanish accent. "I'm sorry I startled you. Chase and I had dinner at the club and are just now joining the festivities."

"You and who had dinner at the club?" Hale asked, coming at them while holding his grandson in his arms. Laidey noticed there were way too many entrances to this very public kitchen.

"Oh, dear boy," Emelina said as if this was nothing. "I'd like you to meet Chase Alexander. Of Phoenix."

Xavier chuckled at the intro.

Chase threw him a watch-yourself glare.

"Of Phoenix?" Hale asked as the two men shook hands.

"I'm in town on business," Chase said.

"He's helping me with Piper's shop," Xavier threw in.

"Ah," Hale said. "Welcome. Henderson is in need of anyone who can swing a hammer."

"So I've been told," Chase shot a look toward Xavier. "My project back in Arizona is on hold. The young man there thought I might be of assistance here this summer."

"The young man is correct. We're happy to have you."

"Chase has invited me to the Champagne and Shackles party the weekend after next. Perhaps we'd return the favor by including him at our table on the Fourth."

Hale's gaze assessed both his mother and Mr. Alexander. "I can't imagine that even with the fireworks, the Fourth of July at our club is going to measure up to my mother at a Champagne and Shackles party. Mr. Alexander, I wish you the best."

"Oh, stop," Emelina insisted. "You'll scare the man off," she said, putting her arm through Chase's. "Now I'm going to introduce him around to the young people. Maybe play a little beer pong."

"Beer pong?" Hale's eyebrows lifted.

"Put my grandson to bed and join us," she suggested.

"Your great-grandson," Hale corrected. He pointed to Vance, Jr. "This is her *great*-grandson," he told Chase.

Chase's grin just widened. "I don't believe Emelina is old enough to have grandchildren, much less great-grandchildren."

"He's a smooth one, Mother. You might have met your match this time."

"Tut," she scolded. "Come, Chase. Let me introduce you to my people."

"Enjoy that beer pong," Hale called after them.

The three of them stood there watching as Emelina introduced Mr. Alexander to Vance.

"Well, this should be interesting," Hale said.

"You okay with this, Mr. Evans?" Xavier asked. "Chase is a great guy. A stand-up guy," he assured him. "I owe him a world of debt. His business in Arizona is—"

Hale cut him off. "Xavier. My mother eats men like Chase for breakfast. I'm far more worried about your friend."

"Oh." Xavier was taken aback. "Ha. All right. Well, trust me. Chase probably won't mind being chewed up and spit out if your mother's the one doing the chewing. Unless you say otherwise, I'll just keep my nose out of it."

"I'm afraid you're gonna have to deal with this—"

Vance came barging through the French doors after having looked so calm during the short span of time he'd been introduced to Chase. "What the hell is going on out there?" he accused both Xavier and his father. "Em's got a man? *Another* man?"

"Heart wants what the heart wants," Hale said rather nonsensically as he handed Vance, Jr. to his father. "Now I need to go fetch Genevra so she can meet this *other* man."

Vance struggled to get Vance, Jr. set up against his shoulder. "What are you doing, Wright, bringing some gold-digging bachelor into town? There was no way Em was not going to fall for *that*."

"That?" Laidey asked.

"That ... hair. Those eyes. Teeth! Geez, the way my grandmother was squeezing the man's biceps, it was hard not to notice he's built for a guy his age. You aiming to strip me of my inheritance?"

It was all said in fun, Laidey could tell. Still Xavier tried to assure Vance.

"He's a good guy. Trust me. Though ..."

"Though what?" Vance turned and shouted up the steps. "Piper."

Xavier shrugged. "I've never known him to date. His wife died. Years ago. So this infatuation with Em ..."

"Infatuation?" Vance all but barked. "Piper!"

"Well, I mean, they met at the club a couple days ago and, you know, seemed to really hit it off."

Vance's eyes narrowed. "What do you mean, hit it off? Pipe— Oh."

Piper appeared at the bottom of the stairs, struggling with the back of her dress. "I told you we needed a babysitter for tonight. I had to change. Vance, Jr. spit up on me while I was putting out the Big Pie Plate dip. Laidey would you mind zipping me up?"

Piper turned her back to Laidey as Vance threw a dangerous glare at Xavier.

"Dude," Xavier said, hands in the air, moving away from Piper and Laidey.

"Bad enough you've set my grandmother up with some roadie. You're not slipping in a glimpse of my wife's naked back."

"Roadie? He's a *business* owner. He owns the premier residential development company in Phoenix."

"Then why is he here to help build out Pipes's insignificant, little pie shop?"

"Insignificant?" Piper stole her son out of Vance's arms.

"Baby Doll, you know what I mean. It's a little suspect that after twenty minutes, Xavier's buddy has eyes for my crazy grandmother."

"Really? Is that suspect?" Piper asked.

"She's ancient."

"She's gorgeous," all three of them—Piper, Laidey, and Xavier—declared.

"Gorgeous and made of money," Vance defended.

"Oh, stop," Piper insisted. "It's not like you or Hale need whatever pennies Emelina has stored at Henderson Bank and Trust.

"Well, whatever she has, I don't want it heading back to Phoenix at summer's end invested in some Ponzi scheme."

"Seriously?" Xavier exclaimed.

"Don't listen to him, Xavier," Piper said. "He's overprotective and clearly doesn't recognize his grandmother as the vibrant, youthful soul she is."

"What I do recognize is a man who has lust in his eyes," Vance defended.

"Really?" Piper asked. "Where is he? It's been a long time since I've seen one of those around here."

All of Vance's attention immediately zoned in on his wife. Laidey watched as his body turned toward her. Saw him lower his head and look Piper dead in the eye. "What did you just say?"

Piper beamed up at her husband. "That it's been a long time since I've seen a man with lust in his eyes."

While she said this, Vance was extricating his son out of his wife's arms. He handed V.J. off to Xavier, who struggled with the kid, moving him this way and that before settling him in the crook of his arm. Vance leaned down and growled—Laidey swore she heard him growl—into Piper's ear before he spun her around and gently swatted her backside to get her moving toward the stairs. Laidey and Xavier stared after them.

"You think she's going to be okay?" Xavier asked. "Should we, like, intervene?"

"Nope," Laidey said, turning a big grin toward Xavier. "I think Piper's going to get exactly what she just asked for. Want me to hold the baby?"

"Why would I want you to hold the baby? I just bought a box of condoms."

"So?"

"Women get all estrogen-y when they hold babies. Their eggs explode out of their ovaries, and it makes them want to procreate."

"Explode? Holding Vance, Jr. will make my eggs explode from my ovaries?"

"Best not to take chances."

She laughed. "So you don't want kids, I take it."

"Sure, I want kids. Like, someday. Not nine months from tonight."

"Tonight?" Her brows lifted.

"Tonight, Tweets. Tonight." He stepped in closer and covered Vance, Jr.'s ears. "I'm sneaking you into my bedroom like we talked about, stripping you out of that fluffy dress, and stuffing a sock in your mouth."

"What?"

"Don't want my parents hearing all those sexy noises you like to make."

"Then come to my place."

"Fuck that. You are fulfilling my horny teenage fantasy. You know how often I thought about sneaking a girl into my room?"

"McKenna?"

His face scrunched up. "No, not McKenna. Definitely *not* McKenna."

That shocked Laidey. And it made her a little incredulous on McKenna's behalf. "Why not McKenna?"

"Long story."

Laidey's face told him she wasn't buying it.

"Look. Someday you and I will have a chat about—"

"Xavier?" McKenna stuck her head in the door, calling his name. *Speak of the devil.*

She gave Laidey a bright smile. "Since your girlfriend gave me all the details everyone is going to want to read in the paper tomorrow, I'm heading home early to write it up. I just need a moment to run some Wright family business by you."

"McKenna, can't you see I'm busy babysitting?"

"What the hell is wrong with Vance Evans letting a guy like you watch over his child?"

"He's Vance's. Clearly, I'm as qualified as he is."

"You might be right. Sorry, Laidey, I just … I just need to borrow him for a minute."

Xavier jostled V.J., reluctantly handing him over to Laidey. "Do not get attached," he warned her.

"I'm a businesswoman. We do our best to beat our ovaries into submission until the last possible moment. I can handle this."

"All right. I'll be right back."

"I'm going to wander over toward Chase and Emelina." She nodded her head toward that end of the pool.

Laidey stepped out into the party as tiki torches were being lit. She couldn't help watching as Xavier followed McKenna down the slope to the parking area. Watched as McKenna turned and reached up to feel his face again. Watched as Xavier stopped and let her, with that cute-boy grin on his face … directed at McKenna.

Laidey let out a big sigh. It's not that she didn't trust Xavier's feelings for her. But history was history, and Xavier and McKenna had theirs.

Instead of making herself crazy wondering what sort of Wright family business had to be kept such a big, fat secret, she turned and folded her way into the crowd with Vance, Jr., telling anyone who asked that she'd offered to show him off while Vance and Piper managed the party. She ran into Lolly, who was holding her half-brother, Beau, so the two of them found an empty lounge chair and sat with their cuddle buddies.

She noticed Xavier emerge back into the party alone. She also noticed he stopped at the bar to get a beer. Noticed how he engaged with several people, stopping to chat, while his eyes scanned the crowd—hopefully for her. Moments later, Vance and Piper emerged from the kitchen, him holding on to the skirt of her dress as they both scouted the crowd.

Oh. Maybe for the baby she was holding?

She got up and headed toward them. She was intercepted by Xavier who practically stole V.J. out of her arms. "He get that estrogen surging?"

"He's cute, I'll give him that," she said. "And he likes his cousin."

"Uncle," Vance corrected as he and Piper joined them. "Beau is his uncle."

"Right," Laidey said. "Hard to remember that when they're both so tiny."

"The Evans family aims to entertain. Speaking of which, my wife would like to apologize for her behavior," he said, reaching in and taking Vance, Jr. from Xavier. "Don't you, Baby Doll."

Piper grinned. "My husband's past serves me well."

"Are you fucking kidding me?" Vance spewed, turning on his wife. "Aw, and now I'm cussin' in front of the kid. Pipes, you're going to be sorry when V.J.'s first word is of the four-letter variety."

"His first word is going to be Momma," she cooed into her baby's face. "Laidey, nice work on having Viper incarcerated today. After all the time and energy Vance and Brooks have spent on trying to shut her down, we're all grateful that her chickens have finally come to roost."

"She's scary," Laidey admitted. "It was selfishly motivated. I didn't want to ever find her sitting at my desk again. Had no idea we'd be celebrating her demise in such grand style."

"You deserve it. Truly," Vance said. "Now you two go have fun. We've got this." He nodded toward his son.

"Everything okay in the bedroom department?" Xavier asked, swinging a finger between Vance and Piper. "I could counsel Vance if you'd like. Share a few pointers."

"Laidey," Vance asked. "Does all that bluster and conceit actually turn a woman on?"

Laidey licked her lips and then leaned in and whispered, "There's been a lot of bluster that's for sure."

"Exactly what I thought." He chin-lifted Xavier. "You go take care of your own woman before you start worrying about mine."

"I don't know," Piper said, assessing Xavier. "Maybe you and Vance should have lunch."

"Baby Doll. *That* is enough."

As the party rode into the night, Xavier marveled at all the people who knew him and yet liked him anyway. And he took great pride in the fact that Chase—the man who practically raised him over the last dozen years—seemed to be making friends and influencing people as he was introduced to this hometown crowd. Hale spent a fair amount of time with the guy, though Xavier noticed Vance kept his distance.

Vance would come around, Xavier thought. As soon as he realized just how much Chase brought to the table, Vance would embrace the guy and his infinite community-planning wisdom. A quick Google search and Chase would be cleared to shackle himself to Mrs. Flores for however long he wanted. Of course, that woman was a force Xavier didn't think either her son or grandson could stop.

The jokes, the camaraderie, the familiar faces. All of it brought a profound satisfaction that settled deep inside Xavier.

He was home.

Xavier Wright had truly come home.

CHAPTER TWENTY-SEVEN

Xavier parked his truck in the usual spot along his parents' circular drive. When he pressed the button to turn off the ignition, he waited a couple beats before saying, "You ready to do this thing?"

Laidey grinned. "Sneaking into your bedroom? Or hoping that my ovaries don't explode at the wrong time?"

"Yeah, that."

She nodded vigorously, biting her lip.

"You hot for me?"

She blushed.

"Shit. I didn't mean that quite the way it sounded. Truly." He reached over, hooking a hand behind her head, and kissed her lips, taking his time, letting her know he wasn't really the asshole his mouth kept trying to prove him to be. He pressed his forehead to hers, having to ask. "Laidey, I definitely want your consent about what's going down tonight. I also kinda need to know that you're with me because you want to be with me. Not because you can't be with *him*."

She pulled back, not looking offended, but rather surprised. "Xavier," she whispered. "You. Of course, this is about you. I've gone a long time without feeling the need to replace my boss. You're the first to turn my head."

His voice rose with suspicion. "In four years?"

She shrugged. "I'm not big on men. I mean, clearly I like big men, but I'm so invisible to most of them that I overhear what they say when they think no one's listening. Men are disgusting."

Xavier laughed. "Tweets, you're right. Certainly wouldn't want you eavesdropping on any of my candid conversations."

"I can only imagine."

"So why me? I mean, you've seen me at my worst. You've heard the stories. You know what I'm capable of."

"Okay, well, I have a two-part answer to that."

"I'm all ears."

"This first part is going to stroke your already overblown ego."

"Bring it on. After dealing with my brothers' bullshit over the last few weeks, my ego could use a boost."

"You—that first night in the club's parking lot—caused me to be startled and intrigued. Because you were magnificent in your desire to get McKenna to play your game. Get her to forgive you. And when you barked at Harry and me? I melted. I mean, I was scared, yeah, but only because I felt your power, your passion, your conviction of self all wrapped up in such a"—she gulped—"magnificent male form." He chuckled. "I'm serious. You worried holding baby Vance would make my ovaries explode? Uh-uh. *You* made my ovaries explode."

"Tweets. You were scared to death of me."

"Yes, but not in the way you thought. I was scared you'd *see* me."

"I did see you. Wanted you to like me."

"So, maybe there was an immediate chemistry between us. Which I fought because, yeah, you beat people up and tried to intimidate me."

"So, what turned the tide in my favor?"

"You asking me to play the piano for your mother."

"Really?"

"Yes. You knew you had screwed up by not calling me—for over a whole week," she emphasized, "You had to grovel to get me to play, and you willingly did it because you thought it would help your mother."

"It did. I think bringing you into the house has really helped my mother. Because she saw how much I liked you. It gave her something to worry about other than her health. Something to pester me about, which put us back where we used to be. Her doing the mothering, me being the sulky kid. Let me tell you, we both like that option far better than me playing part-time caregiver and her being so weak she can't do anything about it."

"I'm glad I could help."

Xavier took her hand, played with her fingers. "I'm not as tough as I used to be. Back in high school, nothing could hurt me. I feared nothing. Because my ma was well, my dad was present, and no matter what shit I pulled, my brothers looked up to me." He took a breath, studying her hand. "Then I left, spent my time thousands of miles away and just assumed it would all be waiting for me whenever I decided to come back."

"And it's not?"

"No. It's not."

"But your mom's alive."

He nodded. "She is."

"And your brothers are coming home next weekend for the Fourth."

"True. Though I'm worried about how that's going to go."

"You haven't communicated with any of them?"

"Yeah, I have. But it's different from seeing them in person. Sharing a meal under the same roof like we used to do day after day after day."

"I understand."

"You miss your family?" he asked.

"Nope. Just saw them."

"You should miss your family."

"Because if I don't my mom will get sick and my brother will forget about me? Is that what this is about? You blame yourself for living your life and not missing your family enough?"

"Laidey. I didn't come home for years. And if I did, it was brief. I didn't bother acknowledging birthdays or my parents' anniversary. I kept up with one brother regularly. Figured he was filling me in on what I needed to know about everybody else. I didn't realize that my relationships with the others were deteriorating. I assumed they were off living their lives while I lived mine. Figured we'd all get together when I found the time to head home."

"None of that is wrong, Xavier," Laidey said while crawling into his lap and snuggling against him. "You living your life is not what caused your mother's illness."

He ducked his face into her neck and held on for dear life. He had to gather himself before he said his next words.

"Stress causes illness. It's a fact. I just thought it was all fun and games at the time. I didn't see how stressful my antics were for my poor mother."

"You don't know what caused this illness. And you've got to remember that you are the oldest of five. Once you left for college, she still had four more just like you to deal with."

"No. No one was as bad as me."

"You might want to check those facts when everyone returns next weekend. I'm sure at least one of the Wright brothers did something just as ridiculous as making his teammates eat live goldfish."

"Probably." He chuckled, sucking in a breath and hissing through his teeth, feeling like such a pussy. He smoothed a hand over Laidey's brown curls, looking into her eyes. "You are such a surprise. I appreciate you talking me down. I really do."

"I'm right, you know. You can't hold yourself responsible for your mother's health. Although you can and probably should take responsibility for your relationships with your brothers. That will help reduce *your* stress. And besides, you did come back, and at the perfect time to help the town you left in your rearview mirror. Everybody loves that you're back."

"Well they haven't tried to run me out of town yet, so that's something."

"I won't let them run you out of town."

"Promise?" He kissed her lips, finding humor in the idea that tiny Laidey Bartholomew, scrumptious, little Tweety Bird was going to stand up to an angry mob trying to tar and feather his ass. "I appreciate that. Come on."

When he started to walk her away from the front door, Laidey balked. "Aren't we going in?"

"Tweets. We're doing this 007 style, remember? Sneaking you in the back window so the 'rents have no idea all the nasty we're going to get up to."

She grinned, tiptoed, and then practically skipped. "I so thought you were kidding about that." She bounced around in front of him like Marnie had anticipating a ride on his motorcycle.

He laughed, swinging their clasped hands between them as they strolled around the house. "Looks like you are up for the challenge."

"Did you leave the window unlocked?" she asked, all giddy.

"I did."

"So how are we doing this? Am I going to get on your shoulders so you can push me up high enough to crawl through? Only, I don't think I'll be able to pull you up and through on my own."

Xavier stopped. "Well, then? How are we possibly going to do this?"

All the joy left Laidey's face. "I don't know. Don't you have a plan?"

"I've had a plan since freshman year in high school. Care to hear it?" Laidey grinned, resuming their stroll. "My original plan was to boost you into the oak tree that's closest to the house. I'll be able to jump up, grab a branch, and hoist myself up to join you. Then, the two of us will carefully climb across the larger branches that head toward the house."

"I should have dressed more appropriately."

"Tweets, you'll look awesome climbing a tree in that fluff. You got your Keds on, right? They'll do ya."

"But what if I fall? What if I break something? Like my back? And you have to call 911? They'll come and roust your parents out of bed to find me lying paralyzed in their backyard."

"Yeah, I do remember how you enjoy tangling with bushes and the like. That's why I consulted my thirty-two-year-old self and came up with this." He pointed to the ladder perfectly positioned underneath his window.

"Sheer genius," Laidey commented.

"Ladies first," Xavier offered.

"So you can look up my dress? No thank you. You go first. Then you can help me through the window."

"Your wish is my command." Xavier grabbed onto the ladder and started to climb. "But once you're in my bedroom, I'm totally looking up your dress."

Laidey snickered, wondering why in the world they were going to such great lengths to do this. Except that it was fun, and clearly Xavier was all about the fun.

She hadn't been all about the fun. She'd been all about the work. Until fun, and sexy—let's not forget about the sexy, she thought—bulldozed his way into her life. Yeah, during that uppity secretary bit, she did not see herself here. Climbing through the Wright's second floor window to get it on with their hot son.

Lord, Grandmother Rowling is probably not very happy with me right now.

"Kiss me," she insisted, whispering forcefully as Xavier took hold of her hand. He helped her maneuver through the window, step down onto a chair, and then picked her up by the waist to set her down on the floor.

"Tweets, you ain't leaving till sun up. What's the rush?"

"I have the original Adelaide in my head, and she wouldn't have approved of this type of behavior."

"There's an original Adelaide?"

"My grandmother."

"Ah. Thus the nickname."

"Right. To differentiate."

"As if people couldn't tell you and your grandmother apart."

"I'm grateful actually. Or I would have been forever called Little Adelaide."

"Well, you are little," he pointed out. "Little and tight. Like your body is just perfectly compact, and your skin feels so good. And fuck, I'm getting myself off just standing here in the dark."

"Yeah, and I'm definitely not thinking about my grandmother anymore," she assured him with a grin.

The two of them stood apart, facing one another. Him tall and fit, her petite and feather-like. She swallowed. "We're a very odd pair."

"We're perfect."

She tilted her head. "Why do you say that?"

"Because I'm a good time waiting to happen, and you're a serious workaholic. I pissed Viper off to the point where she messed with the wrong woman, and you took her down. I was going to build Piper her dream shop, and you made it so much better. Face it, Tweets. This thing between us works pretty good."

"What if …?" She looked over at his bed.

"What if what?" he asked.

"You ever date a short girl?"

"There are no girls as short as you."

"So? What if we don't, you know, fit?"

"Pretty sure we're gonna fit." Then Xavier's entire expression changed. "Are you worried I'm going to hurt you?"

"No. No. Honestly I'm more worried about …"

"About what?"

"Other things."

"*What* other things? Tweets, I promise I'm pretty conventional when it comes to this sort of stuff."

She laughed, but suddenly felt very nervous. She started rubbing her arms and looking around the room, a fresh kind of fear engulfing her.

"Tweets," he whispered, moving in to tug her into his embrace. "Talk to me."

"I'm fine. I'll be fine," she assured him.

"You'll be fine because we're going to talk about whatever you're freaking out over before I begin to pull this dress over your head."

"This one has a zipper in the back," she said into his chest.

"All righty then. Before I unzip this dress." When she refused to say more, he went down on his knees so they were more or less face-to-face. "What's up?"

"I'm concerned that … I mean, what happens if …?"

"Tweets? Seriously, spit it out."

"What if I'm too *little*? What if I can't satisfy you? Enough?"

"What if the world comes to an end?" He shook his head. "Let's just have fun until we hit a snag. Then, we figure it out together. Okay?"

She nodded her head.

"Fuck," he exclaimed.

"What?"

"What if I am too big for you? What if I blow out an ovary or something horrible?"

"Oh, my gosh, what is with you and ovaries?" She pulled out of his grasp and reached back to unzip her dress herself. "You are not getting out of this. We are going to see how things go, and if I bust an ovary, or half of you gets left out of the fun, then we Google the issue tomorrow. Come on. I'm tired of talking about it. Show me some Xavier Wright action."

From a kneeling position, Xavier lunged at the tiny temptress who stood there trying to deflate his stiffy with all her practical nonsense. He swept her legs out from under her, circling her body with his arms so that he could cushion the fall when she hit the ground

"Whoa."

"Yeah, whoa," he taunted from above. "You want action, you got it." His lips landed on hers, not hard, but aggressively as he took control of the situation beneath him. "Arms up, Tweets."

She drew her arms over her head while he kissed her. His hands slid along the cotton fabric over her torso, his thumbs brushing over her breasts, and his fingertips folding around her sides. He was reveling in the feel of her body, and she was reveling in his touch.

When he broke the kiss, she found herself rolled over, face down against the floor. She felt the tug of the zipper sliding its way down her back, and his hands easing under the fabric and on to bare skin.

"Tweets, I swear to God, no woman is softer. You're like holding Vance, Jr. only better. You're fresh and new and sweet smelling, and man, I've wanted to get inside you for a long time now." He kissed along her spine, releasing her bra so he could have complete access. Then he bunched the skirt of her dress up over her hips, rolled her over to face him and sat her up to take off the cutest damn dress he was ever likely to see.

"I don't know when it happened, but I love the shit you wear."

The dress came up over her head, and the tiny lace dropped from her breasts, Xavier sat on his knees, amazed at how much he was feeling.

Fuck. This was it. Had to be.

He grabbed her to him, wrapping one arm around her waist and bringing her against him for the kiss of all kisses. He'd like to suck her tongue into his mouth and make a damn meal of it. She was too good for him. Felt too right. He wanted too much of her, and he wanted it all at the same time. His breathing became labored. His cock swelled against his own zipper, becoming painfully hard. He really didn't know what had him so enthralled, but making her his was a drive that came from deep down inside, an innate desire that was now raging out of control.

"On the bed," he whispered, barely breaking the kiss to say it.

She stood as they kissed. He stood too, working at the buttons on his shirt. The kiss broke, because yeah, he was too damn tall for her, but her fingers went to work on the bottom buttons and together they had his shirt open in record time.

Her warm hands heated him up when they stroked over his abdomen, up onto his chest, up to his shoulders, pushing the fabric back and down his arms. Once freed, he wrapped her up greedily and carried her the few steps to his bed. She sat on the edge, her fingers touching him in spots that shot lust to his groin. Shit. This girl had the touch of all touches.

When she looked up, he just nodded, as if to say, yeah, keep going. When she didn't track to what he was suggesting, he showed her by placing her hands at the buckle of his new belt. She watched his face, licking her lips as she pulled the strap free and unhooked the clasp.

"You ever undress a guy?" he asked, curious.

She shook her head.

"Like it?" he teased.

She grinned. "I like you in your clothes. I like you out of your clothes too," she whispered as she slowly, oh-so-slowly, pulled down his zipper. As soon as it was down, she placed her hand inside his pants, over his boxers, and smoothed her palm up and down the length of him.

"Is that what you're worried about being too big?" He touched her under the chin so she would look at him. "I promise. You're going to feel good."

She gave a hesitant laugh. "I don't doubt that. I want you to feel good too."

"Well, I can tell you one thing. I don't remember a time I've ever felt this good."

"Xavier," she whispered.

"Tweets," he said, his thumb running over her bottom lip. "Scoot back, let's get in bed."

He stripped out of his shoes, his socks, his pants, and his boxers as Laidey backed up against his headboard, smack dab in the middle of his bed.

"Damn," he said, standing there taking her in. "You're a mighty fine sight, Miss Bartholomew. Rest assured, I am aware that I don't deserve this," he said as he placed a knee on the bed. He crawled on his hands and knees, reaching for her ankle to pull her body flat underneath his. "But I'm taking it. You've always brought out the worst in me."

"I think that's all a bunch of fuss," she claimed, her fingers tickling his shoulders as he caged her with his body.

"Because you've learned my secrets. You know I fall for prissy dresses and decorative pencils. How afraid could you possibly be?"

"Oh," she whispered, her eyes glancing shyly into his. "But now I'm truly afraid."

"Of what?"

"Of you," she said softly, "breaking my heart."

He felt his own heart dissolve. "Tweets," he whispered. "I wasn't sure when exactly to tell you this." He licked his lips. "But that kiss we shared after our day on the boat?"

"Yeah?"

"That was your last first kiss."

He saw the moment she understood. She bit her lip, hiding what looked like humor.

"What?" he coaxed.

"That was both romantic and bullying, all at the same time."

"Sorta was. That's why I didn't want to bring it up. But you getting all shy and frightened on me was not going to cut it. I had to bring the old bully into the bedroom."

She licked her lips. "My last first kiss, huh?"

"If I've got anything to say about it."

She pulled his face down to hers so she could kiss him. "What else do you have to say about it?"

"Plenty. But right now, I'm going to let my body do the talking." He spread out over her, lowering some of his weight against her, some to the side. She was little enough that he could easily arrange her however they needed. He just wanted to be sure to be gentle as he did it. He kissed her lips and let his cock do the slow glide against her thigh. Then he shifted his position, and let his cock do that slow glide again, this time hitting the sweet spot.

Ah. Yeah. Fuck, that feels good.

"Condom" he remembered aloud. He reached across Laidey and fumbled for the box on the nightstand, restraining himself from showing Tweets just how big of an investment he'd made in their future. He ripped the package with his teeth and offered it to her. "I would so rather have your hands on me."

"Okay." She smiled as she took it, but hesitated. "Just watch and make sure I do it right."

One eyebrow rose. "Tweets, don't tell me this is your first time."

"For rolling on a condom? Yeah, it's my first time."

"Really?" He grinned in disbelief.

"Are you smirking at me?"

"Sorta. You've definitely kept yourself chained to your desk for way too long."

"Hmm. I was waiting for the proper diversion."

"And then I came to town."

"And then you roared into town on that screaming machine."

"Which got you off."

She didn't say anything else. Was concentrating on sheathing his dick. "How's that?" she asked, observing her handiwork.

"It'll do. Come on, get up."

"Get up?"

"On top," he told her.

"You're supposed to be on top."

"Absolute music to my ears," he said, flipping onto his back and underneath her as he helped her sit. "But the experts say that if you're on top, you're able to control the experience."

"I don't want to be in control. I want the full-blown Xavier Wright experience."

Xavier stopped all movement. "Whatever McKenna has told you, she's lying. I never touched her."

"McKenna hasn't told me anything, but what do you mean you never touched her?"

"Then what Xavier Wright experience are you talking about?"

"The bossy, bully, badass Xavier Wright experience. Do not let me down."

Xavier burst out laughing.

"Shh," she insisted. "Stop laughing. We don't want Big Daddy coming up the stairs and pounding on the door."

"Big Daddy?" Xavier was horrified.

"You know. Your father. He's big."

"Okay. Let's set a few ground rules. First, if you're calling anybody Big Daddy, it better be me. And, really, just leave my family out of the bedroom completely."

"Fine. I'm just saying, shh."

"Got it. Okay. Where were we?"

"You want me on top, and I want you to make me."

"Oh, Tweets. Finally, you've read my mind. Lean down here and kiss me."

Their kiss was long and drawn out, erasing all the chatter they'd worked through, pulling the sensations being stirred up to the forefront of their minds. Xavier couldn't get enough, and Laidey reveled in his exuberance, returning the enthusiasm with her lips and tongue, her fingers and hands. She reached down to stroke his erection and moaned at the hefty length of him. Her thighs clenched together before she started rubbing herself against his thigh.

"Be mine," he said. "Be mine, tonight and always," he whispered. "Let's find a way to make this good."

Laidey wasn't sure if he was talking about sex or life, but she didn't stop to question. She was all in. Whatever the appropriately named Mr. *Wright* wanted, he was going to get. He was definitely her one and only. Now they just needed to figure out if he was the right fit.

Right there with her, he pulled her thigh over his torso, helping her to straddle him. He pushed himself up into a sitting position, the two of them lip locked, his cock rubbing her sex, her sex dripping with desire. She felt that keen awakening in her groin, the desperate longing for physical satisfaction. Her breasts were tight and ached for his touch. She couldn't rub herself against him in enough places.

"Use your hand," he whispered against her lips. "Guide me when you're ready. Take it slow. We'll make this good."

She was ready. So ready. So deliciously out of her mind she didn't think any of it through. She pressed his chest to indicate he should lay back. She pushed up, squeezing his hips with her knees as she stroked his shaft twice before positioning it at her entrance.

They both watched the tip of his penis penetrate her body. "Hot damn," he said, his head collapsing back into his pillow. His hips shifted up, pressing his cock further into Laidey. "Sorry," he gasped. "Sorry. I'll stop. You're in charge."

"I'm fine," she whispered, hands braced on his chest, her head bent, her eyes closed so she could really be present for this experience. If this was her last first time, she wanted to remember every little thing. Like how … freaking … amazing Xavier's body was. The connection was fierce, and slow, and big, and tight, and easy, but hard, and so delicious she wanted to weep. He wasn't too big. He was perfect. Perfect, perfect, absolutely—"Wha—"

Laidey found herself falling, no—whipped around—lying flat on her back, one knee caught up alongside her chest, her other leg spread wide as Xavier took control.

"Too slow, Tweets. Now I'm going to show you how it's done."

It was done hard, and fast, and brilliantly, with heavy breathing and a whole lot of moaning at the end. Xavier Wright was brilliant in bed. He knew how to use his body, every inch of it, to provide pleasure, to string her out until she burst into a million tiny stars and drifted off to a world beyond anything she'd ever known.

Yeah. He was that good.

So good.

Way, way, way past good.

No. The truth was, he was one *o* short of good. Because Xavier Wright was a *god*.

A sweaty, hot, sexy—oh, those noises he made—gorgeous god among men. No wonder the mere mortals of the world couldn't keep up with him. They had no idea what they were up against.

"Tweets." The name burrowed through her consciousness. "Tweets. Baby, you all right?"

Of course, she was all right. She was floating. Relishing. Luxuriating in a state of supreme well-being.

"Seriously." She felt a kiss on her lips. "Tweets. Are you there?"

"Mmmm," she hummed and moaned and tried to stretch, not wanting to give up the luxurious floating. And the gloating, because let's face it, this was worth gloating over. Her eyes fluttered open as she rubbed at her face. Her grin came faster. She licked her lips and just knew that life had changed forever.

Another kiss. "You okay there, Tweets? Can I keep going?"

Going?

"Aren't you? Umm," she tried to force words from her dazzled brain. "Are we done?"

"No, baby. You're done. I'm not done." She heard him laugh.

"Why are you laughing at me?" she wondered, groggy. Like what the hell happened, and why am I groggy?

Xavier kept laughing, but he also kept moving inside her. "Tweets. I swear. You freaking slay me."

"I think I'm the one who's been slain."

"You with me now? You coming around?"

"Did I pass out?"

"I'm not sure. But whatever happened, trust me, you enjoyed it."

"I *so* enjoyed it," she whispered. "Sorry. Carry on."

And he did. On and on and on, and man did she get back into it, her body rocking and rolling right along with his. When he was the one who passed out, she kept going. When she was wrung out, he started it all up again. They couldn't get enough of each other. And the whole time, it was sexy, or fun, or both. It might have gotten edgy, definitely passionate, but it never felt awkward, or odd, or frightening.

At the end ... at the end, it just felt like home.

At the end, the two of them went to sleep.

And for Laidey, in the morning, everything was changed.

CHAPTER TWENTY-EIGHT

There weren't many surprises to be found back in Henderson, but Laidey Bartholomew had definitely turned out to be just that.

A surprise.

A big one.

Like the kind you want to slip a freaking ring on.

Xavier had only known the girl about a month. Had slept with her one damn time. Well, technically that wasn't exactly true, but … you know, had only one good night of lovin' her up under his belt. Not enough time to fall madly in love and want to commit to someone forever and ever.

Only … he sort of did.

Everywhere he looked, it seemed people in Henderson were coupled up. Brooks and Lolly. Vance and Piper. Duncan and Annabelle. Thor and Missy. The Pink One and his Scarlett spitfire. Was he just drinking the Kool-Aid? Or was Ad-el-aide Bar-tho-lo-mew exactly what he thought she was? Perfect. For him. Right along with …

Brilliant.

Effective.

Smokin' hot in bed.

Bent to the serious side of life, which—knowing him—he probably needed.

Sweet.

Cussed when it was uber-called for.

Made him laugh. Especially when she cussed.

Played his favorite instrument better than he did.

Kicked Viper's ass when it was ass-kicking time.

Yeah, he needed to get this girl locked down, and he needed to do it now. He wasn't getting any younger, and there were plenty of young guys—like that *Harry*—who were just waiting on the chance that he'd screw up the good thing he'd found.

Yep. Tweets was his, and he needed to do something about it.

Fast.

"Ma. I'm going to ask Tweets to marry me."

Cutlery clattered to the table. The two of them were sitting in the kitchen, enjoying a midnight pancake session, as had become their habit.

"When?" his mother asked. Not why, or isn't this a little fast, or it's too soon. Just when. "And how?" she asked, her eyes glistening, indicating she'd given up hope of ever seeing one of her boys walk down the aisle.

"I don't know. I just decided. But I can't keep it in. Clearly," he indicated by pointing between the two of them. "Better figure out something before I ruin the surprise attack I'm going to need to get her to say yes. Can't trust myself not to go blurting out something stupid, declaring my intentions before I've got a ring in my hand."

"I've got a ring," his mother offered, sliding her own engagement ring off her hand.

"Ma. No. Hold on." He patted her hands. "That's your ring. You keep it. I can buy Tweets a ring. Oh, fuck." Suddenly the whole process dawned on him. "I haven't met her folks. I bet they've never heard of me. If I'm going to do this, I've got to go talk to her dad, right?" He looked around the kitchen, realizing what this was going to take. His startled gaze landed back on his mother.

She was nodding. Smiling. Her eyes so full of joy she couldn't hold back the tears. "Xavier," she whispered. "This is wonderful."

"I know, right?" He leaned his big body across the table and kissed her on the forehead. "And you and I will convince her to do it quick."

She nodded vigorously.

"Not that I'm thinking we're going to lose you," he assured her. "But yeah, it's time one of your sons gave you a wedding. Let's get this done quick."

"Baby," she patted his hands. "You do this however you want to do this. I'm not going anywhere, I can promise you that. I will be at your wedding, as the radiant mother of the groom."

"Then help me out here. What do I do first?"

Her mother smiled the proudest smile of all smiles. "Go talk to her daddy."

Xavier was going to do that. Right after he talked to Crain. Only he didn't want Laidey seeing him talking to Crain, so he called the man on a Sunday morning and manufactured a reason he needed five minutes of his time—today—and met him at the site Chase had liked best for the multi-unit project.

"You got any plans to show me?" Crain asked as they stood looking at a run-down shell of a building. "I've got a good imagination on a lot of things, but when it comes to concrete, I like to see the schematics."

"Yeah. Sure. When I've got something drawn up, you'll be the first to take a look. In the meantime, I've got a favor to ask. A personal favor."

"Shoot."

Xavier blinked. *That was easy.*

"Ah. Okay. So, I'd like to get in touch with Adelaide Bartholomew's parents." Xavier stood quiet for a moment, letting that sink in. "I want to speak to them without Laidey catching wind of it."

Carraway was a smart one. His eyes got big, and he wiggled something in his pocket. "You thinkin' about havin' a heart-to-heart with her pa?"

"That's my plan. But I've yet to meet him. I'm not sure how things are done in Dallas, and I have no clue how to contact them. So I'm coming to you."

"Well, that's good. Because, trust me, you don't want to do it the way I did. Meeting the parents is a smart move. Real smart. I'll tell you what, doing things by the book, especially in this situation, it's gonna save you a whole lot of time and heartache. Whatever you need from me, you've got it. I'll have their names, numbers, and address to you by noon."

"Great. That's … great. I appreciate it."

"Not a problem. If you're hooked on that little filly, I'm happy to help you seal the deal."

"So you're okay with this? Me and Laidey?"

"I'm okay with it, yeah. Do I think you're good enough for Adelaide Bartholomew? No way. But, man to man, I know what it's like to be in love with a girl who is way out of your reach. Nothin' to be done about it either except leap out there and try to catch her." Crain smacked Xavier on the back. "If you get lucky, I trust you'll appreciate whatever benevolence has been bestowed and do your damnedest to take care of my most important employee."

"I will. I plan to."

"Good. All right. Prepare to book your flight to Dallas. You'll have all the information you'll need by noon."

"Thanks. I owe you."

"Yeah, ya do," Crain teased. "And I will collect somewhere down the line. Count on it."

As Crain drove off, mumbling something about looking at a boat, Xavier wondered which path of mass destruction he wanted to take. Did he confide in his ex about his impending engagement—get her opinion on the style of ring she thought Tweets would be into—or did he consult the man who seemed to know everything? Harry.

That bit of quandary only lasted a few damn seconds because Xavier decided there was no way in hell he was giving Harry the chance to beat him to the punch. If Harry got wind of Xavier's plans, he didn't trust the guy not to propose to his Tweets while he was off bending the knee to her father in Dallas.

Easy decision. McKenna gets the call.

He pulled out his phone and dialed her up.

Besides, he thought as the phone rang, she's the sister-he-never-had, and was probably going to end up in his damn wedding. Nope, he wasn't going to be able to shake McKenna after this went down. He may as well embrace it. Then he'd see about fixing what he'd broken there.

A male voice answered, "Hello."

What the—? Xavier literally pulled the phone away from his head and looked at who he'd dialed. McKenna Blakely, clear as day. He put the phone back to his ear. "Xander?"

"Fuck."

The call was cut off.

"What the hell?" His *Brown-Eyed Girl* ringtone started up and a picture of a naked sleeping Tweets lit up his screen. Really gonna need to change that before she sees it, he thought as he answered. "Sweet Tweets."

"Are we going out on the boat today?" she asked.

"Didn't I say we were?" he countered.

"Yes, but you didn't say what time."

He checked his watch. Shit. He had things to do. Big, important things. Like buy some Margarita mix and whatever brand of tequila Harry liked to serve so he could get his girl all liquored up and have his way with her out in the middle of the lake.

"What time would you like to go?" he asked.

"Three."

"Why three?"

"I want to push through and finish five proposals that are on the brink of being ready. I want them in the mail first thing tomorrow."

"So you want to work on a Sunday instead of going out on the boat with me?" Clearly, he needed to explain the Weekend Rule.

"I want to do both. But I especially don't want to be distracted by work once I'm out on the boat with you."

"Good thought. Does three o'clock give you enough time?"

"It does. I promise."

"Holding you to it, Tweets." Then he sent a kiss through the phone and cut her off.

The day was actually unfolding brilliantly. He now had time to scout out tequila, a shot of which would give him the courage he needed to call Laidey's parents after Crain forwarded him their number. He'd have an appointment in Dallas on the books before he picked up Tweets.

Done.

CHAPTER TWENTY-NINE

Laidey hadn't lived through a workweek like this one since she first came on board at CC Dallas. Back then, things were hectic and tension ran high as Crain worked hard to secure account after account. Her job? Spreading the word that CC Dallas existed. Her job now? Holding CC Henderson together with duct tape and a lot of handholding.

Poppy had chosen this particular week to head back to Dallas and participate in a summer vacation with her family over the Fourth of July. Which, you know, was fine. It was just a shame that it coordinated with the week Mr. Carraway—Crain—wanted to get everything done yesterday.

So Laidey was up early every morning. She worked from Poppy's desk at CC Henderson, so not to miss the sudden shifts in focus for which Crain was famous. These shifts caused a lot of running back and forth to her own office to grab what she needed for the next meeting.

It was bedlam.

Yet, things were being resolved. Mr. Carraway—Crain—was good at that. He'd look at all the research they'd gathered on an issue concerning the sports academy. In nine cases out of ten, he would make a quick decision and they could move forward.

In the tenth case, she and Crain would waltz over to E&E Investments and rally the troops there. Troops being Hale, Vance, and Pinks. Or any combination that included Pinks. Hale and Pinks, Vance and Pinks. Never just Hale and Vance, which Laidey found odd until she realized it was Crain who wanted Pinks in on all of the major decisions.

"He's a sharp one," was all he'd say about it. In the back of Laidey's mind, she couldn't get the conversation from that day on the boat out of her head. Which led her to notice—probably more than she would have if thoughts of Tansy stepping out on Crain weren't dancing through her mind—just how much time McKenna Blakely and her former boyfriend, Xavier Wright, were spending together.

Especially since Laidey had hardly seen him at all this week.

If it wasn't for all those sexy texts he sent while taking a lunch break, and especially those from his bed at night, she'd be concerned. She also reminded herself that she was so busy with Crain she had to turn down Xavier's offer of a lunch date twice, along with his insistence that she come climb the ladder into his bedroom Thursday night.

She told him the truth. That she wanted to. Really wanted to. But she was too tired to get herself there and would probably fall asleep halfway up the ladder if she tried.

When he suggested he could probably manage climbing through her ground-floor window with no problem, she thought long and hard before answering. Having him wrap his strong arms around her while she drifted to sleep sounded like heaven.

She just didn't trust that was all that would happen.

"I need my sleep," she told him, calling instead of texting because she wanted to hear his voice.

"I know, Tweets. Carraway is killing you."

"When he's in town, the rubber hits the road. Which is why I work so hard when he's gone. I need to be prepared for anything."

"The man has a severe case of ADHD," Xavier observed.

"Part of his genius," Laidey sighed.

"You still hung up on him?" he teased.

"Nope. I'm hung up on a brilliant architect who likes to walk around town posing as a motorcycle-riding, construction-boot-wearing badass."

Xavier laughed. "You have me nailed."

"I do, don't I."

"You love my bike."

"I love my own bike."

"Yeah, Tweets. Not the same vibe."

"I know. We're a bit different."

"We complement each other," he countered. "Beautifully. Face it, Tweets. You're never gonna find a better yang to your yin, so I suggest you stop trying."

That made her grin. A big, bottom-lip-biting grin as she snuggled down further into her covers and turned onto her side.

"Tweets?"

"I'm here," she whispered. "I'm starting to think you're my Mr. Right. You aren't planning to break my heart are you?"

"Pfft. Tweets, I'm planning to make you Mrs. Wright," he said lightly, playing off her words.

"Then why are you seeing McKenna behind my back?" she teased.

Silence.

Dead silence.

Oh, no. "Xavier?" she asked, sitting up. "*Are* you seeing McKenna behind my back?"

"No. Tweets—Laidey," he stumbled. "Of course not. Why would you even—how could you possibly—think that?" The grimace in his voice was apparent. The same grimace he always had when he spoke of his connection to McKenna. Laidey didn't understand that. Xavier acted like he was never in love with McKenna, but she knew that wasn't the case. Well, she knew that wasn't the case on McKenna's side. Maybe he never loved her back the same way, but he must have liked her when they were dating. If not, why ask her out?

Laidey stated the present facts. "I saw her coming out of Piper's shop three separate times this week. Xavier, I'm just teasing you, but it's almost as if—thou doth protest too much."

"God, no. I'm protesting the exact right amount," he sounded relieved. "Tweets, you know how I feel about you. You've been busy, and McKenna has issues."

"Issues?"

"I told you at Vance's party. She's worried about sitting at our table on the Fourth. Especially since you're not."

"That's an old story, and I'm fine with it," she told Xavier, although now she was becoming less fine with it. "But I doubt McKenna would come to badger you about that over and over."

"No. But she's been running a lot of errands for Ma these days. The two of them want things perfect when my brothers show up Saturday."

"Oh. Well, is there anything I can do to help?"

"Fuck, no. McKenna has stockpiled enough food and beer to sustain an army. What you can do is stop working so hard and take care of my mother's firstborn. I'm feeling neglected, Tweets."

She laughed, relief surfacing. "CC Henderson has off for the three-day weekend. I just need to get through tomorrow, and then I'm all yours."

"I'm holding you to that. Although I'm out of town tomorrow. Not exactly sure when I'll be getting back. Might have to meet you at The Situation. I hear July third is quite the party."

"I've heard stories. Where are you headed? Raleigh?"

"A little further west than Raleigh. Got some important business to tend to."

"About Piper's shop?"

"Nope. Not Piper's shop. Hey, that's going surprisingly well. If that slave-driver boss of yours loosens your leash a little, stop in tomorrow and take a look. Chase will be there.

"I will. I promise."

"And once I get back, no work. Holiday weekend afoot, and I want your mind, your hands, and that lush, little body of yours all on me."

"All right, Mr. Wright. I'm putting you on my agenda now."

"That-a-girl."

"Good night, Bossy."

"Good night, uppity secretary. Hey, we've gotta do that, ya know."

"Do what?"

"Role-play. Your office, Piper's shop, sneak into that conference room of your hero's, sit my naked ass in his chair and have you get all uppity on me."

"You are absurd." Laidey rolled over and squeezed her eyes tight. "We are not violating Crain's chair that way."

"We'll see, Tweets. We'll see."

Once they hung up, Xavier stared at the ceiling, wondering if he was going to be able to pull this off. McKenna had been in Piper's shop more often than he cared to count this week. No surprise Tweets saw her coming and going. He should have been more careful, but what choice did he have?

McKenna was all over the idea of helping plan his proposal to Tweets. She even had a jeweler friend over in Oxford who let her cart rings back and forth while he worked with Chase on the interior of Piper's shop.

Chase, whom he'd let in on his plan the moment after he told his mother.

"Seems quick," Chase had said.

"It is quick," Xavier agreed. "You don't think she's the one for me?" Xavier challenged.

"I think you know your own mind. If your gut is telling you she's the one you can't live without, then put the hammer to the nail."

Xavier had laughed at the analogy, but in truth, that was exactly what he needed to hear. That was the moment when Xavier's concern about moving too fast changed into determination. Because he hadn't thought about it that way before. He knew he wanted Laidey for more reasons than he was capable of putting into words. Deep down in his gut, he knew she was the one for him. But Chase had done him a solid because now Xavier understood why.

Tweets was the one person he didn't want to live without.

Dallas, Texas

"Mr. Bartholomew," Xavier said, shaking the man's hand. Laidey's father was on the short side, but looked to be a fierce and formidable opponent in this matchup. Joseph Bartholomew was dressed in a business suit befitting the head honcho of this enormous office building. After keeping Xavier waiting no more than three minutes—three minutes that felt like an eternity—he'd come out of his office to personally greet him.

"Thanks for carving time out of your busy schedule," Xavier said. "Your daughter must get her work ethic from you."

Joseph smiled. "Come on back to my office. Let's get acquainted."

And so they did, with Xavier focusing on his credentials as evidence that he'd be able to make a good living and take care of a wife and family. "When I moved back to Henderson recently to help with the care of my mother, I had the intention of starting a business either in town or somewhere in the vicinity. But, honestly, Henderson is a gold mine for someone in my field. Right now, there's more need for experts in design and construction than my partner and I can handle. The ground is ripe for starting my own architectural design firm and simply hiring workers as needed. Same thing on the construction end."

"You asked to speak to Adelaide's mother and me. But I wanted to have a chance to get to know you first, man to man."

"I guess it's pretty obvious why I'm here," Xavier said. "Although I assume Laidey has not mentioned my name. We've only known each other about a month, and for part of that time, I was overwrought with my mother's sudden decline. I'm happy to say that she's doing well at the moment."

"I'm glad to hear it."

"Yes. Well, ah," Xavier faltered, looking at the rug beneath his feet, rubbing his hands together. *Fuck.* This was harder than he'd thought. He shook his head and brought up his gaze, locking eyes with the man who held his happiness in his hands. "Laidey is my everything," the words fell out, surprising him. "I've got degrees and credentials, and I'm good at what I do. I can make money and do it while building a solid reputation. But when it comes to life?" His hands parted. "Laidey makes me better at that. I like to tease her," he confessed. "Because she's cute and intense. She worries and follows rules. Yet she'll throw me a curveball when I'm least expecting it. It's those curveballs that get me looking at life a little less cynically. Laidey comes from this place of focus—so dedicated to her job—yet she wears Keds everywhere she goes."

"Keds?" her father asked, as if he'd never seen them.

"Yeah. Keds. And they're cute too. That's what I noticed first. That's what I ended up falling in love with."

"Her Keds?"

"The fact that she wears them. That she's comfortable being herself. Being Laidey. She doesn't have to look the part of a business executive to be a stellar business executive. She doesn't have to know the right people or show up at the right events. She's kind and she's clever, and she's given a guy like me—a former bully—a chance to live up to my potential. I'm not perfect, Mr. Bartholomew. But Laidey makes me want to get as close as I can."

Mr. Bartholomew smiled. "All right son. I say you've made a damn good case for yourself. Let's go meet Laidey's mother for lunch. See if you can get her to join Team Xavier."

Addy Bartholomew turned out to be a pushover.

One look at Xavier and she licked her lips, just the way her daughter did. All Xavier had to do was open the ring box and place it before Laidey's mother.

Champagne was promptly ordered.

Feeling a total high, with all sorts of thoughts about parents meeting parents and families meeting families tripping through his head, Xavier made a stop at his parents' place instead of shooting off to find Laidey at The Situation.

He handed his mother the ring box, asking her to keep it safe, before he regaled his parents with the adventures of "Xavier Goes to Dallas." The two of them, Xavier noticed, grinned—well, beamed— as he gave them a full accounting. When he realized they were simply reflecting back his own expression, he laughed.

"How am I going to keep this a secret from Tweets? I'm so stoked. Maybe I should just ask her tonight."

"No," his mother said. "Stay the course. McKenna's worked hard planning the setting. What the two of you worked out is perfect. Laidey will love it."

"She will. But with the way I'm feeling right now, she's going to take one look at me and know."

"She won't. Well, she may know that you love her, but she won't guess the rest. It's too soon."

"It's not too soon," he defended.

"I don't mean it's too soon for you to know she's the one. Or for you to ask her to marry you. I just mean it's too soon for her to see it coming."

"True that. Shit." He ran a hand through his hair. "She's not going to say no, is she? I mean, because it's soon? If she says no because she doesn't want to marry me, I'll have to deal. But if she says no, it's too soon, ask me again in a year …"

"Buck up," his father ordered. "You're a Wright. Act like it."

Xavier laughed. "What? Wrights don't take no for an answer?"

"Damn right, they don't," his father said. "Ask your mother. When a Wright asks a woman to marry him, there's only one right answer."

"Poor Tweets." Xavier laughed. "She has no idea what's about to go down."

CHAPTER THIRTY

The bar was packed. Being of small stature, Laidey was jostled while slipping in between people in an effort to maneuver her way off the dance floor and down the hallway toward the back bar.

This was not her scene.

Not that she hadn't been having fun dancing with Scarlett and her friends. She had. Scarlett was a force, and an entertaining one at that. Laidey had a ball trying to keep up. But when the dance floor became so full she couldn't move without being buffeted against one body and into another, she'd had enough. Her plan was to extricate herself from the throng and check the time on her phone. If Xavier didn't make it to the July third bash within the next few minutes, she planned to text him that she was going home.

She didn't actually know how she was going to get there because it was dark, and although the streets of Henderson were safe as far as she knew, she wasn't interested in walking back alone. Everyone she knew was having too much fun to ask them to leave. So she was stuck.

Another drink? Or fresh air?

She'd already had two beers, which really should be her quota, so she opted for fresh air, scooting out the back of the place, not paying attention to the "Emergency Exit Only" sign because she noticed no one ever did.

One step out into the balmy night and she smiled. Because a very familiar, earsplitting nightmare of a roar captured her attention. She turned her head to the left in time to see Xavier Wright—not the architect but the badass, leather jacket and all—roll around the side of the building.

Laidey didn't have to wave him down. He made a beeline and stopped right in front of her. Smiling. Gunning his engine. "Hop on," he said in way of greeting.

She retrieved the helmet off the back, put it on, grabbed ahold of Xavier's arm and shoulder to pull herself up behind him. As soon as she had her arms wrapped around him, off they flew.

It was the ride of her life.

As the wind whipped over them, Laidey realized—because she couldn't get the grin off her face—that her whole worldview had changed. Xavier Wright had changed everything.

How she saw herself.

How she saw him.

How she saw motorcycles and the men who rode them.

Everything.

The ride went on and on, unending, and she was perfectly content to let it. If this was a test of their compatibility, she was passing it with flying colors. Because she got it now. There was freedom in the ride. Freedom in the wind. Freedom in the dark. And with that freedom came a sense of well-being.

Who knew?

They rode with the night, her body against his, connected. When he drove into her drive, she was surprised and a little sad. Until she started to move. Her body revolted, letting her know that even though she'd done nothing but sit and hug Xavier, her limbs weren't happy to be stuck in one position for so long.

"Ouch." She grimaced as she extricated herself from the man and his machine.

"Tweets. You okay?"

"Just sore now that I'm moving. On the ride, I was … perfect."

Xavier sprung the strap from her chin and helped guide her helmet off. "You are that," he offered casually. He took his own helmet off before rubbing her arms, bending them at the elbows, and shaking things out. "Tiny woman. Gonna have to train you right along with Marnie."

"Marnie?"

"The dirt bike thing, remember? I promised Marnie I'd tune up my old dirt bike and show her how it's done. I think you should join us."

She grinned into his face, never imagining she'd find the thought of riding a dirt bike appealing. "Okay."

He grinned back, probably surprised she wasn't fussing about safety and noise. He gripped her chin with his fingers and leaned down to kiss her lips. "Love you, Tweets," he whispered before he took her breath away.

Wait. Did he just say the L word? Laidey's first instinct was to shake his kiss off and ask for clarification. *Did* he love her? For real? But the kiss was too distracting, too delicious, too intoxicating to break free from. She didn't have the will to do it.

Besides, what if he had to backtrack because she'd put him on the spot? Asking for clarification when he'd just said it like … whatever.

"Hey-hey," he breathed over her lips, wrapping his arms around her and pulling her tight against him. "Where'd ya just go?"

"I'm here," she told him.

"No, you're not. You were," he said nodding, acknowledging that the kiss had indeed been awesome until she started thinking. "But then you weren't."

She shook her head. "I'm sorry. It was just my mind spinning like it does sometimes."

He bent his knees so they were eye to eye. "Everything okay?"

"Everything is great," she told him truthfully, leaping onto his body, wrapping her legs around his waist, distracting him before she went ahead and made a fool out of herself.

Because she was in deep.

When it came to Xavier Wright, she was in *way* deep. And yes, even though he had said, "Love you, Tweets," clear as day, Laidey's logical brain felt more and more certain it was simply an endearment. A figure of speech. One intended differently than how she dearly wanted to interpret.

It was early in their relationship, she told herself as she peppered his face with kisses, and even though she was *so* into him and he seemed just as into her, she couldn't expect him to be where she—*oh, man*—just now—*wow*—realized she'd ended up.

Truly, madly in love with Xavier Wright.

She felt a hand at the back of her head, his mouth forcing hers open for a bold kiss. She accepted, gleefully. Relishing the awareness that this was no crush. That she loved Xavier, the former bully, the man who saw her in the parking lot on that first night, forcing her out of a state of invisibility. The man who now held her in his arms like she meant something. Yeah, they had a good thing going, and she planned to eat it up and pray that Xavier Wright would come to realize that the two of them were meant to be together.

"I missed you," she whispered as the kiss ended. He answered with a noise of agreement, with a lick up her neck, with a kiss to her cheek. A squeeze to her ribs. "Eek."

"Sorry, Tweets, just couldn't help myself," he said as he let her feet touch the ground.

"I've got the house to myself. Why don't you come inside?"

Xavier stood there. Grinning. Looking her in the eye and licking his lips.

"Tweets," he breathed, looking away for a moment, and then bringing those sparkling gray eyes back to hers. "Nothin' I'd like more. Believe me. But, I think I'd better go."

"Go?" Her brows lifted. "Go?" she asked again.

"I know." He laughed. "Definitely not the walk on the wild side I'm sure you were expecting. And trust me, this is painful, because I want in your pants, Tweets. And I mean that literally because it's the first time I've seen you in a pair of jeans."

"So come inside," she said, taking his hand and pulling him toward the front door.

He didn't budge.

"Tweets," he said, reeling her back to him, back into his arms and against the comfort of his body. "Here's the deal. I've got a big plan for tomorrow. It's a surprise. If I stay, I'm going to blurt it all out."

"A surprise?"

"Yes. A surprise."

"For me?"

"For you. You like surprises?"

"Is it a good surprise?"

"I hope so. God, I really hope so."

She cracked a grin, because he was definitely not sure of this surprise. "Okay," she relented, getting a sense that whatever he had on his mind was big. "You want to surprise me, I'm happy to be surprised." She moved in and kissed the spot on his chest that aligned directly with her lips. "Text me when you get into bed?"

He grinned, and then kissed the top of her head.

"You got it, Tweets."

CHAPTER THIRTY-ONE

It wasn't until after two o'clock that Laidey was awakened by the ping of her phone.

"Sorry Tweets. Just got to bed. Brothers came home and we've been playing quarters at the kitchen table for hours. I'm fucking old. Hangover has already started and I'm still drunk. Not good. Hitting the hay. Hope I didn't wake you."

Laidey smiled at the message, relieved to have finally heard from him. Happy that his brothers were home and, if the playing of drinking games was any indication, things between them were going well.

She rolled over and tried to go back to sleep.

At six in the morning, she gave up her search for REM sleep, got out of bed, brushed her teeth and hair, flipped one of Xavier's favorite sundresses over her head and loaded the basket of her bike with a thermos of coffee, Advil, and two croissants she'd defrosted from the freezer. In a fit of inspiration, she'd created small containers of butter and jam and wrapped them up with the pastries in a large, red-checked scarf that screamed picnic. She threw in a knife too.

Pleased with her plan, she biked her way to the Wright's home. Instead of pulling up the driveway, she rode onto the grass between their house and the neighbor's, hoping to avoid being noticed.

She smiled when she spied the one detail of her plan she didn't have control over. The ladder was still jammed under Xavier's window. She wondered what his brothers would have to say about that if and when they happened to see it. She didn't want to think about Mr. Wright noticing it.

Still, fear of being caught was less compelling than climbing the ladder with her "Happy Fourth of July Hangover Cure" and surprising Xavier. She quietly stashed her bike against the side of the house realizing non-hungover people might begin stirring since it was now after seven.

With a finger through the thermos and the rest of her hand clasped around her checkered bundle, Laidey carefully ascended the rungs of the ladder, one foot up, then the other, all the way to the top. The window was down, but the shade was up, so she pressed her forehead against the glass to peek inside, right before she knocked.

She swiftly withdrew her hand before it could land against the glass and disturb what was happening inside. What she *thought* was happening, because, honest to God, this did not make any sense.

There was Xavier, his gorgeous brown hair, his clean-shaven cheek, his broad back and muscled arms, lip locked with McKenna.

Lip locked.

With *McKenna.*

In his bed.

McKenna was on top of the covers, Xavier was not. The two were sitting up, but his lips were definitely pressed to hers. In fact, his hand was wrapped around the back of her head, pressing her to him in just the same way he'd done with her not that many hours ago.

Xavier.

And McKenna.

Kissing.

Right there.

Unable to rip her gaze from the two of them, the effort to breathe became increasingly difficult, and her logical brain broke away to run on its own tangent. Did McKenna use the ladder too? Or had she just walked in the front door? Had she spent the entire night? Been in his bed all night long and was just now saying goodbye? Was she planning to climb out the window for her getaway?

Laidey looked down at the ground, figuring she'd better be fast but careful if she didn't want to get caught watching them.

Noise rang inside her ears, like an internal alarm had gone off. Her vision blurred as the incomprehension swirled through her head while she carefully made her way back down the ladder. This couldn't be right, she assured herself. Something was definitely off, her mind insisted.

Xavier said he was drunk.

Maybe he still was.

Perhaps McKenna couldn't help herself now that his beard was gone.

Whatever the reason, her chest now felt as if she was in cardiac arrest, her heart threatening to break even as she tried to hold off that well of emotion so she could sort through the facts.

Xavier.

Definitely Xavier.

And McKenna.

Definitely McKenna.

Kissing.

She'd seen it with her own eyes, and still she couldn't comprehend it. Xavier didn't *love* McKenna. She knew that. He didn't even like her all that much. She knew that too.

"But they were kissing!" her heart screamed.

She was tempted to crawl back up the ladder and look again. Was sure she must have seen it wrong.

But how was that possible?

Laidey dumped her load into the basket of her bike knowing she saw what she saw with her very own eyes. Her own eyes were telling her something other than what she believed possible.

And yet …

She took one more look up at the window. Thought about biking around to the Wright's front door, ringing the bell, and getting to the bottom of it.

Then she remembered.

She wasn't the type to raise that sort of havoc. Not the type to throw a household into an uproar if she truly saw what she saw.

No.

That wasn't her.

She was invisible.

CHAPTER THIRTY-TWO

Xavier checked and rechecked every detail of today's stellar plans.

Much earlier, McKenna had appeared in the kitchen while he was laboring beside Lulu to impress his no-good brothers with a brunch to end all brunches. His way of saying thank you for not ripping his ass a new one last night, but getting him down-and-dirty drunk instead.

"So the club's general manager has everything all set," she said. "And when I say all set, I mean, it will all be handled after the last round of golf today. He'll leave the keys in a golf cart hidden behind the tennis courts as soon as they've roped off the area they don't want people venturing into after dark. The golf cart will be behind the rope, so no one should disturb it. He says he's got the cafe table and chairs all ready to go. He's noted the champagne on ice and given his most trusted caddy the job of setting everything up as soon as the golf course is clear. You'll have your own private viewing spot from the center of the eleventh fairway. Just the two of you. No prying eyes."

"I really appreciate this. Stay for breakfast?"

"Can't. I've got my own day. Oh," she said, turning back to him. "You need to remember the ring, the cookies, and the sail bag I packed for you. I left it up in your room."

"What's in the sail bag?"

"A blanket, bug spray, stuff you may need in case things get carried away under the stars," she said cheekily.

He grinned and tossed a hand up and down his body. "Tweets isn't getting any of this until she says yes. And I'm not asking her until the fireworks start. Want her in the proper headspace."

"That space being the equivalent of stars in her eyes?"

"Yeah. That." He stepped closer and spoke in a low voice. "I don't mind telling you, I'm nervous as shit."

"You'll do fine. Stick to the plan, and she can't say no."

"You think?"

McKenna shrugged. "She told me you do it for her."

He shook his spatula. "I'm going to be doing it for her, you can count on that. Thanks. For everything."

"Sure. What is the sister-you-never-had for?"

"You definitely earn your keep around here," he complimented. "I mean it. Thanks."

Now at the club, Xavier had the ring in his pocket, because like, yeah, who was he going to trust with that? He had spoken to the GM himself, spoke to the caddy who was tasked to set him up, and everything seemed a go. Turns out when you ask people to help you set up a seal-the-deal proposal, they are more than willing to make it go right.

So, ring? Check.

Wright family photo debacle? Done. Thank God. What a pain in the ass that was. All of freaking Henderson strolled by making comments. And let's just say his brothers were one distracting bunch, all in their sporty yachtsmen polos, back in town, determined to cause trouble.

His poor ma.

Not a bad idea proposing to Tweets tonight. The news was bound to take the sting out of whatever hell raising his brothers got up to and give the gossip hounds something better to talk about.

So again, ring? Check.

Brothers raising havoc? Check.

Proposal site in progress? Check.

There was just one big item left to check off his list.

Tweets.

Where the hell was Tweets?

He took out his phone and texted.

"You know, it's unpatriotic to be late for any and all Fourth of July festivities. Where you at, Tweets? Can't find you anywhere."

Twenty minutes and a lot of mixing and mingling later, he texted again. *"Tweets, get your ass to the club. Who am I going to enter the three-legged race with?"*

Finally, a response. *"McKenna."*

"Fuck McKenna. Can't pick her up and carry her the length of the field. I want to win this thing. Where are you?" Oh, fuck. It dawned on him then. *"Do you need a ride? I thought we were meeting here."*

Five minutes later.

"Tweets. I'm calling you. Pick up your damn phone."

She picked up on the second ring. "There you are. I mean, where exactly are you? You here at the club?"

"I'm home," she stated. Then … nothing.

"All right. I'll be there in five minutes to pick you up."

"That's not necessary."

"It sort of is, if you can't be bothered to show up and celebrate our blessed country's birthday."

"I'll pass."

"Can't pass. People will call you names."

Silence.

"Tweets?" It was at this moment Xavier started to feel off. Started to feel unsure. Like the ground beneath him was shifting and out of his control.

He heard her sigh. "Xavier. I'm not sure what the reasoning is behind what I saw this morning. But I did see it. I can't pretend I didn't."

"What did you see?"

"You and McKenna."

Fuck. She overheard their conversation in the kitchen. She knew he was going to propose, and that's why she wasn't showing up. Because she's not ready. Or she doesn't want to say yes.

"Xavier?"

"I don't understand," he said cautiously.

"I saw you and McKenna. Kissing."

"What the fu— Bullshit you saw us kissing." Xavier was right back in his game. "You did not see us kissing."

"I'm sorry, but I did. I crawled up the ladder and looked into your room and there you were. Kissing. I didn't know what to think but I was too shocked to—"

"Wait! Hold on. Say all that again. Slowly."

"I came over this morning. I'm sorry. I didn't mean to snoop. I intended to surprise you with a hangover cure. I had coffee and croissants—"

"Tweets," he interrupted. "That's so thoughtful of you."

"Yeah, but you seemed to be feeling just fine with your tongue stuck down McKenna's throat."

"Tweets. I didn't kiss McKenna." He put the fact out there and left it.

"Xavier. I saw what I saw."

"Whatever you saw, you did not see me kiss McKenna."

"But I did."

"Impossible."

"I saw it, Xavier," she yelled, getting angry. "I'm not an idiot. I may not know why the two of you have been stringing me along, because I sure can't imagine the kind of mean it takes to pull something like that, but I sure as shit know what I saw."

Xavier was baffled. Turning ninety degrees, phone to his ear, seeing nothing of the crowds surrounding him. He started pleading. "Laidey, I swear. I hear you tellin' me what you think you saw, but—"

"But what?"

"Ho-ly *shit.*"

"That's exactly what I thought when I saw McKenna in your bed."

"My bed?" he asked, curious. "Or the one next to mine?"

"Does it matter?" she all but shrieked.

He laughed. Couldn't help himself. "Yeah, sweet Tweets, it really does. Look, what time was it when you saw me allegedly kissing McKenna?"

"Oh, my God, Xavier, seriously?"

"Humor me, babe. I'm making a point."

"Just after seven o'clock this morning."

"And which bed was I kissing her in?"

"The one on the left as you climb through the window."

"Not my bed, but the other one."

"How do I know which bed is yours?"

"Because I fucked your brains out in *my* bed, that's how," he said getting angry. "Now you listen to me, and you listen good. I passed out on the living room couch last night right after I texted you. Passed out looking at the piano, thinking about us making music together. I wasn't in my room at seven o'clock this morning, so you can be sure that if McKenna was there, it was not me she was kissing."

"Xavier," she breathed. He could hear her crying, and it about gutted him. "I saw you. I saw your face, your hands, your back. I saw *you* with McKenna."

"Cheer up, Tweets. You only think you saw me with McKenna. Now, I'll be at your place in fifteen minutes with evidence you need to see before you go and write me out of your life. Put on your party dress, babe, and get ready to grovel."

"Like hell—"

He hung up, cutting her off before he got irritated. Then he rubbed his freshly shaven chin and went in search of said evidence.

CHAPTER THIRTY-THREE

Laidey didn't know what to do with her tears. They wouldn't stop flowing. She didn't know what to make of her conversation with Xavier either, because so little of it made sense. She only knew her head felt split in two, right along with her heart. She needed to lie down.

She'd seen what she'd seen.

Knew what she knew.

Though she had to give Xavier props for being in such complete denial. The man couldn't have acted any more obtuse. She wasn't sure what he meant by bringing over evidence, because frankly, she didn't need any more of that. She sincerely hoped he wasn't dragging McKenna here to try to explain, or to lie, or anything. She needed time before she would be ready to deal with McKenna. Before she had to deal with him.

Ding-dong-ding-dong-ding-dong-ding-dong.

Apparently, she wasn't going to be allowed that time.

Knock. Knock. Knock. Knock. Knock. "Laidey, open the hell up. I've got something to show you."

"Seriously," she mumbled, wiping furiously at her eyes as she stomped through the hallway into the family room. "Unless the guy has a twin brother—" She yanked opened the door.

And there he stood.

Xavier Wright's identical twin brother.

Either that or Laidey was seeing double.

No freaking way.

Two of the hottest-looking creatures God had ever put on the earth stood on her front porch, shoulder to shoulder, sporting their identical dark shades, showing off their identical clean-shaven jaws, owning every inch of their identical six-foot-four, well-built frames, covered in identical shirts, shorts, and shoes. Their hairstyles were similar too. So similar, that if Xavier hadn't started speaking, she would have had to guess which one of the duplicate magazine cover models she was in love with.

"Not a party dress," he commented, looking her up and down. "Tweets, you're gonna have to do a lot better than that if you plan on sucking up to me. How the fuck could you possibly think I'd be caught dead sticking my tongue down anybody's throat but yours? *Especially* McKenna's," he barked. "*This*," he said, taking time to suck in a breath, "is my *brother* Xander. He's got some explaining to do, since I assume he was the one you saw in *our* bedroom, in *his* bed, kissing *my* ex-girlfriend."

"Hi." Xander stuck out his hand.

"Hi," she managed, taking his hand and shaking it, her eyes darting between the two of them.

"It's the shirt," he said. "Can't tell us Wright brothers apart if we're all wearing the same shirt."

"You all look this much alike?" Laidey asked, horrified.

"No." Xander's slow, sexy grin was somehow even more deadly than Xavier's. "I was making a joke."

"Oh." It took Laidey a moment to gather her bearings. Seriously, these Wright boys were lethal. "So, obviously, you two are twins," she stuttered, turning an accusing eye on Xavier. "How is it that bit of information has never come up?"

Xavier shrugged. "Didn't think it was important. Of course, I didn't think you'd be mistaking him for me while he was kissing the bane of my existence."

"So it was you?" Laidey asked Xander, already knowing the answer. "You were the one I saw kissing McKenna?"

"Ah, yeah," he said sheepishly, taking a quick glance at his twin, who was now doing his best to stare him down.

Laidey couldn't get over the similarities. Even their voices. She shook her head, suddenly realizing, "This is why McKenna was looking at you like she was madly in love," she told Xavier. "Once you shaved off your beard, she thought you were *him*."

Laidey's eyes fell on Xander, realizing *he* was the "best friend" McKenna had mentioned. The one she worried Xavier wouldn't be happy she was seeing. *Xander* was the reason McKenna wanted Laidey to date Xavier.

"So," Xavier blurted, turning his attention back to her. "We good here, Tweets?"

She blinked. Blinked again. Then started to cry. "I thought," she stumbled. "I mean, I knew. I *knew* you kissing McKenna didn't make sense, but I couldn't make sense of what I was seeing either. I didn't know—"

"That I had a no-good, lying, cheatin' twin? Yeah, I didn't know that either."

"What the—?" Xander asked. "If you want McKenna, why are you with her?" He threw an arm at Laidey.

"I *don't* want McKenna. I'm just wondering if you do, why the hell has it taken you so long?"

"It's complicated," Xander said.

"How complicated?"

"You're my brother."

"I'm in love with Tweets," he declared. And this time it was loud.

"You are?" Tweets asked through her tears.

"Of course, I am. Ahh—look what you've done," he scowled at his brother. "Gone and gotten my little Tweety Bird all upset."

"Look, man, I'm sorry. I had no—"

"Whatever, dude. Head back to club. We'll be along as soon as I can shove this one in the shower. You really ought to see her when she hasn't been trying to drown herself in tears. She cleans up good, I'm tellin' ya."

Xander fed her his sly grin. "I look forward to seeing the finished product." He winked at Laidey. "Sorry for the trouble. Sincerely."

All she could do was nod before Xavier took her into his arms and slammed the door in his brother's face.

"I didn't know," she sobbed into his shoulder. He lifted her feet off the floor and carried her down the hallway to the bedroom. "I didn't know you had a twin." She smacked his shoulder. "Why didn't you tell me?"

Xavier laughed. "I'm sorry, Tweets. I should have told you. I really should have. But you knew there was no way I was touching McKenna. I still don't see how you believed he was me."

"He looks just like you," she hollered.

"Okay. Yeah, he does. Sit down," he said, placing her on the bed. "I've got a story to tell you. And fuck." He ran a hand through his hair, and then over his mouth and chin as he stared at the ceiling.

"What?" By the way he was acting, Laidey was suddenly more fearful of what he was now going to say than what she thought she saw.

"Okay, listen," he said, taking a seat on the bed beside her. When he finally looked at her face, his expression immediately went soft. "Oh, Tweets." He started wiping at her eyes with both his hands. "This is not the day I had planned for us." He took a deep breath. "Last thing I wanted to do was make you cry."

"I'm fine. And I'm starting to put the puzzle pieces together. Two double beds in one room. You and Xander."

"Yeah. Me and Xander. Always," he groused.

"You don't like him?" Laidey wondered.

"I love him," Xavier admitted. "I missed him more than Ma when I left town. I've seen him more than the others too because, yeah, he's my favorite. My twin. He's, you know, me only better."

"Better?"

"Yeah. Way better."

"He play baseball?"

"Shortstop."

"And you played?"

"First base. It was a good combo."

She smiled. "He's definitely cute."

Xavier chuckled.

"So he didn't make people eat goldfish?" she wondered.

Xavier shook his head. "I was the lone asshole. He had the thankless job of always trying to talk me down."

"Talk you down?"

"From a bad idea."

"Okay."

"Yeah, he was the goody two shoes. Almost as bad as Brooks, although let's face it, nobody is as bad as Brooks when it comes to the saint department."

"So he was the yin to your yang."

Xavier nodded. "He's got my mother's temperament. So you know, people liked him better. I didn't blame them. Didn't really give a shit if anyone liked me or not. Made it a bit difficult being my identical twin, right? People wanted to take a swing at me, but they didn't know if they were marching up to me or Xander. No one could tell us apart. Except Vance. Vance always knew."

"Then how did they know *you* were the bad one?"

"Oh, that they knew. Although every time Xander tried to grow his hair, I'd grow mine. Every time he got his hair cut, I'd cut mine."

"He wanted to look different from you, but you wanted to look the same."

"Right. So I could fly under the radar, knowing no one could be sure just who was who."

Laidey snickered and then really started to laugh. "Xavier, that is perfect."

"Right?" His eyes were bright, happy she understood where he'd been with this look-alike thing.

"Looking exactly like your brother made your life easier and his life harder."

"Exactly. Only Xander was cool about it. Thought most of the shit I did was funny, so he was always on my side. Stuck up for me when I didn't deserve it. Stood beside me when I had a battle to fight, and rarely got into it with me, even when I really crossed a line."

"Sounds like Xander's a great brother."

"Yeah. He was. Is. He is. Which is why what I'm about to tell you may change our relationship."

"Yours and Xander's?"

"No, Tweets. Yours and mine."

Laidey flopped onto her back.

"Tweets?" he asked, leaning over her, stroking tear-soaked ringlets out of her face.

"I just got our relationship back. I like it the way it was. I'm not ready for you to tell me anything that's going to change it."

"I hear ya," he said, flopping onto his back as well. "Trust me, Tweets. I've never wanted anyone to know what I need to tell you."

"Why? Why do you need to tell me?"

"Because I can't bear the burden any longer."

There were a few moments of silence before Laidey turned on her side, tucking her hands under her face, looking at the one she loved more than the rest. "Okay," she said solemnly. "If you need to share a burden, I'm willing to take it on."

"Tweets," he whispered, rolling to drag her against him, enfolding her in his arms. "I love you."

"I love you too," she whispered.

"You do?" he asked against her hair.

"I do." She nodded.

"Well, that's sort of getting the day back on track, then."

"You going to tell me?"

"Yeah, I'm going to tell you, Tweets. Give me a minute."

After a few minutes passed, Laidey sat up. "I'm going to take a shower. You relax. If you don't want to tell me about it today, you can tell me tomorrow. Or next week. Or whenever you're ready."

"I need to tell you today."

She leaned over and kissed him. "All right. Gather your thoughts while I'm in the shower."

Thirty minutes later, when Laidey emerged from the bathroom, Xavier was fast asleep.

CHAPTER THIRTY-FOUR

Xavier groaned, rolling into the warm sweetness next to him. Supple flesh, soft curves, his hands coasting to hips he couldn't wait to get in between. He jogged a knee between her legs, spreading her thighs.

Laidey stretched and purred, complementing her body to his. "Mmm," she hummed. "This is so much better than a three-legged race."

He'd been thinking about how he was going to be able to do this all the time when they were—*Oh, shit!* Xavier's face turned from where he was kissing her neck to look out her bedroom window. "Is that the dark? Is it nighttime?" he asked in a panic, peering out her window. "Oh, no. No, no, no." He pulled out his phone, frantic. "Tweets, it's eight-forty-five. How the hell did we sleep so long?"

She shrugged. "We needed it. Me, after my emotional roller coaster and you, after playing quarters all night. Now come back and kiss me."

"Plenty of time for kissing later, Tweets. Right now, we've got to hustle. Fireworks start shortly after nine."

"I didn't realize you were so into fireworks," she pouted.

"Come on," he ordered. "Off the bed. We're leaving now.

"Xavier. Really? Let's just sit out back. I bet we can see some of the show from here."

Xavier sucked in a long-suffering breath, letting his head drop. When he looked up, his gaze was intense and his voice was deadly. "Tweets. Gonna need you to trust me when I say, we have to leave. Now," he growled.

Laidey must have believed him because she scurried off the bed, tugging off the T-shirt she'd been napping in. In a matter of seconds, she stepped into a signature Lolly DuVal retro-styled dress in red and turned so Xavier could zip her up.

"I'm liking this new frock," he said. "Great color on you, and perfect choice for today."

"Not that anyone's going to see it now that the sun's gone down."

"I see it." He spun her around and took a moment to appreciate the view.

"Do I have a minute to put on mascara and lipstick?"

"You have sixty seconds to handle whatever needs doing. Then we're leaving."

"Bossy, bossy, bossy."

"No big surprise there, Tweets. Just one of the many things you love about me."

"Oh," she exclaimed, turning around with a brush in her hand, beaming. "You have a surprise for me," she remembered.

"Which is why *we need to hurry.*"

Her eyes grew wide and then she whirled, moving in double time, throwing lipstick and mascara into a clutch and stepping into red sandals with a sexy heel.

"No Keds?" Xavier asked.

"Date night," she told him.

He cocked his head to the side and twisted his lips. "I've really grown fond of the Keds."

"You'll live." She took him by his shoulders and turned him, pushing him into the hall toward the front door. "What's my surprise?"

"Oh, now who's bossy?"

"And in a hurry."

Xavier held the door open for her to step through. "We'll make it," he told her. "Right on time."

"We've missed dinner."

"Pfft. Like Harry won't take one look at you in this dress and dive into the kitchen to produce a feast in your honor. The man has it bad," he grumbled, scooping her up and into his truck.

"Everybody loves Harry," she said.

"Not me." He shut the door with a decided thud.

"So what's my surprise?" she asked again as she put on lipstick while he drove them toward the club. "I'm guessing it has something to do with the fireworks."

Xavier found himself getting nervous. What if she didn't like his surprise? Fuck, what if she said no? He looked in her direction, wondering how he was going to survive if she didn't feel it like he did. She had to, right? He couldn't be in this all alone.

Don't take no for an answer, he heard his father say.

Right. And stop being such a chickenshit, he told himself. He reached over and folded his fingers between hers, bringing her hand to his lips for a kiss. "I'm sorry about this morning. I wish I'd been in my room when you arrived. I can't help but think I missed out on something special."

"I was up early. Thought I'd surprise you. Sort of wanted …"

"Yeah?"

She shrugged.

"Sort of wanted what, Tweets? Tell me. Please."

"It's silly. I sort of wanted to be more like you. You know, daring, spontaneous, not afraid to break the rules. It's sort of shocking that the only thing I worried about was finding and handling the ladder. But it was still there, right where we left it."

He nodded. "What did you bring me?"

"A thermos of Kona coffee. Advil for your hangover. And pastries with jam."

"Pastries with jam?" he moaned. "Damn."

"Spend the night with me tonight, and I'll replay it all for you in the morning."

"Done. Hey, look at this," Xavier said as he cruised past all the cars lined up along the edge of the grass and found a parking spot right up front. "Someone must have had to leave early." He felt the day starting to turn in his direction at the same time he felt for the ring down deep in his pants pocket.

When Laidey headed toward the club's front door, he whistled and took her hand. "This way, Tweets."

He led her around the side of the clubhouse and away from the enormous crowd waiting in anticipation for the fireworks to start. It was pretty dark by the time they stumbled upon the golf cart loaded down with McKenna's sail bag. The keys were in the ignition as promised. He assumed they were all set to go.

"What's this?" Laidey asked.

"Part of your surprise. Get in."

Laidey was giddy as he drove them out to the eleventh fairway, slowly, since he could hardly make out the cart path as the lights of the clubhouse drifted off behind them. But once they broke through the trees, he caught the glow of candlelight coming from up the fairway.

"What's that?" Laidey pointed. "My surprise?"

He didn't answer. His nerves had been replaced by anticipation as he drove toward the table for two, complete with a white tablecloth topped with rose petals and champagne glasses. There was an ice bucket in a stand and a chilled bottle of bubbly. He couldn't have been more pleased. Between McKenna and the club staff, the setting was perfect. And the way Tweets was squealing, she believed this was her surprise.

Poor Tweets. She had no idea.

He parked the cart several yards away and helped Laidey onto the damp grass, taking her in one hand and McKenna's bag of tricks in the other. He set the bag down next to the table and helped Laidey into her chair. He remained standing to open the bubbly, sending the cork into midair just as the first boom was unleashed, signaling the start of the show.

"Wow," she said.

"Wow," he agreed as he poured her champagne and sat. "Perfect timing."

"I'm feeling slightly overwhelmed. Xavier, this is so … romantic. Thank you," she said as they clinked glasses. After the two of them drank and looked back toward the glittering sky, Laidey asked, "How in the world did you pull this off?"

"McKenna. She helped me. That's why you spied us together over the past week. We were busy working out the details."

"Oh," she whispered before burying her head in his shirt. "And here I wanted to kill the two of you with my bare hands."

"Tweets." Xavier snorted.

"Well, I did," she said, bringing her head up, sipping her champagne, and glancing up at the barrage of fireworks.

"Shh, baby, come here." Xavier scooted her chair closer to his, guiding her to lean back and relax against him. He wrapped an arm around her shoulders and over her chest, cuddling her to him while they watched the midair explosions burst into spectacular color. "No need to commit homicide. I'd kill myself before I ever sucked face with McKenna."

"Why in the world do you hate her so much?"

"I don't *hate* her," Xavier said. "She's just the one thing I got really wrong."

"How? How did you get it wrong? Because on paper you two were perfect for each other. You're both tall. You're both … assertive."

"Nice synonym for bossy, Tweets."

"I was actually searching for a euphemism for domineering."

"Tomato, tomahto."

They sat for a while in silence, sharing the experience of the stunning light and sound show transforming the summer night. A calm enveloped Xavier—a profound contentment—because the girl he loved leaned solidly against him, the night air surrounding them both. He didn't anticipate the confession, or even understand why the words began spilling from his mouth. Maybe because with Laidey's attention on the sky above, he didn't have to face her as he spoke. Whatever it was, once he got started …

"Remember the night I showed you my Matchbox collection?" He spoke softly, both of their heads tilted toward the fireworks display. "And you figured out how much I liked to one-up my brothers?"

He felt her nod against his shoulder.

"Back in high school, I did that with McKenna," he confessed. "My brother Xander—my twin—was fairly shy around girls. I knew he liked girls, but he'd never talk about any one in particular. However, during our senior year, I noticed he'd picked out a specific sophomore. McKenna. I saw how he looked at her, and had no doubt he was interested. Real interested. And I saw how she looked back at him. Knew she'd go out with him if he ever got up the nerve to ask. Especially after it was announced that he'd been awarded back-to-back honors.

"One had to do with the debate team. They'd gone undefeated since Xander joined his sophomore year. So due to his *undefeated record*," Xavier mocked, "Xander was selected to represent Henderson at the state capital for a reception honoring North Carolina's most outstanding high school seniors. Motherfucker held that shit over my head for weeks. Every night, we'd be lying in bed, and he'd start needling me about it. You'd have thought they'd made him an honorary astronaut and he'd been to the fucking moon."

Xavier shook his head. "I mean, it was just brothers being brothers, him messing with me because, with my reputation, no one was making me honorary anything. He knew it and liked to rub it in.

"Then shit got serious, because my *perfect* twin was awarded the Charles Fleury Trophy. Sort of an all-around-great-guy-of-the-year distinction that was a very big deal in our school. The trophy was enormous. You had to be a leader, an athlete, a scholar, a philanthropist. Hell, I can't remember all the criteria, but trust me, it was big. My parents were beside themselves when Xander won."

"That's cool," Laidey acknowledged.

"It was. And I was really proud of Xander. At first. Then I started taking a whole lot of shit about being the *evil twin*. This from the baseball team—which you know, was all in good fun. But then our other buddies started joining in the razzing. Then people I didn't even know would say shit to me. Of course, it was the worst at home where the rest of our brothers were relentless.

"I laid in bed at night plotting ways to one-up Xander. Not that he deserved it, but my pride was taking a helluva beating. I came up with what I now see was the dirtiest, meanest, most horrible thing any one man could do to another. I stole his girl."

"You mean, you asked McKenna out before he got around to it?" Laidey seemed unimpressed.

"Yes. I asked McKenna out. Wearing my brother's favorite shirt, a pair of his slacks, his belt, and a pair of his shoes."

That's when he felt her soft, little body lift off him and turn to level him with an *Oh-no-you-didn't* glare.

"Honest to God," he told her, hands in the air. "Worst thing I've ever done."

"So, McKenna thought Xander was asking her out?"

"I don't know. I truly don't. But I do know that I hedged my bets as best I could, and it worked like a charm. She said yes. Next thing I know we've been dating a month, and she's at the house having dinner with my family every other night. And they all *love* her. I mean, not just Xander, because yeah, he hung on her every word, but my other brothers, and my dad, and my mom. And oh, my mom. She was so happy to have a girl around the house. She lit up every time McKenna walked in. The two of them were talking prom dresses and hairstyles while I was trying to backpedal my way out of dating her at all.

"The whole thing got away from me, and I was stuck with a girl I didn't really like, just to spite my brother, who would have hung the fuckin' moon for me. I kid you not, I couldn't look in the mirror, I made myself that sick."

"Xavier."

"I'm sorry, babe, but you need to know. I love you, and if this thing between us is going to work, you need to be able to handle the worst in me. Besides, I can't carry this burden around anymore."

"It was over a dozen years ago."

"I know. And they say time heals all wounds. But not one this gaping and ugly. Every time I look at her, I think of how I screwed over Xander. How I cut in on something that might have been great between those two. Because when it comes right down to it, Xander and McKenna could be perfect for one another."

"You might be right. I did see them kissing this morning."

"Right? I mean, what the hell was that about?"

"And … not two weeks ago, McKenna begged me to go out with you. Because she and I are friends, and she was thinking that if you went out with one of *her* friends, she would be able to go out with one of yours."

Xavier's brow furrowed. "Which one of my friends does she want to go out with?"

"Ah, pretty sure that'd be Xander."

"He's my brother."

"She probably didn't want to admit that part, using the term 'best friend' as a metaphor for twin brother."

"I'm confused."

"About what? They were kissing. In your bedroom. This morning. What part of that is confusing?"

"All of it. When the fuck did this start?"

"Does it matter?"

"I don't know."

"Xavier, why aren't you jumping for joy? You just confessed your worst sin to me. This *fixes* it."

"Does it? I stole fourteen years from them. They can't get that back."

"You stole a few months of dating and his senior prom. Then you left town. Whatever happened after that was up to them."

"No. It wasn't. Xander would have *never* gone after McKenna when my back was turned."

"He was kissing her. Today," she stressed. "Oh, my God. You're angry about that."

"I'm not angry, I'm … pissed. He's my brother. What the hell is he doing dating my ex?"

Tweets sprung out of her seat, put her hands on her hips, and leaned in close. "You are insane." She whirled around and stalked off toward the golf cart.

Holy fuck. "Tweets. Wait!" He darted after her, grabbing her up in his arms and hauling her back to the table. "I got off topic. I'm sorry. Yes, I'm insane on this subject, but you're going to help me work through it, I'm sure. Please. Sit." When she refused to do what he asked but crossed her arms over her chest instead, he began rubbing his hands together and pacing nervously. "The truth is, I was planning to talk to Xander about McKenna. See if I could fix what I'd done."

"Well, it looks like the two of them were able to manage things without you. Now you can't be the hero. You can't redeem yourself. And you're just going to have to live with it. All of it."

He licked his lips, studying Laidey, knowing that he'd screwed up royally. With her. On this night of all nights. "I'm sorry," he whispered. "I wasn't like this in Phoenix. But in Henderson, I can't seem to get out of my own way."

"It's not Henderson, Xavier. It's *McKenna*. And *Xander*. It's you, carrying around this one thing from your past and continually beating yourself up over it."

"True. But I didn't think too much about it when I was in Phoenix."

"Because you ran away from your problem. You left McKenna without ending things. You never made amends to your brother. And now, you're pissed he's back with a girl you intentionally stole years ago."

"I'm not. I'm really not. I'm just surprised that's all." The fireworks' grand finale started off with a barrage of pops and booms one right after the other. "Shall we sit? Watch the end. Then ... talk."

Laidey didn't say a word, but she did sit.

Fuck.

This entire day had gotten so far off track Xavier didn't know how to set things right. He sat down and looked up at the sky, not appreciating the brilliant bombardment of fireworks until he reached over to pull Laidey into his lap, snuggling her into his embrace and pushing his nose right underneath her ear. He kissed her there before looking back to the night sky, content to enjoy what was left of the show.

Fortunately, it was a finale to end all finales. It went on and on, blasting away the mood that had gripped Xavier. It also served to soften Laidey so that, little by little, he felt her relax against him. When the end came, she applauded, and when she finally turned her face to his, he hugged her to him intent on making their next kiss the sweetest of apologies.

He kissed her soft and easy, feeling his way by incremental steps toward hot and sultry, remembering they had the blanket and a whole lot of privacy, even though hundreds of people were just around the bend.

"I love you, Ad-el-aide Bar-tho-lo-mew," he whispered, pressing his forehead to hers.

With her arms around his neck, she squeezed him tight. "I love you too," she declared. "And it would be fun, probably for both of us, if you'd allow your twin to date my friend. I suggest you simply step out of the way and let them work this out together."

"You mean, not tell them what I did?"

"Right. Just let that go. You've been away a long time. Unaware of all that's happened since you left. Trust that if McKenna and Xander really wanted to be together, even you couldn't stop them."

"Are you saying the world doesn't revolve around me?"

She laughed before pulling back and giving him the sweetest of gifts. "My world does."

"Aw, Tweets. I so don't deserve you."

"Yeah, ya do. If that was truly the worst thing you've ever done, I've got you beat. I've spent the night in lockup, remember. With an official record and everything."

"Right, right. Well, thank God one of our misspent youths enabled Henderson to put the brakes on Viper. They might erect a monument to you for that, Tweets. Hey? I've got something for you."

"Ooh. Another surprise?"

"Just a little one." He reached down into the sail bag, unearthing the blanket and set that aside. Then he pulled out a small bag with telltale red and white stripes, plunking it on the table. "I thought these might go well with the rest of our champagne."

"Xavier," Laidey said in wonder. "Are these …?" She picked up the bag. "These are from Dallas. These are my favorite-favorite almond cookies from the Petterson bakery in Dallas. You can't get them here."

"I know."

"Had I mentioned these?"

"Nope." He opened the bag and pulled out a cookie.

"Then how did you know about them?"

"I didn't, Tweets." He bit into the soft, gooey center and moaned.

She beamed at his reaction. "Did McKenna? Did she put them in the bag?"

"I picked them up myself. Specifically for this occasion."

"You were in Dallas?"

He nodded and took another bite. She grabbed the bag greedily and pulled one out for herself. Taking a large bite, she grinned as she chewed. "These are absolutely my favorite thing."

"Aw, Tweets. Really? Your very favorite thing?" he said, all hurt.

"My favorite sugar indulgence. Who told you about them?"

"Your mother."

"My mother?" Laidey sat up straighter. "You called my mother?"

Xavier shook his head. "Went to see her. Well, I went to see your father. Ended up having lunch with your mother too."

"What? When?"

"Friday. I mentioned I had business out of town."

"Your business was in *Dallas*? With my *father*?"

He just smiled and then got a little nervous, so he went in for a kiss. "I love you, Tweets. And I need you in my life. Today was a perfect example. You sort me out when I need it. You talk me off the ledge when I threaten to jump. You ease my soul by simply letting me look at you." He scooted her off his lap and into her own chair. Then he stood and moved his chair out of the way.

Getting down on one knee was a simple gesture, but in this moment it felt profound. In this moment, Xavier realized why men had been repeating the act for centuries. It wasn't about begging for someone's hand, but honoring the one who'd stirred up a vision of the future. A vision of a robust life, complete with children and grandchildren. Building a partnership together, and in their case, a town. It was a symbolic expression. Placing the woman he loved higher than himself, because if she agreed to stand by his side, his life would be well worth living.

"Ad-el-aide Bar-tho-lo-mew," he said, as he knelt one knee to the ground.

Laidey immediately covered her mouth with both her hands, suppressing a squeal. Her head was shaking back and forth, but her eyes were huge and shiny. Those eyes—those Tweety Bird eyes—told him she was excited about what was happening. Still, he felt like he should address the obvious.

"Too soon?" he teased, grinning up at her. He reached out a hand and gently pulled one of hers away from her mouth so he could hold on to it. "It's not, Tweets, and I'll tell you why.

"No woman, in all my thirty-two years, has ever tangled up my heart, has ever made me laugh while busting my chops, has ever turned me on by being nothing but cute, has ever inspired me to do right by my family and my hometown the way that you do, Tweets.

These are the facts we're dealing with. I've faced them and come to accept them, and now you will too.

"You're perfect for me," he told her sincerely. "And I'm banking on the fact that after crushin' on the same man for years, since I was able to turn your head in a matter of minutes—although *far* from perfect—I'm right for you too. You get me, babe. And I know where you live. So," he shrugged, "may as well go ahead and say yes to what's comin' at you. You know I won't take no for an answer."

Xavier took his free hand and reached into his pocket. "Laidey, I promise I'll work hard to keep you crushing on me for the rest of your life. Please, do me the honor of becoming my wife."

He opened the ring box and then reached over and dragged the candle to the edge of the table so she'd be able to see his offering.

"Xavier," she squealed. Her knees bounced up and down in excitement as she clapped her hands. "Are you serious?"

"Tweets, do you see the size of that diamond? A man can't get more serious than that. Figured if I wasn't sure of your answer, I'd better pour a little sugar on it. Sweetened the pot. How's it working?"

Xavier didn't really have to ask, because Tweets was grinning from ear to ear, blushing a tidal wave, and making all her cute Tweety Bird noises while she stared at the ring, then up at him, then back at the ring.

"Go ahead," he urged. "Try it on for size."

She practically shrieked, pulling it out of the box and holding it closer to the light. "It's exquisite," she sighed.

"McKenna helped me pick it out. Of course, she brought me measly pieces of crap at first. Apparently, the woman thinks I spent my time in Phoenix panhandling. I had to send her back to the jeweler for serious diamonds." He looked from the ring to Laidey. "Because I'm serious about you, Ad-el-aide. You serious about me?"

Her smile dazzled him. Sent his brain in several different directions. She presented him with the engagement ring. "Put it on me," she requested.

His grin was broad as he took it, polished the diamond against his shirt, and then held her hand as he slipped the symbol of his intent and devotion onto Laidey's finger. "Will you marry me?"

"I will. Yes."

They stared into each other's eyes, grinning. "Wanna go tell people?" he suggested.

She giggled. "I do," she said while leaning in to kiss him. "I really do. But tell me what my parents said. What did you think of them? Oh, my gosh, what did they think of you?"

"Oh, Tweets," he said, pulling her back into his lap. "They love me. Clearly more than they love you, because I tell you what. No way is our daughter gonna be handed off to some stranger who wandered in off the street."

"Xavier." She chuckled. "I'm sure you didn't look like any stranger off the street."

"No," he told her, bringing her in for a kiss. "I represented, Tweets. Wanted to make you proud of the guy you've fallen for." He pulled back. "Of course, I'm a work in progress, obviously. And I'm real sorry about almost ruining our moment."

"You're not a work in progress. You're my idea of perfection," she sighed against his lips. "As long as I get to play your uppity secretary every now and again, I think we'll be just fine."

"I'm leaving the details up to you, Tweets. I may not be easy, but I am all yours."

CHAPTER THIRTY-FIVE

One week later

The heavy click made her insides shiver as Laidey tested the restraint Xavier had just shackled her with. His eyes were a smoky gray and full of mischief as he looked down at her, holding up his right wrist as Harry cuffed the two of them together.

"There ya go," Harry said. "Bring me your empty champagne bottle, and I'll give you another. Finish that and you'll be awarded a key to unshackle yourselves. Until then," he paused and grinned, "this will be a good test of your compatibility."

"You trying to talk her out of marrying me, Harry?" Xavier scowled.

"Wouldn't dream of it, sir. If Laidey's happy, I'm happy."

And Laidey was definitely happy. Because among all the twenty- and thirty-somethings Henderson's theme parties catered to, there were a few couples there who were, if not wiser, at least older. Her parents to name one.

They'd come to Henderson eager to meet the Wright household, which now regularly consisted of more than just Xavier and his parents. It seemed that over the Fourth of July weekend, his brothers had caught hometown fever and all four of them were present and accounted for at the Champagne and Shackles Party where Vance and Brooks continued their not-so-subtle campaign to integrate each one of them into Team Henderson.

Laidey looked over to where her parents, sans handcuffs, were talking to Chase and Emelina, who were tethered together and playing the game. Emelina looked stunning in a flowy Hawaiian-print maxi dress, her hair pinned into an up-do with exotic blooms. She'd look more at home on the shores of Waikiki than surrounded by all these pickup trucks with their lowered tailgates.

Laidey didn't know how old Em was, but she wished upon the first star she saw that she'd look half as good at her age.

"We good?" Xavier asked as he used both of his hands to open their first bottle of champagne. The height difference was glaringly obvious now that their wrists were bound. It was also obvious he was oblivious to the fact that her shoulder was practically yanked out of its socket with every move he made.

"Xavier," she called. "We'll be a whole lot better off if you remember you can't use your arm the way you regularly do."

Xavier looked down, noticing that her arm was pulled up high while he untwisted the wire cage over the cork. "Oh. Tweets. Why didn't you say something?"

"I am." She laughed. "Look, maybe I should take charge of the bottle," she suggested. "Let you be the one jostled around."

Xavier licked his lips, a wicked gleam in his eyes. "I was going to save this for later, but …" He looked over her head and then began backing her up beyond the circle of tiki torches that defined the party and in between two pickup trucks, toward the dark. "What are you doing?"

"Shh, Tweets," he whispered. Pushing her further into the cover of night, her klutzy side surfaced as she stumbled backward. He caught her just in time, pulling her against him by wrapping their joined wrists behind her back, her wrist twisting easily in the cuff to accommodate the move. When he leaned his face down for a kiss, she noticed the stubble she dearly missed already filling in over his chin, jaw, and upper lip. She brought her free hand up to smooth a palm over it as he leaned down to place their champagne on the ground. It was then she felt him fumbling around in his pocket and wondered what he was up to.

"Spin around," he said, as he maneuvered her to do what he wanted. Her tethered hand was behind her back. She felt some tugging.

"What are you doing?"

"This," he said, spinning her back around, plucking up her free hand, and then slapping that into the now-free cuff. He held up his free hands and wiggled his fingers.

"What?" Laidey exclaimed. "Are you Houdini or something? How did you get free?"

He twisted a tiny key between his fingers. "I like this game much better."

"What game?"

"I'm the badass sheriff. You're the sexy prisoner who keeps eye-fucking me from her cell."

"What?" she sputtered.

"Yep. Role-playing, Tweets. It's our thing."

"Me being your uppity secretary is our thing."

"We're expanding the game. You didn't expect me to be stuck in handcuffs all night, did you?"

"Well, yeah."

"Pfft. Tweets. You know me better than that."

She did. She knew him better than that, and she should have seen this coming.

"Besides, those things chafe," he said, rubbing his wrists.

She held her bound hands up to remind him she was still cuffed.

"Stop," he scolded. "Your tiny wrists are fine. Don't be a baby."

"Oh, my God," she laughed. "You're cheating."

"Of course, I'm cheating. Rules are for sissies, and you are marrying anything but a sissy." He kissed her. "By the way, I'm divorcing my family."

"What?"

"Yep. It's just you and me and Team Henderson against the world. Except when we visit Dallas. Your family is cool. We'll keep them."

"Why are you divorcing your family?"

"Because …" he drew out, "when my mother needed a bone marrow transplant, everyone got tested to see if they were a possible match. Everyone except me. They didn't bother me with the process because Xander's DNA and my DNA are identical. They figured they didn't need to double up, and since I was in Arizona, no one told me a damn thing about it. I was completely kept in the dark."

"Okay, but what's the big deal? Makes a little bit of sense."

"Except Xander's freaking bone marrow was a match for Ma. Which means my bone marrow is also a match."

Laidey knew exactly where this was heading. And apparently her face showed it.

"Yeah, so Xander, the *good* twin, stepped up to the plate and saved our mother. *I* was never consulted."

"And you would have liked to have been the one to save your mom."

"Of course, I would have."

"So, you're divorcing your family because …"

"They obviously didn't believe I would rise to the occasion. They didn't even give me a chance."

"Maybe they appreciated how hard you were working in Arizona and knew you would have left Chase without his right-hand man to run back to North Carolina to handle what your twin was willing to do. Your twin, who, by the way, lived right down the road from Duke."

"Don't be confusing my story with facts," he said, backing her up. "Tweets, I'm pissed. I would have gladly done whatever was needed."

"I think they knew that. Which is why you were kept out of the loop. But Xavier, rest assured that if I ever need bone marrow, you're the first person I'm coming to."

"That's why I love you, Tweets. You know I'm more than just the evil twin."

"Right, you're the badass sheriff who I'm going to lure into my cell and have my wicked way with."

"Keep talking," he said against her lips.

"We're going to have to be quick. My parents are at this party."

Xavier pulled up to his full height. "Is that a green light? Did my little Tweety Bird just give me the okay to defile her in public?"

"No. But if we just meander a bit this way," she pointed to the docks, "we might be able to find some privacy on your boat."

"Put those locked hands around my neck," he ordered. He hoisted her and her fluffy dress up. Her legs wrapped around him and he began to kiss her lips as he walked toward the docks. "I love you, babe. Thanks for shifting my mood."

"Don't divorce your family."

"Grrrrr."

"You might not have had the opportunity to help save your mom the way Xander did, but you did come back home. And from the looks of it, you might have started a trend. One that will heal your mother's heart."

He grinned. "Damn, you're good. And you know what will also help to heal my mother's heart? Setting a date for our wedding."

"Lolly's already drawing up pictures for my dress."

"I like the sound of that, Ad-el-aide." He kissed her. "Laidey." He kissed her again. "Tweets."

When they got halfway down the pier, a burst of sound drew their attention to the scrambling that was happening on the back of the Wright family boat. Xavier set Laidey down, took her by the handcuffs, and headed cautiously and curiously toward the craft.

"What's going on here?" he called, finding Xander and McKenna fastening flies and smoothing down clothing.

"Great minds think alike," Xander said, pointing at the two on the pier. "Wanted some alone time."

"When the hell did you two happen?" Xavier asked. "Because honest to God, I intentionally left town the way I did so that you two could figure out, *back then*, that you belonged together."

"What?" McKenna asked.

"Yep. Knew the two of you were far better suited as a couple. My hope was that Xander, being the good twin, would have had the balls to step up and offer to soothe your heart. *Fourteen years* ago."

"Well, now that you mention—"

"McKenna." Xander cut her off.

"What?" Xavier wondered. Laidey watched the interaction. Saw Xavier looking between McKenna and Xander. "You did, didn't you?" A crooked grin slowly appearing. "You were there for her," he accused Xander. "How soon?"

"What?"

"How soon after I left?"

Xander and McKenna shared a look.

"Hmm. That quick, huh?"

Laidey grabbed on to Xavier's arm with both her cuffed hands. She wasn't sure if Xavier was capable of tossing both Xander and McKenna into the lake, but she knew he'd have a more difficult time of it if she clung to him while he tried.

That idea bit the dust the moment he shook her off and jumped down into the boat with both feet. She watched as Xavier stalked his twin.

"You take care of McKenna after I left for school?" he asked quietly.

"Somebody had to," Xander said, standing his ground.

"And you let him?" Xavier asked McKenna. "Right after I left?"

McKenna crossed her arms over her chest, nodding one time. Then another.

"All right. I've got just one goddamn question for the both of you," Xavier said, encroaching on Xander's personal space, not stopping until his chest bumped up against his twin's.

The night got too quiet. The tension raging between them too much. Laidey held her breath, knowing this was a moment Xavier was not going to be able to take back. But she held her tongue, determined not to interfere.

Xavier licked his lips, put his hands on his hips, and said, "How about we give Ma a double wedding?"

The four of them drank beer from a cooler and cleared the air, laughing as they did so. Xavier confessed that he'd intentionally misled McKenna by dressing in Xander's clothes when he asked her out. That led to McKenna's confession that she had indeed thought she was going out on a date with Xander.

"When did you figure out you were with Xavier? Laidey wondered. She was the only one handcuffed at this point, as Xavier continually refused to set her free.

"Drink your bubbly, Tweets," he'd say, reaching for another one of Xander's beers. "You know the rules. No key until you finish the bottle."

"Oh, my goodness," she said, rolling her eyes toward McKenna. "So when did you realize you were stuck with *him*?" She pointed at her fiancé.

"Stuck?" Xavier took exception. Laidey just held up her bound hands.

"About thirty minutes into the date, I realized the *normal* twin wouldn't have honked his horn at Evie Jackson as soon as the light turned green."

"The normal twin?" Xavier protested.

McKenna went on, undaunted. "Which is when I used his name and he responded."

"So why'd you stick out the date?" Laidey was curious.

"I assumed the two of them"—she indicated the Wright brothers—"had talked about it. Figured Xander wasn't that into me." She laughed. "Although he did pay far more attention to me than this one did," she pointed to Xavier, "when I was at their house. I just rolled with it. Happy to be a part of the Wright clan. Until they both left town," she grumbled.

Xavier eyed Xander. "Why'd you leave if you had McKenna?"

"I didn't *have* McKenna," Xander insisted. "What I had was guilt. Huge guilt. For all intents and purposes, she was still your girl when we, ya know …"

"When we, ya know, what?" Xavier pushed, leaning forward, eyeing his brother.

"None of your business," McKenna said primly.

"Well, it kinda is if we both spent fourteen years feeling guilty over the same damn girl," Xavier argued, looking back and forth between the two.

Laidey realized that if Xavier was seeing what she was seeing, it was blatantly obvious what had gone down between McKenna and Xander. She really wasn't sure how Xavier was going to deal with this twist. She silently vowed that whatever his reaction, she would not take it personally.

She ended up being pleasantly surprised.

"Christ, what a waste of energy," Xavier said. "For all of us. I'm sorry, man. I should have come clean. Should have told you before I left. I just didn't have the words."

"Help me convince him to move back, and all will be forgiven," McKenna told Xavier.

"Come on, bro. For Ma, for me, and for this one right here who's done her best to rip our family to shreds by pitting brother against brother."

"What!" McKenna exclaimed, tossing a throw pillow at Xavier.

"Kidding. Kidding." Xavier laughed. "You know I love you like a sister. Just trying to push him into making it official."

"How 'bout from now on, you worry about your own love life? Let me worry about mine," Xander said, putting an arm around McKenna and pulling her in tight against him.

"Deal, you little fucker, because after single-handedly saving Ma's life, if you make McKenna's last name Wright, Dad will not hesitate to leave everything to you."

Xander shot his brother a big, broad, cheeky grin before leaning over and kissing McKenna's cheek.

The four of them partied together for the next hour, joking back and forth, the twins giving shit to one another until Laidey remembered her parents had been left alone back at the party.

"Simmer down, Tweets. I've got it all under control."

"You do?" she asked Xavier.

"I do," he promised, staring down into her eyes. "I really do." He leaned over and kissed her. "Texted Chase. Told him we'd be a while. He and the Big Em are hosting your folks. Introducing them around. It's giving Vance the opportunity to hit your dad up for a large donation to the sports academy."

Laidey's eyes went wide. "Why didn't I think of that?"

"Not your job, Tweets."

"Actually, it sort of is."

"Your job is to take care of me."

"Ha. I think you're perfectly able to take care of yourself." They strolled down the pier, the badass sheriff holding on to the cuffs of his fluffy prisoner with one hand and her half-finished bottle of champagne with the other.

"Yep," Xavier said, grinning into the night. "But it's so much better with you by my side." He looked down. "I love you, Laidey. You and your Keds."

"I love you too, Xavier. You are Xavier, right? I want to make sure I'm marrying the evil twin."

"Evil as in *badass* and *awesome*."

"Exactly. That's the twin I want."

"You got him, Tweets. For the rest of your life, you've got him."

All of my Heroes of Henderson novels and novellas are complete romances in and of themselves and do not need to be read in any particular order. However, it's a little more fun that way.

Heroes of Henderson full-length Novels
Good Cop
Bad Cop
Top Dog
Tempting Vivi
UnderDog
Mr. Wrong
Mr. Wright

Heroes of Henderson Novellas
Playin' Cop
Taming Molly
Kissing Cooper ~ A Christmas Quickie

Listed in order

Countdown to a Kiss
A New Year's Eve Anthology

Playin' Cop
Heroes of Henderson ~ Prequel
Previously published as
The Keeper of the Debutantes in
Countdown to A Kiss

Good Cop
Heroes of Henderson ~ Book 1

Bad Cop
Heroes of Henderson ~ Book 2

Taming Molly
Heroes of Henderson ~ Book 2.5
A DuVal Cousins Quickie

Top Dog
Heroes of Henderson ~ Book 3

Tempting Vivi
Heroes of Henderson ~ Book 3.5
A DuVal Cousins Novel

Kissing Cooper
Heroes of Henderson ~ A Christmas Quickie

UnderDog
Heroes of Henderson ~ Book 4

Mr. Wrong
Heroes of Henderson ~ Book 5

Mr. Wright
Heroes of Henderson ~ Book 6

Mr. Wright Now
Heroes of Henderson ~ Book 7
Coming in 2018

Sign up at *www.LizKellyBooks.com*
to be alerted when new books are released.

About the Author

Growing up every summer in a place where *dancing and romancing* are literally part of its theme song, Liz Kelly can't help but be a romantic at heart. And since her favorite author, Kathleen E. Woodiwiss wrote some of the world's greatest romances, she's just trying to give the world a little more of that. (Okay, maybe a little sexier *that*, but we are now in a new millennium after all.)

A graduate of Wake Forest University, where she met her handsome golf-addicted husband (who is now sporting dark glasses everywhere he goes), Liz is a mother of two grown sons (also sporting dark glasses) and a miniature Labradoodle named Annabelle. They split their time between *The Windy City* of Chicago and the *Fountain of Youth*, a.k.a. Naples, Florida, where dancing and romancing continues on ad infinitum.